For Linda my sister and Lynn my daughter, in a life where birth gave me neither, and for Jeanmarie, whose enthusiasm made it possible for me to say this.

"Stay with me," he whispered.

Her resolve faded. The emotion that had possessed her since meeting him, that had grown ever stronger with each separation, once again controlled her. She nodded silently.

He drew something from his pocket, took her hand, and placed a wide, filigreed gold band on her finger, saying as he did so, "I, David, take thee Eliza . . ."

As though in a trance, unable to look away from him, Eliza repeated the vows with him to the final words. His eyes held her mesmerized. His voice hardened. "Nor death will us part."

"Say it, Eliza," he whispered. "Make the vow."

"Nor death will us part," she swore.

"Miss Richards?"

I heard Martha's voice as the glow from a flashlight flickered into the now dark room. "Are you in here?"

I clutched the edge of the bed as I felt a shudder of pain and regret run through me. What in God's name was going on?

Please turn this page for advance, enthusiastic praise for *Evermore*.

"Refreshingly different. . . . *Evermore* is an extraordinary love story. A real treat for readers!"
　　　—Georgina Gentry, author of
　　　Sioux Slave

"*Evermore* is an unforgettable story of love and obsession and a past that will not die. I couldn't stop reading!"
　　　—Jean Hager, author of *Ravenmocker*

"Unique . . . a special love story with an ambiance and delicate sensibility that will haunt the reader long after the last page is turned."
　　　—Sandra Canfield, author of *The Loving*

"*Evermore* is a love story of unique grace and power. Modean Moon's quietly heroic characters and their poignant struggles are unforgettable. This book is different and special—a richly textured blend of history, fantasy, mystery, and contemporary human relationships. It will delight readers and leave them believing in miracles. *Evermore* is one of the most innovative and endearing stories I've ever read."
　　　—Deborah Smith, author of *Miracles*

MODEAN MOON

Evermore

WARNER BOOKS

A Time Warner Company

WARNER BOOKS EDITION

Copyright © 1993 by Modean Moon
All rights reserved.

Cover illustration by Sharon Spiak
Cover design by Diane Luger
Hand lettering by Carl Dellacroce

Warner Books, Inc.
1271 Avenue of the Americas
New York, NY 10020

W A Time Warner Company

Printed in the United States of America

First Printing: February, 1993

10 9 8 7 6 5 4 3 2 1

PROLOGUE

1 January 1925

My Dear Friend Stephen,

    I write to you after all these years to entreat of you one final request. I can turn to no other; I can trust no other. It is rumored that I am an embittered, half-crazed old man. Yes, even in my isolation, I hear these things. Only you know the truth behind my bitterness. Only you know the deep sense of failure I feel toward the one person whom I could have helped. And only you know that my mind is still clear, although now dedicated to one cause.

    I have done much searching, much reading, and, when I was again able, much praying. The spiritualists and Madame Blavatsky have given me no clear-cut answers, but they have given me hope—hope that is strengthened by the words Eliza spoke to me when she was but a child and again in the hour before she so needlessly left me.

    My preparations are now complete. There is no guarantee this will work, but I have done all that is humanly possible. And if there is a just God, if there is a loving God, Eliza and I will be together again. Here. In the home I built for her. In the home she grew to love in the few short months I was privileged to have her with me.

    I ask—I plead—that you defend my estate, my wishes,

and the Will that I have written. Some will say these are the demands of a deranged man. You have the strength and the position to counter those accusations, to preserve what I have so painstakingly and deliberately established until, God willing, we return.

Before the coming of the white man's religion, our people believed that the spirits of the departed lingered—near their bodies, our people said, but could it not be near persons or places they loved? When once again I felt, other than pain, I became aware of Eliza's gentle touch, of her gentle presence. She is no longer with me, and I am bereft. But I must believe that our separation is temporary. I await only your answer before I, too, can begin the adventure that lies before us.

Farewell, my dear friend.

David

CHAPTER

1

Elizabeth

I found the metal box on the top shelf of my grandmother's closet a month after her funeral, hidden by hats that she had not worn for twenty years and old ladies' orthopedic shoes with black laces.

The influenza that had run rampant through the section of Columbus, Ohio, where we lived, the disease that Gran had refused to give in to until just before it claimed her life, had left me still curiously weak. Other than that—unless the return of the dreams that had troubled me as a child was a result of the illness, of the high fever that had disoriented me, keeping me lost in time and space and unable to differentiate between dream and reality for almost two days—it might never have touched me.

I pushed back feelings of guilt as I went through my grandmother's things; she no longer needed them, and I had never been happy surrounded by the faded remnants of her past.

There was no key to the box, at least none that I could find, and as I knelt on the floor, prying at the lock with a rust-pocked screwdriver, I wondered about the secrets of Grandmother's life that she had found necessary to hide from me. It wasn't her secrets I found, but mine.

Beneath a one-page will leaving anything she might own to me, two small insurance policies, yellowed receipts and tax returns, and long-expired warranties, I found the book I had bought when I was twelve, a moldy old history that I had found in the basement of a used book store and brought home because of a compelling picture it contained.

"Am I related to him?" I had asked my grandmother, hungry for any family, and especially hungry for any tie to the man portrayed, and I showed her the picture of David Richards, a copy of a painting done by the now-famous artist Stephen Ward before the Civil War.

"Richards is a common name, Elizabeth," she told me in the always slightly disapproving tone she used when I questioned her about my parents or when I did something of which she didn't approve. "Don't go borrowing trouble."

The book had disappeared the next day; it just wasn't where I left it when I returned home from school, and Gran denied any knowledge of it. Now, ten years later, I held it in my hands. I rocked back on my heels in front of the closet door in the middle of the jumble of the contents of the box and opened brittle pages, surrendering to the smell of age and history which wafted around me.

I couldn't find the picture at first; I had to search the index. And when I did find it . . . I slumped over the page trying to remember. Had I bought the book because of the name? Or had I recognized him then as I did now? Because the face that smiled at me in recognition was a face as familiar to me as my own. It was the face of the man I now saw nightly—in my dreams. And it was the only face I could recall clearly from those dreams.

I settled onto the floor, clutching the book, before I noticed that the box was not empty. Two other things remained: an age-browned photocopy of a letter from my father to an attorney in Fairview, Oklahoma, and the attorney's return letter to him.

"Am I related to him?" I had asked Gran long ago, and she, knowing that I was, had hidden the truth from me, as she had hidden everything else about my father's family from me, as she had hidden the knowledge that I now knew I had to act upon.

The hill had filled my vision for miles. Shrouded in shadows, it beckoned me onward. The music of Beethoven spilling from the tape deck at a volume loud enough to mute the wind-driven flapping of the car's canvas top seemed a more than fitting accompaniment for the beauty of the view and the ever-growing sense of expectancy I felt.

The cautiously phrased letters from Stanley McCollum, the estate trustee, which had begun arriving after a discreet inquiry from the attorney I hired to handle Gran's tiny estate, lay in a neat bundle on the seat beside me in the well-used little M. G. Midget I bought with the last of Gran's insurance money; bought for three reasons—it was the right size for my less than impressive height, it was cheap, and it fed a sense of adventure I had not realized I had until I tried to persuade myself to buy the sedate, and dull, sedan parked next to it on the lot.

That sense of adventure had grown in the past few weeks; a family connection I had not known of, a home I had not known of, an inheritance I had not known of, and underlying it all, a sense of completion, hurried me through the days and nights until all the details of my past life in Columbus were disposed of and Mr. McCollum was reluctantly convinced that I was who I claimed to be.

I glanced at the directions Mr. McCollum had sent. I had long since decided not to drive into Fairview but to go directly to Richards Spur. *Richards Spur.* An entire town named for an ancestor of mine. I found the turn from the highway and headed toward it, and the hill.

At the base of the hill I drove through the cluster of shabby stone buildings which was all that remained of Richards Spur. Only the post office, an ugly brick square, protested that the town still lived. I hurried past it, unreasonably disappointed by the remnants of the town and intent on finding the road to the top of the hill, but something tugged at the edges of my memory, urging me to slow, urging me to look.

I silenced the music as I braked my little car to a stop in front of the general store. It was impossibly, vaguely familiar. I could never have seen it before, and yet I knew that I had. The board sidewalk sagged under the weight of years, and the roof rested limply on the remains of cedar posts. An empty padlock hasp hung between the double doors, which bore the remnants of rusted metal signs touting "the pause that refreshes." The store was open; I could no more turn away from it than I could have turned away from the information I had found in my father's letter.

Inside, sawdust shavings slipped beneath my feet, and the slowly revolving fan above a bare light bulb churned the musty air, bringing me the scents of old wood and dust and dry rot. As my eyes became accustomed to the darkness, I saw an incredibly ancient woman, dwarfed by the age-blackened rocker in which she sat. Two thin white braids hung over her shoulders, trailing past her waist. Her eyes, alert although clouded by years, were fixed on my face, and I felt myself drawn to her, knowing, but not knowing how I knew, that she was to become terribly important to me.

"Eliza." The voice which came from the depths of the rocker was cracked but still bore a ring of authority.

"Elizabeth," I said, walking toward her, "but how—"

I stopped as another woman stepped from the shadows.

"Can I help you?" she asked, wiping her hands on the butcher's apron that covered her shapeless cotton dress and peering at me with a thin, tight smile.

"We don't get many strangers in here," she said, not bothering to hide her curiosity. "I'm Louise Rustin." Then, noticing my interest in the ancient woman, she added reluctantly, "My grandmother, Marie LeFlore."

The names meant nothing to me. "I'm Elizabeth Richards," I said to the second woman, and watched her smile fade and a strange look come into her eyes.

"I—we heard you were coming." She paused. "Where will you be staying?"

I stared at her, puzzled. "At the house. Of course."

Her eyes wavered, and she once again began wiping her hands on her apron. She turned restlessly toward the back of the store. "I've got to get to work," she said abruptly. "If there's anything you need, just call out." As she edged into the shadows, she hesitated. "Fort Smith is only about a half hour's drive from here. Or there's a motel in Fairview . . . if you change your mind." Then she scurried from sight.

"Child." Marie LeFlore's voice once again commanded me.

She kept her unwavering gaze fixed on me as I went to her and knelt by her side. Then she reached out with one skeletal, quivering hand and touched my hair as it lay across my shoulder.

"Soft," she said. "Like a black cloud framing your face. And eyes the deep blue of mountains seen from a distance." She let her hand linger for a moment on my hair before she spoke again.

"Give me your arm."

I held my right arm out to her, but she shook her head, reaching for the left and pushing back my sleeve. Tentatively she traced the narrow pink birthmark on my forearm. When she spoke, she looked straight into my eyes.

"It must be a very old mark." But it was more question than statement.

"I was born with it," I said softly, puzzled by her actions and by a tug of memory, as I reached to touch her cheek.

"No." Her eyes filmed over, and a smile softened her wrinkled mouth. "I've been waiting for you for a long time."

Waiting for me? I wondered. Or waiting for the woman who would claim the house? I pulled slightly away from her.

"It's all right," she said. "One day you'll understand."

Outside, the smell of dust and the sense of dryness persisted. Even my eyes were dry, but there was a throbbing behind them, a dull ache there and somewhere deep within me. Had it been a mistake to come here? A sudden weakness shook me, and I leaned my head on my arm against the porch post as I looked out over the road.

I knew the road, and yet I didn't know it. The potholed asphalt was wrong, so wrong, and as I watched, it dissolved, becoming the hard clay-packed track the potholes had exposed. I heard voices, at first tiny sounds like those on a cheap radio but gradually becoming clearer, and I heard the vibrations of footsteps on the board sidewalk as people ran from buildings that a moment before had been deserted toward the mule-drawn wagon pulled up in a cloud of dust in front of the new porch on which I stood, unnoticed. . . .

Eliza

The freight wagon finally ceased its jolting, and with stillness the stabbing pain in Eliza's side eased. She heard the Scotsman's voice calling for help and the confusing babble of voices around her.

"My God!" She recognized Wilson's voice close to her. "It's Colonel Richards's lady."

"He'll be up at that house," another voice answered, "if he hasn't already left to go get her."

"I'll catch him," Wilson's voice called, and Eliza heard footsteps running. "There'll be hell to pay if I don't."

Eliza felt the wagon shift as Will MacDougal climbed in beside her. The swirling blackness came again, and only his big hand on her small one seemed to be holding her from complete surrender to it.

His slow voice drifted through the fog. "It's been a hard trip, lass, but it's almost over. Just a wee while longer and he'll be with you."

She saw the faces at the foot of the wagon then, and she read in their eyes the questions their closed lips would never ask her. *His* people. His nation. The nation for which he had fought so hard. The nation for which he was still fighting.

She became aware of how she must look, aware of her torn clothes only partially hidden by the soiled blanket in which she had lain wrapped through the torturous journey.

"Not like this," she whispered to MacDougal. "Not like a whipped dog crawling home."

"He'll not love you less," MacDougal said softly, "and I dare not move you."

In spite of the pain, Eliza felt a strength she had not thought she had. "Then I'll move myself," she said through clenched teeth as she tried to rise. "I'll not lie here waiting for him like a piece of broken freight."

Another pain stabbed her. Not her side this time, but lower. She caught her lip between her teeth to keep from crying out against it, and only MacDougal's arm slipped behind her shoulders kept her from falling.

"Is there a place?" he asked the group at the foot of the wagon.

A tall woman in calico, a flat black braid hanging over each shoulder, her dark features expressionless, stepped forward.

"In the store. Bring her."

Cradled in MacDougal's arms, the pain constant now, Eliza became acutely aware of her surroundings—the two steps up to the plank porch, the sap still congealing on the cedar posts supporting the roof, the double doors being held open, the chill she felt that only deepened in the dim, cool quiet of the store with its mingled odors of sawdust, tobacco, and fresh pine, and a silent, beautiful girl, no older than three, who stood hugging a stuffed doll dressed in orange calico.

"Clear a table," the woman said.

"No," Eliza was barely able to murmur. "Not lying down. Sitting up. And where I can see him coming."

"But lass . . ."

She heard the noises of the woman pushing and ordering the others from the store and away from the doorway and closing one of the doors.

"He would have been proud of me had he brought me here as his bride," Eliza whispered, "and I will not shame him any more than I already have today."

The woman produced a high-backed rocker and placed it facing the door. Eliza saw MacDougal wince when she gave in to a spasm of pain as he settled her into the cushioning pillows in the chair.

She leaned back into the pillows, closing her eyes and tensing her body against the hurt and the memories that would not release her. David! Her heart cried out for him, for his arms around her, for his love to support her.

Oh, God! She shouldn't have come. Not now. Not until the worst had healed. If her need for him had not been so great, she would have realized this before. What would he do? He must not, could not go after Owen.

A tearing at her, stronger than anything she had yet felt, doubled her over, and this time she couldn't stop her cry from escaping. When the pain passed and she leaned back, bathed in perspiration, she felt the coolness of a damp cloth on her face. Through half-opened eyes, she saw that the woman had brought a cloth and basin, and, with a thoughtfulness that brought tears to Eliza's eyes, a hairbrush. The child stood near her knees, hugging her doll tightly and staring at Eliza with wide eyes.

"He's done what he could," the woman said, nodding toward MacDougal, "but he's a man. Now we'll do what we can before the colonel gets here. Out," she said to MacDougal.

"I stay with the lass," he said, but he moved into the shadows.

Eliza felt a smile trying the corners of her lips. The Scotsman's protectiveness had been unexpected, but oh so welcome. She reached for the hairbrush and as she did, the blanket dropped, exposing her arm and shoulder. Her arm fell limply to her lap. The child came closer, but it was not the bruises or cuts that drew her attention. With one tiny brown hand, she reached out and timidly traced the long, ragged scar which still showed pink against the whiteness of Eliza's arm.

"Does it hurt very much?" she asked.

"Marie, go to your grandmother," the woman said.

"No, please," Eliza begged, caressing the child's face. At the woman's nod, she answered the girl.

"No, Marie. It's a very old mark. It doesn't hurt at all."

While the woman tended her, Eliza lay back quietly, fighting the weakness that claimed her and searching the hillside she could see through the one open door. David would come down that hillside, and while her every nerve cried out for him, her mind sought to find a way to spare him, to save him from the temper he kept so closely under control—the temper that could now destroy him and bring disgrace to his people.

She saw dust high on the hill. The cloud of it billowed downward, hidden at times by the trees, and she knew David was coming. She reached mechanically for the hairbrush and saw, without comprehending, that the water in the basin was tinged pink. She tried to lift the brush but could not.

Marie edged closer. "May I brush your hair?" she asked shyly. With a grateful sigh, Eliza surrendered the brush to the child, who in turn thrust her doll into Eliza's lap and started to walk behind her.

"Not there!" Eliza said, remembering the bloody tangle at the back of her head. "Just around my face," she said more softly, "please."

While Eliza's eyes remained fixed on the ever-closer cloud of dust, the child, with infinite gentleness, began smoothing matted waves.

"It's soft," Marie said with a touch of wonder in her voice. "It looks like mine, but it isn't. It has curls." She went on with the brushing. "Do you like Red Feather?"

"Red Feather?" Eliza asked numbly, still watching the hillside.

"My doll."

Eliza glanced down at the doll in her lap. A stuffed fabric doll dressed in orange, named Red Feather. Would she ever understand the people of this nation that was so close, yet so far from where she had been raised? "She's beautiful."

Marie stepped back to admire her handiwork and put down the brush. "Not as beautiful as you," she said.

Eliza forced herself to look at the child. "More so," she said softly, "because she is special to you." She surrendered the treasure to Marie but had to ask, "Why is she called Red Feather?"

Marie's dark brown eyes twinkled with mischief. She lifted the orange dress, exposing a small rip in the seam of the doll's leg. With tiny fingers she poked at it until she drew forth a fluff of red down. "Because that's what we used to make her," she said proudly, "from Granny's red hens."

Eliza fought back the laugh she felt rising, knowing what it would cause her and holding her chest against the pain. *A child is a child*, she thought, *regardless of the race. God grant that our child grow strong and healthy and happy*. Fear clutched at her, chilling her. *God grant that our child be safe.*

She touched Marie's cheek once more before looking back toward the door. She could see two riders now, and even though she could not see their faces, she knew that the one in front was David, riding as she had first seen him, as though that troop of Yankee cavalry still pursued him.

The woman saw them, too. She redraped the blanket around Eliza and began gently exploring the wound at the back of her head. At the first touch, Eliza's stifled moan stopped her, and she gathered the bloody cloth and basin and took them from the room.

Eliza clenched and reclenched her hands beneath the blanket and listened to her heart beating loudly in the silence of the store. The figures grew closer. She could see David's hair now, not straight black and coarse as he would have it, but a rich brown and soft to her touch. She could see the golden bronze coloring of his face, the finely chiseled features which flaunted before the full-blood Choctaw of his people the fact of his English father's blood, the firm, sharp line of his jaw, now tense and unyielding, and the grim, unsmiling set of his mouth.

The two riders reined in, but only David dismounted. Through the crowd that surrounded him, she could still see him, a head taller than the others. His voice rose above theirs clearly: "Damn it! Why not?"—he who so seldom swore. He turned to the other rider, Wilson, spoke to him briefly, and sent him galloping away. And when he turned to the store, she saw his eyes.

Numbness crept over her as David leaped onto the porch and into the store, slamming the door shut behind him. She sat paralyzed as he crossed the room and stood looking down at her.

The silence was unbearable.

"David," she whispered, "am I so horrible that you can't touch me?"

With a groan, he knelt beside her, gathering her in his arms. She reached for him. Through the pain came the comfort of his nearness, and her pulse quickened with the knowledge that this man loved her. In spite of everything, he loved her.

She surrendered to that love, letting her head rest against his chest as she felt his lips moving over her forehead and his hand caressing her hair.

Too late she remembered the tangled mat at the back of her head. David drew his hand away, looking at it as though it were some repulsive thing. Eliza saw fresh blood and realized the wound must have started bleeding again when the woman tried to clean it.

"Who did this to you?" David demanded in a voice that revealed how tightly he held his anger in control—and how close he was to losing that control.

"Not now, David. Please. Just hold me." A sob caught in her throat. "I need you to hold me."

He did, gathering her to him, and Eliza knew that, had the pain been ten times as great, she would not have cried out. For this it was worth it. It was worth it all.

"And if I had come to you when I promised instead of letting myself be kept at council?" She heard the bitterness in his question.

"You did what you had to do," she said. Thank God he had not been there. She crept closer to him, but as he tightened his arms around her, a spasm she could not hide made him draw away.

The blanket had slipped again, and he folded it back from her, looking for the first time at the marks that covered her, at the truth he had not known. She would have given anything to take the suffering from his eyes, but all she could do was wait passively while he covered her, all but her left arm. He bent his head to her arm and, as in times past, touched his lips to the pink scar.

"Am I never to bring you anything but pain?" he murmured without looking up at her.

She freed her hand and pressed her fingers to his lips, silencing him.

"Love," she said softly, turning his face to hers. She looked deeply into his eyes. "Love and the joy of living. Happiness, and the promise of more happiness to come. That's what you bring to me."

He placed his fingers gently over a bruise on her arm.

"You didn't do that," she said. "You have never hurt me. None of this should be on your conscience."

The woman reentered the room, and as David looked up at her he saw the big Scotsman for the first time. "Who are you?" he demanded, rising to his feet.

"William MacDougal," the man said, moving forward from the shadows.

The woman stepped between them. "He brought your lady, Colonel."

"What do you know about this?" David asked, less sharply.

"Just that she came to the freight yards," MacDougal told him, to all appearances unintimidated by the leashed anger of the man who stood as tall as he, "asking for someone to bring her to you."

Eliza breathed a silent prayer that he not tell the rest—it was not necessary to tell the rest—even though she would forever owe him a debt of gratitude for his intervention.

"My wagon was empty. I brought her. She would not let me stop for a doctor."

"Well, there's a doctor coming now," David said. He turned to the woman. "We'll need a place for a few days, Jane, until she's ready to travel."

Eliza groped for his sleeve. "Home," she whispered. "Take me home."

"May I talk with you, Colonel Richards?" the Scotsman asked, glancing at Eliza. "By the door." She watched the two men walk across the room. They talked in a tone so low she could not hear their words, but David never took his eyes from her. When they walked back to her, he was still looking at her, but he spoke to the woman behind her.

"You'll come, Jane?"

"With the doctor."

David gathered Eliza in his arms. When he started to put

her in the bed of the wagon, among the pillows MacDougal had carried out, she protested.

"On the seat with you," she said as firmly as she could. "I want to see our home as we drive up."

David hesitated so long she thought he was going to refuse, but with a look on his face she had not seen before, he nodded. With William MacDougal's help, he lifted her to the wagon and nestled her in his arms.

As the Scotsman drove carefully up the hill, cursing under his breath each rock and hole in the roadway, Eliza could no longer hold back her tears. They welled in her eyes and slid silently down her cheeks.

"Talk to me, David," she whispered, turning her face to his chest. As though sensing she needed the sound of his voice as a lifeline, he began talking, softly, melodically, about the orchard, the herds that were almost back to full number, the house.

"I've planted a magnolia for you at the gate to the terrace," he told her, "and on the terrace, all the roses you love."

Her head sank lower on his chest.

"They don't look like much now," he went on evenly, "but on each side of this road, all the way to the main gate, I've planted young pines. In a few years they'll be . . ."

The blackness swirled around her, more demanding now, and at last, safe in David's arms, she let herself surrender to it.

Elizabeth

I lifted my head from the post and looked at the double row of giant pines leading up the hillside. I still felt a throbbing behind my eyes, but my weakness was gone, replaced by the chill of—not fear, but something so close to fear that I couldn't put a name to it.

What had happened? The potholed asphalt stretched in

front of deserted buildings in a dying town. I leaned against the dry remains of a cedar post on a sagging porch. *I knew those people*. David Richards, yes, but more intimately than I could ever have known him from a book. And Eliza. And the others. But I couldn't know them, could I? Were they the ones who moved through my dreams? "Control your imagination, Elizabeth," Gran had said long ago. "Reality is all you need." Why? Why had she said that? I searched my memory for something she had insisted I deny, but all I found was the image of a young girl in a blackberry patch. A dream I had tried to tell Gran about? Or more? And then I remembered: A series of dreams that were more than dreams, memories that were more than memories, so much so that, in the innocence of my childhood, I had felt them to be a part of another life I led—a life as real as the one I shared with my grandmother. That was what Gran insisted I deny, and I, hungry for her love, had done so.

This hadn't been a dream. That much I knew. Had I been there? Because I felt I had *been* Eliza, feeling her love for David as well as her pain, knowing her thoughts, moving through her actions, and—for the time—I *was* her, having no knowledge of *me*.

Impossible. I knew that, too. I felt tears on my cheeks and raised my hand from the post to wipe them away. I looked at the post—old, dry, long ago having given up all of its juices—just as it had been when I first saw it before I walked into the store. "Impossible," I whispered.

Reality. I needed reality. I walked on slightly shaky legs to my car and slid in. My glance fell on the letters in the seat. I had come with only clothing and personal things, as David Richards's will specified, and with only the money Mr. McCollum had sent for the trip. It hadn't seemed so long when I first learned of the other specification in the will. In fact, surprising myself, I had looked upon it as something of a lark, but now the year I had to live in the house, without a job, without any independent income, before inheriting, stretched ominously before me.

Why? Why had he made such a provision in his will? Mr. McCollum didn't know, or, if he did, he hid his knowledge behind a veil of ridicule. And I? Why did I feel that the answer was within me?

I pushed those unwelcomed thoughts from my mind. Grateful for a fresh breeze on my face, I turned my little car away from the town and started toward the hill.

I, too, wanted to see it as I drove up, I realized. As much as Eliza had. I squared my shoulders. Nothing on the hill would hurt me. I sensed the truth of that as I sensed the truth in the words I heard myself repeating. "I *have* come home."

CHAPTER
2

I found the red clay roadway littered with beer cans, bottles, and discarded paper. At the remains of an old fence, a pile of abandoned appliance bodies and unidentifiable trash backed up a pool of stagnant water from which something small and furry scurried as my car approached, and I questioned the mentality and morality of anyone who would willingly desecrate such beauty.

Inside the fence, though, to my relief, I found no litter. Beneath the pines, a cool quiet reigned, broken only by the groaning engine of my little car as I shifted into a lower gear for the climb.

Not all of the trees in their bare winter drab were familiar to me. There were notable absences of those I had considered my particular favorites, and I had to remind myself that I was much farther south than I had ever been before. Still, I sensed that in the glory of fall, the colors here would be every bit as vibrant as those of central Ohio, with the added beauty of hills and gentle mountains. And even in January, the weather was mild. The gaily colored poncho, also bought in a moment of defiance, which I wore over slacks and a soft sweater, was more than adequate. *It will do,* I thought, surveying the few tan oak leaves clinging tenaciously to the gray-brown of their branches, the bleached silver heads of winter grasses, and the deep green of the pines which rose up along both sides of the roadway and which seemed to beckon me onward. *It will do*.

I also sensed an isolation, a feeling that could have been overwhelming had it not been so welcome. For years, Gran and I had lived in a second-floor walk-up apartment in a crumbling building, hearing our neighbors growing louder and less considerate as each year passed. Because of that, the idea of living in a single house far from human intrusion seemed like a private slice of heaven.

The winding road was little-used, enhancing the sense of isolation. Saplings and wild grasses encroached, claimed the roadbed as their own, and softened the once raw wound until all that remained to mark my way upward were the tall pines and two lines of bent grass showing me the path of another car.

Finally, though, I passed through two ornate iron gates, now streaked red and hanging heavily from bent hinges in a stone fence, then rounded an ancient elm with drooping branches, and I was there.

I don't know what I had expected; I really don't. A large house, yes. That much had been intimated in the letters. But not a miniature fairy-tale castle, turreted, many-windowed, outlined against the sky and the backdrop of distant mountains.

I felt a suspicious lump in my throat and fought back a flash of bitterness. "Oh, Gran," I whispered. "Why? *Why* did you try to keep me from this?" For a moment I was with her again, in the darkened apartment I had known all my life, where she allowed no sunshine for fear it would fade the already faded upholstery, a lonely little girl begging for her approval, which was as rare as sunshine in the place I had never called home.

Well, I had a home now. Across a broad lawn, waist high with grass and briars, the house stood, waiting, welcoming me. Silence surrounded me as I drank in the unexpected beauty and as, slowly, I began to see the ravages time had made on the house and the careless repairs that had followed. I released a shuddering breath and gripped the steering wheel. For a moment perfection had beckoned. For a moment I had been blinded by hope.

It made no sense, I thought as I eased my foot from the brake and once again followed the tracks through the weeds, past leaning outbuildings with gaping roofs, around two still substantial stone barns. There was money in the estate; that much had been made chillingly clear. Enough for seven other women to have tried to claim it. In addition to the house, the bequest included self-sustaining income properties to provide for me for the year I must live here, to provide maintenance for the house, to provide, as Mr. McCollum had informed me in that one telephone conversation I had with him, "more than adequate" financial recompense for someone who had once had no prospects or knowledge of the inheritance, and no true claim to it other than the accident of birth. Why then the waste? I wondered as I reached the back of the house and pulled to a stop in the shadow of a battered white sedan. Why the needless waste?

A woman opened the back door. She stood there and watched me as I parked. She was in her fifties, possibly even her sixties, around Gran's age when I had first been thrust upon her. Life had not been kind to her, but her hesitant, welcoming smile as she approached me destroyed forever any further comparison with my grandmother.

"Miss Richards?"

She wiped her hand on her apron and held it out, catching me just as I turned to take one of my two bags from the car. I turned back to her, clasping her work-worn hand in mine. I didn't know what to expect from her. I didn't even know who she was. But she had made an overture. Years of deeply ingrained habit took over. I smiled. "Yes."

"I'm Martha Wilson," she said, as though that explained

everything. "Let me get that bag for you." Competently, she reached into the car and dragged out my heaviest suitcase. "I imagine it's quite a shock for you," she said, nodding toward the house. "You ought to be prepared. It's no better inside."

When we reached the back step, she bumped the door open with her hip and took from me the suitcase I was carrying. "I expect you're ready for a rest and some coffee after your trip. We can get these later," she said, setting Gran's ancient luggage on the floor. "Did you have any trouble finding your way from Fairview?"

"I haven't been there yet," I told her. "I came directly here." I stood in the doorway looking around the cavernous kitchen, at the pair of massive ranges, antiques now, that lined one wall, at the door to what had to be a walk-in cooler, at the sunlight playing over the glass-fronted cabinets, paint-blistered and empty except for a few dishes in one corner. The room was clean; every available surface had been scrubbed regularly and frequently, but an air of disuse and a hushed expectancy seemed to hover over everything. I stepped into the room.

"I'd like to see the house."

"Of course. Just a few minutes won't hurt, though. You look like the trip wore you out, and I've already got the coffee made, and a cake. I hope you like apple spice—"

"Now," I said, prompted by something beyond my conscious knowledge, but at Martha's hastily concealed look of disappointment, I did add, "Please."

Silently she led me through the large, empty rooms, and I, as silent as she, surveyed the crumbling varnish of the rich, delicately carved woods, the stains on imported marble mantels, and bare electrical wires hanging from the high ceilings. The only noise was the click of my heels on the spotless hardwood floors. And with each step, I felt the house enveloping me, wrapping itself around me. Not unpleasantly. Oh, no, far from unpleasantly.

I leaned against a wide, multipaned window and looked out over the valley to the south, trying to absorb the feeling, and trying to absorb the magnitude of the neglect. The window I looked through sparkled. Absently I ran my finger along the frame. The varnish had bubbled with age, but it was clean and recently oiled.

I looked at the woman standing by my side. She stuffed her hands into the pockets of her apron and stared at the floor.

"No, it isn't," I said, sighing.

"What?" she asked.

"As bad inside. It is bad," I told her, "and disappointing, although I really didn't know what to expect, but at least inside someone *cared*." I caught the glimmer of pride in her pale eyes before she masked it. "You?"

Martha caressed the window facing with roughened fingers. "I do the best I can," she admitted reluctantly.

"Who are you, Martha Wilson?" I asked. "You're not the housekeeper, are you?"

"Not . . . not officially."

I felt the chill inside the house for the first time and rubbed my arms beneath the poncho. Martha might have shown me a genuine welcome, she might have food and coffee waiting for me, but I saw that she wasn't the type to spew forth information, not unless it was carefully solicited, and not unless she thought the information was needed. Seeing the rest of the house could wait, at least for a little while longer.

"Apple spice cake?" I asked.

She nodded a yes.

"I love it. And I'm starved," I admitted.

She seemed to accept that I knew so much more than I did. About the house. About the entire bizarre chain of events that had brought me to an abandoned hilltop. About the family I had never even known I had. That would help in freeing her tongue, but not as much, I realized, as my being honest would.

The cake was wonderful, an elusive blending of spices and textures that almost melted in my mouth and left me longing for more. The coffee was rich, black, and strong, the way I had only recently begun brewing it. But sitting with Martha Wilson at the scarred kitchen table was a strange experience, if only one of the many that day. Because I had the strongest sense of having done it, time and again, for all of my life. Maybe that feeling was what finally freed my tongue.

"When you say you're not officially the housekeeper, what do you mean?"

"You don't know, do you? They let you come into this with no idea of what you were getting into."

"I don't know anything," I admitted, "except what was in two letters in my grandmother's lockbox and the little bit of information Mr. McCollum revealed. And who David Richards was, of course. And I understand even less. Especially why, if he went to such great pains about providing for this house in his will, it has been neglected like it has."

She studied me silently for a moment, the signs of an inner debate evident in her pale eyes. "There hasn't been hired help in this house for seven years," she said finally. "Longer than that, from the looks of things when I moved in, just someone here drawing a paycheck. I did apply, though." She threw her head back, letting what I suspected was an inherent pride show itself for a moment. "Got myself up in my Sunday best, made an appointment, and drove into Fairview, to the bank. With my Jim gone, well, I just didn't have enough income to keep the place we had then, didn't have enough to keep from being a drain on what family I had left. And there always had been someone up here before, you see. Always.

"Stanley McCollum was a tightfisted, mean little boy. And he's a tightfisted, mean little man."

She looked at me and smiled, a smile at odds with her words. "I'm not telling you anything to prejudice you against him," she said. "It's something you'll find out, if you haven't already. He treats that trust money like it's his own, and like he's down to the last two nickels. And he has since his daddy died and he took over as trustee; that's when things started going downhill. If it wasn't for John Richards looking over his shoulder, no telling what he'd have done up here. Of course, he couldn't have done much less.

"I went to him looking for a job," she said, her voice quivering with remembered indignation, "and he treated me like I'd gone asking for charity. And it was charity he finally offered me—not then, but weeks later. To give the devil his due, it was probably John who persuaded him to do it. To protect the house from vandals, Stanley said." She snorted in derision. "I could live here in the servants' quarters to protect the house from vandals."

"He doesn't want you here?" I leaned my chin on my fist and felt a bubble of unexpected laughter as I remembered his frosty and tenuous acceptance of me. "He doesn't want me here, either. You and I ought to get along just fine."

"That's what I had hoped." A warm, generous smile lighted her face.

There were other questions to be asked, other answers to be gleaned. About the house. About the family. Who, for example, was John Richards? McCollum had never mentioned him. Gran certainly hadn't. Because of the age of the probate, I had assumed I was probably the last of the family, a distant last. I was distant, but not the last, I discovered as I sat with Martha in cozy intimacy in the cavernous room. There were two of us remaining, me and John Richards, the only living descendants of David Richards's two nephews.

"What's the upstairs like?" I asked when she filled my cup still another time.

"I don't know. Except for the quarters, I've never been up there."

"You haven't?" I stopped, speechless. "But you—I'm sorry. I realize it isn't your job, but you've taken such loving care of the downstairs, I just thought—"

"It wasn't for not wanting to," she said. She pushed her cup away and stood up. "Come with me. I guess you might as well know the rest of it."

I followed her through the house, retracing our earlier steps but going farther, into the front hall, dim in the fading afternoon light, to the huge curving staircase. Halfway up, barely visible in the shadows, a metal grate—the old, strap-metal type once used in jails—had been bolted into the walls. In the center of the grate was a small door secured by a massive padlock.

"Why?" I asked.

She studied her hands, work-roughened and worn, then stuffed them into the pockets of her apron. "You're not the first, you know."

The first? The first to ask why? And then I realized what she meant. The first to try to claim the inheritance. "No. That much I do know. I'm the eighth."

She nodded brusquely. "I'd made up my mind if you were like the last one, the only one I ever met, all hard and grasping and demanding, I was going to pack up and leave you with it. I have places I can go. Now. But you're not."

She nodded toward the grate. "Everything of value is upstairs. They put it up there after the last caretakers left. Patched up the storm damage and put that grate in and locked the upstairs doors off the servants' stairway. Said it was to protect it from vandals, too. Vandals!" She repeated the word with the same derision she had voiced earlier, in the kitchen. "By then most of the county had heard about that fool girl running down the hill, pounding on Frank's door in the middle of the night, screaming about ghosts."

"Ghosts?" I asked weakly. I had sensed a presence in the

house since entering; not until that moment had I considered it threatening. Now I felt a chill along the back of my neck.

"Real quiet ones," Martha said. "So quiet that in all the time I've been here, by myself, I've never heard them. But they sure do keep the superstitious thieves and the curious away. That's the reason I never bothered to deny the rumors. Until now."

She turned, and I followed her back through the darkening house. "I think she was unbalanced when she came here," Martha continued. "I know she was when she left. Stanley wasn't any more welcoming to her than he's going to be with you. The caretakers at that time weren't too bright and they were a whole lot greedy. And to top it all off, the one night she tried to stay, we had the worst storm this county's seen since statehood. A tornado took out half of Richards Spur, and winds knocked down trees and power lines and took off roofs from here to Fort Smith.

"She wanted too much," Martha said when we reached the narrow back stairs that she had told me led to her quarters. "And that's what she got. Too much."

The hardest part was removing the boards that covered the door from the servants' stairwell. Rationally I knew I should listen to Martha's request that I wait until morning. Rationally I knew that at some point McCollum would have to give me the keys. I was tired from the drive, confused by the strange experiences of the day, disappointed beyond any reason at what I had found, and frustrated. But above that, something else was urging me on. I didn't consider myself much of a lock-picker—my one experience had been with a dime store lockbox—but for some reason I knew I had to try.

Martha brought me her small supply of tools, and I worked carefully at prying each of the large nails out of the underlying woodwork. The old lock stood firm. None of Martha's pitifully few keys even fit the opening. But the hinges were on our side of the door. I removed the top hinge pin and started tapping on the bottom one. Martha put her hand on my shoulder.

"You may think I'm unbalanced, too," I told her, "but this is something I have to do."

"Do you want me to come with you?"

I shook my head. "Not this time. Do you mind?"

She almost laughed but disguised it with a cough, then shook her head and helped me lift out the door. She took a flashlight from her toolbox and handed it to me. She didn't say be careful, but I felt the weight of those words as she put her hand on my shoulder, passed me her keys, and then stood back out of my way.

Inside, an expectant silence surrounded me as I threaded my way through piles of boxes and furniture, past doors, all locked, through the gentle restraint of gossamer webs, deeper into the heart of the house.

A dim beam of light from the main stairwell penetrated the gloom of the upper hall, and I at last found my bearings and headed toward the light. A door stood at the top of the landing, a door like all the other doors I had passed, but I felt drawn to this one.

The door was locked, as the others had been locked. Against what? Martha's story about that other woman's one night in this house echoed in my mind, and I wondered, were they all locked to keep someone out? Or something in? I pushed those thoughts away as I knelt by the lock with the small ring of keys. I found a key that would fit into the opening and forced it, first one direction, then the other, until I recognized the words I now heard: my words, my voice. "Please. Please. Please."

"Oh, please open," I said, and as I did, the lock gave and the door eased open.

The room was empty. Oh, there was furniture there, carelessly shrouded against dust as though whoever had done it had spent no more time than necessary within the circular walls, but to me it was empty. Alone, I walked through the room, avoiding the covered rolls I recognized as carpets and mattresses, only glancing at the brighter places on the faded walls where paintings had hung, to the boarded window. Angrily I tore the weather-warped plywood from the window and looked down into the jungle the terrace had become. The magnolia growing by the gate passed the window where I stood and grew still taller. In the distance, a line of trees marked the meandering river. Between the river and the base of the hill lay farmland, rich, reddish brown, waiting for its new crop. Beyond, smoky in the fading light, were the mountains. To the east, on the hilltop, sprawled what was left of an orchard.

Through filming eyes I looked back to the lonely room. Gently I removed a canvas drape from the headboard of the bed and ran my fingers over carved rosewood. I threw the cover on the floor and sank onto it, leaning against the bed, looking at the grayness of it all—the twilight filtering through coated windows to touch the grime that covered the fireplace in front of me.

"Why?" I whispered. Why had the deterioration been allowed? And why did I feel so much pain that it had? And then—then I felt it happening again.

Eliza

She opened her eyes slowly. She felt a curious tightness around her chest, but except for a dull throbbing in her head, she was at last free of pain. Her hand flew to her stomach. Then, sighing, she sank more deeply into the pillows and looked around the room.

David stood at the fireplace, his back to her, one slender brown hand gripping the mantel. His knuckles showed white against the pale pink veining of the marble. She saw his reflection in the mirror in front of him, and his dark, brooding scowl sent a shudder through her.

"David?" she whispered.

Instantly he was beside her, only tenderness showing in his eyes as he caressed her face. He bent to her and kissed her forehead. She reached for him, but he pushed her down gently. "You mustn't move."

Fear returned to her then. "The child?"

"The doctor doesn't know yet." The calm in his voice broke. "Eliza, why didn't you tell me?"

"I wanted to." She turned her face from him. "But at first I wanted to be sure before I said anything, and when I was, you were so worried about what was happening to your nation and about leaving me to meet with the council that I couldn't put any more on your shoulders." She felt tears gathering in her eyes and willed them not to fall. "I've made such a mess of things for you."

"No." He silenced her with a kiss. "Never you."

She lay quietly, drinking in the comfort of his presence, and he sat beside her, caressing her with the tenderness she had learned to expect from this strong, willful man.

"What were you staring at?" she murmured drowsily. "While you were standing the mantel?"

A grim smile crossed his face as he held out a long lock of raven hair. "It seems your wild savage has finally scalped you."

She reached for her head, but he caught her hand. "Lie still," he said. "Not all of it. Just where necessary."

His mood changed abruptly. "It was Owen, wasn't it? Tell me what happened."

"David," she said, searching the stern mask his face had become, "you must promise me something."

"It was Owen," he repeated. "You've told me that much."

"You must swear to me that you will never cause him any harm because of me."

"Tell me what happened," he insisted in a dull monotone.

"Swear," she said, as firm as he on this point. "It could only bring destruction to you and the nation if you seek revenge. Swear to me."

His eyes met hers and held them. He gave a quick, curt nod. "Now tell me what happened."

He had never lied to her before; his silence now was eloquent. She knew she could never tell him the whole of what had happened. "He found me," she said. "We always knew that was a possibility. I—I got careless."

David rose from the bed, his face blanched of color, and stalked across the room. At the mantel he stood poised.

"David," she said softly, "you swore."

"I swore." He whirled to face the fireplace. "I swear." He clenched his fist and beat at the mantel with enough force to overturn a candlestick. "Damn his soul!"

A light tap sounded at the door and Jane entered. "Reverend Smith is downstairs."

David turned dazed eyes toward Eliza. "Give us a few minutes, Jane. Then send him up."

Methodically he righted the candlestick. Methodically he walked to the far end of the fireplace and stood there, his back once again to her. He seemed to be struggling with something. She sensed his hands moving on the mantel but could not see them. She saw his shoulders slump, then straighten. He threw his head back.

"Since you cannot be moved, I've asked the minister to perform the service here. If you still wish to marry me."

She stared at his rigid back. "Can you doubt that I do?" she whispered.

He turned to her, his eyes still troubled. "No, but I can wonder at it." He crossed to her. "As I can wonder at you and the love you have given me so selflessly."

She raised her hand to his face. "We were meant to love each other."

The minister looked as though he had never had to suffer the hardships of life in Indian Territory. He was pale but well fed, a tall man, though not as tall as David. Eliza felt the stirrings of fear when he entered the room and spoke brusquely to David, not looking at her. "The doctor gave me your message, Colonel Richards."

David had pulled a chair to the bedside and seated himself there, clasping her hand reassuringly. "I'm glad you could come so quickly."

"Colonel, I'd like to speak with you a moment."

She felt David's hand tense on hers at the command implied in the man's tone.

"What is it?" David asked.

The minister looked toward her for the first time. She recognized in his eyes an emotion she had seen too often: zeal, misguided or otherwise, driving him. The fear within her flared.

"Privately," he insisted.

David's hand clenched hers.

"What is it?"

For the first time the man faltered. He looked at the ceiling above their heads before taking a deep breath. "Is the lady divorced?"

"Yes." She heard David's reply, clipped and cold in the silence of the room. *Don't!* she pleaded silently, without knowing whether the plea was for the minister or for David.

"Then I'm afraid, sir, in view of that and the lady's advanced—" he paused, hesitant only in his choice of a word, "confinement, I cannot be a party to this sacrilege."

Unaware of his strength, David grasped her hand, holding it until it numbed in his. "You what?"

"I cannot officiate at any wedding ceremony between the two of you," he said with more determination.

"The child is mine, Smith," David said in a tone Eliza had never heard him use, soft but with the promise of power behind it, one which countenanced no argument. "And Eliza will be my wife. Do you understand?"

"Yes," Smith told him, his voice rising slightly, as though to overcome or deny what she had heard in David's. "And I understand that you'll have to find some other way to make that so. This mission is just getting started in the community. There is a great deal of dissatisfaction being expressed against the church sanctifying your relationship with this woman. Your own people have reminded me of your law, not the church's, which forbids marriage between a citizen of the Choctaw Nation and a white man—" once again he glanced at her, and Eliza read condemnation in his eyes, "and a white man of poor character. I have been assured by members of my congregation that this law also applies to white women. I cannot risk the integrity of my church by defying public sentiment in this matter."

"And what about the integrity of your God?" David asked coldly.

"The one whose laws you flaunted?" Smith asked.

David released her hand. His voice was low, but it chilled her with its deadly calm. "Get out."

Smith's eyes glowed and his face was flushed, but he stood firmly planted at the foot of the bed. "Richards, you are a powerful man, but you are not above God."

"And you, sir," David said, "are not *of* Him. Get out," he repeated softly. "Out of my house, off my land, out of this nation. Because I promise you that you will have no church to pastor here. When I have finished what was started today, there will be no community to need your church."

Eliza stared at Smith's back as he left the room, at the

finality of the door closing behind him. But his words remained to mock her. She should have known.

"He doesn't matter," David said. "None of them do. We'll find another minister. We'll have a civil ceremony if necessary."

"You can't marry me," she said dully.

"What are you saying?"

"I'm not worthy of you."

"Eliza, look at me."

"That's what *they* are saying," she told him, still staring at the door. "Your people. And if you do find someone who will perform the ceremony, that is what they will say the rest of your life—that you married a divorced woman with child, and unclean . . ." She felt her voice break and stopped until the tightness eased. She began to tremble and fought against it. "I will leave as soon as I can."

He caught her face in his hand and turned her toward him, forcing her to look at him. "Eliza, you are my wife," he told her, "the wife of my soul. You have been for many years. I don't need a minister to say the words to make it so."

"All your plans," she began, "all you've worked for—"

Placing his fingers on her lips, he silenced her. "For years we've been separated because of those plans. For years you've suffered because of them. You've given so much for them, can't you give some for me now?"

Eliza stared into his eyes, not daring to hope.

"I need you," he told her. "The nation can do without me, but I can't do without you. Not any longer."

She felt moisture gathering in her eyes and knew that she should turn away from him while she still had the strength to do so.

"Stay with me," he whispered.

Her resolve faded. The emotion that had possessed her since meeting him, that had grown ever stronger with each separation, once again controlled her. She nodded silently.

He drew something from his pocket, took her hand, and placed a wide, filigreed gold band on her finger, saying as he did so, "I, David, take thee, Eliza . . ."

As though in a trance, unable to look away from him, Eliza repeated the vows with him to the final words. His eyes held her mesmerized. His voice hardened. "Nor death will us part.

"Say it, Eliza," he whispered. "Make the vow."

"Nor death will us part," she swore.

Elizabeth

"Miss Richards?"

I heard Martha's voice as the glow from a flashlight flickered into the now dark room. "Are you in here?"

I clutched the edge of the bed as I felt a shudder of pain and regret run through me. What in God's name was going on?

"Miss Richards?"

I found my voice and the strength to answer her.

"Over here, Martha."

"Are you all right?" she asked, searching my face as I rose to meet her. "Did something happen?"

"No," I told her, feeling drained, alone, and too confused to say anything. To anyone. "Nothing happened."

CHAPTER

3

I awoke to silence and the feeling that I had slept much too long. The feeling grew, and with it came a heavy sense of something that had to be done. I sat up abruptly, and as I did, the memories of the previous day flooded over me.

I was home.

As irrational as that thought might have seemed, even yesterday I had known it was true.

I plumped the pillow into the corner of the sofa and pulled myself into a sitting position against it, looking at the room I had first seen the night before. A square gas heater sat in front of the fireplace, its flat metal top painted to give the appearance of wood grain. On top of the stove sat a bucket, steam rising from the water within it. From behind the stove, copper tubing snaked along the wall, disappearing through a neatly taped opening in a window. A spotless aluminum coffeepot sat on a nearby propane burner, and I became aware of the aroma of freshly perked coffee.

Even the servants' quarters showed the care that had gone into the building of the house, and the neglect it had endured. The room I studied also bore signs of Martha's caring. The glass in the windows sparkled; no gray here. The wooden mantel, smaller, less elaborate than those downstairs, glowed from recent polishings, and the hardwood floor, although worn, was clean and freshly waxed.

The coffee summoned me from under the quilt at last. I wondered about Martha's absence. The coffee was hot. A clean cup sat beside the hot plate, next to the kerosene lamp we had used the night before. I started to wander into the adjoining rooms but felt suddenly reticent about invading Martha's quarters without her, even though she had already given me a tour.

I took my coffee back to the couch and snuggled under the quilt, knees drawn up, while I studied the room. An electric light fixture, brass, with two etched glass globes, hung from the ceiling. There were two electric outlets, but nothing was plugged into them: no radio, no television, no clock, no lamp. Behind one of the doors across the room was a large, old-fashioned bathroom, complete with a floor of tiny ceramic tile, a claw-footed tub, and a separate shower. Also inoperative. No electricity. I remembered Martha's words as she had shown me the bathroom, before leaving me there with a bucket of water heated on her makeshift stove.

"It's the pump," she had said. "It won't work without electricity, if it will work at all now, and the power company won't agree to turn on the service until an electrician checks out the bare wires in the house."

"Even if McCollum asked them to?"

She looked at me and sighed.

"And he won't have the wires checked?"

She avoided my eyes.

It seemed that nothing in this enigma of a house worked without electricity, except for the huge coal-fired furnace in the cellars I had not yet seen. That simply didn't work. And except for Martha. I didn't understand why she expended so much effort on the house. Or maybe I did, after listening to her last night as we stood in the bathroom, as she ran her hand, almost caressingly, over the gleaming fixtures.

"They used to talk about this house when I was growing up," she had told me. "About how the colonel kept adding to it, modernizing it, and keeping it so fine, even at the last, just as though he was waiting . . ." She suddenly became very interested in the spot she was polishing, but her eyes didn't lose their faraway look. "And I used to dream about how it would look, dream so hard I could almost see inside without ever coming up the hill."

I heard a door slam below, bringing me back to the reality of hot coffee and bright morning sunshine. Footsteps paused outside the door, and then Martha entered, lugging a pail of water.

"Oh, you're awake," she said pleasantly as she put the bucket she carried beside the other one on the stove. "I should have seen that you got to bed proper last night, but you were so tired I just covered you up and let you sleep. I hope you don't mind."

I shook my head, and she turned back to the first bucket, testing its contents with a tentative finger. "Good," she said. "The water is just about right."

I shrugged out of the quilt and walked over to where she stood. She wouldn't take my thanks for the extra effort I caused her; I had tried to offer them the night before and only embarrassed her. I looked out the window. A solitary hawk circled over the slope of the overgrown hillside. Other than that, the hilltop was still. Still, quiet, and lonely. Waiting. Or so it seemed to me. As the colonel had waited? As I had waited? And then I wondered where that thought had come from.

Closing my eyes, I threw back my head, twisting it, trying to ease the sudden tightness in my neck. In my throat. In my heart. I hugged myself against the chill I felt standing in front of the lighted stove.

"I'd better get dressed," I said finally. "It's time for me to meet Stanley McCollum."

* * *

Richards Spur did not appear as inviting as it had the day before. A harsh, cold wind blew, pounding a loose shutter against an unseen wall as I parked in front of the general store. The yellow dust and grit flung by the wind bit into my face and hands and tore at my hair beneath its restraining band as I hurried through the door.

Marie LeFlore waited in the rocker. Hesitantly I walked to her and dropped to my knees beside her, taking her hands in mine.

"Good morning, child," she said, tightening her fragile fingers around mine. "Did you sleep well?"

"Beautifully," I told her, wanting to ask her what she had meant by her last, cryptic words to me, wanting to tell her about the strange occurrences that had shaken me, and sensing somehow that this woman held a key that I needed.

"You did?" Louise Rustin's voice broke in before I could begin.

"Yes." I rose to my feet, trying not to let my annoyance at her interruption show. She stared at me dumbly, as though I were lying, and when she remained silent, I sighed, remembering my reason for being there. "May I use your telephone?"

I thought for a moment she was going to refuse. Instead she agreed grudgingly, then busied herself nearby, listening, I was sure, to every word as I placed the call.

Mr. McCollum was in conference and couldn't be disturbed before noon. At least that was what his secretary coolly informed me.

I felt a knot of frustration lodge within me as I replaced the receiver. He had expected my arrival this morning; surely it wasn't too much to presume that he would see me. Think *power*. The thought came uninvited. Toward a penniless orphan from Columbus, Ohio, his actions were still rude, but as the possible heir of a large estate, one for which he was responsible, wasn't I entitled to a little more than "poor relation" status?

"Eliza." Marie's voice stopped me as I reached the door.

"Elizabeth, Grandmother," Louise snapped. "If you're going to call Miss Richards by her first name, at least get it right." She glared at Marie and at me before disappearing into the rear of the store.

"Eliza."

I went to her and took the quivering hand she held out to me.

"He never meant it to be this way," she said, answering my unspoken questions and creating more in my mind. "He wanted everything to be perfect for you."

I clasped her frail hand, wanting to ask so much more and yet afraid of what I might hear. "Thank you," I said, meeting her smile.

The drive from Richards Spur to Fairview didn't take long. It didn't take long at all, because the farther I went, the angrier I became at McCollum's attitude, and the angrier I became, the harder I pushed the accelerator. Along with the anger came questions. David Richards had built the house and maintained it in style until his death. He had left it in trust, meaning for it to be maintained until claimed by someone—a specific someone. Why? And who? And what I was experiencing was nothing new to me, I knew that now, just more intense. Memory? It felt like memory. More real, more clear than any memory I had from my childhood. But if it was memory— was I Eliza? Marie LeFlore seemed to think so. My hands shook on the steering wheel. Marie LeFlore was ancient.

Reality. Reality. Gran's words hammered at me. I gripped the wheel. *This* was reality. A stingy trustee was reality. A neglected house was reality. And I held on to all of them until I reached Fairview, a town that was a curious mixture of the very new and the very old. I drove past acres of earth-moving machinery and oil-field drilling equipment, past bright new shopping centers, modern schools, and sleekly designed housing developments, to the heart of the town, which, except for traffic lights and parking meters and false fronts on some of the buildings, could have been the model for a turn-of-the-century painting.

I located the bank building with no trouble. It was the tallest in town, three stories, with a clock and a beautiful stone front which, unlike the surrounding structures, wasn't hidden by metal paneling. Inside, though, the building was new. Electric heat surrounded me, and my feet sank into plush carpet. The noises of calculators and typewriters were subdued behind soundproofed walls and insulated glass.

The young woman at the front desk looked at me, clearly wondering who I might be. She appraised me and decided to be pleasant. "May I help you?"

"Mr. McCollum's office."

"Second floor, front office." Her telephone buzzed discreetly, and she turned to it, forgetting me before I crossed the hall and mounted the stairs. A lovely old banister graced the stairwell, and I had a sudden vision of those other stairs, with their crumbling varnish and crude bolts marring the paneling.

McCollum's secretary was as cool and impersonal as her telephone voice, and just as firm. "I told you. He is in conference. He cannot be disturbed before noon. If you'd care to leave a telephone number where you can be reached, I'll contact you for him at his convenience."

At his convenience. It seemed to me that too many things had been done at Stanley McCollum's convenience, or not done at all. He didn't like me, he didn't want me there, and I doubted there was anything I could do to make things better, or worse. I looked at the closed door behind her and walked toward it.

"You can't go in there," she said again as I opened the door.

He sat behind a large teak desk. "None of the others—"
His voice broke off as I entered.

He studied me silently for a moment, as I studied him, then
nodded at his secretary. Quietly she left the room, closing the
door behind her. I approached his desk, not sure now what I
would say. He was younger than I expected, handsome in a
manner some women would find appealing, carefully and
expensively tailored, styled, and turned out.

"Mr. McCollum," I said, choosing my words and keeping
my voice as low and controlled as I could. "That house is
uninhabitable."

What could have passed for a smile crossed his face, and
he visibly relaxed in his oversized leather chair. "Miss Richards. I heard that you had gone directly to the house last
night. I wish you had listened to my advice or had at least
seen me first; we might have been able to save you some
discomfort." He shuffled through the one folder on his desk
and brought forth a typewritten document which he held toward me. "But since you didn't . . . please sit down. Now,
as I explained previously, since you have been unable to
stay in the house, it will be necessary for you to sign this
relinquishment."

I stared at him in amazement. He thought—he actually
thought—I would give up this quickly, this easily? "I'm not
talking about my ability to stay in the house," I told him,
brushing aside the paper and refusing the chair. "I'm talking
about the condition to which you have let it deteriorate."

"Living there for the required year does mean sleeping
there, too," he said, the condescension in his voice giving
me yet another reason to dislike him.

"I slept there last night."

His smile faded. "All night?"

He ought to get himself a direct line to Louise Rustin, I
thought; their questions were remarkably similar. "Thank
you for the concern over my sleeping patterns," I told him.

"but I will say this once more, and only once. I slept there last night. I slept as comfortably as possible considering the lack of heat, electricity, or running water. I slept soundlessly, dreamlessly, and late."

A bead of perspiration popped out on his upper lip.

"Now it's my turn to ask a question," I went on, prompted by a strength and a knowledge that I didn't understand. "What is the annual allowance for maintenance of the property?"

He leaned back in his chair, studying me. His eyes narrowed, his lips thinning in a parody of a smile. "The figures are none of your concern at this time. The amount is . . . adequate."

I seemed to have tapped some inner source of courage that I'd never known I had. "Then I'd like to know what you've done with the money, because you certainly haven't spent it on the house."

He sat up in his chair, a retort framed, but I continued. "Not this year, nor the year before, nor the year before that. You haven't spent a cent on the house in the past seven years, and very little before that."

I took the paper he still held, glanced at it, and tore it in half. "No. I'm not relinquishing anything. On the contrary, I'm demanding what I think must be available. Funds to make the house livable. A cleaning crew, electricians, skilled laborers to undo some of the damage you have allowed to happen, and the keys, because I don't intend to spend the rest of this year taking doors off hinges and picking locks."

Picking up the pieces of the paper I had dropped on his desk, he glanced at them, at me, then at some point over my shoulder. "I'm sure you know that most of your demands are unreasonable."

I shook my head. "What I am sure of is that not once in the past seven years have you been as negligent in deducting your fees for management of the trust as you have been in fulfilling your obligations."

"Young lady," he said, rising to his feet. "I don't know who you think you are to—"

"I'm Elizabeth Richards," I told him. I looked at him steadily. Then, with a deep, quiet confidence, I said, "I meet those requirements for inheritance set out by David Richards in his will. I have come to claim what is mine."

Once again he glanced behind me. His lips tightened to no more than a thin line against his chiseled features.

"The keys, please," I said in the same calm voice that had carried me through the past moments.

He looked at me then, his eyes cold and angry, and nodded abruptly. "They're in the vault. I'll see that they're brought up." Then, without another word, he left the room.

"Well done, cousin."

I stiffened at the softly spoken, lightly mocking words as I realized who must be standing behind me. McCollum's interrupted conference. John Richards? The cousin I had not known of until the day before? I turned to face him and then had to grasp the edge of the desk. I stared at the long, lean figure posed so confidently across the room, at the face that had become so familiar to me. "David?" I whispered the name before I could stop myself, knowing even as I did so how wrong it was.

"Hardly." He laughed harshly and moved closer to me. "Thank God I don't have the name, too."

Then I saw his eyes and the look of possession that claimed me before he masked it. "It's a remarkable resemblance, isn't it?" he went on. "A genetic fluke, a throwback. One more thing to keep his memory alive."

The bitterness in his voice denied the heritage for which David had fought so hard, denied the goodness I now knew he had possessed.

"But don't hold the fact that I look like our crazy ancestor against me, will you? I assure you, I've hated this face since I first saw it reflected in a history book."

His gaze raked over me, inventorying each inch of my appearance, and then returned to my face. "Do you know what it's like to have people constantly comparing you with someone long dead? To know they're saying, 'He looks just like crazy David Richards who built his own castle and still couldn't be king'?"

I was incapable of speech, reacting completely out of proportion to what the encounter demanded. The desk supported me as his words and his bitterness battered at me.

"Of course you don't. But take care, cousin, that they don't say, 'There goes crazy Elizabeth Richards, who thinks she has a right to live in that castle.' "

McCollum returned. Somehow I took the box of keys from him. Somehow I walked across the room. When I opened the door, I paused, gripping the knob as I had the desk. My breath, rapid now, scraped in my chest and grated in my throat. The expression in John's eyes once again claimed me. I turned, avoiding the image I now knew I had longed to see, and faced the once again self-assured man who stood between us.

Somehow, my voice didn't break. "I believe there are provisions for a housekeeper's salary. I also believe that Martha Wilson has earned that salary."

Somehow, holding on to the beautiful old banister, I made my knees hold me upright as I started down the flight of stairs. They seemed to stretch endlessly ahead, and the faintest glimmers of a memory began hammering at my mind, echoing as relentlessly as John Richards's words.

Somehow I was in my car, through the city, and on my way back to Richards Spur. When I neared the hill, his face appeared before me, blinding my vision. I felt tears creeping down my cheeks, although I didn't know the reason for them. A fresh load of trash had been dumped on the pile near the gate, spilling out into the road, but I didn't see it until I was upon it. I swerved, and the car skidded on the loose dirt and into a leaning fence post, which snapped with the impact. The car came to a shuddering stop beneath the pines, and I leaned my head on the steering wheel, surrendering to what I was very much afraid was inevitable, to the images crowding against me. . . .

Eliza

"You don't go into the woods, now, you hear me? That hell-born horse of your father's can just stay lost before I let you get hurt lookin' for him."

"Yes, Bessie," Eliza said patiently, but she didn't heed the warning. Bessie was always worrying about her. She wandered across the narrow neck of the forest and sat beside a creek overlooking a clearing and the fence that separated her father's land from Jameson's. That vile stallion had destroyed the vegetable garden before escaping, but she was half-inclined to thank him for it, because only fear of her father's wrath had prompted Bessie to let Eliza leave the tenuous protection of the house's grounds by herself.

Oh, drat the roan! Her father was going to have an absolute fit when he came home if the stallion was still missing, especially after having gone to so much trouble to hide the horse from both armies.

She heaved a sigh, rose and dusted her skirts, and was taking one final look at the clearing when she saw him. At first she thought it was the roan, running free, but as it came closer, she saw that it was not her father's horse, and that there was a rider, one who rode as she had never seen anyone ride before. He seemed a part of the animal, crouched low against it, urging it onward.

"Oh, don't try that fence," she whispered as he drew near the briar-covered barrier.

Shots rang out behind him as a troop of Yankee cavalry

broke from Jameson's woods. The rider's speed never once checked as he raced toward the fence. Another volley of shots sounded as the horse cleared the top rail, and she thought she saw the rider fumble, but onward he came, never slowing, toward her.

The Yankees' horses balked at the fence, and she laughed with delight as one soldier was unseated into the briars.

"Come on," she silently urged the lone rider. "You can make it." She saw his dark hair caught by the wind, his long, slender hands on the horse's neck, the red spreading across his gray jacket.

For the first time, the war came close to Eliza. For the first time she realized it was more than parades of young men marching gaily off to whip the Yankees, more than the privations that her household was finally feeling in spite of her father's hoarding. For a moment it stunned her.

She saw the spot where the soldier would enter the woods and hurried toward it. She reached it just after he did. He had turned to look back over the clearing. His breath came in ragged gasps and he slumped in the saddle, his lips compressed against pain. His horse was lathered in sweat, its sides heaving. A twig snapped beneath her foot, and the soldier whirled, revolver drawn.

"That fence won't hold them long," she told him. "Send your horse on and follow me."

"You're little more than a child," he said, panting.

"Will a Yankee bullet know that?"

Without another word he slid from the saddle, turned the horse into the woods, and slapped it on the flank, sending it clamoring through the underbrush.

He stumbled. Instantly she was beside him, guiding his arm over her shoulder. She slid her arm around him, feeling the warmth of his blood through her sleeve. As quickly and quietly as possible she led him through the forest. He tried at first to walk alone, but by the time they reached the edge of the woods behind her home, she was supporting most of his weight.

Bessie stood beside the barn, looking toward the trees, and when they came into sight, she ran to them, her huge bulk and aprons flapping.

"Lord, child, what have you gone and found?"

"Just help me get him into the house," Eliza said, now breathing almost as raggedly as the soldier.

Upstairs, in her ruffled white bedroom, Eliza pulled out the chair before her dressing table, and the soldier collapsed onto it. While Bessie prepared the bed, Eliza removed his gun belt and helped him out of his jacket. She saw him bite back a moan as she worked the jacket off his shoulders and reached into her embroidery basket for scissors to cut away his shirt over the wound. She drew back when she exposed the ravaged flesh, and had to turn her eyes away. Taking a deep breath, she tossed the bloody fabric beside the washbasin and searched the basket for a strip of linen. Finding it, she turned back to him, her hand once again steady. She had just dampened the cloth and started to cleanse the ragged wound when hoofbeats sounded on the drive.

"They must not find me yet," were the first words he spoke. There was no fear in his voice, but it was low and hoarse.

"They won't," Eliza promised him, promised herself. "Bessie, turn back the mattress on the far side."

He shook his head, trying to smile. "That won't work, girl. That's one of the first places they'll look."

She helped him to his feet. "No gentleman is going to search a lady's bed when she's in it."

There was no time for anything else. Pressing the linen against his wound, she helped him into the bed, placed his revolver in his hand, his belt beside him, his jacket under his head. "Whatever happens, don't move until I tell you to."

Quickly, she and Bessie spread the feather bed over him, smoothing the covers. The horses were at the door.

"Hurry, Bessie. Downstairs. Tell them he stole father's roan stallion and rode east."

Bessie started out the door.

"Your apron," Eliza whispered. "Give me your apron. It's bloody."

Voices sounded from the porch. "Here's fresh blood, Captain." They were pounding on the door. Eliza looked at the bloody scene around her, at her sleeve that was soaked through. No time. There was no time.

"Try to stall them, Bessie." They would not find him. No matter what, they would not find him.

The front door was flung open; Bessie started down the stairs.

"Where is that rebel savage?" a voice called out.

Eliza heard Bessie trying to talk to them, trying to keep them from searching the house, and then she heard their steps on the stairs. She reached for her scissors. If she couldn't hide the blood, maybe, just maybe she could explain it. With the strange sensation of having lived through all this before, she put the tip of the scissors to her arm, feeling the point even through the sticky wet cloth. Gritting her teeth, hearing the sound of footsteps over her own heartbeat, she dragged the blade along her arm and slid the scissors into the already pink water of the basin. She fell onto the bed, her weight pushing the feathers even higher to cover the soldier, just as a Yankee captain, gun in hand, kicked open the bedroom door.

Bessie's eyes widened when she saw Eliza's arm, but she said nothing. Eliza looked at it, wondering why it didn't hurt, watching her blood mingling with his.

The captain stopped. "I beg your pardon, miss." But there was no apology in his look. Sunlight through the open window glinted against his golden hair and highlighted the harsh arrogance in his eyes as his look traveled from her arm to her face and then down the length of her body.

Bessie pushed between them, snatching up the basin and the forgotten piece of the soldier's shirt and moving to Eliza's side. "I told you there wasn't no soldier up here," she huffed as she hid the bloody cloth beneath the basin as she placed it on the bed. "He's done gone on that red devil of a horse." She cut away Eliza's sleeve and pressed a cloth against the wound.

The officer stepped farther into the room. "How did that happen?"

Eliza bit her lip. She'd already had Bessie call him a horse thief. Surely one more lie wouldn't hurt. "I did not want him to take my father's stallion."

"You're lucky you still have your scalp," he said. "He's not one of your gentleman soldiers. If you should see him again—"

"Do you really think we will, Captain?"

"Markham. Owen Markham," he said, and still his eyes lingered on her.

"Captain Markham." There had to be some way to get him out of the room. Eliza threw her free arm over her eyes and spoke tremulously. "Bessie?"

"My apologies, miss. I'll send my medical officer to see to that."

"No," she said. She knew it had come out too fast, too harsh. She caught herself and resumed her pose. "No, thank you, Captain Markham. There will be no need for that, but . . ."

"Yes?"

She looked demurely away from him. "It does hurt frightfully. Could you please leave me something for the pain?"

Eliza hid behind the curtains, a compress pressed against her arm, and watched while Bessie claimed the medicine.

When the riders turned down the drive and rode away, she released her breath, aware for the first time that she had been holding it.

Bessie came lumbering back up the stairs and pushed the medicine toward Eliza. ''It's not for me. It's for him.''

She stood to one side while Bessie pulled the mattress back. His eyes were closed. He lay so still.

''Is he dead?'' Eliza whispered, kneeling beside him.

He opened his eyes. He saw her sleeve. He reached for her arm, caught it, and drew it close to him. He looked into her eyes and held her still. ''Very brave,'' he murmured.

''I promised you,'' she said simply.

With the last of his strength he raised his head and pressed his lips to her wrist, just below the torn flesh.

He healed quickly—too quickly, Eliza thought as she kept vigil while he slept, realizing that soon he would be strong enough to leave. Gone were those terrible hours when he had been near death, when the strange, musical language had broken incoherently from his lips, when she had grasped his hand as though her strength could hold his soul within his body, could keep him from sliding from this life.

Gone, too, were the hours when she had watched him in restless sleep, her glance lingering on the strong, proud lines of his face until drawn by some power stronger than her will to his lean, graceful body.

The memory of his lips on her wrist brought a warm glow to her. She wondered what it would be like to have his arms around her, holding her close, to have his lips pressed against her lips, to have his eyes look at her with love.

He moaned and turned in his sleep. His arm slipped from under the sheet and dropped to the side of the bed. She put aside her forgotten mending and lifted his arm onto the bed. She let one hand remain on his bare shoulder. With the other, she smoothed the soft hair from his forehead. She bent closer to him, aching to touch her lips to his face. Just this once, while he slept. He need never know.

His shoulder tensed. His eyes opened. She felt her blood rushing to her face. Could he have read her thoughts? His eyes met hers with an intensity that frightened her, but with a gentleness she had not thought possible in a man.

He raised his hand and touched her face.

"Thank you," he said.

CHAPTER
4

Elizabeth

I could not forget the derision and bitterness in John's eyes, in his voice, as he spoke of David. And just now I had seen Owen Markham speak of him, with different words but the same emotion. And the expression, the *ownership*, I had seen in John's eyes for one brief moment was the same I had seen in Owen's eyes. Or had I? God! Was it possible?

I cranked my car into a protesting start and urged it up the hill, not allowing myself to think again until I passed through the rusted iron gates and again confronted the house.

This was real. I was here. I fought against the memories of the morning and reached for the house keys on the passenger seat. Memories? Or fanciful imaginings? Whatever. This was my home now. And it would be the home that it was obviously built to be. It *would* be.

I looked for the path through the weeds. It was gone; the weeds were gone, chopped close to the ground and lying in scattered clumps, drying in the weak afternoon sun, while dust hovered heavily above. With the underbrush cleared, I saw stones marking a drive, and what had appeared to be a vine-covered stump a few yards from the front entrance had been sheared of its briars and now revealed the graceful lines of a small fountain in a circular bed.

I tapped the horn once, hesitantly, as I started uneasily along the drive. McCollum couldn't have done this, not this soon.

A gray tractor sat parked at the gate to the terrace, and Martha stood beside it, talking with a tall young man. As my car approached, she waved, and I parked in front. I walked the short distance to them, studying the young man.

Here was the Indian of my imagination: tall, erect, with straight black hair framing his face, high cheekbones, skin tinged with bronze, and a knowledge of himself that showed in the way he held his head, his shoulders, his entire body. He and Marie LeFlore. Two. Two alone in all the faces I had seen in Richards Spur and Fairview. Two left of the nation David Richards had known.

Martha's entire face creased with her smile. "My nephew, Mack Wilson," she said, pride gilding the simple words and telling me of her affection for him.

"Thank you, Mack," I said, extending my hand. He looked at it for a moment before wiping his on his jeans and taking it. His grasp was as confident as his posture, and I felt instinctively that Martha was justified in her pride.

"It wasn't much," he said. "Things are kind of slow at my place now anyway." He scraped a worn boot over the ground. "You've got good grass. It won't be as hard to get it back in shape as I first thought." He nodded toward the terrace. "That's going to be a little tougher. I can do some now, but I'd like to wait awhile on the rest, until it greens up some and I can see what I'm doing."

His words were matter-of-fact, a farmer talking about something he knew, but there was an expression on his face, a strange blending of reluctance and determination, which seemed to suggest some inner conflict.

"You don't have to do this unless you want to," I told him. "Do you?"

"Sure," he said. A smile broke across his face as he apparently resolved his conflict. "Sure. My father told me there was always a Wilson or a MacDougal with Colonel Richards, and I guess it's my place to do what I can." He draped an arm over Martha's shoulder, giving her a gentle hug. "Besides, with Aunt Martha and Marie LeFlore both after me, I figure it has to be the right thing to do."

He cast a quick glance at the sun. "I'd better get going or my wife will start worrying, but I'll be back in the morning."

Martha smiled up at him, and I glimpsed a faint glint of moisture in her eyes. "Give my love to Joannie."

He bent his head to her. "Take care of yourself," he said softly. "And thanks for lifting the ban on visiting you."

Martha and I watched the tractor disappear through the gates. I wanted to question her on all that had just happened, but I couldn't find words that would ask without prying.

"Well," she said, sniffing surreptitiously as she straightened her shoulders and started toward the rear of the house.

I stopped her. "Not this time." I reached into the box of keys I held. "This time we go in the front."

With anticipation and a now familiar emotion that still I refused to acknowledge as fear, I fitted the key into the lock, turned it, and pushed open the massive, complaining doors. Taking a deep breath, I stepped through the doorway and crossed the great hall to the stairs. There I turned, looking out the open doors to the fountain, the lawn, the stone wall, and beyond that to the blue of the mountains.

Martha stood silently for a moment before closing the doors, and then, as though reading my thoughts, she asked softly, "Do you want me to go upstairs with you now?"

I shook my head and started up the steps.

"Miss Richards?" She forced a troubled smile as I looked back at her. "I'll be in my room if you need me."

"I'll be all right, Martha," I said, reassuring her, if not myself.

I unlocked the padlock, opened the gate in the hateful grate, and wound my way up the staircase. Here, too, I found boxes and crates piled carelessly, leaving only a narrow path.

The door to the tower room was open, as I had left it. I followed the beam of light falling through it. What would the room hold for me in the daylight? Nothing, I hoped. Or did I?

Gone were the dustcovers and rolls of carpets and mattresses. Gone was the gray, replaced by rose, faded but still delicate. I recognized Martha's apron beside a small box of cleaning supplies and sent her a silent blessing. The graceful rosewood furniture glowed, the delicately carved mantel showed fine veins of marble, the rugs gleamed like silk against the dark floor, and the brighter squares of color against the lighter walls had been covered with paintings. Except one.

A wing chair sat near the drapeless window, and I sank into it, looking over the valley. As I sat there, loneliness overcame me, stealing upon me, enveloping me before I realized what was happening, loneliness so intense it seemed to drive the desire for life from me. The valley lost its beauty. The one bright spot on the wall mocked me. My eyes, dry and burning, sank back into my head, and I felt old, so very old, weak and defeated. I could not fight it. I felt no desire to fight it. I surrendered, drawing back into the chair, back into myself, feeling the weight of countless disappointments, countless empty years bearing down on me.

Thoughts of death came then, inexplicably, but they did not frighten me. They brought glimmers of hope, of release from the pain of loneliness, and I welcomed them to me.

"Miss Richards!"

The spell shattered. I turned, dazed, to look at Martha's contorted face.

"Why, Martha, what is it?"

Her face relaxed, but her lips remained fixed in a frown.

"You shouldn't sit there by that broken window. You'll catch your death in this cold."

She turned, tied on her apron, and busied herself with the cleaning supplies. "It's for sure you're not going to be able to sleep in here for a while. This is the coldest room I've ever been in."

I followed her across the room and put a hand on her shoulder. "That isn't the reason. You were frightened. Won't you tell me why?"

She avoided looking at me and walked to the window, taking care not to touch the chair. "It must be the silence of this place getting on my nerves," she said slowly.

I took her hand and led her to the bed, where I urged her to sit beside me.

"That didn't bother you yesterday. It must be more than that."

She looked steadily at the fireplace but didn't speak.

"Martha, ever since I came here, I've sensed that something is being kept from me. Yesterday, you started to talk about it, but you really only hinted around the edges of what you wanted to say. If you know something, don't you think I have a right to know it, too?"

She bit her lip and nodded. "Of course you do," she said hesitantly, groping for words. "Yesterday it was just rumor, silly superstition that I had grown up with, half believing, half accepting, but never sure. Today . . . today when I came into the room and saw you sitting in that chair, you looked so different, so not yourself that I—I . . ."

She twisted her hands in her apron and still would not look at me. "I'm not a superstitious woman—never have been. I haven't had the time for that kind of thing. But I haven't done one thing today because *I* wanted to. Not that I wouldn't have wanted to make it nice for you, but it was as if something was inside me, making me do it.

"When you left this morning, I started unpacking your things and putting them away in a room in the quarters, but this something, whatever it is, wouldn't let me finish. Before I knew what I was doing, I was in here with my cleaning stuff.

"And when I saw that I couldn't do it all by myself, that same something told me to go get Mack. Not just anyone—Mack. So I went and fetched him. I told him it was to knock down the weeds, but that wasn't the only reason, or even the main reason. It was to work in this room.

"And he came, and beat the rugs, and carried the featherbed out in the sun to fluff up, and arranged the furniture. And he felt it, too. He didn't say anything; he wouldn't want to scare me. But I could tell.

"And then, when we were finished in here and glad to be leaving, he stopped at the door and looked back at that chair. It was over against a wall. He went over to it, and moved it to the window, and straightened it, and—"

Her voice broke. One worn hand formed a fist.

"And when I asked him why he'd done it, he didn't know. Mack's too young to have heard, and most other folks, if they did hear, have forgotten. But I heard. And I remember. They said . . . they said David Richards died in that chair, in front of that window. He was very old, but not sick. They said he just got up one morning, sat down in that chair, looked out over the valley, and died."

Ghosts. For the second time in two days, Martha had brought up the subject. The first time had caused merely a tingle of anticipation, but that was before so many other things had happened to me. Was what I was experiencing the effect of ghostly intervention? Somehow it didn't seem so. And for the first time I wished I had listened to some of the New Age beliefs that had been so prevalent on the campus of the University of Ohio while I was there. But like Martha, I had never been superstitious—I hadn't had the time for it. And Gran would never have allowed any reference to it, or study of it, in her house. An English degree with a teaching certificate had been my goal on campus, and I stuck to it with dogged determination, because with it, ultimately, would come my emancipation.

I took Martha's hand in mine, unclenched it, soothed it. I had to work to speak around the catch in my throat. "And you think he may still be here?"

"I don't know!" she cried. "I don't know what to think anymore."

I spoke carefully. "I can't tell you that there is nothing here. I don't know, either." But how I wished I did. "I can tell you that superstition and rumor and coincidence feed on themselves. If you had not already heard the stories and had a seed of doubt planted in your mind, what happened here today might seem strange but not frightening, and you would either forget about it or search until you found a reasonable explanation."

"But if it's true?" she whispered.

"If there is a . . ." I stumbled over the word, "a spirit here—Oh, look around you, Martha. The man who built this house was sensitive and caring and appreciative of beauty. Could someone like that possibly wish to cause us harm?"

Although I had no desire to leave the room, I clasped her hand and rose to my feet. "Come on. We'll finish in here later. Right now, I need a cup of coffee."

She jumped to her feet, either instantly solicitous or seizing on any excuse to leave the room. "Have you eaten today?"

I admitted that I hadn't.

"Whatever am I thinking of? You come right along with me, Miss Richards."

I almost laughed. Although the walls were not yet crumbling around us, here we were in a vast mausoleum with no utilities, no running water, no indoor plumbing, and she was treating me like the lady of the manor. And we had been through too much together for me to allow that to go on.

"Martha?"

"Yes."

"I'd really like for you to call me Elizabeth."

The days raced by. With Martha in tow, I explored room after room, taking delight in each new wonder I found. In jeans and boots Mack's sister had left behind when she moved to Tulsa, I prowled outbuildings and the woods nearby, never seeing the vicious rattlesnakes or silent, deadly copperheads that Martha constantly warned me about. Sometimes I would jump in my car, fly down the hill, and sit for hours at Marie LeFlore's feet while she told me stories of David Richard's successes with the orchard, the railroad, the coal mines—stories I had read in the few weeks since finding my book and before coming to Oklahoma but now needed to hear from someone who had known him.

The workmen came, hesitant at first, but my exuberance must have been contagious. I watched enthralled as they erased the scars of time from the house.

Mack came every day, and his ready laugh rang through the halls as he helped me prowl through boxes and make plans for arranging the treasures I found, while Martha watched over us, and fed me, insisting that I make time for rest, for fresh air, for sleep.

True, there was one locked door I refused to open, unwilling to learn what was behind it; true, Mack's smile faded when I asked him to bring Joannie to the house; true, alone at night in the spare white bedroom where I would sleep until the heavy work was completed, I would awaken, listen but hear nothing, look but see only the familiar shapes of the furniture around me. But I was happy. For the first time in my life, I was truly happy. Except—except for those unexplained

occurrences the first days of my arrival. Except for the nig-
gling little feeling I forced to the back of my mind that
something was not quite right.

I was in the larger of the stone barns, digging through bins
of orchard equipment, most of which I couldn't recognize,
crawling over the cultivators and mowers to get to the spring-
seated wagons, when I heard a persistent horn honking as it
came up the hill. I worked my way to the barn door in time
to see Martha's car appear through the gates. I waved at her,
and she sped toward me.

"Where's Mack?" she yelled as she braked to a stop.

"He had to go into Fairview. What's the matter?"

"They're cutting the pines."

The giant pines that lined the drive up the hill. The pines
David had planted for Eliza. I didn't even ask who. I jerked
open her door and motioned for her to get out, then slid
behind the wheel. "If I'm not back soon, go for the sheriff.
My keys are upstairs."

I was gone before she could protest, tires squealing as I hit
the roadway, and driving much too fast for the hill.

There were four of them, rough-looking and unshaven.
One yanked at the starter cord of a chainsaw. I skidded to a
stop behind their flatbed truck and was out of the car and in
the middle of them before they realized what was happening—before *I* realized what was happening. I grabbed for the
saw, and the man holding it, in his surprise, let it go.

"Get off my land," I said, brandishing the saw in front of
me.

They recovered. The man reached for his saw, but I held
on to it, dodging his reach. "I said get off my land."

He threw his chest out and strutted toward me. "I've got
a lease that says I can cut all John Richards's timber I want,"
he said, "and if you ladies will just stay where you belong,
that's what I intend to do."

He reached for the saw again, and I sidestepped him, trying not to think about his bloated face, his overweight, unwashed body, his ham-sized hands. "I am where I belong. Now, you take your lease and find some trees that belong to John Richards, because these don't." I walked to the truck and threw the saw on it. "And if so much as one branch is cut, I'll have you all in jail."

Three of them had scattered, climbing in and onto the truck. The one held his ground, glowering at me from rheumy eyes. I was terrified, but I knew I couldn't show it—not if I wanted to survive this encounter intact. He was another version of McCollum, rougher, probably more physically vicious, but it appeared that he, too, took his orders from John Richards. But I wouldn't be bested by him, either. I stiffened my back, jutted out my chin, hooked my thumbs over my jeans pockets, and glowered back at him. His eyes finally slithered to focus somewhere left of my shoulder. Still I stared.

"I'm going to get Richards and straighten you out," he threatened.

"Get anyone you want," I said evenly. "But don't come back."

He swaggered to the truck, muttering something about "meddling women," and, grinding the gears, tore off in a cloud of dust.

I reached for the support of a pine and leaned against it, watching my hand tremble. I thought I felt the forest breathe a sigh of relief but knew the sigh must have been mine.

John Richards again. I didn't want to think about him. I wouldn't think about him. Not in these woods. This property was not his, would never be his. If it had been intended for him . . . A curiously shaped stick lay on the ground at my feet, and I reached for it idly, my headband snagging hopelessly on a briar as I did so. I slipped out of it, leaving it hanging there for the moment, and shook my hair free.

Did David Richards haunt this hill? Had he grown up here, wandering through these woods in his youth? I could almost see the young David beside me as I took aim at a pine cone and with a twist of my wrist sent the stick sailing toward it. I could almost hear his laughter echoing with mine as the stick struck the cone and knocked it from the tree. I could almost feel his presence as I wandered more deeply into the timelessness of the forest.

I picked up another stick and was aiming at a broken branch when the sound of a car drew me back from fantasy into responsibility. I hurried back toward the road, expecting to see Martha in my car. Instead, a new pickup truck blocked the road going uphill, and a tall figure in jeans and a suede jacket stood by Martha's car. He honked the horn and called out.

"Martha! Mrs. Wilson, are you all right?"

I stepped back into the shadows when I recognized him. John Richards. What was he doing here? Resentment welled up within me but faded as I looked at him. From this distance I couldn't see his eyes. From this distance I could allow myself the painful luxury of . . . of what? Of pretending that he was David?

He left the car and glanced at the road in front of it, the weeds beside it. He followed the broken grass to the tree where I had stood, studied the ground, and started into the woods. My headband waved from the briar in front of him, and his face darkened when he saw it. Snatching it from the briar, he stared at it intently for a moment, then called out.

"Elizabeth! Where are you?"

I could put it off no longer. Reluctantly, I stepped into his view. He scrambled through the brush to me and caught my shoulders in his hands. "Are you all right? Did they hurt you?"

For a split second his eyes, searching for any sign of injury, seemed almost crazed but then I realized he was merely examining me as he would any possession that had somehow been threatened.

I shrugged loose from his hold. "Well, cousin," I said, forcing myself to adopt the casual bantering he had used in McCollum's office, "have you come to finish what your men started?"

"My men? They don't work for me."

I twisted the stick in my hand. "They might as well, cousin; they had your lease."

"Is that what they told you?"

"You know it is."

"No," he said. "I don't. What I do know is that I wouldn't let scum like that on my land to kill snakes."

I aimed the stick at a pine cone and missed.

"Be honest with me, John. They left to go get you, and now you're here." I walked on ahead of him, but he stopped me with a hand on my arm.

"I was talking with Louise Rustin at the store when I saw them barreling down the road from this direction, and I knew that whatever they had been doing up here meant trouble. That's the only reason I came."

I felt as though the breath had been knocked from me. I fought to keep from sagging against him. "Then they really were timber thieves?"

He nodded. "And from the looks of things, you protected your sacred pines with nothing but a stick and righteous indignation."

"I didn't have a stick," I said weakly. "I took a chainsaw away from one of them."

He looked at me strangely and then his laughter rang out. Before I knew what he was doing, he had his arm around me, hugging me close to his side. "Oh, cousin," he said, "these woods really must be haunted for you to have managed that."

I tried to free myself, but he tightened his arm around me and guided me to the road. I was only human—how else can

I explain the flush that started deep within me, growing until it forced out even the January chill? And no one could deny that John Richards was an attractive man. For the moment, he even seemed . . . companionable, with a trace of a smile softening what only days before had seemed a cold, harsh face.

Companionable. Not intimate. Not passionate. Not anything to explain the need I felt to have him tighten his hand on my shoulder, turn me in his arms, and hold me safe. Safe at last.

I slipped from his grasp and escaped instead into the safety of Martha's car, aching with the tension of not letting him know just how vulnerable—to him—I had suddenly become. He leaned against the open door, the smile still playing across his features as I tried to start the car and the engine refused to catch.

"We're going to have to talk, you know."

"Are we?" I tried the key again, pumping the accelerator. "Is that one of the requirements I haven't heard about yet?"

"No. Just everyday family courtesy."

Who was he kidding? Nothing since my arrival had been of the "everyday" variety, and I certainly hadn't seen anything to indicate the Richards family even knew what courtesy meant.

The engine still refused to catch. John reached across me and turned off the key. "Now you've flooded it. You'll have to wait awhile."

I sat there in silence, staring through the windshield.

"Are you cold?"

I shook my head but felt him close his hand over mine. I tried not to flinch, to give him any indication of the unexpected and unwelcome, although not unpleasant, physical sensations that casual touch caused.

"You're like ice," he said, tugging on my hand. "Come and sit in the truck where it's warm."

I started to pull away from him and then realized how childish that would seem. He couldn't possibly know. Unless I struggled. Unless I made more of a scene than the situation warranted. I allowed him to lead me from the car and to his truck. I slid across the seat and leaned against the passenger door.

He started the engine, and heat poured into the cab. I hadn't realized how cold I really was until that moment. I eased my toes in my boots and held my hands to the warmth flooding from the dashboard.

John stretched his long legs across the center hump, leaned back against his door, and looked at me.

"It would be better if you didn't mention your encounter today to Mack."

That was the last thing I had expected him to say, and suspicions darted through my mind. "Oh? Better for whom?"

He grimaced. "I'll take care of the problem in my own way and in my own time. Mack has a tendency to be overprotective, at least where some persons are concerned. He doesn't need any more trouble than he already has."

"Can't anyone in this part of the country make a simple, declarative statement?" I asked. "Why is it that you people act as if life is one big secret that I'm not entitled to know anything about?"

"Maybe if you stopped thinking of us as *you people* you'd know the answer to that. But that's not going to happen, is it, Elizabeth? Because, in spite of ties of blood and birth, you are the outsider here."

"That's . . . that's feudal," I protested.

"It may be feudal, but it's a fact. It's the way things have been since this territory was settled, and it's the way they'll continue to be until long after our lifetimes.

"And I'll win, you know."

The smile was gone from his face, the chill was back in the truck, and we had arrived at what he had wanted to talk about all along.

"What do you mean?" I asked, forcing him to be the one to continue the subject.

"You'll never inherit the house. I've planned this too carefully and for too long. I would have had it by now if you hadn't shown up."

I turned to him, puzzled. "But the trust—"

"Can be broken."

He studied me for a moment and then spoke slowly. "I've seen enough of you to know you've got the Richards stubbornness, but I think you've also got more than a share of common sense. I've given you time to see the problems up there; now I have a proposition for you. If you won't fight my breaking the trust, I'll split the trust lands and money with you." He stopped, looking into my eyes, which I knew held nothing but questions. "Half or nothing," he said levelly. "I'll even let you have the hill."

"If?" I managed to ask. There had to be a catch to this outrageous proposal.

"If I can have the house."

I looked away from him. Was this man ever going to do or say what I expected of him? "I don't understand. How could you have let the house fall into such disrepair if you care for it so much?"

"Care for it?" The harshness in his voice shocked me. "You wanted to be let in on the secrets around here. This is one of mine." He continued in a calm, controlled voice, emotionless except for the content of his words. "I want to destroy that house. I want to watch while a demolition expert blows it to rubble. I want to watch that rubble covered by a bulldozer. I want to watch while briars and underbrush take over again, until there is nothing left but wild land no different from thousands of other hills."

"But why?" I asked.

"So that in a few years, when anyone thinks of—*if* anyone thinks of—David Richards, it will be only his financial successes they remember. They won't be idealizing a man who betrayed a nation to gain those successes. They certainly won't be thinking about crazy old King David and his castle.

"And maybe, just maybe, I can get out from under his shadow."

The only sound in the truck was that of the fan motor churning out stale, heated air. How awful it must be to hate a man, a dead man, so intensely. Especially when one carried that man's name, his blood, his face. And how mistaken John was in his hatred. I searched for something, anything to help. John? David? I didn't know who. I only knew I had to speak.

"David was a strong man. He spent his life helping his people, because he believed in them. He wouldn't have betrayed them. Not for personal gain."

"You haven't read the same history books I have, Elizabeth. That won't wash. If you were right, he wouldn't have turned from them at the end. He wouldn't have worked so hard at bringing in the railroads and coal mines, things he had fought before, things he knew would ultimately destroy the sovereignty of what you so devotedly call *his* people. They weren't *his*, he was *theirs*. He failed them, and he knew it. You can tell by looking at what few pictures there are of him late in life. And that house is a symbol of his failure."

He put the truck in gear. "To hell with the car. I'll send someone back for it."

Suddenly I understood. "Why, John Richards, you feel guilty because of that failure."

"Do I?" He shifted gears and concentrated on the roadway. "Perhaps," he admitted. "Does it really matter now? What Choctaw blood I have has been so diluted it wouldn't even have gotten me on the tribal rolls." He shook his head and stared straight ahead. "But he could have had it all. He was strong enough, and popular enough, and vocal enough that he could have made a difference. And the council that chose him to act as delegate to Washington again and to stand for principal chief could have seen him elected. He was too strong, had too many depending on him for him to have thrown it all over because of a woman. No. There had to be some deeper flaw in him.''

This was important to me, so very important, and I had to keep him talking no matter how much I hated what he was saying. "What woman?"

"Your books didn't tell you that, did they?" he asked. "No. I suppose they wouldn't. After his involvement with her had ruined his political career, and with it any real chance for the survival of the Choctaw Nation, he kept her a carefully guarded secret.'' He glanced at me, then back at the narrow road. "The family kept the secret.''

No, my books hadn't told me anything about her, and my part of the family hadn't lived long enough to do so; the only thing that had told me about her was myself.

"So he wasn't a god, is that what you're saying?" I asked tightly. "He was a man. He fell in love.''

We passed through the gates. Martha stood on the terrace, watching for me. Her face relaxed only slightly when she saw me, and who I was with, and she went back into the house before we came to a stop.

"Love?" John went on mercilessly. "He loved her so much that when she came crawling to him, pregnant, he wouldn't marry her to give her bastard a name.''

A child. There had been a child. Nothing could have told me that.

We were stopped now. John reached over and caught my jaw in his hand, forcing me to look at him while he looked deeply into my own eyes. "And she loved him so much that she abandoned him and her son. And only later did guilt, or shame, or God knows what force him to acknowledge the child was his.''

"David had a child . . ." my voice broke, "a son who—"

"It doesn't seem fair, does it? Heroes are supposed to be

perfect, strong and brave and larger than life. And their children are supposed to be the same. But I'm telling you what it was really like. David was no hero. And his son was an idiot, brain-damaged from birth.''

"No," I whimpered. There was no way I could have known about Eliza or her pregnancy, but I did. And I didn't want to know what John was telling me. But there was proof of that, too, within myself, within the one remaining locked room in the house. How, *how* did I know? "No."

"Elizabeth? What's wrong?"

I shook my head, breaking the contact of his hand against my face, fumbled behind me, and opened the door. Not speaking, I jumped from the truck.

"Elizabeth!"

I heard John calling my name, saw Martha and the workmen staring at me as I burst into the hall, and ran up the stairs. I bumped into a packing case in the upper hall, knocking tools in all directions, but that didn't stop me. The keys. The keys were in the tower room. I snatched them from the chest and raced back into the hall.

The door was as formidable, as frightening as it had been when I first saw it, but now I had to see what it hid. The lock was different, higher than the others, and my hand trembled as I lifted the ring of keys to it. John's words and my own futile denials rang inside my head. None of the keys fit. I threw them to the floor and ran back to the pile of tools, clawed through it, and grabbed a pry bar. He had to be wrong; *I* had to be wrong, I prayed as the bar bit into the door and facing, sending splinters flying. The bar finally caught at the lock, and I pushed against the door, stumbling into the room as it gave.

The pry bar dropped forgotten from my hands. Metal restraints in the form of lightly wrought circus wagons barricaded the windows which ran the length of the room. No one pane of glass remained; they lay in shards on the floor, and furniture. A branch had crashed through the center window and its bars, and lay rotting across the remains of a tiny crib. A miniature lion's cage sat in the center of the room, its doors open, and it was to there that I felt myself drawn. A bed. A twin-sized bed completely enclosed by bars, the covers still on it, mildewed and rotten. I knelt beside it.

"I can't know this," I heard myself saying. "This isn't real." I touched the crumbling linens. "Not real." A gray, shapeless lump lay beside the pillow, and as I picked it up, I saw a strip of unfaded orange before it crumbled in my hand releasing mats of red down.

I must have cried out, because Martha reached out for me, lifting me to my feet, cradling me against her. She smoothed my hair and rocked softly with me before turning with me, still holding me close. I saw the shocked and questioning faces of the workmen clustered outside the nursery door. John Richards stood in front of them, looking even more stunned than the others.

Martha put herself between him and me as we entered the hallway. "Haven't you done enough for now?" she hissed at him. "For God's sake, leave."

She knew without my telling her that I wanted to go to the tower room. She closed the door behind us and helped me to the bed.

"Something else has happened, hasn't it? One of those things between you and this house. One of those happenings that if I search hard enough, I can find a logical explanation for."

I choked back a sob and gave a quick nod.

"Do you want to tell me what it is?"

"I . . . I don't think I can."

"Elizabeth, let me take you to Mack and Joannie's. You can stay there. Give up this house. Whatever is happening isn't natural. It can't be worth it."

"I think it's too late." Too late. The secrets of the living were still hidden from me, and most of the secrets of the dead. But not the big one. How could I remember Eliza and her love and her pain? I had been Eliza; I was Eliza. And for some reason I might never understand, I was here again, reliving that life. I had loved David Richards; I had given birth to the child that existed in that travesty of a nursery for how long? How many years?

"Elizabeth, are you safe here?"

The horror of the tiny jail struck me again, and I twisted away from Martha, ignoring her question as I gestured impotently toward the nursery. "I want it gone. all of it. Burned, buried, I don't care. I don't ever want to see any of it again. Will you tell them, Martha? Now?"

"Can you do that? Won't Stanley make trouble for you if you destroy trust property?"

"I don't care. I just want it gone. Please, Martha."

She put her hand on my shoulder, sighed, then rose and left the room. When she returned, I raised eyes that felt bruised, then watched her face, concentrating on the errand I had asked of her in an effort to force all other thoughts from my mind. "Did you tell them? Will they do it?"

She nodded and held out her hand. Two pills rested in her palm. "Take them."

I shook my head. The picture of the nursery swam before my eyes, and thoughts I couldn't yet let myself accept swirled through that picture. Martha held the pills closer. I took them.

She sat beside me until the medication took effect, and with that came loss of my control of my thoughts. Scattered through my visions of David caring for a child who would never know him, I have vague memories of her removing my boots and covering me, softly repeating the question I still couldn't answer. "Are you safe here?"

CHAPTER
5

*There were lions, and tigers, too, hideous caricatures in
shades of rotting gray, mottled with the black of mildew. On
silent feet they circled the cage where I was trapped. I reached
for my baby, but he grew man-sized before my eyes, crying
that pitiful, melwing newborn whimper. Where was David? I
fought the bars, but they held, and the cage started moving
toward the tiny crumpled crib while ants crawled over the
decaying log.*

*"Don't think of that," he whispered. "Think of our times
together. Hold on to them."*

There were so few of them; too few for this.

"Share them with me. It's been so long."

In spite of the turmoil of the war, their house remained
unharmed. Eliza suspected that her father's politics changed
as necessary to protect his plantation. She also suspected that
if their neighbors ever discovered his treachery they might do
the damage the Yankees so far had not.

But that day Eliza was happy the house remained unharmed
and that her father was still away on one of his frequent
"business" trips. Was she "house proud," as the vicar's
wife had once accused a neighbor? Perhaps. But perhaps
she only took natural pleasure in the beauty her mother had

surrounded herself with, the beauty Eliza could now share with David.

Rain had fallen steadily for the past two days, causing David to chafe at his inactivity, so when the sun had risen, bright and clear, he had insisted on adventuring outside. He refused her help, but leaned heavily on the banister as she accompanied him down the stairs.

As they stood on the veranda, David took deep breaths of the fresh morning air and smiled at the antics of birds bathing in the shallow puddles left in the drive by the rain.

"I hate to admit this," he told her after only a few minutes, "but I'm not as strong as I thought."

Eliza looked at him in alarm. "Do you need some help?"

"No." He laughed softly. "But I don't think I can manage a hike through the woods today after all."

Eliza hid her relief, at both his assurance and the fact that he would not soon be leaving.

"Should we go inside?"

She saw him wince with pain as he forced himself to resume his former military posture. "I'm afraid so," he admitted.

Her mother's piano dominated the small drawing room to the right of the entryway. As David eased himself onto a chair, from long habit Eliza seated herself at the piano.

"Do you play?"

"Not well," Eliza admitted, grimacing but seizing on any topic to draw his mind away from his pain. "My mother told me that all properly reared young ladies had to play, but I'm afraid I must not be properly reared."

"And for that, I shall be eternally grateful," David said. "Otherwise, I might not be here. Will you play for me?"

Eliza turned to the piano, hiding her flush of pleasure. "There is something I do fairly well," she said, beginning to finger the familiar keys. "My mother told me this was my song, probably in an attempt to ensure I learned at least one melody."

She played competently through the short piece and as she rested her hands on the keys at the conclusion, she felt David's hand drop onto her shoulder.

"That's beautiful," he told her. "As any song that is yours should be. Are there words?"

As the warmth of his hand spread through her, Eliza felt once again those strange emotions that had assailed her as she watched him sleep. She found her voice. "None that I know of."

He placed his hand beside hers on the keyboard. "Will you teach me?" he asked. "That way I will always have something to remember you by."

I could see David. He was at the end of a long hall, holding something wrapped in a blanket. I ran to him, but a wall of bars stopped me, encircled me, imprisoned me. I struggled against them, but they refused to open. I called to him, but he did not hear me. He looked at the blanket in his arms, and his expression was infinitely sad, infinitely lonely. If only I could get to him. Why was I locked away?

"Don't think of that. Not now. Remember . . . remember. . . ."

The days had stretched slowly into months since David had left. In spite of Bessie's care, Eliza's arm had scarred, but when she looked at it, it wasn't the pain she remembered— it was the touch of David's lips on her wrist. And when she remembered David, which was often, it was the way he had looked when he awoke and found her bending over him.

When Eliza was strong, she pushed those thoughts from her mind, telling herself that if David remembered her, he remembered her as a child who had helped him, nothing more, for she had been a child until he came. When she was not so strong, she surrendered to the thoughts, dreaming of the day he would return and take her to that wild and beautiful land in the West that he had described to her during their few short days together.

Summer was dying. The leaves, dry and colorless, rustled to the ground, and the air had a bite to it that told of a bitter winter to come.

When Eliza first saw the rider approaching, he seemed so much a part of her thoughts that she was not fully aware of him until he turned into the drive. Then, for one agonizing moment while her heart pounded furiously, she was unable to move or speak. He saw her, a smile flashing across his face, and waved. The spell shattered into crystal shards of joy.

"David!" she cried, gathering her skirts, rushing toward him. "Bessie, come quick. David has returned!"

Eliza ran, unmindful of her hair, which had slipped from the pins and fallen free, forgetting the decorum that Bessie had tried so hard to instill in her, aware of nothing but David and the fact that he really had returned. He stepped from his horse, waiting beside it, but as she reached him, she remembered that her dreams had been only hers and that she didn't know if he felt the same. She stopped in front of him, looking up, suddenly very shy.

But then she was in his arms, being lifted high, and his laugh was ringing out with hers. His eyes met hers. The laughter died. He put her down, his hands falling from her waist.

"You're not a child anymore, are you?" he asked.

She shook her head, once again unable to speak, the feeling of his arms around her being added to her treasure of memories. She wished for a moment she were a child, because then he could have gathered her to him—but that wasn't the embrace she wanted.

"You're thinner," he said.

Eliza managed a smile and found her voice. "You're looking well." And then, unable to say what she wanted, not knowing what else to say, she walked silently with him toward the house.

"Mr. David!" Bessie's greeting rang from the house as she hurried toward them. "Oh, Mr. David, we're so glad to see you back here safe."

"Thank you, Bessie," he said. "I'm glad to be back. Have you been taking good care of Eliza?"

"I've been trying," Bessie told him with a laugh, "but sometimes that gets mighty hard to do."

David was looking at her again, and Eliza felt herself flushing.

Bessie took charge. "Come on in and get some food in you."

In the kitchen, while Bessie and David bantered back and forth, Eliza sat silent, stealing glances at him from under her lashes when she thought he wouldn't notice.

"I'm sorry all we have is this skimpy old soup," Bessie apologized as she set a bowl of the steaming vegetables before him, "but I killed our last scrawny rooster a week ago. If I'd known you was coming, I'd have saved him for you."

"Don't worry about me, Bessie. This is better than I usually get," he said, laughing, but his gaze lingered on Eliza's face before he turned to the soup.

He is truly beautiful, Eliza thought as she watched him. But was his face a little more lined, or was it just that he was tired that made him seem different somehow? Not vulnerable—he had never seemed vulnerable, even when he had lain unconscious—but less the bronze god she had made him in her dreams. More human, more open to hurt, and, she thought, bending her head to hide the color she felt staining her cheeks, easier to love.

David finished his meal and rose to his feet. "That was just what I needed, Bessie," he said slowly. "Now, if you two will excuse my bad manners . . ." He looked steadily at Eliza, forcing her to meet his eyes. "I must go."

"Not so soon!" Eliza cried, forgetting her shyness. He couldn't leave her again.

He stared down at her. "No," he said in the same soft voice, still looking at her. "No, you're right. It is too soon to leave."

He turned to Bessie with a smile. "How would you like some meat for supper?" he asked.

"I'd like it so much, I'd think the good Lord had done us a special favor. But you don't dare go shooting around here."

"Let me worry about that." He started for the door.

"Wait," Eliza said breathlessly, surprising even herself. "I'm going with you."

Bessie frowned, and David looked at her strangely, but nothing mattered except that she had to be near him, if only for a little while, even if he never cared for her.

In the woods, her shyness began to leave. "I'm glad you're here," she said.

"I was beginning to wonder." He smiled at her, easing the sting of his words, as he picked up a branch and began stripping the bark from it with his knife. "You've become more . . . quiet."

As they walked, he whittled almost absently at the branch and began humming a tune under his breath. She listened, entranced, as she recognized the melody. "You remembered."

"How could I forget your song?" he teased her gently. "I may not be able to play it, but I'll always remember your trying to teach me."

"Oh." He had remembered her as a child. Only a child would have been so excited about a silly melody. She blinked back tears of disappointment. Well, she wasn't a child, but he would never know that unless she got over her speechlessness.

"What . . ." She began. He turned from his whittling to her.

She refused to be silent any longer, but what topic was safe? The image of him lying on her bed, near death, swam before her, and as she looked at him, so strong now, she knew that at any moment he could be torn by another bullet. . . . She chased the thought from her mind.

"What are you doing in this war?" she whispered.

Was it her imagination, or did his expression soften?

"Right now?" he asked. It must have been her imagination, because his words were impersonal. "Acting as a sort of glorified courier between the Choctaw Nation and Richmond."

"No," she stammered. "I mean why? Your land seems so far away, so different. Why were you drawn into this war? You can't be fighting for the same reasons we are." She stopped, but her fear found words. "Why do you take the chance of being wounded or—or killed for a cause that isn't your own?"

"Isn't it?" he asked. He leaned against a tree and started whittling once more, speaking as carefully as he shaped the stick. "It isn't the slavery issue, although some of us do have slaves. It isn't state's rights, because we certainly aren't a state and don't want to be. What we're fighting for is more basic than either of those issues."

His hands stilled, and for a moment the grimness of his expression gave her fear of another sort. "We're fighting for the survival of our nation, for our land which the government in Washington already wants to take from us, for our wealth which is controlled by someone other than ourselves and which has been invested in southern banks, for our integrity as a free people. If the Confederacy doesn't win, we stand to lose more than a war. We could lose everything."

"David, I—"

He silenced her with a quick gesture, took aim, and sent the carved stick sailing through the air. She heard it strike something behind her. With a triumphant chuckle, David walked a few feet into the brush and returned with the stick and a dead squirrel.

"Who are you, David Richards?" she asked when her laughter had passed. "At one moment you seem no different from a southern gentleman, and the next you're a wild little boy."

"I'm both," he said. "A product of two proud nations. Sired by one, born to and raised by another. Educated in the woodlands and mountains of my mother and the universities of my father.

"And you? Who are you, Eliza?"

"I don't know," she said slowly, meeting his eyes and realizing as she spoke that she really didn't know. "Sometimes I feel as though I am living for a definite purpose. Sometimes I almost know what it is. Sometimes, though, I feel as though nothing new will ever happen, that I'm living a life I've already known in another time, another place." She studied his face for any reaction.

He spoke quietly. "Was I in that other life, too?"

"You must have been," she said, her shyness gone completely. "Do you think—do you think me very strange?"

He shook his head and, taking her arm, led her deeper into the woods.

By the time they reached the creek where she had been sitting when she first saw him, David had a number of squirrels in his catch and had begun teaching her to throw the squirrel stick.

"Is this more of your education in the woodlands of your mother?" Eliza asked, falling to her knees beside the creek and holding her cupped hands to the water for a drink.

"Definitely," David said, dropping down beside her and stretching out on the grassy bank.

She was aware of his presence beside her, but it was as though he had always been with her. The silence between them was not heavy and strained as it had been, but calm, peaceful, as though their thoughts were flowing together without the need for words.

"I know a hill," David said, breaking the silence, "sitting alone in the middle of a wide river valley. From the top of the hill you can see, in the distance, mountains surrounding you. And the soil is as rich and fertile as that found in the bottomlands.

"When the war is over, I'm going to clear the top of that hill and plant an orchard, but first I'm going to build a house—not just an ordinary house, but one fit for a princess."

Eliza listened to the music of his voice and saw, as in a dream, the house rising on the top of that enchanted hill.

"There is a story my people tell of a woman so beautiful that the only way her suitor won permission to marry her was by promising her guardian that his people would lie upon the ground so that she might walk upon them as she came to him as a bride. I cannot promise that, but I can promise my bride—"

The vision before Eliza's eyes shattered. Of course he would marry. But why did he have to tell her now? Why did he have to spoil this one perfect day? Once again the tears welled in her eyes, and she stared at the creek, her back to him so he would not see.

"—that when she and I go to church on Sunday, people from miles around will comment on David Richards's beautiful lady."

Oh, he was cruel, she thought. Cruel to torment her. She could see the woman, a woman of his people who shared his beautiful bronze coloring, long, straight black hair, and flashing eyes that wavered under no one's gaze.

"And when I am elected principal chief, she will be first lady of my people, as she is already first lady in my heart."

She felt numb. Try as she would, she couldn't stop the tears from streaming down her face. She heard him moving behind her and then he was beside her, his hands on hers. She tried to twist away, but he touched her cheek with one slender, tanned hand, and turned her to face him. His eyes read hers.

"That is," he said, "if you wish it."

"If I wish it?" she whispered. She thought her heart would burst within her. The trees, the creek, the ground itself seemed to be spinning around them. "Oh, David . . . oh, David." She could barely speak. "I thought . . ."

He spoke lightly, gently teasing her, and yet hesitantly. "Is that a yes, or a no?"

"Yes," she said. It was so right, so very right. "Yes, yes, yes."

"You're not afraid to go so far away with me?"

She wasn't. "I'd go anywhere with you, or for you."

And then, as had happened so many times in her dreams, even as she marveled at the sensation of having done the same thing at some other time, he drew her face to his and gently touched his lips to hers. All thoughts of that distant time faded. There was only the present. Her arms crept around him. A warmth she had never known spread through her, and she arched closer, eager to savor its glow. The forest sounds died away. There was only the two of them reaching for each other, needing each other until, with a long, shuddering sigh, he lifted his head and held her tightly against his chest. She listened to the thunder of his heartbeat and marveled at the needs pulsing though her, pushing their way through the confusion in her mind.

Finally he helped her to her feet and reached for the squirrels. She retrieved the stick, and silently they walked back toward the house.

"Take me with you now," she pleaded as they reached the clearing.

"Would that I could," he said, "but there is no safe place to take you. Word has reached Richmond that Fort Smith ha fallen to the Yankees. They already occupy the Creek and Cherokee Nations. By the time I get home, our nation will probably be occupied.''

''But you could be—''

He silenced her. ''Nothing is going to happen to me. Nothing would dare happen to me. And as soon as I can after the war is over, I will be back for you.''

''You're leaving now?''

''I have to, Eliza.'' He flashed a wistful smile at Bessie, who had come from the house to stand beside them. ''Take good care of her for me, will you?''

''I sure will, Mr. David. I took care of her mother, I'll look out after her, and I reckon I'll be caring for her little ones, too.''

He turned to Eliza and, laying his hand against her cheek, looked down into her eyes. ''I love you,'' he told her. ''In this life, in all that have gone before, in all that are to come. Evermore. Remember that.''

And he was gone, leaving only the memory of their last, desperate kiss and the promise, ''after the war.''

After the war. After the war. The words echoed through empty hallways, past deserted rooms and around an overturned crib.

I was alone, with only ravaged dreams to remind me of all that had been lost, of all that the Yankees, and Owen Markham, had taken from me.

''You're not alone. Not alone. Not. . . .''

Eliza had wandered to the edge of the woods picking blackberries. Bessie wouldn't let her go any farther, saying it wasn't safe. Of course, she'd said that the day Eliza had found David. David. Eliza's thoughts turned to him again, as they did so often. The war couldn't last much longer. She couldn't quite picture the life they'd have together in the

West, but she wasn't the least bit scared. She found herself humming. Her song. And she smiled. Life would be wondrous, wherever they were, because they would be together.

She had stripped the last of the berries from the cane before her and put them in the now full bucket when she saw the two riders. They came from the woods just beyond the thicket and were galloping in her direction. Yankees! Eliza cast a glance at them and then at the house, too far away to reach before they overtook her.

"Well, well, what have we got here?" one asked in a harsh, nasal voice, as they reined in their horses.

"Looks to me like we got a nice reward for a long day's ride," the other said, laughing.

Guiding their horses between her and the house, they dismounted and stalked toward her.

"Not much meat on her bones," the first one said.

"Hell, not much meat anywhere in this part of the country," his partner answered. "But a scrawny chicken is better than no chicken at all."

At last freed from her paralysis, Eliza threw the bucket of berries at them and ran, screaming for Bessie at the top of her voice. One of the soldiers tackled her, knocking her to the ground. She scrambled up, clawing and kicking.

"I'm coming, Miss Eliza," she heard from the house. "Hey, you white trash, leave my little lady alone!"

"Jesus!" one of them said. "It looks like a mama bear coming for her cub." He twisted Eliza around. "You her cub, girl?"

"Naw, Jenson. She's white. You like 'em fat; want to try the black bear?"

Jenson snickered. "Let me get a closer look at her first."

Bessie lumbered toward them, a butcher knife waving from her hand. "You let go of her or I'll cut your hearts out and feed them to the rats."

Eliza heard the shot ring out from beside her and watched Bessie crumple to the ground. Jenson holstered his revolver.

"What the hell'd you do that for?" the other asked.

"I don't like them ugly." He yanked Eliza closer to him.

"Bessie!" she screamed, struggling to free herself.

"Ain't no one going to help you now, little gal." He reached for her bodice, but stilled his hand at the sound of another shot. The second Yankee slumped to the ground.

A small band of soldiers emerged from the woods. Eliza gasped when she recognized the captain at their head. Owen Markham stepped from his horse, his gun aimed at the man who held her.

"Move away from her," Markham's voice grated through the waiting silence.

"Now, Captain, we didn't mean no harm. We was aiming to come back, just as soon as we had some fun with the gal."

"Move away from her."

Eliza felt the hands release her.

"Even our deserters don't make war on women or children," Markham said as he pulled the trigger. Eliza watched the man fall, but it wasn't real. Bessie was real, and she lay motionless on the ground.

She stumbled toward Bessie, but Markham caught her.

"I've got to help her," she protested.

He snapped an order to a soldier. "See to the Negress."

The soldier walked to Bessie and nudged her with his boot. "She's dead."

"Bury her."

Eliza struggled against him, but he held her. "Be still," he said in the same voice he used with the soldier.

He took her arm and half led, half dragged her to the house. "Stay here," he commanded. "I'll leave orders. You'll be safe."

Eliza raised tear-filled eyes to his face. "Why?"

Markham answered a question she had not asked. "I don't want someone else pawing over what belongs to me. And I will have you."

Marie LeFlore appeared beside David at the end of the hall, her long, black hair hanging down her back, Red Feather clasped in her little girl arms. I called to her and she waved at me. She took the bundle from David and brought it to me, smiling as she did so. The bars parted to allow the blankets to pass through. I took them eagerly, uncovering the baby's face, but the face of Owen Markham stared up at me. As I screamed, the bundle deteriorated into a mass of red feathers swirling about me, blinding me.

"Don't think about Owen Markham. Don't think about the Yankees."

I have to. They were part of it.

"They don't matter anymore."

Eliza went downstairs reluctantly, puzzled by her father's summons to join him in the library. But her wonder at the strange command paled beside the joy that enveloped her, putting color in her cheeks and a brightness in her eyes, a joy which, since the arrival of David's letter, had covered everything with a blanket of sweet contentment and breathless anticipation.

The letter lay tucked beneath her bodice, but the words were written on her heart, to be called forth or to creep forward on their own, to thrill her again as they had when she first saw them in his beautiful, flowing script.

The message was brief. He was in Washington City. Finally, ratification of the treaty seemed imminent. His nation was safe. And he missed her. "I shall come for you in midsummer," the letter read. "The home I have promised you will not be completed by then, but I can wait no longer. Each day seems an eternity."

She paused by an open window. The moon bathed everything with its silver glow. A warm breeze carried into the house the familiar spring sounds of crickets, bullfrogs, and a solitary owl, and the fresh, newly washed scent left by the late afternoon shower. The smell of death was gone, the war was over, and David was coming for her. Could the night be anything but perfect?

With a smile she realized that she was humming. Her song. How David had laughed as she tried to teach him to pick out the melody on the out-of-tune piano in the drawing room.

With a sigh, she drew herself away from the window. Her father waited. Tapping lightly on the closed door to announce herself, she entered the library. Her father and another man sat in a pool of soft light near the fireplace with their cigars and brandy. At first she didn't recognize the visitor. Without his blue uniform, he seemed only vaguely, disturbingly familiar, the candlelight muting the golden highlights in his hair and throwing shadows across his strong, chisled profile. But when the two men rose to meet her, she saw the mockery and possession in his eyes. A band tightened around her heart, and she hesitated.

"Come, come, daughter," her father said as he motioned her to his side. "Now is not the time for feminine modesty."

As Eliza walked to him, she glanced at the almost empty decanter on the table; obviously her father had again, as so often lately, had far too much to drink.

"I understand that although you have met our guest, you have never been properly introduced." He spoke too rapidly. There was a precision in his usually casual drawl and he radiated a tension that made her back stiffen. "Eliza, may I present Owen Markham."

She nodded coolly, a light frown creasing her brow. "Captain."

"Now, now, Eliza. Not 'Captain.' The war is over. Mr.

Markham is with the Department of the Interior now. In a highly responsible position, I might add.''

Eliza tried to conceal the embarrassment she felt for this man who was her father. Why was he fawning over this— this Yankee?

A smile of secret amusement played over Owen Markham's lips as he advanced toward her. ''You will excuse me, Eliza? Sir? I must see to the horses.''

Eliza felt a chilling band of fear tighten within her as Markham left the room. His words had not been a request, but a command. It was no longer ''Miss Eliza'' when he addressed her, but ''Eliza.'' She tried to hold on to the contentment with which she had entered the room, but she felt it being stolen from her. She turned to her father. He filled his glass and smiled at her as he resumed his seat, but she felt no reason to return the smile.

''Mr. Markham has done me the honor of asking for your hand in marriage.''

The band twisted. The contentment shattered. She felt the blood draining from her face.

''And I have assured him you will accept.''

''Father!'' It was a ragged cry, full of disbelief and horror.

''You could do worse, Eliza,'' he said, staring at the brandy he swirled in the snifter before taking a long drink. ''The war is over. He is an influential man. You will be well cared for.''

Her father had never allowed her to argue with him, to in any way defy his wishes, but now she knew she had to. ''I do not wish to marry him.''

''Many women do not wish to marry the man selected for them. I fail to see that as a valid objection. In time, you will learn to care for him, or at least to care for your position as his wife and the mother of his children.''

Eliza closed her eyes, suppressing a moan, and the letter near her heart rustled against her flesh. Her father had never permitted secretiveness from her, either, yet she had kept

from him the most important secret of her life. "I love someone else," she said softly, "and I have promised to marry
him."

"Who?" he asked sharply, slamming his snifter on the
table. "Damnation! What went on in my absence? What did
that uppity and slatternly Negress allow to transpire?"

Eliza's head jerked up at his words, but she bit back her
angry denial, knowing it would only fuel her father's anger.
Bessie had been neither uppity nor slatternly; she had been,
until David, the one person to show Eliza love since her
mother's death. But Bessie was not the issue here; David
was, and her love for him.

"We gave comfort and sanctuary to a wounded Confederate officer, a gentleman, as I know you would have done had
you been here."

"A gentleman?" he asked incredulously, but she saw the
gleam of speculation in his eyes. "Someone who courted you
and proposed marriage to you under the protection of my roof
and has not bothered to make himself known to me? What
kind of gentleman is that?"

She dropped to her knees beside his chair, pleading with
him. "He's coming in midsummer to speak with you, Father.
He would have spoken sooner, but you were away so much,
and he had to return to his nation. He was needed at home so
badly after the war."

"His nation?" he asked. "France? England? From which
nation does your *Confederate* gentleman come?"

Eliza hesitated. Too late, she heard the warnings clamoring
in her heart, in her head.

"I'm waiting."

Yes, he was waiting, and she had said too much not to
speak now. She readied herself for his reaction, praying that
at least the common cause of the Confederacy might sway
her father. "The lands to the west."

"The lands to the west?" he repeated blankly. Then his

face contorted. "Indian!" he roared, pushing her away from him. "You've soiled yourself with a savage?" He rose from his chair and stood looking down at her. "I was concerned about a Yankee," he said bitterly, "but I would rather see you married to a Yankee, I would rather see you ruined, than squatting beside some redskin's teepee."

"Father, it's not like that. He's not like that," she cried, but he turned from her and paced the room, heaping verbal abuse upon her and overriding her words.

None of it mattered to him. He wouldn't understand David's nobility or his gentleness or his dedication to his people and the nation they were trying to save, any more than he would understand the love the two of them felt for each other. She would not expose any of it to his sarcasm.

When he paused in his tirade to draw a deep breath, Eliza rose to her feet and interrupted him. "I do not wish to displease you, Father, but this is one thing I cannot do. I will not marry Owen Markham. I have promised myself to another, and I intend to keep that vow."

She turned to leave the room, almost reaching the door.

"Eliza, Owen Markham is with the Department of the Interior."

She faced him. "His position does not impress me."

"The Department of the Interior, Eliza," he repeated, and she saw triumph in his eyes. "His duties include dealing with the rebel nations. They are at this moment negotiating treaties which could spell the end for those so-called nations." He shook his head. "You won't go to your Indian. And even if you did, he wouldn't be foolish enough to take you in."

She felt the room closing in on her. She could not endanger David, but there had to be some escape from the horror of belonging to Owen Markham. There had to be. "And if I do not marry anyone?" she whispered. "If I simply refuse to take the vows?"

"Which tribe, Eliza? There weren't so many of them that

fought against the government in Washington that, if this conversation were made known to him, Markham couldn't take vengeance on all of them, if he so desired."

"No," she whispered. "You wouldn't."

"He wants you. Badly." His eyes raked over her, and she saw the gleam of victory burning feverishly in them. "Enough to offer me a way to save what my family spent generations building. I don't know, however, if his wanting you would extend to offering marriage if he knew about your past indiscretions, and I hesitate to put it to the test. Unless you force me to. I do know this. I will tolerate no further opposition from you. You will leave with Owen Markham tonight to become his wife, or you will leave with him tonight to become whatever he wants of you. I would advise you to be grateful that so presentable a man has offered matrimony."

He brushed past her and stopped at the door without looking back. "I'll leave you now to compose yourself while I tell Markham that you have accepted his very flattering offer."

As he closed the door behind him, she heard the key sliding in the lock. For a moment she was unable to think. Locked in the room, with no one to turn to, panic held her immobile until one word screamed itself at her over the confusion in her mind. *Run!* she heard. *Run from this house!* But she was not to be allowed that, either. From beneath the window a low laugh drifted upward, and she realized that her father and Markham stood below.

Frantic now, she searched the room for any means of escape and found none. That knowledge forced her to recognize a single truth: She couldn't run. Had every door and window been open to her, she could not leave. She had given her father the one weapon that could hold her here.

Numbness crept through her. She drew David's letter from her breast and reread it; then, knowing that not even this would be left to her, she touched the corner of the letter to a candle and knelt beside the empty fireplace, watching her future curling into one black ash. The last word to blacken was "eternity," and it taunted her, "eternity, eternity, eternity," as the numbness overwhelmed her.

She felt a hand on her arm, although she had not heard the door open, and it tightened, lifting her to her feet. His face still mocked her. His eyes still held possession, and now something else. "I told you that one day you would belong to me."

The numbness lifted once—later that night, when he took her, painfully—and she prayed for it to return, to seal her away from a shame she hadn't dreamed could exist, to give her the only escape she would ever know from the prison her life had become.

"Shhh. Quiet, now. Remember our afternoon. The water is bubbling in the creek. The grass is soft beneath you. The air is crisp and fresh."

But my baby. . . .

"You are on that creek bank. Life is full of promise and just beginning. Remember that. Hold that to you. Sleep now, and dream. Dream of that autumn day so long ago. Sleep."

A lamp near the door cast a dim glow over the room. My eyes felt as though I had ground sand into them, and my head pounded furiously when I awoke, but I felt curiously rested.

Eliza's music ran through my memory. I knew the music. Like someone who had seen something too overwhelming to comprehend, I held on to that one inconsequential fact. I knew Eliza's song. Beethoven's *Für Elise* was the third selection on the first side of the tape I had played almost continuously during the drive from Columbus, Ohio, to Richards Spur, Oklahoma. It was a melody so familiar, even the ice-cream vendors in Columbus blasted it from loudspeakers to summon neighborhood children to their trucks. And it was a melody had loved since childhood. The rest—the rest I could not even consider at that point.

But at last I could answer Martha's question. Yes. Here, of all places, I was safe. The wing chair was turned toward the window and someone was seated in it. For a moment it seemed almost a part of my dreams, but I recognized Mack's worn boots.

"Won't Joannie be worried about you?" I asked, pulling myself up to a sitting position. The sound of my voice made my head pound even harder.

"Aunt Martha said it was time for you to be waking up," Mack drawled casually. "She didn't know what your state of mind would be, so I was elected to sit with you. She left some things for you on the bed table."

I noticed the tray then, took two of the aspirin, and placed the damp cloth over my eyes. It didn't seem a bit unusual for Mack to be there.

"Where is Martha now?" I asked.

"Where she always is when she has a problem to solve," he said with a gentle laugh. "Cooking."

After a few minutes I felt the aspirin beginning to work.

"Mack?" I asked. "Did she tell you what happened?"

"Just that John Richards was mixed up in it some way." While there was no curiosity in his voice, I thought I detected a bitterness that seemed foreign to the easygoing Mack I knew.

"Watch out for him, Elizabeth. Even if he is your kin, I don't think you can trust him."

CHAPTER
6

The door to the nursery remained closed. I accepted Martha's word that the room had been cleared and the windows replaced, but I had no desire to see the inside again. The splintered facing was reminder enough.

The money involved had certainly played a role in my decision to come to Richards Spur, but only a small one. In what now seemed to me to have been unthinking naïveté, I had wanted a family, a home. Those were here, all right, but so was so much more. Now I had to ask myself if I, too, like the last woman who tried to claim the estate, had wanted too much.

A vague dissatisfaction replaced the joy of discovery that had carried me for so many days. I was eager to learn more of what had happened in the past and why I was now here, but I was also terribly afraid.

Gradually the lower rooms of the house took shape, and the neatly marked and taped movers' boxes were emptied and disposed of. Gradually the stacks of draped furniture from the upper halls were diminished as chairs and sofas and tables found their way to what I hoped were their proper places. But for the while, at least, there were no more memories.

We found a beautiful Steinway grand piano stored in an upper bedroom, and the workmen carried it down to the drawing room. I thought briefly of my childhood dream of learning to play the piano, but as I ran my fingers over the out-of-tune keys, I knew that was a dream that would still have to be postponed. At least for a while.

Even the discovery of a door that had been hidden behind a pile of storage didn't lift my dissatisfaction. Martha was obviously excited as we tried the keys, and I tried to make her believe that I was, too, but I think she knew my smile was only for her benefit.

The door opened onto a narrow, curving stairwell leading upward to a circular room, cedar-lined and sweet-smelling in spite of the dust. Long rods hung suspended from the ceiling as in an enormous closet, shrouded and ghostly in the dim light of the lamp Martha held. I took the lamp from her, and she lifted one of the dustcovers.

"Draperies," she cried. "Oh, look, Elizabeth. Can they still be any good?"

Now she was the one who dug excitedly through treasures; I, the one who stood by watching. She found a sweep of delicate white lace with small embroidered roses. "These have to be the ones for your room."

"Those are the undercurtains. There ought to be some old-rose draperies," I said without thinking.

She freed the sheers and continued searching, but I could read in her eyes the silent questions my words had raised.

"Here they are," she said finally. She didn't ask me about my careless comment. To be honest, I don't think she wanted to know. I set the lamp on the floor and helped her free the heavy draperies.

We were laden with our discoveries and leaving the room when I saw the other stairs. On impulse I followed them upward, and Martha came with me. When I opened the door at the top, light flooded the stairwell, blinding me for a moment with its brightness.

As my eyes adjusted, I realized that we were on top of the

southeast tower, directly above my bedroom. The view was awesome. I found the row of pines with its scattered green outcroppings leading down the hill and the dull green of another pine standing in solitary splendor among the winterbare oaks on the southern slope. Behind me was the hilltop, now overgrown and wild, and all around was the lush river valley, surrounded in the distance by what seemed to be an unbroken wall of mountains. The squalor that was Richards Spur was too close to the hill to be seen from this height.

"Can you imagine what it must have been like when that was all Richards land?" I asked, a little humbled at the thought of how much effort it had taken to clear and claim the valley.

"It still is," Martha told me, and in her voice I thought I heard the same touch of bitterness I had detected in Mack's.

"But surely it was broken up when he died?"

"It was." There was no mistaking the inflection. Martha was bitter.

"John Richards," she went on. "He's put it all back together. Any way he could. The only thing he doesn't own around here is this hill."

"There's Mack's place," I began, but she turned to me.

"I thought you knew," she said. "I supposed that somehow you knew that, too. His orchard is on the hill. It's been in his mother's family for years. The colonel deeded it to the MacDougals before he died."

"The MacDougals."

"William MacDougal and his wife Jane, Marie LeFlore's mother." And another piece of confirmation clicked firmly into place. The gentle Scotsman had married Jane and stayed

I apparently gave no outward sign that Martha's words meant more to me than they should have. If I did, Martha didn't notice. She pointed to a field bordering the river where some slow-moving black cattle grazed. "The house is gone, but that used to be our place."

"You told me about the place you were renting when your husband died, but I had no idea it was so close."

"No. That's the one we used to own." She turned abruptly and started down the stairs, and not knowing what to say, I followed her.

Martha's habit was to go into Richards Spur each morning, to check the post office for mail, to pick up what few things we needed from the store, and occasionally to visit with Joannie. I usually didn't accompany her, but the next morning I felt a need to talk with Marie LeFlore. Martha parked in front of the store and went about her errands.

Marie was sitting in her rocking chair, but there was a marked change in her appearance. Her eyes seemed sunken and, for the first time since I had met her, lifeless. I drew up a stool and sat beside her.

"Are you all right?" I asked.

Her voice was cracked and lacked her customary authority. "It's just age, Eliza. I was only waiting for you. Now I can go."

I took her frail hand in mine. "I found your doll," I told her, at last able to speak about it. "Red Feather."

"No. Not my doll. His," she said, glancing listlessly about the room. "My doll is in the ground. Under the magnolia. Such a sweet doll he was."

"Marie, why didn't you tell me?" But she didn't answer. She seemed lost in a faraway thought. I released her hand, smoothed a tendril of hair from her forehead, and rose to leave.

Martha had come into the store and stood by the door holding a letter in her hand. I recognized McCollum's letterhead. Martha's eyes were moist.

"What has he done now?" I asked her.

Martha shook her head and handed the letter to me. "Thank you, Elizabeth. I didn't know how we were going to make it."

It was the check I had demanded for her.

"I'm going to Fairview," she said. "No. No, I'm going to Fort Smith and buy a carload of groceries, and some linens for the house, and—"

I stopped her. A thought was forming—one I didn't like. Had I been so wrapped up in myself that I hadn't even considered what now seemed obvious?

"Martha, have you been supporting me?"

"Everyone knows you can't spend any money or you lose the house."

What had I been thinking of, not to realize before that moment just whose money was being spent? "I can't spend any of my money, but the trust is supposed to provide for me. You didn't have to. If you hadn't been there, or if I hadn't been so inconsiderate . . ."

I broke off in midsentence and reached for the telephone. "We're going shopping," I told her, "but not with that check. That's for you."

I dialed the number and stood impatiently tapping my foot. As before, Louise Rustin suddenly decided to clean the front of the store and busied herself nearby. As before, McCollum's secretary did not want to put my call through. But this time, she did.

"Mr. McCollum," I told him as soon as he was on the line. "I appreciate that you have finally sent Martha Wilson her salary, but we seem to have an additional problem. In spite of the fact that you do not like me, and that your fondest wish is to see me gone, I do have to eat. Martha has to eat. We require a certain amount of cleaning supplies and a few amenities, such as towels, sheets, that sort of thing. And I'm relatively certain that David Richards did not intend for anyone to have to live here without the basic necessities for life. What is the provision for an allowance?"

After a moment of intense silence, I heard his voice, if possible even more condescending than before, and his face wavered through my memory, superimposed now on the body and the self-indulgence of Eliza's father. "Miss Richards, you seem inordinately concerned about dollar figures which are not at this point any of your business. When—if—you inherit, all of that information will be placed at your disposal. Not until then."

I couldn't speak to him for more than a minute without wanting to rage at him, but I held on to my temper as best I could. "I am concerned about eating. I am concerned about maintaining not a luxurious but at least a moderate standard of living. And the more I think about it, I'm concerned about the way you have been handling the trust. In fact, I wonder if an audit isn't necessary. But that can wait, because what I am most concerned about right this minute is gaining access to a reasonable amount of the allowance. And I expect that no later than Friday."

I hung up on him. He couldn't know that I was trembling inside, and I refused to let Louise Rustin see how shaken I was.

"I used to see him," Marie said absently.

"Who, Marie? The child?" I asked, kneeling beside her.

"No. The colonel. I'd go to the top of the hill. I'd go to the graves. I'd see him in the tower window. Watching. Just watching. And waiting. I know he can't really be there, that he's in that box, but I'd see him."

As I looked at her, I knew that she wouldn't be alive much longer. I bent to her and kissed her withered cheek before I took Martha's arm and hurried her from the store. I didn't want Louise Rustin to see me crying.

The broken windows were replaced. The curtains and draperies were hung. A matching old-rose bedspread covered the bed. The tower room had been thoroughly cleaned, but I couldn't bear the thought of anything but cleaning being done to it. Not yet. Except for the one bright spot on the wall, the room was complete.

The workmen had finished with the lower floor and moved upstairs. We could walk through the halls now without scraping our shins or tripping. The rooms downstairs, though showing their age, showed it gracefully. I knew that I had never seen a lovelier house, and I began holding my head a little higher and my back a little straighter because it was mine.

And when the electricity was restored and the pump once again working, I reveled in the luxury of soaking chin deep in the enormous tub in the marble-walled bath of my room, of wandering in my robe to the delicately carved mantel, of knowing that the room, the house, and the hill were meant for me.

Each day when Martha returned from Richards Spur, I met her with two questions. Each day the answers were the same: Marie wasn't any better, and no, the allowance hadn't arrived. Friday came and I knew I would have to confront McCollum again. I was dressing for the trip to Fairview when Martha came into my room.

"He's here," she said in the voice she reserved for speaking about John.

I felt my heart give a strange tug, my throat become dry and tight. I pushed the unwanted, unneeded feelings of anticipation aside. What could he want? He hadn't been back since the episode in the—a picture of the nursery flashed through my mind; I pushed that aside also—since the episode of the timber thieves.

He waited in the drawing room, standing at the Steinway, picking out a melody with his left hand. He must have heard my step, for he began banging out a discordant version of chopsticks. Then he turned, smiling, and his attitude was that of a genial host welcoming a guest to his house.

Raising one dark brow, he inspected me. "You ought to wear that shade of blue more often," he said. "It's extremely flattering."

Even after the debacle of our last meeting, I was susceptible to the attraction I had felt for him, to his glib compliment, and I hated that.

"Mr. Richards, I am quite busy this morning. Would you please tell me why you're here?"

"*Mr. Richards?* I believe you must be as cold as this house today." He turned to the fire and prodded it. "I thought I remembered a furnace in this place."

"It isn't working yet, but even if it were, it would have no effect on my attitude. Martha and I are planning to do some shopping in Fort Smith today, and I've just learned that I have to make a trip to Fairview first. So let's make this visit as brief as possible. Why are you here?"

A smile worked at the corners of his lips, and somewhere within me, I swear something fluttered. Anger. I told myself that was what it had to be, although I had never felt it so intensely before. I drew on that, straightening to my full height and summoning my iciest voice. "I'm afraid I must ask you to leave."

He walked over and stood looking down at me. "Why, cousin, would you be so rude when I've driven all this way just to save you a trip to Fairview?"

Why, indeed? When looking at him brought to life memories of all that had been lost, and why. But John couldn't, mustn't know that. I focused instead on the last part of his statement. "What do you mean?"

He reached into his inside jacket pocket and pulled out a small package. I knew what it was but not how to battle the defeat I felt.

"I mean, I've brought you your checkbook."

"Does Stanley McCollum always ask you before he does anything?"

He smiled grimly but didn't answer my question. "Martha?" he said.

She stepped from the hallway into the room.

"Get Miss Richards's coat," he told her. "I'm taking her into Fort Smith."

"Wait a minute, Martha. Mr. Richards is not taking me anywhere."

He made a slight movement of his head, and then I heard her steps going down the hall.

His face relaxed into a smile. "Come on, Elizabeth. This is my way of making amends."

There was no fighting him, not when I needed so much of my strength to fight my reaction to him.

Martha returned with my coat. "Martha goes, too," I managed to say. He nodded, and while she went for her coat, he helped me into mine.

"And I promise," he said quietly, "that the past will stay in the past unless you bring it forward.

He ushered us outside to a silver Continental. He held the front door for me, opened a rear door for Martha, and drove down the hill before I had found an appropriate retort.

Martha had been preparing her list for a week. When John asked and she told him what we needed, his laugh rang out. "You never would have been able to get all that in your toy car, cousin."

He could be charming. He proved that. By the time we reached the interstate highway which looped around Fort Smith, even Martha seemed to have thawed toward him. He knew all the shops she wanted to visit and acted as though his sole purpose was to see that she found everything on her list. During lunch, she even relaxed enough to laugh at one of his stories. And I? I wondered at his motives, and at my own for enjoying the day in spite of myself, but I said no more than necessary to maintain polite conversation.

We were on our way home, driving through the center of town on the wide main street, past unfamiliar buildings, when

John suddenly made a right turn and stopped in front of a building under construction.

"I know I said I'd keep the past in the past," he said, "but this is a hard city to do that in." He seemed to be inspecting the building the way he had me. "We almost didn't get started on that. This used to be a freight yard, and you would have thought I was tearing down the Confederate soldier on the courthouse lawn when I decided to put an office building here."

"Freight yard?" I asked, looking around for some landmark.

"Before the railroad," he said, noticing my search. "Over a hundred years ago. I don't understand it, but this whole area has become some sort of shrine. In the residential section between here and the river, half of the houses aren't fit to live in, and the other half are either antique shops or shrines to the past. The whole area is desperately in need of new life—but don't try to infringe on the integrity of the neighborhood by constructing a decent building."

"Could we—" I knew, without knowing how I knew, that there was something here for me to learn. Oh, Lord, could it possibly be? "Could we drive through that area?"

"You'd like that, wouldn't you?" John put the car in gear and drove slowly through the neighborhood. He was right. Most of the houses looked as though only a bulldozer could help them, but many of them stood proudly in their restoration paint. I had never been here before; how could I possibly recognize anything? And then I saw it.

"Stop," I said, and John did.

It was a small house, just four rooms and an attic, with wide porches wrapping around it and massive brick chimneys at each end. It gleamed with its fresh paint and new brick sidewalk, and I was glad that it did. A small sign stood near the coach step.

"Are antiques on your list?" John asked.

I shook my head. "But I'd like to look."

The inside of the house gleamed, too, from the pegged floors to the hardware on the doors, even to the bricks in the fireplaces. I leaned against the mantel in the parlor while a woman in costume explained the restoration of the house and the extent of its former disrepair. I didn't correct her when she said that the family parlor had been in one place and the dining room in another. I didn't question John as to why he was watching me so intently, watching as though he expected me to say or do something completely outrageous at any moment. The memories, good and bad, were coming so fast I couldn't sort them. Martha walked to where I stood and touched the cupid carved on the mantel.

"It's pretty," she said, "but nothing like what we have at home."

"Are you folks from around here?" the shopkeeper asked.

"Across the river," Martha said.

"Then you might be interested in this part of the history of the house," the woman went on. "Legend has it that one of the wealthy Indian planters from across the river kept his mistress in this house."

"Legend?" I asked, feeling myself growing cold. "Don't you mean gossip?"

John turned his head to one side as though he meant to shake it. A negative gesture? For me? For what? He stopped himself, walked to my side, and began studying the mantel.

The woman was oblivious to anything but the enjoyment of telling her story. "Oh, no. It isn't gossip. The widow of one of our founding ministers told all about it in her memoirs—without names, of course. It seems that after the death of her husband, she was forced to find work, and she was hired as a housekeeper in this house. You can imagine how she must have felt when she realized what the situation was."

"Yes," I said, feeling the coldness creeping into my voice. "I can imagine."

"She was really quite distraught about it. She said that she fought with her conscience for a long time until she found that she really had no choice."

I clutched at the mantel. What had she done? I didn't want to hear more, but I couldn't stop her.

"She wrote the woman's husband and told him what his wife was doing, pleading with him to save his wife from the life of sin she was leading."

I was like ice, frozen, unable to think or feel.

"Of course, by today's standards it might not be the right thing to do, but I think that back then her motives were honorable."

I broke the spell. "I think her motives were vicious. Let's go." And I walked from the house, not waiting for the others.

They joined me in the car, and John again looked at me strangely. "What's the matter, cousin?" he asked softly so that Martha couldn't hear. "You acted as though she was talking about our King David and his Bathsheba."

What a short time it had taken to make the trip to Fort Smith. Now it seemed as if it would take as long to go home as it had by wagon all those years before.

Neither Martha's nor, especially, John's attempts at conversation on the return drive did anything to lift my heavy mood. John helped carry our packages in, but when I didn't invite him to stay, he gave me another of his maddening smiles. *Secrets*, that smile seemed to say. *You have them, too, and before I'm through, I'll know all of them.*

Either Martha wasn't aware of my mood or she ignored it, and I was glad for that. She seemed happier than I had ever seen her as she busied herself putting away her new household treasures. I helped her, not wanting to spoil her excitement.

She chattered pleasantly but incessantly as we unwrapped the new linens. I tried to follow her words, but images were flashing behind my eyes so rapidly, so insistently that only an occasional comment penetrated my consciousness. This was memory, the common, ordinary variety, if anything about what I was experiencing could be called common, not the flashes of complete and detailed involvement that still had the power to shake the foundations of everything I had thought I believed. Nevertheless, I knew Eliza had lived in that house in Fort Smith as surely as I knew . . . as I knew that she had lived in this one.

". . . so nice today, just like . . ." A stray phrase caught my attention. The subject seemed important to her.

"I'm sorry, Martha." I gave myself a mental shake. "What were you saying?"

"Why, John. Today he was almost the way he used to be. When he was a boy."

I didn't want to talk about John Richards, but it seemed that Martha, too, was bothered by memory.

"I had forgotten," she said slowly. "So much has happened, I had forgotten what a good child he was. So well spoken and serious, and always having a kind word for me."

A smile softened her lined face as she delved back into her past. "He used to practice his piano lessons up here—of course, being a Richards, he always had the run of this place—and on his way home he'd stop at the ranch for a drink of water, for a little visit, and then he would be off again on that black stallion of his, riding like he was part of the horse.

"But that was a long time ago," she said abruptly, turning again to the linens. "Too much has happened between then and now."

She tore a wrapper from a sheet. "No. That John Richards is gone. When he changed, he changed."

I took the sheet from her. "What made him change, Martha?" I asked, more to quiet her than because I wanted to learn. Or maybe I did. What had he done to her?

"I don't know," she said. "I know when it happened, but I don't really know what. It was his sixteenth birthday. He'd gotten a new saddle and was going to try it out, but for some reason that stallion of his threw him. Threw him into the corral fence. It knocked him out for a while, but everybody said it didn't really hurt him all that bad.

"They didn't even keep him in the hospital. But he got rid of that horse. Never rode it again—well, one time, my Jim said. He got up on the horse with his hand still bandaged and rode till the horse was just about dead. Jim said he did it to prove he was still boss. But he got rid of it right after that.

"Maybe it was the first time anything or anybody crossed him. I don't know. Maybe he thought that because he was a Richards, he couldn't be hurt like the rest of us. Whatever it was, it changed him. It was like overnight he grew up, and he's been a hard, cold man ever since."

We finished with the linens in silence and then I pleaded the need for a nap as an excuse to be alone.

In my room I sank into the wing chair by the window and thought about Martha's words. "Why, God?" I whispered, not truly understanding my own question. But I had to ask someone, and there was nowhere else to turn. "Why would You allow that face and that body to belong to that soul? Tell me I'm wrong; please tell me it isn't so."

A hard man ever since, Martha had said. She had no way of knowing how hard he could be, or how long he had been that way. And I? Did I know? Oh, God, it felt as though I did. I moaned and shrank more deeply into the chair. The images had been pushed back for too long. They would no longer be denied.

Eliza

Eliza sat stiffly, ill at ease in the carriage. A long line of other carriages paraded past the gleaming whiteness of the nation's Capitol. People called to each other and waved greetings while she waited, as silent and still as her Negro driver, for Owen to join her.

Owen's latest actions puzzled her. For years his commands had been simple. She was to remain in his house, unseen and not speaking unless he required it of her, oversee the household, and accommodate him in her bed when he so desired. Now, suddenly, he wished her to become a hostess, to accompany him to the social activities from which he had always excluded her. Suddenly, she must have an extensive wardrobe, be seen shopping, be seen calling for him at the

Capitol. He had even insisted she be in the Senate gallery the following day, although he didn't tell her why. These things frightened Eliza, for Owen demanded perfection from her and when she failed in any way his punishments were cruel and often painful.

Eliza was acutely aware of the inquiring glances cast her way by the passing parade of unknown persons, just as she was aware of the stiffness of the new blue gown she wore and of the unyielding band of her ridiculous hat and of the silly little frilled parasol which did nothing to protect her from the heat of the July sun.

Would Owen never arrive? The thought stunned her. This was the first time she had ever wished him to hurry to her. No, she told herself, she didn't want him; she just wanted to be gone from where she was. Strange. Within the confines of his house, Eliza found it almost possible to accept the emptiness of her life. There, habit and what will she had left pushed down those feelings of frustration, anger, or loneliness that still struggled within her. Only outside the house, where she could see real people, living real lives, did those feelings threaten to overcome her.

What was Owen's latest game? Politics? Perhaps. He hadn't risen as rapidly in the Department of the Interior as he had wanted. He wouldn't long be satisfied with remaining in the same position. His ego couldn't stand his not advancing in power and prestige.

She looked impatiently toward the steps of the Capitol. A group of men emerged from the building, started down the long line of steps, then paused near the bottom, engaged in an animated conversation. One, taller and slimmer than his companions, stood slightly apart from them. Something about his stance caught Eliza's eye, and she glanced toward him. She felt her heart leap, but she fought against leaning forward to see better.

"It isn't David," she whispered through clenched teeth.

"It never has been. It never will be. Never." But she stared, feeling the blood drain from her face as she recognized long-remembered mannerisms.

One of the other men spoke to him. He shook his head and turned to start down the remaining steps. He was looking right at her. She felt her breath imprisoned within her and forced herself to exhale. *Oh, God*, she thought, *he's seen me.* He had. Her eyes locked on his face. She couldn't move. She wanted to run. To him? From him?

He stopped. Not twenty feet from her, he stopped, his eyes taking in the frivolous hat, the expensive fabric of her gown. For a second he looked as if he were going to call out to her, and then he seemed to draw into himself.

She felt the weight of the carriage shift and knew that Owen was climbing in beside her.

"Those damned Indians kept me a good hour longer than they should have," he swore loudly. "You don't look half bad, dear," he said in a lower voice. "A little pale, and the gown could be livelier, but I think you'll do."

Eliza said nothing. She tore herself away from the sight of David and focused on the back of the driver's head.

"You could smile," Owen whispered. When she didn't, he hissed at her. "Smile, I said."

She forced her lips into a smile as Owen shouted to the driver, "Get us to Mrs. Carmichael's, Jericho. We're late already."

A crack of the whip, a lurch of the carriage, and David was left behind, a blur against the larger blur of the Capitol.

Something long repressed stirred within Eliza. She felt moisture gathering in her eyes. No. She had not shed a tear in four years. She would not cry now.

Amanda Carmichael was the widow of a senator who had died in office two years after the end of the war. Josiah Carmichael had been powerful, and Amanda had enjoyed that power. After his death, Amanda declared that Washington City was her home and refused to leave. Quietly at first, because of the prescribed period of mourning, she began building her own position and was now the acknowledged queen of Washington society. Owen, although not a member of her inner circle of friends, had often been invited to gatherings at her home. Eliza had never been included in the invitations—until now.

"Remember, you are a lady, and you are my wife," Owen reminded her needlessly as they were led into the drawing room. "The wrong word from Amanda Carmichael to the right person can ruin my career."

Owen guided her through the crowded room to an incredibly beautiful woman dressed in maroon satin. She wore her dark blond hair piled regally atop her head, framing patrician features. A choker of diamonds circled her slender neck. As she turned toward them, Eliza thought she saw a flicker of something—distaste? distrust?—in the woman's eyes, but it was gone in an instant, and when she spoke her voice was warm and welcoming.

"Owen, I'm so happy you could come this afternoon." Amanda extended a hand to him and then turned to Eliza. "And I'm especially happy you could come, too, Mrs. Markham. I do hope we will have an opportunity to visit."

From Owen's tightening grip on her arm, Eliza felt sure that no visit would take place, but she murmured what she hoped was an appropriate comment.

Owen glanced around the room. "I see your other guests have not arrived."

"No," Amanda said, "but they did have the grace to send a messenger saying they'd been detained." Her hand rested lightly on Owen's arm. "I'm counting on you today. You know these people; I don't."

"I hope you never know them as I do, Mrs. Carmichael."

Eliza wondered briefly who those other guests were, but

Amanda Carmichael excused herself at that point, leaving Eliza with a silent Owen. There were a number of other women present, but Owen did not introduce her. He saw her to a chair near the doorway and left her seated there while he visited from group to group, but she frequently felt the intensity of his gaze upon her.

She knew he was using her, but she didn't know how or why. *Be patient*, she told herself, *you'll know sooner than you really want to; just be on your guard*.

Even with that warning, she was not prepared for the group that entered the room. She started, then forced herself to sit quietly, showing no more than mild curiosity as the men who had been with David on the Capitol steps were greeted by Amanda Carmichael. Eliza's heart pounded furiously with fear that she would be faced with meeting David here, but she had long ago trained herself to hide behind an inexpressive facade. She did this now, and when Owen joined Amanda Carmichael and looked quizzically at Eliza, she felt sure he read nothing in her face.

David did not appear. Eliza felt a strange sense of relief and disappointment at his absence. She was too far from his associates to hear their conversation. She was almost too far from them to see them clearly. There were five of them, all dressed in socially acceptable black suits. The oldest, obviously a full-blood, betrayed his discomfort only by the erectness of his carriage. Their features, their hair, their coloring set them apart from the rest of the gathering. Eliza wondered how differently they would look out of the confinement of the Washington drawing room. She also wondered if she were reading her tension in their actions, for they seemed to her to be on the alert, ready to flee should the throng of gaping onlookers turn hostile. It must have been her imagination, she decided, for one of them, a heavy man of about fifty, said something to Amanda Carmichael, and the woman's delighted laugh rang through the room. She linked her arm through the Indian's arm and led him to a cluster of chairs, where they sat and held a lively but obviously friendly conversation.

Eliza willed herself to sit impassively through the rest of the long afternoon. Finally, the guests were leaving. Finally, Owen was at her side, and they were making their polite farewells. But Eliza did not relax. She knew from Owen's expression that the evening would require all her strength.

It did. A supper she did not taste, served by the housekeeper who had also learned not to speak unless Owen asked her a direct question. Owen asked no questions. He called for whiskey and dismissed the housekeeper, who went gratefully, Eliza knew, to her room.

Owen filled his glass repeatedly, not speaking, studying Eliza all the while, until the silence was as heavy as the heat, a physical force in the room, pressing her down, squeezing the life from her.

He rose abruptly from the table. "I want you to play for me," he said, and walked into the adjoining room.

He never asked that of her. Eliza sat in stunned disbelief until she realized that he had settled into a chair waiting for her to respond. She followed him into the parlor and seated herself at the piano, hesitantly placing her fingers on the keys.

"What would you like to hear?" she asked, the calm in her voice giving lie to the turmoil she felt.

"Surprise me. Something a loving wife would play for a husband who has had an involved and trying day."

She had no idea what to play. A waltz, perhaps? She began playing softly.

"Not that," he said, interrupting her. "Play the one you used to play when you didn't know I was in the house. It's repititious and rather sweet."

Her fingers froze in place on the keys. When had he heard that melody? It had to be the one he meant, but she hadn't played it for years.

"Eliza. Play it for me."

How could she, when the memories that music evoked were only painful now? But he waited, and she couldn't refuse to do as he asked. Perhaps if she concentrated on the mechanics of the melody there would be no room in her mind for anything else. It almost worked. Owen's presence in the room kept her from surrendering to the call of the past. She played through the piece, her fingers stumbling only when her concentration faltered, and sat with hands on the keyboard as the final note echoed through her mind.

Owen reached for the decanter again, poured the last of the whiskey into his glass, drained the amber liquid, and set the glass beside the decanter with a clatter.

"You're tired, my dear," he said carefully. "Shall we go upstairs?"

He stumbled only slightly as he rose from the chair, assisted her from the piano bench, and, with a cruel grip on her arm, guided her up the stairs to her room.

The soft glow of a lamp near the bed provided the only illumination. Owen bent his head to hers in the beginnings of the too familiar ritual. Eliza's eyes closed. Her memory turned to another kiss an eternity before. What would it hurt, she thought, to pretend, just this once? Owen's mouth was claiming hers, but it was David she remembered, longed to respond to, until the memory of his face at the Capitol swam before her eyes. *My God, what am I doing?* she thought. Passion drained from her and she endured Owen's embrace until he pushed her from him with an oath.

She stared at him in amazement as he went to each lamp, lit them, and filled the room with light.

"Come here," he said from across the room.

When she didn't move, he walked to her and pushed her into a circle of light.

"Owen!" Involuntarily, against all her knowledge of how he expected her to act toward him, she protested.

"Shut up," he told her. "I want to see. I want to see just what you are."

Trembling inwardly at this new violation, Eliza stood rigidly before him, her vision fixed firmly at a spot on the carpet.

He loosened her hair. She felt it cascade around her, the softness of it falling below her waist.

"You look like a woman," he said. His voice changed, the chill of it penetrating her to the bone. "Look at me." When she failed to do so, he clenched his hand in her hair and jerked her head up. "Look at me!"

He stared into her eyes as though he could find answers there. "Other women find me attractive. What is there in you that won't let you respond?"

She remained mute, her eyes locked on his.

"I've given you everything." He spoke evenly now. "My home, my name, a place in society."

He pushed her toward the wardrobe. "I've bought you clothes other women only dream about," he said as he opened the doors and began pulling dresses from their hooks. "But you dress like a widow. You only go out when I insist upon it. You never smile. You never thank me." He tore her new blue riding habit from its hanger and it joined the pile of velvets and satins on the floor. The strap of the small riding crop caught on his ring, and, swearing, he released her hair to free his hand. She fought back a long-battled urge to tell him why she could never respond to him, knowing he was dangerously close to losing all control.

"I want you, Eliza, but I want more than just your shell. I want your warmth. I want your comfort. I want you to want me. Other women would give me that. I have a right to it from you."

She closed her eyes against the demands in his. "Go to one of them," she pleaded softly. "I can't help you that way."

His blow caught her beneath the right eye, his heavy signet

ring biting into the skin between cheek and temple. Her head snapped to the side, and she stumbled backward.

"You will," he groaned, catching her, jerking her to him in a travesty of an embrace. His mouth closed on hers, and she tasted the warmth of blood as her lips were forced over her teeth. "Damn you, you will," he muttered as he began fumbling with her clothes.

Eliza knew that she should submit passively, so that this evening could finally be over, but something in her was alive for the first time in four years. Each touch of his hands, his mouth, and his body against hers was a violation she could no longer tolerate. She began struggling, quietly, desperately, until she was able to push away from him. Her feet tangled in the riding habit, and she sprawled on the floor.

He walked to her slowly and deliberately, with a look she had never before seen in his eyes. He bent over her but did not touch her. Instead, he picked up the riding crop and stood toying with it while he studied her.

"You saw him today, didn't you?"

She fought the panic clawing at her throat and forced herself to look up at him. "Who?"

The whip slashed into her shoulder, tearing the delicate fabric of her dress and leaving a narrow line of blood on the exposed skin.

She tried to rise from the floor, but he pushed her down.

"I know he exists. Your father told me that much when I visited him this spring. He came once, looking for you. Did you know that? Your father was so drunk he couldn't remember anything about the man, except the lie he told him to get rid of him. God, I wish I had been there. I want to know who he is."

Her voice caught in her throat. She had to force the words out. "There is no one else. You know I have never broken my vows."

She saw his movement and threw her arm up to protect her

face. The leather bit into her arm, curled around the old scar, then scraped her flesh as he yanked it away.

She waited for the next blow, but he stood transfixed, staring at her arm.

"The courier," he said. "That's who it has to be. You lied to me even then."

He grabbed her arm, pulling her from the floor. "He's in the city, isn't he?" he demanded, twisting her arm until she cried out.

"I thought I could find out who he is without asking you, but that was before I knew how deep the lie went." He bent over her. "Have you been with him? Is that why you won't have me now?

"He is a member of the Choctaw delegation, isn't he?" he asked, his face so close she felt the harshness of his breath against her. "They're going back to their wilderness in a few days, and I will have his name before they leave."

At her continued silence, he pushed her away from him, still holding her arm. The whip sliced across her back. She jerked away from the pain of it, but still he held her.

"His name, Eliza." The whip bit into her back again. "Tell me his name."

Eliza caught the cry which nearly escaped her. She clenched her teeth against any sound slipping from her. Now Owen only suspected that David was a member of the delegation. If he were certain—No. Her mind refused to consider what he might do if he were certain. She had known, dimly, what he was capable of doing to David and his people four years ago when she married him. For him to find out now, to exert the full force of the influence he now possessed, would mean that she had endured the last four years for nothing.

It was as though she were watching herself from across the room. Her voice betrayed none of the tumult within her. "I'll see you in hell first."

As the whip cut repeatedly into her back, she could no

longer remain the calm, detached observer. She felt every biting blow, endured every agonizing second, until she found herself on the floor, her arms protecting her head.

Please, God, make me mad, she prayed through a red blur of pain. *Give me the peace of madness so that I don't know what is happening, so that I don't have to be strong any longer.*

The lashing stopped, but still she knelt, waiting.

She felt the toe of Owen's shoe in her side, nudging her around. She forced her eyes to focus and looked up at him.

"There are other ways, Eliza." He took a step closer to her. "I will know his name. Before I finish with you, I will know everything about him that you know."

He would, too. She knew with sudden clarity that he would abuse her until she betrayed all she had ever loved, unless he killed her first, unless she . . . She felt hysterical laughter rising within her. Was this, then, madness? If so, where was the peace she had prayed for?

He leaned closer. She drew herself as upright as she could. The laughter bubbled in her throat and escaped into the room. She saw him draw back the whip to strike her again. She threw her arms in front of her face. The leather bit into the palm of her left hand, but her fingers closed on it, and with her right hand she grabbed for the slender strip. She felt it sliding against her palms as she tried to hold it, as Owen tried to reclaim it. She felt her flesh burning as she lost her grip and felt the knotted end of it bite into her hand. Then, with more strength than she had, she tore the whip from Owen's hand. With an oath, he sprang for her.

She flailed at him with her only weapon. The tooled leather on the handle caught him just above the ear, and he fell to the floor.

Eliza stared at him for a moment. Then, with a whimper, she dropped the whip.

He had fallen facedown in front of her. *I've killed him*, she thought without feeling, until the enormity of what she had done slammed into her.

"Owen?" she whispered. "Owen?" She reached for him, not daring to touch him. When she saw the pulse beating at his temple, a great sigh escaped her and she realized that she had been holding her breath.

I've got to get help, she thought, struggling to stand, but as quickly as that thought came there also came the knowledge of what he would do to her when he regained consciousness. She stood utterly still, torn between her instinct to give aid and the surety that she had to flee even though she had no money, no one to turn to, and no safe place to go.

Her glance darted from object to object in the room, as though searching them for answers, before falling on the whip at her feet.

"I have to," she whispered. With trembling hands she reached into Owen's jacket, drew out his wallet, and took a few bills from it. "I have to," she repeated. She took all the bills and held them tightly in her fist as she ran from the room.

She was at the front door of the house before she remembered her torn dress. Panicked now, she knew there was no time to change. She hurried to the door beneath the stairs, tore it open, and fumbled inside the closet for something to cover her. An old black cloak hung from a peg at the back. She grabbed it, throwing it around her and drawing its hood over her hair as she escaped from the house.

She had no plan for her flight other than putting as much distance as possible between herself and Owen Markham. David. The thought of searching him out, of losing herself in the safety of his arms, beckoned to her, but she cast aside that idea. Owen would expect her to do that. God help anyone he found her with.

CHAPTER
8

Elizabeth

Icy rain beat fitfully at the library windows. Occasional flakes of white splattered against the panes, dissolving into puddles of water that gathered at the mullions, then streamed downward.

I was alone in the house and glad of it, for in this very masculine room on the ground floor of the southeast tower I didn't have to worry about Stanley McCollum's continued pettiness, about the conflicting emotions I felt each time I thought about John. I didn't have to worry about David and Eliza's still incomplete story, or why I, who had never had a moment of drama in my life, had been chosen to relive a life that seemed to have been steeped in tragedy. Here in this room, I could simply surrender to the power that had been David Richards.

The day before, four men had carried a massive walnut rolltop desk downstairs and placed it against the south wall, and we had hung brown velvet draperies over fourteen-foot-tall windows. Every box tagged for the library and every other piece of furniture I thought might belong to this room had been piled in the center of it the night before, and I had spent the day unpacking, arranging, and cleaning.

The drapes were open now, drawn back against the stone walls to admit as much of the weak afternoon light as possible, and a fire glowed from the hearth. But as the storm increased in intensity the room grew dimmer, and it became more and more difficult to read the titles of the books I had piled onto the shelf beside me.

I paused, unwilling to climb down from the ladder until I finished with the books I had brought up, and looked over the room. Overall, I was pleased with my work, although I had not found any of the room's accessories, and I wished I knew how David had arranged the furniture, just as I wished I knew how he had arranged the hundreds of books now resting in stacks of rough groupings I had created as I unpacked them. I now understood how Martha had felt the day she cleaned my room, because I could almost describe what drove me as obsession: obsession that I be the one to restore this room, and that I do it properly.

With a sigh, I turned back to the books. For the most part, David's collection delighted me. I had chosen to major in English because I loved books—old, new, and in any stage in between—and the notion that their contents opened new pathways to anyone willing to step between their covers. Also, if I were willing to teach grammar as well as literature and if I were willing to teach in an inner-city school, I could almost guarantee I'd have a job.

I recognized many of the titles in David's library, now classic, beautifully bound volumes, few of them bearing printing dates later than 1900. But these with which I now worked were unfamiliar, both titles and authors, and delving into them, I learned that their subject matter was unfamiliar, too.

For some reason David Richards had amassed an extensive collection of what I could describe only as metaphysics. Nineteenth century and earlier metaphysics. I, in my ignorance, had supposed the New Age movement to be the product of a much later generation.

Not knowing where else to turn, I had asked God for answers but had received none. Now, it seemed, I had been provided with volumes, thousands of pages, of answers. All I had to do was find the right questions.

I picked up a book, peered at the barely visible title on its spine, and positioned it on the shelf just as light flooded the room. I whirled around, almost losing my balance on the ladder.

John stood by the light switch holding a mug of steaming coffee in each hand.

Grateful for the distraction of having to regain my balance, I used the next few moments to try to bring my thoughts under control. Why was he here? I turned my back to him and began worrying with the books to hide my confusion, but one slipped from my hand and fell to the floor.

John walked across the room, set the mugs on a side table, and picked up the book. His right eyebrow lifted slightly. "The Secret Doctrine? Helena Blavatsky? Don't tell me King David was a theosophist?" He glanced at the titles on the shelf where I was working, and his eyebrow quirked even higher. "Or a spirtualist?"

I had no clear-cut understanding of those terms, but I did understand the derision in John's voice. I said nothing.

"I don't remember these books," he said, running a finger along the spines of those already in place.

"That's not surprising," I told him, and gestured to another shelf. "Do you remember Hawthorne and Emerson, either?"

"No." He grinned then, and walked back to the table where the coffee waited. "The truth is, I spent as little time as possible in this room. As a child, I found it extremely oppressive.

"You might as well come down," he added. "I'm staying until we finish our coffee."

I repressed an oath but climbed down from the ladder.

"What are you doing here?" I asked pointedly. *Spying for*

McCollum? I wanted to ask. But I knew that wasn't right. John didn't work for McCollum; McCollum worked for John.

John held on to his maddening grin. "We're in for some bad weather. I thought you might appreciate knowing in time to put in some extra supplies."

I softened, a little. That was a kind gesture on his part, no matter what his underlying reasons were. I took the coffee he handed me, appreciating its warmth in the room I suddenly realized was cold.

"Thank you, John, but you didn't need to make the trip. Martha has gone to Richards Spur for groceries." And to mail my carefully composed letters, but I didn't tell him that; I hadn't even told her what the letters contained.

"I know," he said.

I looked at him over the edge of the cup.

"I saw her in town."

His eyes darkened. I saw the frosty gust of his breath as his laugh echoed around me. "If you could see your face . . ."

Anger shot through me. How dare he laugh at me?

"You knew there was no reason to come here, yet you came anyway?" I asked. "You walked into my house without knocking? You made yourself at home in my kitchen? And now you're laughing at me? What do you think gives you the right to do that?"

His laughter died and, at last, so did his grin. "I've never had to ask permission to enter this house," he said. "I was working a few miles from here. Yes, I saw Martha in town but I decided to come up anyway. I was cold and I was wet. I knocked on the kitchen door. No one answered. I opened the door and called out. No one answered. The kitchen was warm. I poured myself a cup of coffee. I poured you a cup of coffee. And I brought it to you.

"Now tell me, cousin, just what have I done to spark that kind of anger?"

What had he done? What had *John* actually done? Besides

threaten this house. Besides threaten my own newly found faith in what was happening to me by the impossible attraction I felt for him. Why had I so quickly identified him with Owen Markham? Did I really have anything to base that identification on other then John's own denial, his hatred, of David? "Nothing, John," I murmured. "I . . . Nothing."

He wrapped both hands around his cup, warming them. "Elizabeth, you saw me for the first time at the bank. Before that we hadn't even spoken to each other. But since the minute we met, it's been as though you were fighting me. Why? What did I do in no more than thirty seconds to irritate you so much?"

How much could I tell him? How much did I understand myself? Not much. Not yet.

I searched for safe, sensible reasons. "You were with Stanley McCollum," I said slowly. "That's bad enough. You mocked me. You threatened me. You looked at me. . . ." I drew a deep breath. I'd never forget that look. "And the way you looked at me . . . appraised me, disregarded me and my feelings, and told me that you felt you could control me."

"In thirty seconds?" he asked cautiously. "Are you sure that's all?"

I nodded abruptly and stared into my cup, not daring to speak or look at him.

"Cousin, I don't know what you knew about us when you came here, but you ought to realize by now that I do have some control over you—not because I want it but because I am who I am.

"As for appraising you, why should I be different from any other man in the county? You're certainly the best-looking stranger around.

"And," he added confidentially, "I've been told I'm the most eligible man in three counties."

"Why, you . . ." I spluttered, jerking my head up to look at him.

Which apparently was the effect he'd been aiming for. He laughed again, softly, and without much humor. "It's not fair to tease you," he said finally. "You rise to the bait too fiercely."

He shook his head. "I may not be your only living relative, but I'm the only one in this area. And you're the only family I have here, too. Truce?"

I was drained by the encounter, frustrated and confused, and something within me nagged of the inevitability of his getting what he wanted. To fight now was senseless.

"Truce," I said, sighing.

"Good." He reached over and patted my hand. "We have to keep up appearances. The gossips have already paired us off."

I jerked my hand away from his and stared sharply at him. His grin was back, softening his features. I wanted to cry, but a part of me wanted to laugh with him, to join in this game he insisted upon playing, regardless of the outcome.

"But not victory," I whispered.

"No." Once again he became serious. "I'm not sure either one of us can really win."

John wanted to see the house. Puzzled, and more than a little reluctant, I led him through the lower rooms and up the main stairs. He paused at the place where the gate had been and ran his fingers over the now restored wood, but he didn't say anything.

Feeling strangely defensive, I followed him while he wandered, aimlessly it seemed, through the halls of the upper floor, peering into those rooms which still held shrouded furniture and boxes, glancing at the shattered doorjamb of the nursery but not attempting to enter, to my room, where he stopped near the wing chair and studied the room.

"You've done a remarkable job," he said at last. "This room . . ." he ran his hand over the back of the chair, "this room is just as I remember it."

"It is?" I asked, surprised at the approval I thought I heard in his voice.

"When I was a child," he told me, "I used to practice on the Steinway downstairs. I don't know that it made my playing any better, but at least my father didn't have to put up with the noise. I spent every minute I could in this house. Now I know that I was allowed free rein of the house because I was a Richards, and my father's son, but then I didn't understand why we couldn't live here, why we had to wait for some as yet unknown female Richards to inherit. But I suppose you must have wondered the same thing. Why this house stood vacant with just a caretaker when there were heirs to the rest of the estate."

"No, I didn't," I told him. "I didn't know it really existed until my grandmother died this fall."

"That's strange," he said, looking at me with the same questioning expression I had noticed about him before. "When I first heard of you, I imagined you as a little girl being groomed to take your rightful place when you came of age, being force-fed stories of David Richards and his castle with your peanut butter sandwiches."

"I'm sorry to disappoint you." I wandered to the window. The snow fell steadily now, large wet flakes which curtained the view and made lacy patterns on the enameled green of the magnolia outside the window. I felt as though we were shut off from the rest of the world. An aura of unreality surrounded us, and it seemed not at all strange to want to talk with this man.

"I was always drawn to the history of the Five Civilized Nations, the Choctaw in particular, because it seemed that they were the most . . . courageous . . . of the five. I found a picture of David Richards in a history book when I was twelve and felt that I ought to know him. I pretended we were related, because of our names, but I didn't know we were until just after grandmother died.

"The books I read didn't devote much space to his personal life, and Gran, my mother's mother, didn't know or didn't want to tell me very much, but it seems right that he had a home like this, and it seems to me that I have always loved the view from this window.

"I even—" I broke off, bewildered by the realization that I had been willing to say far too much.

John didn't seem to notice. "What about your father?" he prompted gently. "Didn't he—"

"I don't remember my parents. My father was a race car driver. Gran didn't like him; he was 'irresponsible.' He and my mother were killed when a truck ran into their sports car. I don't think Gran ever forgave him. I know that other than her bitterness about him taking my mother from her, she only told me what she absolutely had to about my father, and nothing about his family, even to the point of lying to me."

"And now you . . ." He hesitated, watching the swirling snow. "And now you drive a sports car yourself."

I felt a bittersweet smile quirking my lips at his question, even as I wondered what he had started to say. "It's hardly that," I told him. "Although Gran wouldn't know the difference. No, I don't think she'd forgive me for the car any more than she would forgive me for being here, for abandoning her like she felt my mother had."

The silence deepened around us in the darkening room.

"I've always loved this view, too," John admitted.

I watched his familiar profile as he gazed at the falling snow, and a sweet, sad yearning began within me. I longed to touch his face.

I shoved my hands into my sweater pockets and snapped myself back to reality. I studied him a moment longer. I didn't want to be indebted to him, but he was the only one I knew who was familiar with the house. And he had been the one to call the truce, although I had no idea how far the truce would carry either of us.

"John? Will you help me?"

He turned without speaking, the questions back in his eyes.

"Will you tell me how the house was, before? Will you show me how the rooms were arranged?"

There was just a suggestion of a lifted eyebrow, a twitch near his jaw. "But you're doing well without my help."

"Not really. And there's so much I can't find, so much that seems incomplete."

I had his full attention.

"Such as?"

"Such as the desk accessories, the china and silver, the decorations that would complete the rooms. Things I feel should be here." I indicated the bare spot on the bedroom wall and the real reason I asked. "Even the painting that belongs there."

Again I saw the barely perceptible twitch near his jaw. "You haven't found them?"

"If I had, would I be asking for your help?"

He studied me for a long time before speaking. "Yes," he said finally. "You should know. Come with me."

He took me by the hand, back through the hall, up to the room where the draperies were stored. He went to the wall beneath the stairs leading up to the roof. It, like the rest of the room, was paneled by wide cedar planks marked at regula intervals by narrower vertical battens.

"During the Civil War," he said, "the Creek and Cherokee Nations were occupied by Union troops. A number of refu gees fled south. Some of them, unfortunately, stayed after the war, starving, and stealing what they could find. It was two years before the government had any control of the situa tion. Then, later, there were white outlaws who hid in the nation to avoid capture and prosecution.

"This had to have been built during the first part of con struction."

He ran his fingers along the edge of a batten and lifted

on hidden hinges to one side, revealing a lock in the underlying board.

"When I helped close the house, I put the things I considered most valuable in here."

"You helped?" I asked, remembering the jumbled piles of possessions.

"Naturally." He took a ring of keys from his pocket, slipped one from the ring, and handed it to me.

I looked at it suspiciously. "Why do you have this?"

"I stole it," he said simply. "Over twenty years ago when I first found the room, I stole the key from the caretaker. He didn't know what it fit; he probably never missed it."

"And no one ever asked about it?"

John hesitated. "No one but I knew it existed. Until now."

I turned the key over in my fingers. "You don't like me—"

"That's not—"

"In any event, you don't want me here. You've made that more than clear. Why are you giving this to me now?"

He put his hand on my shoulder but remained silent until I looked up at him. "Let's just say that I want to even things up a little."

I stepped away from the physical contact, my suspicions growing. "In what way?"

John dropped his hand to his side. "Stan McCollum has had his attorneys examining the trust agreement since shortly after you arrived. He's decided that restoration is not provided for in the agreement, and he's cutting off all but maintenance funds at the end of this month."

"He can't do that!"

"Yes," John said. "He can. Open the door, Elizabeth."

I was trembling with anger. "Is there going to be a constant battle for the rest of the year?"

"Probably."

"Is this part of your bribe, then? Look what you can have,

Elizabeth, if you just give up and let me win? See what you stand to lose if you fight?''

He was angry, probably as angry as me, and no doubt, in his eyes, with better reason. To my chagrin, he controlled his anger better than me. He started to say something, stopped, and then said very distinctly, ''Open the door, Elizabeth.''

The door opened outward on hinges hidden by another batten, a heavy metal door disguised by the cedar panels which covered it. Inside was total blackness.

John took a book of matches from his pocket, struck one, stepped inside the door, fumbled with something, then held a lighted candle in a holder toward me.

''Won't you come in, Miss Richards?'' he asked, giving me a mock bow. Belatedly I remembered our truce, the one John seemed determined to maintain.

As my eyes adjusted to the darkness, John lighted another candle and walked farther into the shelf-lined room. Cartons in neat stacks filled the shelves, with only glimpses of cedar-lined walls visible between them.

I visualized the house, trying to see the room from the outside. ''I would never have found it,'' I said finally.

''You have to be a child, playing where you're not supposed to, to find anything this well hidden,'' he told me.

He walked to the boxes and scanned the labels. ''These are the library things.'' He pointed to a shelf and walked on. ''Here are the china, the crystal, and the silver.''

''The painting?'' I asked hesitantly.

He turned to me, and the flickering light from his candle cast odd patterns of shadows across his face. ''I believe you'll find something acceptable near the door.''

To the right of the door stood what appeared to be a cloth-draped chest. When I lifted the drape, I found a wooden rack holding framed paintings. I knelt beside it, holding my candle close to the first canvas, a beautifully executed landscape. I searched for the artist's signature.

"Why, it's a Stephen Ward." I could only guess at the value of the painting. Ward was considered one of the finest nineteenth century western artists. His work, though different in emphasis, was ranked with that of Russell and Remington.

I pulled the painting forward and looked at the next one. "So is this," I said, scrambling to my feet and pulling that one forward. "And the next."

I turned to John. "They all are," he said. "It's the most extensive Ward collection I know of, from his earliest work on."

"But they should be in a museum," I protested. "Not locked up in the dark."

"Once they are yours, you can do what you want with them." He paused, and I could have sworn it was for dramatic effect. "Until then, I'd leave them where they are."

I thought his words and his emphasis strange, but I turned back to the paintings, looking through them for the one I felt I must recognize. "It isn't here," I said, more to myself than to him.

"What isn't?"

"The one for my room. It isn't here." Surely he would know. "Where is it, John?"

He took my candle from me and placed both of them on the table near the door.

"Are you positive?" he asked, looking into my eyes.

I nodded dumbly, disappointment washing through me with the unreasonable intensity that so many of my emotions now held.

John raised his hands, touching, smoothing, and then lifting my hair to the top of my head. His eyes were black in the flickering light and gave no clue to his thoughts as I stared helplessly up at him.

"I can't help you," he said reluctantly.

I felt his hand tightening in my hair as he bent toward me. I couldn't move, I could barely breathe as he bent closer.

"I can't help myself." With his other arm, he pulled me to him as his mouth claimed mine. With the first touch of his lips I felt myself falling into an abyss of longing, a longing John shared. His lips became more insistent and, reluctantly but unable to stop, I responded to that longing and to him. Eventually, it was John who pulled away, because God help me, I couldn't.

He gathered me to him in an imprisoning embrace, my face buried in the rough suede of his vest, and I leaned against him helplessly while trying to sort out the need that raged within.

I pushed away from him and found my voice. "You'd better go," I said, but the indignation I tried for sounded more like a plea.

CHAPTER 9

After locking the vault, by unspoken agreement John turned to leave, and I accompanied him, strangely unwilling to be parted from him. I knew I'd have to sort through the physical and emotional needs that were hammering at me. I wouldn't be one of those silly women who let physical attraction hold her in thrall. No, I—I felt a bitter laugh forming and forced it down. No. I had the knowledge of a hundred-year-old love to keep me rooted in reality.

When we reached the warmth of the kitchen, we found that Martha had returned. The tension between us was so heavy, Martha would have seen it if she hadn't had her back to us, unloading a sack of groceries and throwing canned goods into the pantry.

John took his coat from the hook but stopped at the back door. I went to Martha's side.

"What is it?" I asked her, concerned over her behavior and, knowing how she felt about John, half fearing a retort about unexpected company.

"That woman," she muttered, throwing another can onto the shelf.

I knew exactly who she meant. Although I'd never heard Martha refer to her in quite that way before, that was how I often thought of Louise Rustin.

John waited at the door as if he, too, were concerned about Martha's uncharacteristic behavior. I took the sack from Martha and put it on the cabinet.

"What has she done now?"

Martha was near tears. "Oh, Elizabeth, Marie is so sick. Louise has her there in the store and won't send for a doctor."

"Let's go," I said.

"I'll drive," John said from the doorway.

I looked up at him, surprised by his offer of help. Apparently our truce still held. But I was uneasy about accepting and worried that Martha would reject his offer as interference. He spoke again. "How bad are the roads, Martha?"

"Bad," she told him. "And getting worse."

"Then, if you want to get home tonight," he said, canceling any objections either of us might have, "you'll go with me in the truck."

No longer falling gently, the wind-driven snow blew almost horizontally as we left the house, drifting high against anything that blocked its passage. I waded through it to the truck, slipping once on underlying ice.

The solitary elm near the gate groaned heavily under the weight of ice-covered branches and snow built up in each fork of the tree.

The three of us were silent all the way down the hill. Even with the four-wheel drive of the pickup, I felt the truck sliding on the roadway and knew John had to focus his attention on keeping us out of a ditch. I was glad he had insisted on driving; my skills would never have gotten us down safely.

I pounded on the door of the darkened store until I saw a light come on inside. Louise opened the door only a crack. "I'm closed."

I pushed past her into the store. "Where is she?"

"In the back room," Martha said, following me inside, with John immediately behind her. I started toward the back.

"Wait a minute. You can't just barge in," Louise complained. I didn't stop; let her complain all she wanted.

As I opened the door Martha indicated, a wave of heat and the odor of unburned gas and unwashed body blasted from the room. An unvented stove blazed in one corner, and the heat in the room sucked the breath from my body. I turned off the stove.

Marie, frail and even more shrunken, lay on an old quilt on the unmade bed. I knelt beside her and touched her cheek.

"She's burning with fever," I told Martha. "We have to get her to a hospital."

"You're not taking her out of here," Louise snapped. "Not unless you want her death on your conscience."

"She's right." John stepped in front of Louise. "We can't take her out in this weather."

Such a feeling of frustration came over me that I was immobilized for a moment. John was Marie's only hope. "Are you influential enough to get a doctor here?"

A blast of icy wind rattled the windows at the back of the room. John looked first at the windows and then at Marie. "I can try."

I saw him at the telephone when I returned to the front of the store. I pulled the chain on each light I came to until I found what I needed, grabbed sheets and a nightgown from the counters, and handed towels to Martha. "Please see if you can find a basin and water," I told her.

"What do you think you're doing?" Louise demanded.

I didn't even try to hide my disgust. "What you should have done. Get out of my way."

She followed me back into the room. "You can't just come in here and take over." But she immediately fell silent when she noticed that John had entered the room.

"Any luck?" I asked him.

"Not yet."

While John held Marie, I stripped off the old quilt and put a clean sheet on the mattress. John settled her back in bed, and I covered her with another sheet.

"Can I do anything else?"

I shook my head. "Just keep trying to get a doctor."

Louise started in on me again. "I don't need you here. I don't want you here——"

"Louise." John's voice left no question of his authority. "I want to talk with you at the front. Now."

Martha joined me then. Together we removed Marie's stained clothing, sponged her body, and dressed her in the clean nightgown. Her fever-glazed eyes opened. "Eliza?"

"Yes, Marie," I said calmly, determined that she would see none of the fear I felt for her. Martha slipped from the room, leaving us alone.

I smoothed Marie's hair from her face and straightened her braids over her shoulders. In spite of my resolve, tears welled in my eyes.

"It's my time," she said softly.

"But I just found you. Please don't go yet. I need you so much."

"You're sturdy. You don't need me. Trust your feelings."

Trust my feelings? Which ones? The ones that said run to John? The ones that said I loved David? The ones that said that none of this could be happening?

"Is it real?" I asked.

"Oh, yes." She was slipping away from me by the second. "More real than anything you've ever known."

"But if it is . . . is David here, too? Where, Marie? And why don't I know?"

"Oh, child, you have so much to learn. And so does he." Her eyes closed but she continued, almost in a whisper. "I told him he couldn't play God, but he had to try. . . ."

Through the tears I could no longer hold back, I saw Ma-

rie's image blur, grow darker, soften. In a misty vision, I saw
Marie caring for Eliza's child, I saw Bessie caring for Eliza,
and I knew this was not the first time I had watched this dear
friend die.

I fought back a sob, knowing the answer, knowing I
shouldn't ask. "You are Bessie, aren't you?"

With her eyes still closed, she smiled as if at some ancient
memory. "I was Bessie. I *am* Marie." Her smile faded.
"That's something you have to learn, too. Oh, my child,
have I done wrong? Have I done wrong by telling you?"

She was silent.

"Marie? Marie?" I took her fragile hand in mine and held
it to my cheek. "I love you."

Her smile returned for only a second before pain twisted her
mouth. "I know. But I'm so tired, Eliza. Please let me go."

I leaned over and kissed her cheek. Her hand fluttered in
mine, and then she was still. I sat beside her, holding her
lifeless hand, alone as except for a few brief weeks, I had
always been.

Eliza

Eliza reached the railroad depot just as a train was boarding
and managed to board, clutching a ticket to St. Louis, just as
the train was pulling out. She had asked for a compartment
but was told there were none available unless the conductor
could locate one.

She waited now in the almost empty coach for the conductor to return with an answer for her, and as she waited the
strength that had sustained her during her flight began to drain
away. She longed to throw off the heavy cloak and collapse
against the seat, but to throw off the cloak was to be discovered, and to lean back was torture, for now every nerve in
her body cried out.

"Mrs. Griffith?" She felt a hand touch her shoulder. Startled, she tensed forward.

"Mrs. Griffith?"

It was the conductor, using the name she had given him. She caught her breath and turned toward him.

"There are two gentlemen traveling together who have offered to share a compartment so that you can have one of theirs," he told her.

"I didn't mean to put anyone out," Eliza protested but breathed a prayer of thanksgiving as he brushed aside her objection.

"It's no trouble for them, I assure you. Please follow me."

To her surprise, she found that she was barely able to stand and less able to walk. She followed him haltingly down the aisle until a wave of weakness washed over her. She leaned against a chair, clutching it with her burning hands so she would not fall. At the coach door, the conductor turned to wait for her, and she straightened, not wanting him to see her weakness. Somehow she managed to go on, into the next car, where he tapped on a door, opened it, and stepped aside for her to enter.

A man knelt on the floor, closing a case, his face hidden from her.

"I'll be out in just a moment," he said in a rich, melodic voice which stopped her in midstep just outside the door.

David! What was he doing here?

He rose and turned to her, and she lowered her head, relying on the anonymity of the hooded, shapeless cloak, knowing that he must not recognize her.

"The conductor told us of your loss, Mrs. Griffith," he said softly. For a moment she was puzzled, until she remembered the story she had told of recent widowhood to explain her strange attire. "I know how difficult it is when you lose someone you love."

She dipped her head in acknowledgment, wanting nothing more than to look up at him, to drink in his closeness, but knowing that she could not. Then he was gone, and with him yet another part of her.

The conductor remained outside until she entered. "The porter will be here in a few minutes to make up your berth," he said before closing the door.

Alone. She sank onto the seat, grateful for the dimmed light of the compartment, but she couldn't divest herself of the cloak. Not until the porter had made his rounds. She rested her cheek against the window.

Why now, David? she thought. *Why here?* Oh, God, to be so close and not to be able to go to him. The next car? The next compartment?

There was a hollow feeling behind her eyes, another in her throat. This had been his place, if only for a short while. He had sat in this same seat, breathed the same air, looked out this very window. She looked around the compartment furtively as if this, too, were something forbidden to her, and yet feeling that if she looked hard enough she could see the essence of him still here.

She found something wedged in the corner of the seat and pulled it toward her. It was a slim, dark leather portfolio with gold initials on the clasp. D.R. She placed the portfolio on her lap and touched it lovingly. "Oh, David," she moaned, "do you ever think of me?"

A tap on the door reminded her of the porter. "Come in," she said, not looking up from the portfolio. She heard the door open and waited for the noises that would tell her it was time to make way for the porter. She heard only silence and then the sound of the door closing.

"Eliza?"

It had been years since she had heard him speak her name, but as she turned to him she had the strangest feeling that this meeting had been predestined.

He stood just inside the door, his features taut, the expression in his eyes . . . guarded. "I don't understand."

There was no way to hide, no place to run, and she was too weary to have done so had there been. "You weren't supposed to leave for a few more days," she whispered.

He glanced at the portfolio in her lap. "Perhaps I do understand after all." David had never spoken to anyone in her presence the way he now spoke, and nothing Owen had ever done to her had the power to hurt her the way the cynicism she heard in David's voice did. "I came back for that, but if you need it so badly, I'll wait while you read its contents."

"What . . ." she stammered.

"I didn't think even Markham could sink low enough to send his wife to spy," he said. "He must be more desperate than I thought." He laughed, a mockery of the laugh she remembered. "When I left early, did he decide I must be carrying plans for a new strategy back to the nation?

"What are you wearing under the cloak, Eliza? A party dress? That blue froth I saw you in earlier? Wasn't there time to change? Is that the reason for the elaborate story of mourning? Get you on the train, with me, and if all else fails play on old relationships to gain the information he thinks I have?"

His words struck her like blows. She could only stare at him, hollow-eyed, as he hammered away any hope she had that he still loved her.

"No," she whimpered, pushing the portfolio to the floor.

As he looked at the portfolio, a shadow flickered across his face. He dropped to the seat beside her, resting his head in his hands, and sat silently massaging his forehead with strong, tanned fingers.

"I'm sorry, Eliza," he said finally. "I know better than that. Markham might try, but you wouldn't go along with it. You can't have changed that much."

He shook his head. "And there's nothing to learn. The delegation is in shambles. They're worrying about what they lost, not that our nation may lose its entire invested wealth, and its identity. That's why I left—in disgust. Perhaps once I'm home we can reach some decision about what to do next.''

He looked so disillusioned, so lost. She reached out and touched his shoulder. *Oh, my poor David,* she thought. *What's happened to your dreams?*

It was as though he read her thoughts. ''We're not beaten, you know. We've just had a pretty heavy setback.''

''I am sorry,'' he said again. ''You must have important reasons for what you are doing.'' He reached for her hand, but she quickly tucked it inside her cloak.

''I do,'' she said softly.

''Where are you going?''

She saw a picture in her mind of a solitary hill in the middle of a wide valley, with the home he had once promised her rising from that hill. Perhaps it was only her dreams that had died. ''I can't tell you,'' she said.

He closed in on himself again. ''I see.''

She couldn't tell him, but she couldn't bear the lack of expression on his face. ''No. No, you don't see,'' she murmured. ''I can't tell you, because it's better for you not to know.'' She drew a ragged breath. ''I've left Owen.''

She saw expression in his eyes then—incredulity.

''Why?'' he demanded. ''You had everything you wanted—a beautiful home, an influential husband, money, a place in society.''

Where had he gotten those ideas? From her father, of course. But why had he believed them? ''Oh, David.'' She shook her head in angry denial. ''I have the clothes on my back, a little money, and a railway ticket.'' Her cloak had slipped away from her face, and a loose strand of hair fell over her eye.

''Are you positive this is what you must do?'' David asked, reaching to smooth back her hair.

Oh, God, couldn't he tell? ''Of course I'm positive!''

He put his hand under her chin and turned her face toward the light. She watched his eyes darken and narrow as he smoothed her hair behind her ear and gently probed the wound on the side of her face.

"Did he do this?" he asked tightly.

She heard noises in the room, strange, choking sounds, not sobbing, not laughter, and realized they were coming from her.

"Did he strike you?" he demanded.

She couldn't speak, couldn't breathe. His hands were on her shoulders now.

"Eliza, answer me!"

He clenched his fingers on her shoulders, and a bright burst of pain forced a cry from her. The noises stopped. His hands fell away.

He reached for the fastenings of her cloak.

"Please, don't," she whispered. She reached out to stop him, and he caught her hands in his.

Tears welled in her eyes as he looked at the marks on her hands and the burns on her palms caused by the leather pulling across them. The tears began falling as he raised her sleeve and saw the angry banding of welts across the old scar.

He bent his head to her arm, touched his lips to the scar, and placed a whisper-soft kiss in the palm of each hand.

The tears streamed silently down her cheeks as he unfastened the cloak. Only a twitch near his jaw betrayed that he felt anything as he pushed back the cloak.

As the cloak fell from her, so did what little control she had left. She collapsed against him, great gasping sobs tearing from her.

"David," she moaned, "Oh, God, David, please help me."

He knelt motionless beside her for endless moments, then slipped one arm around her, tentatively, as though afraid of hurting her further. He eased his other hand in her hair, holding her head to his chest as she cried.

"I'll help you, Eliza," she heard from a distance. "I owe you that much."

Owe, she heard. Not love. Evermore, he had once promised her, in this life and the next. But her father's lies, and time, had killed what David had once felt for her. Could she have expected more? *Yes!* she longed to cry. *Yes, please God, yes.* But she couldn't, no more than she could refuse the help David now offered her.

Elizabeth

A knock at the door jolted me back to the present. John entered the room carrying a blanket, which he handed to me.

"The doctor is on his way."

I took the blanket and covered Marie.

"It doesn't matter now."

John called for me, two days later, to escort me to the funeral service. Martha had declared the roads passable and, although she didn't know that my throat was scratchy and my head dull with the persistence of a low-grade fever, she warned me to bundle up warm so I wouldn't catch cold, and drove over to Mack's place to gather with the rest of her family early that morning.

My mood demanded gray, dripping skies, but the sun refused to cooperate. It glinted with uncomfortable brightness from the sky and from the melting snow.

The service was held at the small, one-room church in Richards Spur, a white frame building with a bell-less tower which leaned dangerously away from the building. A surprising number of persons attended the brief service in the church and then waded through the red clay mud to the graveside.

Mack was there, looking grim and uncomfortable in a dark suit and well-polished cowboy boots. In a whisper, Martha explained that Joannie was not feeling well and Mack had insisted she stay home.

Stan McCollum was also present. I caught sight of him, once looking disdainfully at the mud which spattered on his trousers legs, and another time looking at me with a speculative expression in his eyes. When he saw me return his stare, he glanced away.

Louise Rustin did not look away. I felt the heat of her ill-repressed anger often through both services.

John remained silent, as he had been since we first entered the church.

In the past two days, I had delved into the densely printed pages of David Richards's books seeking answers that still evaded me. And I still had nothing to go on but my own instinct, although that was much stronger now.

Well, Marie, I asked her silently, *what happens next?*

After the few words of the graveside service, McCollum started toward us. John stepped forward, almost, it seemed, to intercept him.

Unwilling to confront McCollum, I eased away from the remaining small gathering of people and wandered into the older part of the cemetery. Mine was not aimless wandering, but it would have seemed so to anyone watching.

I found the family plot at the back of the cemetery, a large, well-tended area not fenced but outlined with narrow flat stones. From the center of the plot rose a large white obelisk bearing the name Richards. The newer graves were marked with flat head markers; the older ones with small, upright, carved marble monuments.

Snow still covered the ground, but the stones were easy to see from the edge of the plot. I wandered around the boundary until I came to a marker which bore the name Jonathon David.

I walked to it and knelt beside it, brushing the snow from the dates. It was too new.

"My father," John said. I hadn't heard him walk up.

I looked back at the dates. "You must have been very young."

"Almost eighteen."

"And your mother?"

He knelt beside me facing the grave to his right and touched that stone.

"Mary Catherine," I read, and then the dates. She had died seventeen years before her husband.

"Complications after childbirth," John said, rising to his feet.

I stood beside him. He obviously didn't want my sympathy. "I'd like to see David Richards's grave."

"Sorry," John said, but he didn't sound as though he were. "It isn't here."

"Oh, well. . . ." I couldn't argue with that. "Perhaps when I go into Fairview, I can stop by the cemetery there."

He shook his head. "I don't know where he's buried. Dad said something once about a private cemetery, but I wasn't interested at the time, and I didn't pay much attention."

"The child?" I asked hopefully.

His eyes turned hard and dark in the glare of the sun.

Only one other question remained, but did I really want to ask him? Yes, I decided. This was something I had to know. "What about Eliza?"

"Who?"

"Eliza, his . . ." I hesitated, "the child's mother."

He took my arm and pulled me toward the church. "I don't know how you dreamed up that bit of nonsense," he said tersely. "No one still living has any idea what her name was, or where she went after she presented him with the child."

I shrugged away from his hand. "She didn't go any-where."

He caught my shoulders and turned me to face him. For an instant I felt we were back in the shadows of the attic, with John about to kiss me, with me unable, unwilling to refuse. Then reality intruded. "You obviously have better sources of information than I do," John said. "What makes you so sure of that?"

I tried to meet his eyes but couldn't. I wasn't sure. Lord, I wasn't even sure of *my* actions at the moment. "I just don't think she would have," I said in a futile attempt at defense.

John was quiet for a long time. "Don't let anyone else hear you talking like that, especially Stan McCollum."

"Why would I say anything to him?"

"He wants to talk with you."

"But I don't want to talk to him."

"Elizabeth, he is trustee for the estate. You can't avoid him."

"I've been doing my best."

"He knows. Just try to cooperate with him."

John and I drove back to the house in the silence that marked so much of our time together. I tried to warm my feet against the car heater but couldn't escape the chill. I had managed to get snow in my shoes, and my stockings were sodden. I wanted only to soak in a hot tub and then curl up in front of a fire, in a flannel nightgown, drinking hot coffee. But John was with me. And McCollum was right behind.

I resisted the temptation to make my trustee as uncomfort-able as possible by taking his coat and leading him into the frigid drawing room. Instead, I led him and John to the library, where the remnants of a fire glowed in the fireplace.

John stirred the coals and fed the fire, and I waited for McCollum to say something. He glanced anxiously at John.

"Oh, for goodness' sake, John. Give him permission to speak and let's get this over with!"

McCollum shot me a malevolent glare and slammed his briefcase down on the desk. "I've written you asking you to contact me, but you've not seen fit to do so."

"I've been busy." Busy grieving the loss of a friend. Would McCollum understand that? Probably not. He'd probably never grieved for anyone.

"Obviously. In any event, it is necessary from time to time to contact you, so I've arranged to have a telephone installed."

What? He was actually giving me access to the outside world without the ever-present ear of Louise Rustin? "Thank you. Martha will appreciate that."

"But not you?"

"I have no one I wish to speak with."

With a grimace, he opened his briefcase and drew forth a sheaf of papers. "I have a number of invoices."

I remained silent. John seemed preoccupied with the fire.

"I want to examine the work that's been done before I pay these."

"When do you want to do that?" I asked, but I already suspected his answer, suspected it would be hours before I would be warm, before I would be rid of him.

"Right now. I also want to check the inventory."

McCollum prowled through every room of the house, from cellars to attics, examining pictures and furniture, making marks on his typewritten lists. I was torn between wanting to stay in the library, warm and out of his presence, and an uneasy feeling that he should not be allowed the freedom of the house. Comfort lost.

John accompanied us for a while, but he soon abandoned the tour. I couldn't watch both of them. I stayed with McCollum.

I couldn't follow him into the nursery. I waited in the hallway, listening to his footsteps on the bare floor, hearing the opening and closing of what was probably a closet door.

"Where are the contents of this room?" he asked when he joined me in the hall.

"I had them destroyed."

"You had no right to do that."

I didn't want to discuss the nursery with anyone, especially not with him, and my scratchy throat by this time had become painful. I ignored his comment and turned my back on him.

"I'm talking to you."

"Mr. McCollum, I'm freezing. If we must continue this . . . discussion, let's do it in the library."

John had pulled a chair close to the fireplace and sat with his feet stretched to the edge of the coals. He glanced at me before turning to McCollum. "Was your tour satisfactory, Stan?"

McCollum shuffled the papers and replaced them in his briefcase. "Not entirely. There are several items on the inventory I couldn't find."

McCollum apparently didn't know about the vault. Well, if John wanted him to know, he'd have to tell him.

"As you noticed," I said, "there are a number of boxes I haven't unpacked. If you'll leave me a copy of the inventory, I'll mark off any items I happen to find."

McCollum snapped his briefcase shut, taking his time before turning around. "Miss Richards, when you inherit this property, if you do, you will receive a copy of the inventory. Not until then.

"There will be no more work done on this house until that unlikely event, either."

I studied him, wanting to lash out in anger and knowing somehow that was what he wanted.

"The masonry work? The furnace?"

"The house has stood for over a hundred years. It won't fall down this winter."

John rose and stretched his hands toward the fire. "What about the furnace, Stan? Even you will have to admit it's a little bit chilly today."

"I don't consider major furnace repair this late in the season a reasonable expense. The house was designed to be heated by fireplaces, but if Miss Richards is not satisfied with those, I suppose we could rig up a few propane heaters."

I remembered the plain brown heater with the exposed copper tubing in Martha's sitting room. "No, we can't," I said. "Either it's done right, or it's not done at all."

"As you wish. I want your checkbook."

I blinked back my astonishment. What now?

"Your checking account has been closed. I have an arrangement with Louise Rustin. She will allow you an account with her for your household needs."

I held myself in the appearance of calm. "And if I should need something Mrs. Rustin doesn't stock—a tank of gasoline, for example."

McCollum picked up his briefcase. "I'm not at all sure that your automobile falls within the intended meaning of personal property. I've asked my attorney to render an opinion on that point. In the meantime, Martha can submit mileage claims for any necessary driving she does in connection with her work, and should you have need of other incidental sums of money, my secretary will process your requests."

John spoke softly. "That's a pretty tight rein, Stan."

"Don't bother, cousin. I know what's happening." I crossed to the desk where I had tossed my purse. A worthless checkbook would do me no good. "Here." I held out the checkbook, making McCollum reach for it. He took it and walked across the room, preparing to leave, apparently having nothing further to say to me.

"I would like to see a copy of the will," I said. "I'm having a little trouble relating this conversation to my concept of the trust provisions."

McCollum stopped at the door and turned to face me, his animosity palpable even from this distance. "I assure you, I'm following them explicitly."

"Oh, I'm sure you are." The effort of speaking tore at my throat, but I continued slowly, distinctly. "I am also sure that I will remain the year, no matter how uncomfortable you try to make me, and that I *will* claim my inheritance."

McCollum had one further, parting shot. "Miss Richards, you have already destroyed a room full of furniture. If you remove one more item from this hill, I will instigate legal proceedings against you."

Neither man said good-bye. John just joined McCollum and closed the library door as they left. I sank into the chair he had abandoned, curling into the warmth of his lingering body heat.

McCollum's secretary would process my requests! Louise Rustin would allow me an account! And my car? I thought over our correspondence. Yes, I had told McCollum I would be driving to Richards Spur, and he had sent money for the travel expenses and given instructions for driving from Tulsa. I would have to put those letters in a safe place. As soon as I thawed out. God, I was cold. The air in the room felt like ice against my cheek.

The library door opened and John returned. "He's gone."

I rose to meet him and all the anger I had fought down rose with me, but when I started to speak I was wracked by a cough that left me clutching the chair for support.

He took me by the shoulders. "Come to the kitchen with me. I made coffee and lighted all the burners and ovens while you were on your grand tour. The room ought to be warm by now."

* * *

I was grateful for the warmth and for the rich, hot coffee John poured for me. I wrapped my hands around the mug and breathed in the rising steam as we sat at the kitchen table.

"I do want a copy of the will."

"He'll send one. If he doesn't, I will," John told me.

"Without a fight?"

"There's no point in refusing. All you'd have to do is go to the courthouse and ask to see it."

"I didn't know that."

John rose from the table and poured both of us more coffee. "It's public record. Probates, divorces, most lawsuits can be seen for the asking."

Another cough shook me just as the outside door opened, admitting a gust of frigid air, and Martha.

John didn't bother to sit back down. He walked to where his coat now hung and lifted it from the peg. "She's managed to get sick," he told Martha, opening the door she had just closed. "See that she gets to bed."

Martha gave him a long, appraising look before doing just what he'd told her. She managed to keep me in bed for a full day, cosseting me with hot tea and homemade soup, before I rebelled. The cough was better but not gone, my throat was still irritated, and my fever came and went, but I was not sick enough to tolerate the inactivity of bed rest, not for the second time in less than six months. At least that was what I told myself to explain my overpowering need to escape my bed . . . to be free. So, against Martha's protests, I resumed my work in the library.

CHAPTER

10

"Spring is the most beautiful time of the year," David had told Eliza over a hundred years before. "It comes stealing upon you, full of promise, long before you expect it."

Spring came in mid-February that year, first with patches of green clover in the lawn, followed in a few days by the purple of the clover blossoms. It came gently and as unexpectedly as he had warned. I awoke one morning and found the tangled terrace ablaze with the yellow of forsythia and jonquils, the leafless forest filled with the pink of redbud and white of wild plum. Masses of delicate lavender wisteria appeared on the bare twisted vines climbing the walls of the house. In March, chartreuse bangles of incipient acorns pushed the remnants of last year's dead leaves from the branches of the oaks, and a palette of greens announced new leaves on other trees on the hillside.

Although I welcomed a fire at night, I put aside my jacket and, in spite of Martha's admonitions, wandered coatless through the vibrant, pulsing rainbow my hill had become.

The telephone was installed, at my insistence, in the quarters. No response had come to my carefully phrased inquiries in the letters Martha had mailed for me the day Marie died, and I began to doubt that one ever would. But a copy of David Richards's will arrived by mail in a plain manila envelope. From McCollum? Or from John? I wondered, but decided that it made no difference.

The will contained generous provisions for his two nephews, apparently his only heirs, and then the trust. Stephen Ward had been named as first trustee, with the bank in Fairview to succeed him, provided that no Richards held controlling interest of that bank.

I pored over the trust provisions until my eyes blurred, but other than the feeling I already had, that David Richards had preserved this home for Eliza, the provisions made no sense to me. Otherwise, why must the heir be a female Richards?

And why the one-year residency requirement? Why the insistence on providing for the claimant? And other than the obvious, legal age to inherit, why the insistence that the claimant be at least twenty-one? Why? Why? Why?

The biggest question was still David. If I were Eliza, and strange as it seemed, I had to accept that I was, David had to be somewhere near. But in the almost three months since my arrival I had found not one clue to where he was, or even if he was, other than Marie's dying assurance.

I shut the papers in the desk and wandered to the library window. Mack had started work on the terrace the week before, and most of the jungle was gone. He worked with an easy grace, identifying weeds and wasted plants, spading the rich earth, separating and transplanting those shrubs and bulbs which crowded each other, and filling the bare spaces where only weeds had survived.

When he started the work, I had offered to help, but he had declined my offer with his quick laugh.

"Joannie wanted to help me once," he told me. "She was just a little, bitty girl, but she was so serious I gave her a hoe, showed her what Johnson grass looked like, and asked her to hoe a row of new corn." His eyes sparkled with the memory. "She worked all morning on that row and was so proud of her work I didn't have the heart to tell her."

"What?"

"That was the neatest row of Johnson grass I'd ever seen. She'd taken out everything else, even the corn."

I laughed with him, knowing he was telling me I didn't know weed from flower and not minding his gentle mockery.

"I'll get the grass out," he had said. "Then you can tend the corn."

I drew open the drapes, flooding the room with afternoon sunlight. Mack wasn't on the terrace. Instead, Martha knelt on the ground beside a box of plants.

I slipped outside to join her, enjoying the warm breeze on my face.

"Where's Mack?" I asked.

"Trouble with his irrigation lines. He asked me to get these plants back in the ground for him."

I dropped to my knees beside her, stifling a cough as I did so.

"You're determined to catch your death, aren't you?" she asked, but a concerned smile softened her words.

"Oh, Martha, please stop worrying. It's a beautiful spring day. Let's enjoy it."

"It's not spring yet. We've got at least one more frost coming, maybe tonight if the weather report is right. Now you get off that cold ground."

"It's not cold." I buried my hands in the warmth of the freshly turned earth. "And how can you say it isn't spring? Just look at the new life around you."

I reached into the box for a plant. "You know, we even have trees alive in the orchard. When I looked out the window this morning, I saw a mass of blossoms."

"Oh, no." Martha sank back on her heels clutching a forgotten seedling. After a silent moment, she stood, picking up the box. "Can you take care of yourself for a while?"

"Of course, but what's the matter?"

"I've got to go to Mack's. If the peaches are in bloom and it frosts tonight, he's going to need his irrigation system. He's going to need all the help he can get."

I scrambled to my feet. "Then I'll go with you."

For a moment I thought she was going to tell me I wasn't wanted. Finally, though, she nodded her assent. "But get a jacket."

Mack's orchard was on the eastern end of the hill. Martha drove through Richards Spur, but where the asphalt curved left toward the highway, she veered to the right and followed a gravel road around the base of the hill.

Bright orange flags on small stakes dotted one side of the road and spread over into a field.

"What are those?"

Martha glanced at them and then back at the road. "They look like survey stakes. I guess the county commissioners have finally decided it's time to do something about this road."

I looked in awe at the lush valley to the left. The grasses already stood knee high, and sleek, fat cattle grazed behind well-tended fences.

"It's all Richards land," Martha said in the same tone she might have used to tell me it was all snake-filled swamp. Her recent softening toward John had apparently hardened once again to hatred.

"This, too?" I asked, trying to ignore her bitterness and remembering her once pointing out other Richards lands to the south.

She nodded. "Everything you've seen since we left the hill. Except the church."

"You mean except for the town, don't you?"

"Everything. If he doesn't own it, he holds the mortgage, and with him that's just about the same as owning it."

She turned right onto a narrow road, and her car groaned up the hill, drowning out any further conversation, if any had been offered. It wasn't.

My first impression of Mack's place was that it was immaculate—a picture postcard version of an ideal country homestead. A rambling one-story bungalow faced the south, sheltered on the north by a grove of towering oak trees. A cluster of barns and outbuildings lay to the west of the house, and the orchards stretched out in neat rows to the south and to the west.

We saw Mack loading a length of pipe into the back of his battered truck at one of the outbuildings. Martha pulled up near him. A strange expression crossed his face when he realized I was with Martha, but his easy, familiar smile had replaced it by the time he walked to the side of the car.

Martha spoke as he walked up. "We thought we'd see if you needed any help."

"I appreciate that, Aunt Martha, Elizabeth, but I don't think there's anything you can do right now. I'm pretty sure I've got all the leaks fixed, except for this last piece of pipe, but I won't know until I can turn the water back on."

"Is Joannie in the house?" Martha asked.

Mack nodded.

"Do you think she would mind if we went in and waited to see if you're going to need us?"

I thought he looked at me, but it may have been a play of the sunlight. "No," he said. "Go on up and tell her I'll be in as soon as I can."

Martha tapped on the front door, opened it, and called out before going into the house. I hesitated a moment, then followed her.

The inside of the house was as immaculate as the outside. I longed to see the glow of wax on the spotless, dark wood floors and thought colorful throw rugs would have added to the charm, but other than that, I found the house delightfully welcoming. Martha led me to a large room with two walls of windows overlooking the orchard. Across the room a woman sat in a high-backed chair facing the windows.

"Joannie?" Martha spoke from the doorway. "This is Elizabeth. Mack said to tell you he'd be in as soon as he could."

Without pausing, Martha crossed to the back of the room, which was a large country kitchen. "Coffee ready?"

"Yes, Aunt Martha." Joannie's voice was as soft as a whisper. "Please bring some for Elizabeth, too." She was knitting an afghan which spilled over her lap to the floor. She made no effort to rise, but crossed the needles in her lap and indicated a couch next to her. "Won't you please come over here, Elizabeth?"

As she spoke, she turned partially toward me and I saw her clearly for the first time. I was speechless for a moment. A cloud of golden hair haloed exquisite, delicate features and dark, fawnlike eyes.

"Please," she repeated.

I took the seat she indicated. I couldn't help looking out the windows. Mack was in view, and I realized there were few places in the orchard where he could not be seen from where Joannie sat.

Joannie followed my glance. "He's been working all day. He didn't even stop for lunch."

Fleetingly, I wondered why she wasn't outside helping him, but that seemed disloyal to her, and I had the strangest need to protect her from any disloyalty, from any discomfort or pain. That need was overpowering, and alien to anything I had ever felt for anyone before. I tried to name the feeling, but the closest I could come to identification was wondering if this was how a mother would feel about her child.

Martha brought coffee and returned to the kitchen. I heard

the noises of dishes being placed on the table, but Joannie
still made no effort to rise. Another nibble of disloyalty. I
pushed it away, but it didn't go so easily.

"Mack told me you were very pretty," she said. I wondered how Mack could think anyone else pretty when he had
her to compare them to, and told her so.

Her childlike laughter bubbled into the room. "Thank
you," she said shyly. "I do so want to be pretty. For Mack."

Martha brought a tray bearing a bowl of stew and a glass
of milk and set it on the table near Joannie. "You didn't have
your lunch today, either, did you, young lady?"

Joannie shook her head. "I wanted to wait for Mack. I
didn't realize until you came that it was so late."

"Well, remember, you've got to keep your strength up."

"Are you ill?" Concern, as unexplained and as intense as
my desire to protect her, rocked me.

"She's going to have a baby," Martha said firmly.

"That's wonderful. When?"

An expression I would have called fear in anyone else
darkened Joannie's eyes. "In June."

While she ate, I watched her, trying to visualize this girl
as a mother, for, though she had to be at least as old as me,
she seemed a child herself, protected and loved and unaware
that some people in this world could be harsh and uncaring.

We talked then, or rather Joannie talked and I listened. She
talked about Mack. He filled her world. She saw through his
eyes, dreamed his dreams. And when she talked, she seemed
to glow.

When I heard a heavy step in the hall, I realized that the
room had grown dim, brightened only by the light from the
kitchen behind us. I glanced outside. The sky had turned an
ominous shade of gray, although it was too early for nightfall.

Joannie turned toward the sound, her face radiant.
"Mack."

His clothes were crusted with mud, and his face showed

exhaustion and frustration, but as he crossed the room carrying an armload of blossom-laden peach boughs, his gentle smile erased all signs of frustration.

Mack placed the boughs in Joannie's lap and kissed her upturned cheek.

"You shouldn't have cut them," she chastised gently.

"Yes, I should have."

"Did you get the line fixed?" Joannie asked, holding the blossoms to her face and breathing deeply of their perfume.

Mack knelt beside her. "Let me get some of this mud off before we talk." He looked at me. "I see Aunt Martha has supper on the table. I'd be real pleased if you'd stay."

I nodded my acceptance. Mack ruffled Joannie's hair and excused himself.

Joannie clutched the peach boughs without seeing them, obviously lost in thought. I watched her for a moment, but it seemed an invasion of her privacy. I stood and reached for the boughs. "I need to go into the kitchen. Can I put these in water for you?"

She smiled at me, but some other unexpressed emotion darkened her lovely eyes.

In the kitchen Martha handed me a vase. I filled it with water and arranged the boughs. "Should we leave?" I whispered.

"No." She held out a cup of coffee.

I leaned against the sink, nursing the coffee, wondering about the mixed signals I was getting from Joannie. I heard voices from the front of the room—Mack's saying, "You have nothing to be ashamed of," and Joannie's, a little sharper than I had heard before, an insistent, "No!"

Martha busied herself then, placing last-minute dishes on the table and directing traffic. "Mack! You get over here before this gets cold again. Elizabeth, you sit there," ignoring the fact that Joannie still sat in her chair, half turned away from us, until the three of us were seated around the round oak table with thick stew, golden steaming cornbread, and rich, creamy milk, all crying for our attention.

Mack's face once again showed frustration. I felt as though I shouldn't have come, much less stayed. Martha seemed bent on pretending that the tension in the room did not exist by passing dishes and urging the two of us to eat.

"Is the line fixed yet?" I asked abruptly.

"Part of it, yes. The rest, I don't know. Aunt Martha, after we finish supper, will you turn the valves while I check the sprinklers?"

Martha nodded.

"I don't know anything about orchards," I said. "Why do you need your irrigation lines so badly now?"

"Frost," Mack told me, and then must have realized that told me nothing. "There are a couple of ways to fight frost," he said. "The old way, with smudge, is still used in some parts of the country. The way taught now is with irrigation. If I can wet down the blossoms, that moisture will insulate them against a light freeze. If not . . ." He shook his head as if denying that alternative. "If not, I'll have no peach crop."

Martha spoke briskly. "Then you hurry and eat your supper and let's get out there, young man. We don't have a whole lot of time before dark."

"It doesn't make any difference, Aunt Martha. If it works, it works. If it doesn't, there's nothing I can do about it now."

A movement from the room in front of us caught my eye. Joannie had thrown off the afghan and was reaching under the couch beside her. Mack's attention remained focused on the design of the tablecloth.

"I should have replaced the line last year," he said softly. "It was a gamble I had to take. In the same situation, I'd do it again."

The objects retrieved from under the couch, Joannie began to rise. I didn't mean to stare, but I couldn't turn my eyes away as she labored upright and balanced herself on crutches. Her right leg twisted at an unnatural angle as she made her way with painful slowness across the room.

"I just didn't believe I was going to lose," Mack said.

Joannie stopped beside his chair. "We haven't lost yet," she said, resting her slender hand on his shoulder. He clasped it and held it to his cheek.

"No, we haven't, have we?"

Mack's chair scraped across the hardwood floor as he rose. "Aunt Martha, if you're ready, let's go turn on the water."

I watched Joannie as Mack settled her into his chair. I couldn't remain in the house alone with her and not question her.

"Let me help instead," I said quickly.

The temperature had fallen at least fifteen degrees since we'd arrived. Mack cast a wary eye at the sky as he led me to the control house. He opened the main valve behind me, explained the smaller valves to me, and after brief instructions left me there. He was to drive to the end of each row and on signal I would turn the valve controlling those sprinklers. If all was well, he'd move on to the next set of sprinklers. If not, he would signal, and I'd turn off the valve.

"It's an artesian well," he told me. "I've never run out of water, but to be on the safe side, let's start with the lower slopes."

I don't know what went wrong. I held my breath as I turned each of the first three valves on signal and the sprinklers began pulsing out their life-saving water. Mack was on his way to the fourth set when water began hissing from the first valve. I reached for it, uncertain as to whether I ought to turn it off, when the second one began hissing, and the third one blew completely off. I ran for the door, screaming for Mack. His truck was tearing toward me. All the outside sprinklers were silent.

When he reached the control room, water was trickling from the main valve. Mack took one quick look around the room, grabbed for the main valve, and shut it off.

He stood silently before it, holding it for a second, before he turned to me. "That's it," he said finally.

"Isn't there anything we can do?" I asked helplessly.

The expression on his face told me there were no other options. "Not if we get a freeze."

Martha and Joannie were quiet when we returned to the house. A small radio sat on the kitchen table, but it, too, was silent.

"Any change in the weather forecast?" Mack asked.

Joannie said bleakly, "They're predicting temperatures in the low to mid-twenties."

Mack poured himself a cup of coffee, pulled out a chair, and slumped into it. Joannie looked stricken.

"Don't worry, honey," Mack said. "We still have the apples."

"But you'll have to work for Richards again."

"That's okay," he told her. "One more year, and this place will be paying for itself."

"Mack?" I asked hesitantly. "Did I . . . could I have done anything?"

He shook his head. "No, you did fine, Elizabeth. The system is just worn out. It's been patched too many times." He took Joannie's hand in his.

"What about smudge?" I persisted, unwilling, unable to see him lose his crop.

He looked at me, a question in his eyes.

"You mentioned that some people still use smudge to fight frost. Couldn't you?"

"I thought about that earlier. I have the fuel, but I don't have anything to burn it in. When I took over this place, there wasn't a smudge pot on it. Then I had to make a choice between spending money on pots or on the irrigation system. This afternoon I had to decide whether to spend time looking for containers or trying to get the lines in order.''

I thought of all those buildings full of equipment on the other side of the hill and felt hope beginning to grow. ''What does a smudge pot look like?''

Mack couldn't understand my intensity, but he answered, gesturing. ''It's about so big, made of metal, and you fill it with coal oil, diesel fuel, kerosene, just about anything you have that will burn.''

I began to relax. ''Do they look a little like bowling balls?''

In spite of his exhaustion, Mack laughed outright. ''I hadn't thought about it that way before, but yes, they do. Why?''

''Because,'' I said, ''I think I have more smudge pots than you will ever need. Do we have time to go get them?''

I had everyone's attention.

''Are you sure?''

I had to shake my head. ''No. I only know there are crates of round metal pots—crates of them, Mack—in a barn behind the house.''

''I'll get the truck,'' he said.

Surprisingly, the opposition came from Martha. ''Maybe I ought not say anything, but I can't not say it. I know what Stanley McCollum told you, Elizabeth, about filing charges against you if you took one more thing off the hill. He will.''

Mack stopped, halfway to the door.

''We won't tell him,'' I said. ''We'll have them back by tomorrow. He need never know.''

Martha bit her lip and stammered slightly. ''Somebody keeps track of everyone who goes up your road, and everyone who comes down. There's no way McCollum wouldn't learn about a truckload of equipment coming down.''

''Oh, no,'' Joannie moaned.

I hadn't realized Louise Rustin was reporting my activities, but the knowledge came as no surprise. McCollum, with his insistence on following not the spirit but the letter of the trust provisions, would have to have someone to help him keep his checklist.

Damn him! It wasn't fair for him to force me to choose between sacrificing Mack's crop and jeopardizing my inheritance.

"I won't!"

Mack started back toward the table. "I understand," he said.

"No. No, you don't," I hurried to explain. "If he insists on my following the provisions to the letter, I will. We won't take the pots off the hill. If there's any way we can do it, we'll bring them across the top. Can we?"

I saw a speculative look in Mack's eye, and I knew then that while Mack was normally honest and straightforward about his activities, he wasn't averse to besting McCollum at his own game.

"Maybe," Mack said. "There's an old wagon road that hasn't been used for years. It's all overgrown, and there are a couple of fences across it on your side, but I might be able to get over it with the tractor."

There was one more, brief opposition from both Martha and Mack when I insisted on going with him. He had hitched a trailer to the back of the tractor and was ready to leave when I asked him where I should ride.

"Even if I could tell you where they are, you'd have to spend valuable time just looking for them. I'll have to show you."

Martha reluctantly acquiesced, and I climbed onto the tractor, standing on the frame below and behind the seat and holding onto the seat as Mack instructed. The temperature was still dropping, the sun only an outline of silver in the gray sky.

It was exhilarating at first, the coolness against my face as we jostled along the track. I was happy to be defeating

McCollum in even this small way and, at the same time, feeling somehow that I was repaying a debt long owed to Mack. But as we went on, the air became biting, small daggers cutting into my face and hands and later seeming even to stab into my lungs and my ears. The noise of the tractor engine made it impossible to talk without shouting, so we were silent. At each of the two fences Mack had to stop to cut, he asked me how I was doing. I smiled reassuringly at him.

The relative warmth of the barn came none to soon. I stumbled from the tractor, cupped my hands over my mouth, and breathed into them for a moment, then placed them over my ears until the worst of the tingling ceased. I looked longingly at the welcoming glow of a light in Martha's sitting room, but Martha had the door key with her, and besides, we had no time to spare.

Mack put his hand on my shoulder. "Are you all right?"

"Umm. Just let me get my bearings." I glanced around the barn, unfamiliar in the dimming light only slightly brightened by the tractor's headlights. "They're in a side room, behind some other things."

I found a familiar wagon, and after that it was easy. They were in the back of the second room we entered.

Mack breathed a deep sigh. "You were right. They are smudge pots, and, Lord, there are hundreds of them!"

He pulled the tractor close, and we loaded the trailer until he insisted we had enough. Then it was back across the hilltop, with the sun sinking rapidly behind us and the temperature dropping almost as fast as the sun.

Joannie and Martha waited by the fuel tanks with the pickup truck. As we offloaded the pots, they began filling them and setting them in the back of the truck. Mack and I left in the truck, and, because I could drive it, I drove the truck through the orchard while Mack set the pots among the trees and lighted them. When we emptied the truck, we returned and took the tractor and now loaded trailer. I didn't know how to drive the tractor, so Mack drove and I set and lighted the pots. It was a silent operation, saved from being grim by the few words of encouragement we had time to give each other. It was dark when we finished, the stars bright in a clear, cold sky, but throughout the peach orchard we saw the glow of burning fuel, the warm black smoke rising among the blossoms.

Mack clasped my shoulders. "We did it," he said. He hugged Martha. "We did it." He turned to Joannie, grasped her to him, and twirled around with her in his arms. "We did it!" he shouted.

Back inside the kitchen I sank into a chair and gratefully accepted the coffee Martha offered. I huddled into my jacket, refusing to take it off, and only then did I realize how deeply the chill had penetrated. I felt as though my bones were frozen, and I held myself stiff to keep from trembling.

Martha glanced warily at me. "I think I'd better get you home," she said.

"Not yet," I protested. "Let me get warm first."

She brought an afghan from the front of the room and put it around my shoulders. I snuggled into it, still holding the coffee but having neither the strength nor the energy to drink it. I felt a cough rising but stifled it because I knew it would only cause her worry.

Mack and Joannie were talking happily about other adventures, and Martha joined in their reminiscences. How nice it would be, I thought as I shrugged deeper into the afghan, to be a part of a family this close. How nice it would be to belong to someone, as Mack and Joannie belonged to each other. How wonderful it would be, I added as much more than an afterthought, if I could just get my body as warm as my spirit felt. A deep lethargy stole over me as I watched the diffused glow from the orchard through the fog-covered windows.

Eliza

Eliza remembered little of the remainder of the train ride to St. Louis. David found a woman on the train to dress her wounds and tend her during the trip. They reached St. Louis with barely enough time to make a few necessary purchases before boarding the steamboat for Little Rock. David, Eliza, and Wilson, who was traveling with David, reached Little Rock in record time, only to learn that the Arkansas River was too low for passenger boats to work their way upriver to Fort Smith. David sent Wilson on by horseback and found accommodations for Eliza in a boarding house, in spite of the shortage of rooms because of the earthquake earlier that month. He insisted that she see a doctor while they were there, so she did, knowing what the doctor would tell her. Her body was healing.

The ache she felt was not caused by physical pain. It was brought by the betrayal she had seen in David's eyes when he thought she was spying on him, and the memory of his words, "I owe you that much."

What had she expected? That he would declare his undying love for her? That was too much to ask, even if his love for her hadn't died. The fact that her own tightly concealed love for him threatened to make itself known was another matter. The years had hardened him. Just as she was no longer the innocent child he had known, he was sterner, and grimmer, than she remembered.

The wonder was that he could bear to look at her at all. Not only was she another man's wife, she was the wife of a man who had proven himself to be an enemy of David's people.

The tears unlocked on the night she had collapsed in his arms came often now, but he never saw them again. They came at night, when she was alone in her room, when she remembered their brief moments of happiness and realized

they would have no more. They came when she admitted that
once he had helped her establish a life without Owen, David
would also be gone from her life.

The first two weeks of August were dry, with the Arkansas
remaining low, freight piling up on the docks, and stranded
passengers searching for rooms all adding to the chaos of
the damaged town. Eliza felt strong enough to suggest they
continue their journey overland. David vetoed the suggestion,
but she noticed his growing preoccupation and his increasing
irritation with various articles appearing in the newspapers.

The rains came. She watched as the river rose slightly and
then became too swollen for river traffic. Finally they booked
passage on the first steamer able to move upriver and arrived
in Fort Smith late in August, five weeks after her flight from
Owen.

Wilson met them at the dock. David greeted him sol-
emnly. "Were you able to take care of everything here?"
he asked.

Wilson nodded. "I found a house and a housekeeper, and
I've made inquiries into the other matters."

David helped Eliza into the carriage as Wilson collected
their trunks. "Do you have the reports from home?"

Again Wilson nodded.

"Then take us directly to the house," David told him. "I
want to go over them as quickly as possible."

Wilson turned the horses onto a broad thoroughfare. Eliza
stared about her. She had expected a garrison encampment,
a frontier outpost. Instead she found a small city. Shops and
houses lined each side of the road they traveled until they
reached a pile of rubble marring the pleasant drive.

"Pull up," David said, looking at the rubble, concern
evident in his voice. "What happened to the mill? I didn't
think the earthquake damage reached this far west."

"That's not damage, Colonel," Wilson grunted. "That's
progress. Kanady's torn down his mill and shop. They're

going to build a block of brick buildings there. Three stories high, the newspaper said."

David shook his head and leaned back in the seat. "Have you been saving the newspapers for me?"

"Yes, sir. Just like you asked."

Wilson turned left off the avenue. The street now was narrower, bordered by large houses set back in well-kept lawns. Wilson pulled up in front of a small, porch-lined house.

"The housekeeper is going to take some getting used to," he said. "She's a preacher's widow, and just about as dour as they come." He cast an apologetic glance in Eliza's direction. "But with her around, there won't be a chance of any kind of scandal."

"Thank you, Wilson," Eliza murmured. Then David helped her to the carriage block and down to the brick sidewalk.

In the shadows of the porch, Wilson produced a ring of keys and handed them to David. David turned to Eliza, holding the keys out to her. "Your home, Mrs. Griffith," he said softly.

Eliza took the keys with trembling fingers and opened the door. Wide-planked pegged floors gleamed softly. The walls wore new paper; the mantels and trim, new paint.

"It's lovely," she exclaimed.

"I'll get your trunk." Wilson left the house and returned with the small camel-backed trunk they had purchased in St. Louis. He indicated a door to the right of the entry. "This is the room you'll want to use," he said as he carried the trunk into the room and set it at the foot of a high-post bed.

Eliza thanked him and had just knelt to open the trunk when the noise of an ominous throat-clearing drew her attention. She hastened to the doorway, accompanied by Wilson, to see a gaunt woman, dressed in unrelieved black, staring at David, who had remained in the parlor.

Wilson spoke. "Mrs. Jenkins, this is Mrs. Griffith, the

lady you'll be looking after. I expected to find you here when
we arrived.''

"I've been to church, Mr. Wilson, as I should have been.
I did not realize anyone would be traveling on the Lord's
day.''

Foreseeing a confrontation, Eliza interceded. "Of course
not, Mrs. Jenkins. And under different circumstances, we
would not have been.'' She attempted a smile, but the woman
facing her was formidable. "I'm going to freshen up, but I
wonder if you would be kind enough to prepare coffee for the
gentlemen?''

Mrs. Jenkins nodded stiffly and strode from the room.
Wilson rolled his eyes upward, Eliza stifled a smile, and
David said, grinning ruefully, "I think your reputation will
be well guarded.''

With relief Eliza changed from her heavy traveling costume
into a lighter dress with loose, flowing sleeves. She bathed
her face and the back of her neck with water from the pitcher
waiting on the marble-topped washstand and sank into a chair
near a window. A few moments—that was all she needed,
she told herself. Just a few moments alone.

She glanced curiously about the room, and a smile curved
her lips as she did so. This was a pleasant room: airy, taste-
fully decorated, and feminine without being frilly. Two doors
other than the one by the entry opened from the room. She
wondered about them but remained seated.

"Enough," she said with a small shake of her head. It was
obvious that her future was being planned. She might as well
find out now what those plans were. She squared her shoulders
and returned to the parlor.

David had papers scattered around him and sat scowling at
a document in his hand. The coffee had been served. The tray
sat on a small table near the fireplace, but Mrs. Jenkins, Eliza
saw gratefully, had left the room.

David looked up, his scowl deepening as he looked at her, and she shrank inwardly from that look. "Should I leave the two of you alone a while longer?" she asked.

David shook his head impatiently. "No. We have to talk." He indicated a chair, and Eliza crossed the room hesitantly and sat facing him.

He continued to look at her for a moment, studying her, examining her features for . . . for what? Then he tossed the papers he held to one side, rose, and paced restlessly about the room. He paused at the tray, poured a cup of coffee, and handed it to her.

"Wilson," he said abruptly, "please tell Mr. Grimes that we have arrived and would like to see him today."

"Yes, Colonel," Wilson said. He nodded in Eliza's direction and hurried from the room.

David leaned against the mantel and stared at her again, a penetrating stare that she could not meet.

"Do you want me to notify your father of your whereabouts?"

"No!" She glanced quickly at him to see if he had noticed her sharpness, then lowered her lashes. "He would only tell Owen where I am."

"Do you want me to get word to him that you are safe?"

Eliza thought of what her father had said to her the night he let Owen take her away. "It's better that he knows nothing about me."

"He must be concerned about you."

"It's better that he knows nothing," she insisted.

David gripped the mantel. "I've been away from home too long," he said. "There are matters that must be taken up with the council. I have to return."

Eliza kept her head averted so that he could not read the despair she felt at his words. "I expected as much," she said softly. "When must you leave?"

"Tonight, if possible."

Not so soon! she cried silently. But of course she couldn't say that.

"That's why I've asked Grimes to come here today," David continued. "I want to be certain that you are taken care of before I leave."

"Who is Mr. Grimes?" Her voice surprised her. It sounded almost natural.

"He's an attorney. He will advise us as to how you can obtain your divorce."

Her head jerked up at his words. "Divorce? Oh, David, I can't!" she cried.

He crossed the room and gripped her hand. "Eliza." His voice bit into her. "Do you still love Markham?"

She closed her eyes against the anguish of the last four years. "No," she whispered.

He released her hand and rested his lightly on her shoulder. "There is no alternative," he said firmly. "If Markham finds you, he can demand that you return to his home. You have no recourse, no protection from him as long as you remain his wife."

"But David, the scandal . . . the shame—"

"Will that be worse than what you went through the night I found you?"

She buried her face in her hands and shook her head mutely.

Jeremiah Grimes was about thirty, with a shock of white-blond hair and clear blue eyes and an accent that was unmistakably northern. Wilson introduced him to David and Eliza and excused himself, going into the dining room and pulling the doors shut behind him.

"Minnesota," Grimes said, smiling. "The next question is usually, what am I doing down here? I came to Fort Smith to muster out, but we had to wait for the Choctaw Nation to surrender before the army would let us go home. That's not a complaint you hear in my words, Colonel Richards. If anything, it's gratitude. Because while I was waiting, I discovered I had a real affinity for this country. I had an opportunity to read for the law, and I stayed."

"You come highly recommended," David told him.

"Thank you, sir. So do you."

"Did Mr. Pike explain the circumstances to you?"

"No. He told me that he normally handles your legal matters in the States, but that there was a conflict of interest at this time and asked if I would assist you." He glanced at Eliza. "He did say that it was a matter of personal urgency for the lady."

David leaned toward him. "It is. Now I must ask for the cloak of your professional confidence, because I consider her safety at stake if what I am about to tell you becomes known outside this room."

Grimes's joviality faded. He became all business. His clear blue eyes met David's dark ones without wavering. "Of course, Colonel Richards."

"Other than Mr. Pike, only Wilson and I know her true identity at this time. Everyone else, her housekeeper included, believes her to be Eliza Griffith, the recent widow of a kinsman of Wilson's."

Grimes nodded his understanding.

David went on slowly, "It has become necessary for her to leave her husband and seek a divorce."

"Will her husband agree to a divorce?" Grimes asked.

"Obviously not," David told him, "or this subterfuge wouldn't be necessary."

"Can he be found for service of a summons?" Grimes asked.

David's smile was brittle. "Quite easily. He's Owen Markham, undersecretary with the Department of the Interior."

"Oh, my God." Grimes cast an apologetic look at Eliza. "Pardon me, ma'am," he said before proceeding intently.

"Colonel Richards, do you realize what a compromising position you're in? If Markham should discover your involvement, he could discredit you in Washington, perhaps even with your own nation."

Eliza had to speak. "No, please. David is involved in this only accidentally."

"She means that she did not actively seek my assistance," David interrupted, "but I have offered it, and I mean to follow through. I owe—I owe Mrs. Markham a debt of long standing."

"This could be an extremely expensive way of repaying that debt, Colonel."

There was no trace of emotion in David's expression. "I owe her my life."

Grimes was silent for a moment. "Very well." he turned to Eliza. In a gentle voice, he carefully chose his words. "Mrs. Markham, please understand that I have to ask you some questions."

"I understand." Eliza swallowed back her fear of answering those questions and waited for him to proceed.

"Good. The most important one is, are you sure—are you very sure—that you want to do this?"

Eliza cast an apprehensive glance at David, then at Grimes. Did she want to do this? There was no question that she wanted to be free of Owen, but could she deny her vows to him?

David answered for her. "She does not want to do this, Mr. Grimes. She has no choice. Show him your arms, Eliza."

"Must I?" she whispered.

David's answer was firm. "Yes."

She turned to one side, fumbled with the buttons of one cuff, and slowly pushed up the sleeve.

"Both of them," David insisted.

She drew a ragged breath, turned toward Grimes, and reluctantly bared both arms, exposing red slashes which, though healing, still marred her pale flesh and the remains of angry bruises which, though faded to a dull yellow, still showed where Owen had gripped her.

"That is sufficient, Mrs. Markham," Grimes said in a reassuring voice. Eliza drew the sleeves down over her shame and rapidly refastened the buttons.

"When did this happen?"

"It was the evening of July the thirteenth," she murmured, unable to look up from her hands, unable to face the pity or the derision she felt sure she must see in Grimes's eyes.

"That would have been five weeks ago?"

"Yes."

"Did your husband do this to you?"

"Yes."

"Did you give him any provocation?"

Eliza looked up in astonishment at the question.

Grimes smiled at her and choose new words. "Did you do anything to him to cause him to—"

Provocation? Was not loving a man provocation for the pain Owen had caused her? "I gave him no reason to do this to me, Mr. Grimes."

"All right," he said. "Had he ever been violent with you before?"

Eliza's voice was so low it was almost inaudible. "Not to this extent."

Grimes went on, persistent, probing. "When was the first time he was violent with you?"

She saw David's dark, brooding scowl. He didn't know. He mustn't know. There was no way she could ever tell anyone of the brutality Owen had shown her on their wedding night.

"Isn't this enough?" she cried. "Isn't what he did to me this time enough? Why do you keep asking these questions?"

Grimes took her hand in his and went on in his measured, even tone. "Because the courts have held in some cases that a single act of cruelty is not sufficient grounds for granting a divorce.''

David's scowl was still firmly in place as he spoke from across the room. ''Her injuries were not confined to those you saw on her arms, Mr. Grimes. Her clothing was shredded in the assault. Her back was severely lacerated and will probably bear the scars of that evening as long as she lives. I have affidavits from the woman who tended her during the trip to St. Louis and from the doctor who examined her in Little Rock.''

Voices intruded from the dining room. Immediately following a staccato rap on the door, the dining room door slid open. Mrs. Jenkins stood stiffly in the doorway, Wilson behind her with his hand raised in ineffectual protest.

''Mr. Grimes, I didn't know you—''

''Mrs. Jenkins,'' Grimes said pleasantly, revealing no trace of the seriousness of their discussion as he rose to greet her. ''I heard that you had found a position. I'm delighted to know that it is with such a charming employer.''

''But I don't understand. . . .''

''I knew the lady's husband during the war. I've come to pay my condolences.''

''Oh.'' Then, apparently remembering her excuse for entering the room, the woman faced Eliza. ''Mrs. Griffith, I'm sorry for interrupting, but I need to know if you want me to prepare supper. It's getting late and I'm expected at evening services.''

Eliza forced herself to think about something as trivial as an evening meal, or as mildly irritating as the fact she heard no apology in her housekeeper's voice in spite of her words. Long years of practice came to her aid. Mrs. Jenkins was upset by the change in her schedule and would need special treatment for a few days.

''It's much too hot for a heavy meal,'' Eliza said, ''but I

would appreciate it if you would set out a cold supper and make another pot of coffee before you leave.''

''Very well.''

''And Mrs. Jenkins?'' Grimes said.

''Yes, Mr. Grimes?'' Her voice was decidedly softer when she spoke to him.

''My wife will be at church. Will you be so kind as to tell her that I'll be a little late but that I will join her there?''

When Mrs. Jenkins left, Eliza sank back into the chair, her smile fading. Wilson pulled the door shut behind him, leaving the three of them alone again.

''Did you know him?'' she asked.

Grimes was no longer smiling, either. ''Yes. I did.''

''Does that mean you won't help me?''

''Not at all.'' Grimes seemed to regain his earlier good spirits. ''I have a few more questions—easy questions. When and where you were married, where you lived, if you have any children, and what kind of property settlement you want.''

Eliza answered his questions. They were easy after his earlier ones. He seemed surprised when she said there would be no property settlement.

''But you're entitled to something.''

''I want nothing from him. I would prefer not even to keep his name.''

David had remained silent during the last of the interview. He now walked to Grimes's side. ''How long will it take?''

''The divorce itself, if Markham doesn't fight it, shouldn't take much longer than three months.''

''So long?'' David asked.

''No, I'm afraid it will take much longer.'' Grimes turned to Eliza. ''Before we can even ask that you be granted a divorce, you must have been a resident of this state for at least a year.''

''I can't hide from him that long,'' she said dully.

David refused to be defeated in this. "You have to."

"In the meantime," Grimes continued as though they hadn't spoken, "your guise as a widow will explain why you're not out in society." He took a sheet of paper from his folio and wrote a name on it. "I want you to consult with this doctor. He will give you what treatment your injuries require, and he will testify as to the extent of them if it becomes necessary. I'll tell him to expect you tomorrow afternoon, and I'll send a driver to take you to his office."

It was quiet when Grimes left. It was as though he took the life from the room with him. Unspoken words hung heavily in the air. Eliza could not look at David.

She broke the silence. "I must find work."

"Don't be a fool, Eliza. You're not able to work, and you can't take the risk of being among people who might learn who you are."

"But I have no money," she said. "I can't support myself for a year."

"I'll take care of you."

"I can't live on your charity!" she cried.

"It isn't charity, Eliza."

"It is if I have no way of repaying you."

"When did you start keeping a ledger sheet?" he asked. "How much do I owe you? So much for each meal, so much for each night you sheltered me, so much for lying to the Yankee soldiers." He grasped her left arm. "How much did you charge me for the scar you will always bear?"

She felt tears gathering in her eyes, fought to hold them back, and lost.

He released his grip on her arm. "Let me do this, Eliza. After you're free from Markham, after you're safe, I'll help you to establish yourself in any place you want to go. Then if you insist, we can talk about repayment."

She longed to reach out to him. Every fiber in her cried

out to tell him she didn't want to go away from him. Instead, she wiped angrily at the tears which still fell.

"Very well," she said.

Elizabeth

The cough tore from me. I couldn't fight it. It left me shivering and weak, huddled in the chair. Martha was at my side instantly, her fingers icy probes against my forehead.

"Mack, you start the car and get the heater going. I'm taking Elizabeth home right now."

Joannie grasped my hand when I said good night to her. "Thank you," she murmured.

Mack met us at the door. "I don't know how I can ever repay you."

Memories I didn't know how I knew told me I owed this man, this family, more than I could ever repay.

"You already have," I told him.

Martha remained quiet during the drive down the hill. I was coughing so hard she couldn't have said much, anyway. When we reached Richards Spur, she pulled to a stop in front of the store.

"Why are we stopping?" I managed to ask.

"We're out of aspirin, and I'm going to get you some stronger cough medicine, young lady, and some cold tablets and whatever else I can find in there for you."

I shook my head, knowing it would do no good to argue with her, and leaned back against the seat to wait. My eyes felt as though they had sunk back into my head, and I had absolutely no strength left. I was glad to be going home.

A blast of cold air roused me from a light sleep.

"Do you have any money with you?" Martha asked.

"No," I murmured groggily.

"Then I'll have to come back down," she said. "I left my purse at home."

I forced myself awake. "Just sign the ticket," I said.

Martha muttered and got into the car.

"Can't you sign the ticket?" I asked, now fully awake. "Martha, what happened in there?"

Martha stared at the steering wheel. "She said you'd have to sign it yourself, that my signature won't do anymore."

"Oh, good grief."

"Don't worry about it," Martha said. "I'll come back down with the money."

"No, you won't," I told her. I spoke carefully. "We're going to play their game as long as necessary. If she wants me to sign, I'll sign."

I felt the bite of ice in the air as I walked across the porch and then a wave of stale, overheated air as I entered the store. Louise Rustin stood near the cash register.

"Where's the charge ticket, Mrs. Rustin?"

"I'll get it ready," she said stiffly. She pulled a book from the drawer and began writing.

Martha reached across her for the telephone. "Your phone's off the hook, Louise."

Louise glared at her. "On purpose. Pesky kids."

I leaned against the counter. It seemed to take forever for her to fill out the few items of information. A box on the counter held a jumble of items. I reached idly into the box.

"Are these for sale?" I wondered aloud.

Louise stopped writing. "Yes. They were Marie's."

I found a hairbrush with an ornate, flower-entwined E engraved on its age-blackened back.

"You can't afford it." Louise didn't even look up from the charge book when she spoke. "And even if you could, wouldn't sell it to you."

I couldn't repress my sigh. Reluctantly I replaced the hair brush. "Is the charge ticket ready?"

She pushed the book toward me. I glanced at it and scrawled my signature. I started to speak. Why? I wanted to ask. Why are you treating me this way? But then I realized that even she probably did not know her reasons.

Martha picked up the purchases and hurried me toward the door.

Home had never looked so good. Totally dark, a looming shadow in the night, it welcomed me. Martha followed me to my room, lighted a fire in the fireplace, fed me various medicines when I was dressed for bed, and covered me with extra quilts. I didn't mind. For once I wanted to be comforted and pampered, and warm.

CHAPTER
11

Eliza

Her first days in Fort Smith passed with awkward slowness. After Eliza had unpacked and arranged her few belongings and explored the house, she had no new experiences to look forward to. Each day became like the preceding one.

Of the two other doors in her bedroom, one led to the service area of the house and the other onto the wide wrap-around porch. She had chairs placed on the side porch and sat outside for hours, enjoying the long Indian summer.

Mrs. Jenkins's presence in the house was not companion-ship. It was a disapproving cloud that followed Eliza from room to room, from hour to hour, from day to day. Eliza felt partially responsible. The first night in the house, after David and Wilson left, she retired to her room and began dressing for bed. She was rubbing medicated lotion into her skin when she heard noises in the house. Fear held her immobile. She knew it was impossible, but her mind screamed that Owen had somehow found her.

A knock on the service door of her room freed her from her paralysis. She grabbed for her dressing gown, covering herself just as Mrs. Jenkins opened the door.

She had hidden her emotions too long, and fear of discovery

made her voice sharp. "Don't you ever enter this room again without my permission."

She regretted her words the moment she heard them. "Oh, Mrs. Jenkins, I'm so sorry. I didn't mean—"

The older woman's eyes glinted darkly. "There's no reason to apologize, Mrs. Griffith. I forgot my position. I assure you that I won't do so again."

She did not forget, nor did she allow Eliza to do so. She performed her duties with a correctness that bordered on but never crossed the line into rudeness. She offered no warmth or sign of friendliness, nor would she accept any from Eliza.

The only bright spots in Eliza's life were David's visits, but once past her initial joy at seeing him, they, too, were clouded. Every few weeks, when he could find time for the trip to Fort Smith, he and Wilson—always with Wilson, never alone—would arrive in the early afternoon. Wilson would excuse himself and retire to the dining room, where he invariably busied himself with paperwork, while she and David made desultory conversation until dinnertime. The men would stay for dinner, visit for a short while afterward, and then leave. The pattern was always the same.

Eliza held herself in tight control during those visits, although she thought at times she would not be able to bear the lack of any sign of emotion from David. He was always polite, but it was the politeness of a stranger. He had loved her, she told herself. She knew that he had—she had worn the knowledge of that love as a protective armor through all the years of separation. How could he have turned off that love so completely? But as quickly as she asked herself the question, she knew the answer. Because of what he thought she had done.

She longed to throw herself into his arms, to beat on his chest, to scream at him, "I did it for you! I went through it for you!" Instead, she busied herself with the coffee service, or with a piece of needlework. Owen was between them; he would always be between them. But even if he were not, she could not, would not beggar herself by offering her love to a man who obviously no longer wanted it. Nor would she attempt to buy his love by revealing the sacrifices she had been forced to make.

Each time David left, she watched from the doorway until he disappeared into the dark, then turned and faced Mrs. Jenkins's unyielding disapproval. She locked herself in her room and hid her face in her pillow. At those times the emptiness within her was so great she wondered why she must continue living. But continue she did, through the long Indian summer, through the brief, blustery fall, until even the small pleasure of sitting on her porch was denied her, into the winter, when night came early and lasted and lasted and lasted. The bitter chill outside matched the desolation within her, and she sat for hours, forgotten needlework in her lap, before the fire in the parlor.

On one such night, footsteps on the porch and a loud knock at the front door roused Eliza from her apathy. She started upright at the sounds, her heart pounding furiously. No one ever called this late. No one ever knocked with that tone of authority. Her mind jumped from one possibility to another. Another knock reverberated. She raced for the service area, searching for Mrs. Jenkins, and met her as the older woman entered from the hallway to the kitchen, her frown fixed firmly in place.

"Who can that be?" she grumbled.

"I don't know," Eliza said, "but please, please, if you don't know them, don't let them in. If you don't know them, don't tell them I'm here."

Mrs. Jenkins pushed past her with a snort of displeasure. Eliza turned in the hallway, uncertain as to whether she should flee, or hide, or return to the parlor to face whatever awaited her there.

"Eliza?"

She couldn't stifle her gasp of relief when she recognized David's voice. She ran her hands over her hair and smoothed her dress, giving herself time to appear more composed before she turned to him.

"I didn't mean to alarm you," he said.

"It's just that no one ever visits this late," she told him with an attempt at a smile.

"We've been in council at Okmulgee." His dark eyes studied her too pale complexion, her too thin body. "I've been away so long." He took her face in his hand and turned her toward him so he could look more deeply into her eyes. "Are you all right?"

His touch was heaven, and agony. He was so close she could feel his breath warm on her cheek, so close that if she would but sway forward she could be in his arms. Memories of their times together flooded in on her, and her lonely longings stirred to life. She closed her eyes briefly against them, but the touch of his fingers still burned her skin.

She stepped back abruptly. "Of course I'm all right," she said with forced brightness. "My nerves are stretched a little thin, that's all. As soon as the weather changes and I can spend some time outside again, I'll be fine."

Mrs. Jenkins entered the hallway, closing the dining room door with a resounding slam.

"Have you had your supper yet?" Eliza asked David.

David couldn't see Mrs. Jenkins's disapproving scowl when she heard the question, but Eliza did.

"Yes. We stopped in Fort Smith."

"Then just some coffee, Mrs. Jenkins, and perhaps some dessert for the gentlemen." She turned to David. "Wilson is with you, isn't he?"

David smiled. "No. But I have brought someone I want you to meet."

Aware of the housekeeper's lingering presence, Eliza waited until the woman left the hallway.

"You didn't bring a stranger here?" she whispered.

"An old friend of mine, Eliza. Someone I've known since he was a child. You'll enjoy meeting him."

"I can't meet any of your friends. What will they think?"

She saw a nerve jump near his temple, but he spoke softly. "Stephen will think you are a charming lady whom I have befriended. Unless, of course, we stand here arguing about it so long that he feels he isn't welcome."

Chastened and chagrined by her lack of manners, Eliza dipped her head. "I'll do my best to make your friend feel welcome."

She found that she did not have to work at making Stephen Ward feel welcome. If anything, the young man put her at ease. He had a ready smile and sparkling eyes that danced with humor, and he didn't embarrass her with speculative looks or disturbing questions. A small man, not much taller than she, he already bore the signs that by thirty he would be stocky and prosperous-looking, but there was gentleness in his pleasant round face, and patience, and perception.

He was quiet as Mrs. Jenkins silently served the coffee but became animated again when she left the room. "She would make a study," he said, smiling. "All blacks and whites and angular lines."

"Stephen is an artist," David said in answer to Eliza's puzzled expression.

"Starving artist," Stephen amended.

"I thought for sure you would get at least one commission from the men at council," David said.

"The trouble was," Stephen told him as he helped himself to a piece of pie from the waiting tray, "they couldn't decide whether they were there to be founding fathers of a new, great state, or to toll the death knell for five great nations, and none of them wanted to commemorate themselves as being a part of it until they were sure what it was."

"I don't understand," Eliza said.

"There is talk of combining the five 'civilized' nations—the Choctaw, Chickasaw, Cherokee, Creek, and Seminole—into one 'Indian State,'" David told her. "So far it is just words. I think there are enough of us opposed to it to keep it from happening. The Council at Okmulgee drafted a constitution, but I don't believe it will ever be ratified by all the nations."

He cast an appraising glance at Stephen. "I think you ought to paint Peter Pitchlyn."

Stephen choked on his pie. "Oh, you do?" He laughed. "Well, I don't. Every portrait of that man is going to be compared to the one George Catlin did of him. I don't want to be in that shadow. I want people comparing other painters' work to mine, not mine to someone else's."

He saluted David with his pie plate. "I have another subject in mind. Someone who will be equally well known. Brilliant military career, illustrious delegate to Washington, youngest principal chief—"

David shook his head. "Not now, Stephen." He softened his voice. "You'll have to do him at some later date."

"You are right, of course." Stephen did not seem the least disturbed by David's sharp words. "And I've already painted him once, so there is no great hurry. One commission at a time."

"You do have a commission?" Eliza asked. "How exciting."

"Yes, it is," Stephen agreed. "I've painted landscapes and stodgy old men long enough. It's time to find out if I have enough talent to do justice to a beautiful woman." His gaze lingered on Eliza's face. "And you, Mrs. Griffith, are a very beautiful woman."

Eliza felt the blood draining from her face as the meaning of his words became clear. "Me? You want to paint me?"

"Very much," he told her. "We'll start tomorrow evening if you have nothing else planned."

In her confusion Eliza couldn't give voice to her real objection. "I thought painters wanted bright sunlight."

"No. Not for all subjects. I want to try to capture your image softened by candlelight." He looked at her studiously. "Do you have a dress, white, perhaps, or a light color, with lace high at the throat?"

She nodded.

"I wish you would wear it for me."

She looked to David for help. He just smiled secretively and brought her fresh coffee. "You can't argue with Stephen, Eliza. He's a very persuasive young man."

After they left, her objections rose to torture her sleep. She could not pose. After supper the next day, though, she changed into a white summer dress with lace at the throat, rehearsing her arguments as she did so.

While Stephen set up his easel, she drew David to one side. "This is madness," she whispered. "What if . . . what if someone should see the painting?"

"No one will," he assured her. "I'll see to that. Stephen is a talented artist, Eliza, but he needs encouragement. Please let me do this for him."

She looked at Stephen happily arranging his paints and wavered in her resolve.

David spoke softly so only she would hear his words. "Many of our people are talented, but only a few have received recognition. Stephen has it within him to be a great artist, but he feels he must earn his own way. He has many obligations. If he cannot meet those obligations with earnings from his paintings, he will put his art aside. And that will destroy him."

Eliza stood before David, feeling that she shouldn't give in to his wishes in this, yet recognizing it was wrong for her to deprive Stephen Ward of this opportunity. Of course, deep down, she knew she wouldn't deny David anything he asked of her.

Stephen spoke from across the room. "Would you mind standing? It will be more tiring for you than if I posed you seated, but I'd like to paint you in front of that wonderful mantel."

"It's time to decide, Eliza," David told her.

She managed a brief smile for Stephen as she walked slowly to the fireplace. "How do you want me to stand?"

Stephen hurried to her side. "Like this, I think," he said, placing her left arm on the mantel and turning her face to one side. "Not a full profile. Just look toward David."

He stood back and examined the effect. "The hair," he said. "Not so severe. May I?"

Without waiting for an answer, he loosened the tightly drawn knot she wore at the base of her neck. He piled her hair in abandon on the top of her head and framed her face with a few soft curls.

"One thing more," he added. From his satchel he produced a dusky rose-colored shawl of soft wool and draped it over her shoulders, leaving her gloveless arms bare below the abbreviated sleeves of her dress. He arranged a lamp near her and stepped back again. After a moment of study, he glanced at David, who nodded in approval.

"That's it," Stephen said. "That's the effect I want to try to capture."

After the first evening, Eliza found that she looked forward to their sessions. Stephen's gentle wit eased the grim expression from David's face and allowed her to relax. Although she grew tired from standing in one position and often the fire became much too warm for comfort, she enjoyed Stephen's lightly told stories of growing up in the woodlands, and she took secret delight in the attention David paid her when he tended the fire or brought her fresh coffee.

She was never sure whether she extended the invitation, or whether David or even Stephen did, but after the first evening they began taking their meals together. Except for Mrs. Jenkins's dour countenance as she served them, there was almost a festive air in the small house from just after sunset until Stephen rubbed his eyes late in the evening and said, "That's it. That's all I can do tonight."

There were times, though, when David seemed preoccupied, brooding about some problem that he could not or would not discuss with her, and there were other times when, feeling particularly happy, she would glance surreptitiously at him and feel a pang tear through her as she realized these evenings could not continue, that these evenings were just an interlude, but that, had things been different, this was the life she could have had.

Eliza had no idea how fast the painting was progressing. Stephen made her promise not to look at it until it was completed. He covered it each evening and left it on the easel. She longed to look at it, not from vanity but to have some idea of how much longer the sessions would continue. She was afraid, though, of finding it nearly finished, knowing that soon David must return to his nation and that soon she would be alone again.

One night Stephen was unusually silent as he worked, concentrating intently on his task. The next evening he approached his easel with strange reluctance. About an hour into the session he looked up and shook his head.

"I can't quite get it," he said. He looked at Eliza, perplexed, then spoke. "David, would you mind holding that lamp closer to her face? There are too many shadows."

David brought the lamp as he moved closer.

"That's it," Stephen said. "Right there. Please. Now, Eliza, just look at David. That's good."

He began working steadily.

While Eliza looked at David, she tried to remain detached, but as she studied each well-remembered feature she saw the changes that time had wrought—the firm set of his once smiling mouth, the deepening lines of care about his eyes

and the strands of silver flecked through his dark hair—
memories of a younger David, an innocent Eliza, came rushing back. A sense of tremendous sorrow, of unbearable loss
welled up within her, and it took all her strength not to cry
for the things that could have been.

With relief she heard Stephen's chair scrape across the
floor. "You can rest now," he said.

She tore her gaze from David's face, embarrassed by the
raw emotion she felt, and turned to Stephen. He crossed to
the coffeepot and started to pour himself a cup of coffee.

"It's empty," he said.

David put the lamp down. "Do you want me to call for
Mrs. Jenkins?"

Thankful for any excuse to leave the room, Eliza picked
up the tray. "No. I'll go. It won't take but a minute," she
said, hurrying from the room.

In the hallway she leaned against the door. There was a
tremor in her hands she couldn't control, and her breath came
painfully fast.

"Oh, God, David," she murmured to herself. "Why do I
still love you?" A sob broke from her, and she whispered,
"Why can't you love me?"

Elizabeth

A cough racked me into consciousness. Cramped by my
position, I turned carefully in the bed, each bone, each muscle
protesting. The sheets were ice against my skin. The fire had
burned down until only a few coals glowed from the fireplace.
I fumbled with the lamp on the bed table until I finally found
the switch and turned it on. Then I forced myself to push
back the covers, cross the room, and add more wood to the
fire.

Strangely weak and yet reluctant to return to bed, I curled
into the wing chair, tucking my feet under me, and watched

the shifting patterns of shadow and light caused by the moon on the valley below. When even sitting upright became too much of an effort, I moved back to the bed and sat on the edge of it.

Now I knew what painting belonged on the wall in my room, but not where it was, or even when it had been taken. But I had little time to reflect on that. Another spasm of coughing tore through me. There was no fighting it, and when it passed it left me exhausted and frightened.

Martha had left an assortment of medications on the bed table. I shook out two aspirin and swallowed them, but the chilled water irritated the raw wound my throat had become. I knew that only something warm would ease it.

I struggled into my robe and slippers and made my way through the darkened hallway toward the service stairs, puzzled by my lack of strength. I paused about halfway to catch my breath. A faint light shone from the hallway. Martha? No. This was the flickering light of a small candle. Silently I approached it. A tall figure cast in sillhouette by the light, made its way carefully down the hall.

I could barely breathe as I recognized the long black coat and dark hair tied at the neck. David? I couldn't move. I had heard the stories about his ghost, but hadn't believed them— surely, since I'd come back, he must have, too. If not, why was I here? But now I had to believe. My fear vanished. "David," I called softly. The light snuffed out, and when I hurried to where I had last seen it, I found nothing.

I leaned helplessly against the wall and gave in to another coughing spasm. Of course I had found nothing, I realized when the spasm passed. There was nothing to find. There was only my loneliness and my weakness conspiring to show me the one person I wanted to comfort me.

I went down the service stairs, stumbling on them, to the dark kitchen. I flipped on the overhead lights and stood blinking against their glare until my eyes adjusted. I lit all the burners on the stove and managed to find the teakettle, fill it, and put it on to boil before sinking wearily into a kitchen chair, resting my head on the table.

The whistle of the teakettle nagged at me as I struggled to remember where I was and why I was there.

"Tea," I murmured finally, feeling a small victory at recalling that much. "Hot tea for my throat."

I forced myself to my feet, rattled dishes in the cabinet as I found a cup, saucer, spoon, located the tea bags, and carried them all back to the cabinet beside the stoves.

I eased the kettle off the stove, held it for a moment until it stopped its fierce boiling, and turned to fill the cup. I watched in fascination as the water, in slow motion, poured from the spout to the counter beside my cup.

A muffled exclamation escaped me, and I hurriedly set the kettle on the stove. "What's the matter with me?"

I snatched a dish towel from a nearby hook. As I wiped at the counter, I picked up the cup by the saucer, intending only to get it out of the way of the dish towel. The cup flew from the saucer, shattering on the floor at my feet. "What is the matter with me?" I asked again, staring at the broken china.

I was still standing there, staring at it, when Martha came into the kitchen. She took one look at me, and another at the broken cup. "Elizabeth," she asked, "what's wrong?"

Frightened now by my lack of coordination, my weakness, and confused by my inability to do even a simple thing like pour a cup of tea, I could only stare back at her.

Tears of frustration welled in my eyes. "I don't know, Martha." It was a little girl's voice I heard, not mine.

Instantly she was beside me, her arm supporting me. Her cool fingers trailed across my forehead. " 'Sakes alive, child," she said, "you're burning up. Let me get you back into bed."

"I only wanted a cup of tea, Martha. My throat hurts so terribly," I protested, but even to me it sounded like a whimper.

"I'll bring your tea to you," she promised as she led me from the kitchen, "but first let's get you covered up and warm."

CHAPTER
12

Eliza

As Eliza feared, once the painting was finished, the nightly visits ceased. Stephen seemed pleased with the painting, as did David. Secretly, Eliza felt that the artist had portrayed her as too lovely. There was a youth reflected in the painting that she no longer felt, and something troubled her about the expression which stared back at her from the canvas.

The winter was fierce, but brief. The early spring David promised her finally arrived and when she was able to get out of the house for even short periods of time her spirits lifted. With the assistance of Jeremiah Grimes she obtained bedding plants and seeds and hired a man to spade up the overgrown flower gardens which bordered the porch and walk.

She enjoyed feeling the warm sun on her back and the moist coolness of earth between her fingers. The hours she spent in her garden each morning were precious because she found that there she had the ability to lose all track of time.

David's visits were once again sporadic. Eliza sometimes wondered if it would be easier for her if he didn't return, but when weeks stretched by with no sight of him she knew that separation was not the answer for the ache always within her.

She played out scenarios in her mind in which she confessed her love to him, but too often, even in her fantasies, he scowled at her and said in clipped, measured tones, "It's too late, Eliza."

His face was lined now by the frown he so often wore. Heavy marks creased his forehead and each side of his mouth. She frequently found him staring at her, a brooding look in his eyes. She wondered why he came. He seemed preoccupied and impatient. But when he spoke to her, his voice was always gentle.

On a steamy late afternoon in mid-July he seemed more preoccupied than usual. As usual, Wilson remained in the dining room after supper, papers spread before him on the table. Eliza and David went outside, onto the porch.

There was no breeze, and the heat did nothing to allay the discomfort she felt as she watched David lean silently against the porch rail, staring vacantly into space. When he began to pace restlessly up and down the length of the porch, she could stand it no longer. "David, what is the matter?"

David stopped his pacing and turned to her. A bitter smile twisted his mouth. "A question? Eliza, you never ask me questions. You never ask what I'm doing, what I'm thinking, where I've been, where I'm going. Why is that?"

"I wasn't—" She stopped herself before telling him that she hadn't been allowed to ask questions of Owen.

He watched her intently. "You weren't what?"

"I wasn't—" Oh, Lord, if she looked at him any longer she would be lost. She turned away from him and stared over the wilting heads of her heat-parched flowers. She forced into her voice a calmness she was far from feeling. "I was trying not to pry."

"Pry, Eliza," he said softly. "If you're not interested, pretend that you are."

Pretend to be interested? It took all her strength to pretend not to be. Her voice caught in her throat. "Of course I'm interested."

"Of course," he said dully.

She heard his footsteps cross the porch and the scrape of chair legs as he sat down.

"I've been appointed to fill a Senate vacancy," he said.

She kept her back to him as she felt moisture gathering in her eyes. "I remember your once telling me that someday you would be principal chief."

"If I ever am," he said in a tone that tore at her heart, "it may be an empty honor."

"No," she protested.

He didn't hear her. "Our nation is dying. And not dramatically. After all the promises, after all our work in building a new home in this wilderness that they happily pushed us into to get our lands in the South, after all the pain of the Civil War—not even our war, as you once reminded me—after all our 'brilliant' negotiations following that war, we're still being nibbled away. They're like mice after cheese—a little piece here, a little piece there, a concession here, a compromise there. Soon there won't be anything left of our nation except perhaps a word or two of the language.

"*Oklahoma*," he said bitterly. " 'Land of the red men' is how they translate it. If they have their way, one day there won't be enough 'red men' here to remind the world that these were ever separate nations.

"The Council at Okmulgee is a start. The editorials that question whether our land is too valuable to be held for so few. The railroad—already in the Creek Nation, bringing white men who will want our timber and our valleys. The growing pressure to survey our lands and allot them to individuals instead of holding them for all. The warnings are all there, but I don't know what we can do. I don't know if there is anything we can do."

She turned toward him. He leaned forward in the chair, resting his elbows on his knees and massaging the furrow in his forehead.

She went to him and knelt beside him, hiding the pain she felt. "Last summer," she said firmly, "you told me you weren't defeated. This winter you told me that you thought you had enough support to keep the constitution of the Okmulgee council from being ratified. Surely, now that you are a member of the legislature, you will be able to exert even more influence. Won't you have some say in what your government does with its land? Won't you have some influence over the railroad as it crosses your country?"

He looked up at her with an expression in his eyes she couldn't interpret. Speculative? Pensive? She forced herself to continue in an even voice.

"You won't give up. You are not able to give up. Your nation has cost too many people too much to be allowed to die."

He took her hand in both of his. "No. I won't give up. I can fight the survey. I can fight allotment. I can be highly critical of those railroads that want the east-west line through the nation. But I'm only one person."

"But you are not the only person who cares."

Eliza lay awake long after he left, staring into the shadows of her room. David's nation couldn't die now. It couldn't!

Something shook at my shoulder. I tried to ignore it, but the pressure returned. The quilts were so heavy I couldn't breathe.

"Elizabeth?"

Why, it was Jane. What was she doing here? She should be down at the store taking care of Marie. Such a beautiful daughter she had. One day I would have a little girl just like her.

"Elizabeth, here's your tea."

She was one of his people; she could help.

"You won't let him give up, will you, Jane? You'll help him, won't you?"

"Elizabeth?"

"Where's Marie? You shouldn't leave her alone. She's so little."

It was so hot. Why was it so hot? *I'd be all wilted by the time David arrived, and I did so want—no,* needed *—to look nice today.*

Eliza dressed with special care. It was the first time since last winter that she had known with certainty when David would arrive. He had promised to be with her. Today her year of exile was over and she could formally ask to be released from her marriage vows. Her hands trembled as she arranged her hair. It wasn't wrong. Surely it couldn't be wrong to end a marriage that had been forced upon her. She pushed the final hairpin into place with a defiant gesture.

Mrs. Jenkins's unsmiling presence at breakfast reminded Eliza of how severely she would be censured should it become known that she was divorced. The woman disliked her now, for no valid reason. If she knew the truth . . .

Eliza couldn't tolerate her presence any longer, not if she were to go through with what faced her today.

"Mrs. Jenkins?"

"Yes?"

"Do you not have any family in Fort Smith?"

The woman looked at her quizzically. "Of course I do."

"You never mention them."

"It's not my place to discuss my family with you," Mrs. Jenkins said, sniffing.

Eliza's composure was daunted by the woman's barbed response, but she had made up her mind to be rid of her for at least this day.

"Would you like to visit them?"

"Why?"

Why did this woman have the ability to infuriate her? It was impossible to be subtle.

"I would like for you to take the day off and visit your family."

"I have work to do. I don't neglect my work."

Eliza didn't scream at her to get out of her house, that she didn't want her around to cast a pall on what must be done. She looked at her steadily. "I insist."

It seemed hours before David arrived. She went through agonies of indecision. It was not too late to stop Mr. Grimes; no papers had been filed. She had promised, before God, to be Owen's wife. *Till death do us part* kept running through her mind. Perhaps if she could remain hidden from him, it wouldn't be necessary to take this step. No. She had to sever all ties with Owen Markham. If only she didn't have to face the rest of her life alone. If only David still cared, it would be easier.

But David didn't care for her, and she would be alone, forever. Where could she go? What could she do? She had not been able to face those questions before. There had always been time, later, for making decisions. Now there was no more time, and she had no answers.

A parade of empty years stretched before her, lonely and joyless. A sob broke from her, and she pressed her hand to her mouth to keep another from escaping. "I will survive," she vowed.

That vow sustained her when David arrived, accompanied only by Jeremiah Grimes. It sustained her through the brief reading of the complaint. It kept her hand from shaking as she signed her name where Grimes indicated.

"Now," Grimes said as he tucked the papers back into their folder, "we have a problem."

Eliza looked at her hands. They were trembling again. She clasped them together.

"In a case like this I would ordinarily suggest that we try for what is known as constructive service of summons. It's quicker, and, in your case, it might be safer for you. We would simply have to publish a notice for four weeks, and in thirty days it would be all over. Your husband might not ever know he had been sued for divorce.''

''But you can't risk that with a man of Markham's position?'' David interrupted.

''No. We can't. Someone will have to be appointed by the court to take the summons to him. Someone who knows him.'' He turned to David. ''Do you know anyone who can do that?''

David was studying Eliza. He spoke to her. ''I can't be gone that long at this time.''

''No,'' Grimes said. ''Under no circumstances, Colonel Richards, should you even consider going yourself.''

''It's a great deal to ask of someone else,'' David said. He rubbed his forehead with the fingers of both hands, a gesture Eliza now recognized as one he used unconsciously when in deep thought. ''Stephen Ward has wanted to return to Washington. Would he be acceptable?''

''I'll have to research the law, because of his citizenship. It may be necessary to appoint someone to accompany him and actually serve the summons, but I believe the court will accept him.''

Grimes was especially solemn as he took his leave. He clasped Eliza's hand. ''If your husband should contact you, or if you become frightened for any reason, please let me know. We can protect you.''

She held her head erect and spoke with deceptive calm. ''Thank you, Mr. Grimes.''

After Grimes left, David lapsed into silence. Eliza was afraid to speak, afraid that if she opened her mouth words which she must never say would pour forth.

''Have you decided where you will go?'' David asked abruptly.

Must they discuss it now? She shook her head.

"You could go home."

"I have no home," she said.

"To Virginia. To your father."

"I have no home."

David stood facing the mantel, gripping the ledge. "Perhaps you would like to visit friends in Washington before you decide."

She stared past him into the brick of the unused firebox. "No."

"You'll just go off to a new city, a new life, and put all this behind you?"

She felt a constriction in her throat and pressure behind her eyes. "I suppose."

He beat his fist against the mantel once before turning to face her. "How very calm you are," he said slowly. "Haven't you heard? We're the ones who are supposed to be stoic. And yet you constantly amaze me with your ability to show no emotion at all.

"Was it this easy for you to forget me when you married Markham?"

She felt her heart twisting and the pressure in her throat growing.

"Do you know that in the year you've been here you've not once voluntarily spoken of the man you lived with for four years? Nothing bad. Nothing good. Nothing."

He walked toward her as he spoke. Her eyes were trapped in the bitterness she saw in his. She was too stunned to respond, too stunned even to think.

"Your friends in Washington don't exist for you any longer, do they?" He stopped in front of her. "It's as though your father isn't even alive."

She stood and tried to push past him, but he caught her by the shoulders.

"How do you do it, Eliza? How do you turn off love?"

Oh, David, she cried inwardly. *Don't do this. Please don't do this. I can't take much more.*

His fingers bit into her shoulders. "Was I so wrong about you? I remember you as warm and vibrant, but most of all . . . caring."

She felt tears rising. She turned her head and strained away from him as his words railed down on her.

"When did you change? Why did you change?"

He forced her to face him, and she knew the pain in his eyes would haunt her forever.

"What have you done with the girl I loved?"

She could stand no more. "Please let me go," she moaned.

"No! I have to know."

"She's dead!" Eliza cried, and once she spoke she could not stop. "She died the night her father sold her to Owen Markham."

David released his grip on her shoulders. She stared into his stricken eyes and then, as she had longed so often to do, she threw herself against his chest.

"I don't want to go away. Please don't make me leave. I know you don't love me, but I can't go on living if I lose you again."

"Oh, God," she heard him groan. "I should have known."

A shudder ran through him before he grasped her to him.

"You're not going away. Nothing is ever going to take you from me again."

He held her pressed to him, her face buried in the fabric of his coat. She felt the beat of his heart beneath her cheek, the heat of his body mingling with hers. His arms were bands holding her ever tighter, ever closer to him, and she prayed they would never release her.

He held her away from him and she murmured in protest. He looked down at her face, unspoken questions shadowing his eyes, and bent toward her, his warm mouth kissing the tears from her cheeks.

Groaning, he pulled her to him, and his mouth claimed hers, searching, needing, and within her stirred longings she had felt but once before. She was fifteen again, with David beside a creek, in a world without pain, feeling anew the wonder of wanting to be one with this man, of knowing he felt the same.

She felt weak, without the strength to stand alone, and a warmth flowed through her body. Her arms crept around him, pulling her closer to him. She was floating, she was drowning, she was dying, but she had to go on. This delicious agony must continue.

He tore away, his voice a ragged imitation of the one she knew. "We can't do this."

She reached to touch his face. With tentative fingers she explored each beloved feature and smoothed at the lines which now marked him.

"Please love me," she whispered. "David, I need you to love me."

"Eliza, do you know what you're asking?"

In response she slid her hands behind his head, her mouth seeking his, and when she kissed him, it was with the hunger of seven years of separation, seven lonely years of longing.

How could she have pretended, even for a moment, that Owen was David? She felt David's need, yes. But that need was tempered by love, a love she could feel even though David had not spoken the words.

He pulled away from her again, slowly and reluctantly, and looked into her eyes.

"I've waited for this moment forever," he told her.

"And so have I."

With a smile which, for so many years, she had seen only in her dreams, he lifted her into his arms.

"I love you, Eliza. I never stopped loving you. I never will."

"Nor I you," she promised.

She felt one moment of panic as David lowered her to her bed. She had never known love in the act of love, only pain.

But David did love her. She felt it in the gentleness of his touch, even as he trembled with the demands of his body. No, not Owen, she thought, never Owen. Lifting herself to David's caress, she surrendered to her own needs.

An unbearable weight pushed down on me. A band tightened across my chest and refused to let me breathe. I reached out beside me and found only cold, empty sheets.

"David?" My voice rattled in my throat. "David, where are you?"

The face that stared back at Eliza from her dressing table mirror was softer than she had seen it since childhood. She found herself smiling at her reflection and realized with a little start of surprise that the smile was becoming as familiar to her now as its absence had been for so long.

In less than a week she would be David's wife. In less than a week she would be home, in the house on the hill he had promised her.

"It isn't completed," he had warned her. "I stopped work on it when—when I thought you weren't coming."

David had stayed in Fort Smith, near her, until the legislature convened in early October. Bit by bit he drew from her as much of her story as she was able to tell. In scattered fragments she learned of his life since the end of the war, of his disappointments, and of the mistaken impressions of her marriage that he had formed after talking with her father.

David had rejoiced with her when the telegram came from Stephen advising that Owen was on an extended tour of the western tribes and not available to be served with summons, making constructive notice possible after all. Together they laughed at the added message, "Am painting second most beautiful woman in the world."

The only dark moment came after Stephen's affidavit about Owen had arrived by mail. "If I sit with the Senate," David told her, "I can't be with you at the time of the divorce."

Alone? Was she strong enough to go through that alone? Eliza pushed those thoughts from her mind. Of course she was. David loved her, and they would be together forever, soon.

She took his hand in hers. "What do you mean, *if* you sit with the Senate? Too many things require your attention. And you told me there would be dissension over the selection of the new delegates to Washington and the new candidate for principal chief. You must go."

He drew her to him. "I know. It's only for a month. I'll be back by early November. I just don't feel right about leaving you alone at this time."

"What can go wrong?" she chided. "Owen doesn't know where I am. I have Mr. Grimes to take care of any emergencies, and"—she laughed gently—"I have Mrs. Jenkins to protect my virtue."

He held her close.

"I don't want you to leave me, either," she told him, "but I know why you have to go, and I know that if you don't, you will never forgive yourself."

A rap at the door startled her, and Eliza looked up from the mirror and her memories in surprise as Mrs. Jenkins entered her room, her black coat buttoned up to her neck and her stiff black hat perched primly on her head.

"I have to go out," she announced.

How very strange, Eliza thought. "Of course, Mrs. Jenkins. Is something wrong?"

"No," the woman denied quickly. "No. It's a—it's a

matter of an unfortunate woman who needs my help. It shouldn't take too long."

"Take as long as you need," Eliza had told her. This surprising sign of compassion in the housekeeper came much too late, but the woman had lost her power to irritate Eliza. Perhaps because she knew that soon she could say good-bye to Mrs. Jenkins.

Nothing could bother her now, Eliza thought as she dressed for bed. As if to reassure herself that it really had happened, she took the blue-backed legal document from its place in her trunk and read it again. After all the waiting, the dread and the anticipation, it had been too simple. Without Owen to contest the divorce, it had amounted only to a formality, a few questions asked in the privacy of the judge's chambers. There should have been a drum to toll the knell for that part of her life, or perhaps a woman pointing an accusing finger at her and shrinking away in horror. There was nothing but a scrawled signature across an already prepared page.

"But it *is* over," she said as she replaced the papers in the trunk.

She walked through the room gathering the little things she would take with her, things she could easily pack now, and found herself humming half-remembered melodies her mother had once taught her. She suddenly realized it had been years since she had felt happy enough to sing.

When Wilson had made a special trip to Fort Smith on the first of November to tell her that David had been detained, his message had bothered her at first. "An additional three days," Wilson had said. "At the most. It's important that he stay."

Of course it was important. David wouldn't be kept away if it were not. And now the waiting was over. Even at this moment he might be riding toward home.

Eliza stopped humming and went back to the mirror. Her eyes shone with the joy of her secret surprise. When David left, she had not been sure. Now she had no doubt. Her complexion glowed. She rested her hand on her no longer flat stomach. "A boy," she prayed, "one who looks just like his father."

She heard the sound of steps on the porch outside her room. It was too soon for Mrs. Jenkins to return, but perhaps she had forgotten something. No. The steps were too heavy. They stopped at the door to her bedroom. *David!* she thought as she heard the knob being tried. *He's come early.*

She ran to the door, words of welcome on her lips. The door slammed open, and she froze in midstep, her mouth forming a silent scream. Owen stood there. His eyes raked over her. His handsome face twisted in contempt. He spoke with quiet, deadly cold. "You whore."

Cold. Now I was cold. How could that be? I was going somewhere; I knew that, but not where. But when I tried to rise, to run, something held me down. "No," I moaned. "Let me go. Please! Let me go."

Eliza huddled behind the fence. She held her breath for fear that her ragged breathing or the sight of it in the chill night air would give her hiding place away. Her heartbeat seemed to echo in the darkness, and she was afraid it, too, might tell him where she hid. After an eternity, Owen's footsteps had faded into the night, but the memory of his words rang loudly in her ears. "There's no place for you to hide, Eliza. I'll find you wherever you are. He'll never have you."

She tried to straighten her tattered dressing gown and discovered that she couldn't raise her right arm. She pulled her clothes together as well as she could with one hand and crept down the alley, scraping her bare feet on the stones of the roadway.

She had only one clear thought. David. She must get to David. He would help her. She felt tears cold on her cheeks.

She couldn't go through this again. *David!* she cried silently. *Don't let him find me!*

The houses were unfamiliar now. Somehow, though, she knew she was going toward the heart of town, toward the road to David.

Surely she was far enough away from Owen to risk standing, to risk running. There were lights ahead, and voices carried through the sound of wind-driven leaves.

She crept cautiously past a row of small stores, dark as the night they were outlined against, toward the freight yard. She peered through the gate, making sure Owen was not there. She saw three men outlined by the torches in the yard. One stood alone, unloading a wagon. Two stood by another wagon, involved in a heated argument.

She staggered into the yard. The two stopped their argument to look at her.

"Please. Help me." She forced the words through her bruised lips.

The taller of the two, bearded, broke into a broad grin. "Damn, girl, if they catch you this far uptown you're going to go to jail for sure. What are you doing off the row?"

Not understanding him, she repeated, "Please. Help me."

The bearded one walked toward her, calling back over his shoulder, "So much for your argument that we didn't have time to go to Jean's place." He stopped in front of Eliza and inspected her, still grinning. "You like it rough, girl?"

There was a film before her eyes. It was painful now to breathe, difficult to stand. She stumbled, and the man caught her around the waist.

"Well, come on," he said. "If you're looking for business, you found some."

"No," she whispered, finally understanding his words. "Have to get away."

"Come on, I said." His hands tightened on her waist. "We've got to get this wagon out of here before daylight."

"No," she cried, beating with her one good hand against his chest. His grin was gone as he lifted her from the ground.

"You'll be putting her down." A man's voice, a broad Scot's brogue, cut through the night. The man who had been standing alone strode toward them carrying a blanket over one arm.

The bearded man turned toward him, still holding Eliza. "And why would I do that?"

The Scotsman looked warily at him, and at the other man now poised nearby.

"Because she's not a harlot."

The bearded one broke into a laugh. "Are you crazy, man? Look at her."

"I'm looking," the Scotsman told him, "and it grieves me. She's my wife, and she's not been right since I got her back from the Comanche."

The bearded man released her as though he had been struck, and the Scotsman hurried to her side, draping the blanket over her, speaking softly to her. "Come, lass. You know I've told you not to be wandering off alone." He helped her toward his wagon, and Eliza went thankfully, feeling only gentleness flowing from him.

He lifted her into his wagon. When she tried to speak, he silenced her with a quick gesture. "Rest now, lass. We'll be leaving soon," he said in a voice loud enough to be heard by the other two. She nodded her understanding and lay back against the side of the wagon, still trembling.

When the noises in the yard told her that the other wagon had left, the Scotsman joined her.

"My name is William MacDougal," he told her, "and I'll be helping you if I can."

"Why?" she asked, sensing the danger he had so quietly confronted and the deep sadness that seemed to have come over him.

"For my wife," he told her. "Because there was no one to help her. Because . . . because I never got her back."

"Elizabeth."

Jane leaned over me. I could barely see her in the dim light, and her voice seemed to come from far away.

"Elizabeth, we're taking you to a doctor."

"No." Why would she do that? "Will promised to take me to David. He's got to do that. We can't stop now. I have to get to him."

"Elizabeth, listen to me." Another voice intruded. "This is Mack. Aunt Martha is here with me. We're going to take you to the hospital."

His words penetrated slowly. I tried to focus my vision, but I couldn't see clearly. Martha leaned over me.

"Martha?"

"Yes, dear."

"Isn't it morning yet?"

A smile trembled across her lips. "It's late afternoon. I've been so worried about you."

"How are the peaches?"

"Oh, thank the Lord," she said. She pressed her hands to her face and turned away, her shoulders shaking.

"They're fine," Mack told me. "We saved them." His voice sounded curiously patient and controlled. "Listen to me. You are ill. We have to take you to Fort Smith, to the hospital. Do you understand what I'm saying?"

The hospital? No. It was out of the question. "I can't go."

"We don't have any choice."

I shrank back into the pillows, hearing the rasp of my own breathing. "Oh, but I do. I can't be away from here. McCollum would use it against me. Mack, don't do this to me."

Mack's voice was firm. "Not even Stanley McCollum would do that."

It took all my strength to speak. "You know he would."

He turned to Martha. "She may be right."

I was drifting, but I had to hear what was said. It was so difficult to listen. Martha's voice was softer. "But what can we do?"

Mack's deeper tones were almost inaudible. "I don't like it any better than you do, but we'd better call him. He got a doctor for Marie. If he will, he can help us."

Eliza awoke to the touch of David's hand on her cheek and his lips on hers. She slid her arms around his neck and pulled him even closer to her as she returned his kiss before she reluctantly opened her eyes.

He looked down at her, a teasing smile in his eyes. "Good morning, sleepyhead."

Still not fully awake, Eliza pulled herself awkwardly up against the headboard and sank back against the pillows with a sigh of gentle protest. The feather mattress sagged with his weight as David sat beside her.

"Are you sure you want to get up now?" he asked as he handed her coffee from the waiting tray.

"No," she murmured before taking a sip of the steaming liquid, "but I won't miss this time with you."

He traced the hollows beneath her eyes with slender, tanned fingers. "You had another dream last night, didn't you?"

Eliza's breath caught in her throat. He knew. How she wished she could hide this from him, but he always knew.

He took the cup from her and set it on the tray. "Can you remember the dream?"

She leaned forward and circled his waist with her arms. When she spoke, she spoke against his chest.

"No. It's like the others. All I know is that something horrible was going to happen, something so bad I couldn't even see it in the dream."

A shudder ran through her, and she held him tighter, grateful for the strength and comfort he so selflessly gave her.

"It will get better," he promised. "After the child is born. And after a little more time has passed."

She managed to smile as she pulled away from him, touching his lips with a whisper of a kiss before she sank back against the pillows.

"I know," she said. "It's just that I resent the dreams so much. They intrude on my time with you. They have no right to do that."

He rested his hand on her swollen stomach. "How is he acting? Is he giving you any trouble?"

"No," she said with a laugh, "he's no trouble at all. Just growing every day." Pride touched her voice. "I've shown them, haven't I? All those people who said I'd never carry this baby are going to be so surprised."

David turned to the tray, taking extra care as he lifted her cup and handed it to her.

"What do you want to do today?" he asked.

"Are they gone?"

"All but one, and he's leaving this morning."

She looked toward the window, where sunlight filtered through the sheer curtains. "Is it warm enough yet?"

David's chuckle echoed through the room. "All right. Today, definitely, we walk in the orchard. But not for very long." He touched her cheek. "Not long enough to tire you."

She dressed warmly. Although the sun shone brightly, David had told her often that the winds still carried a chill. She smiled as she replaced her brush next to his razor on the washstand. Now, at last, their things were mingled, just as their lives must always have been. She stopped by the window, looking over the valley. It was a scene she could summon with her eyes closed, one which she never tired of:

the valley below, the river winding its way through it, the mountains in the distance.

"It's almost too perfect," she said to herself.

She took a shawl from the wardrobe and made her way carefully down the curved staircase, feeling very awkward and yet so very thankful that the baby still grew within her.

The door to David's study was closed, but the sounds of voices carried through to the hall. Eliza shook her head. These men who came so often now, what did they want?

In the kitchen she found the old Indian woman who served as David's cook muttering over a tray. Short of breath from even this brief exertion, Eliza eased herself into a chair, feeling strangely weak.

No. Not today. She didn't have time to be weak or ill or anything else that would interfere with today's walk in the orchard. She had waited too long.

Something twisted uncomfortably within her. She placed her hand on her stomach. Was that movement? She felt it again, sharper this time. *David,* she thought triumphantly through the discomfort, *our son is finally kicking me*. It seemed important that he know that.

The old woman finished filling the tray and picked it up to leave the room.

"Is that for David?" Eliza asked.

The woman nodded, and Eliza stood and reached for the tray. "I'll take it to him."

She paused at the study door to shift the tray to one hand. The voices inside were louder now. Should she disturb them? Of course she should. She tapped firmly on the door. The voices stopped. She waited impatiently for David to call out for her to enter. Instead, he flung the door open, his scowl softening when he saw her.

"We're almost finished," he told her as he took the tray from her.

"David, I . . ." She wanted to tell him about the child, but this obviously was the wrong time to interrupt him.

"What is it?" He put the tray on a nearby table and took her hand. "Is anything wrong?"

"No." She smiled at him. "I'll tell you later."

"By all means, tell him now," a bitter voice said from inside the room. She looked up in surprise at the man standing behind David. His scowl was as deep as David's had been, but it didn't soften when he looked at her. If anything, it deepened. "Apparently you're the only one he will listen to."

David drew her closer to him. He did not turn but spoke in clipped words. "You will not talk to my wife in that tone of voice."

"Your wife?" The derision in the man's voice tore at Eliza's heart, but David's eyes were locked on hers. She could not show the pain. She could not turn and run.

David put his arm around her shoulder as he led her from the room. He stopped at the door and spoke without looking back. "I have nothing further to say to you. I expect you to leave immediately."

With his arm still around her shoulder, David led her down the hall to the front doors, which he threw open, not stopping to close them. She stumbled in her effort to keep up with his determined stride.

"David," she protested with a gentle laugh as they crossed the lawn, "I am slightly less than graceful these days. Can we please slow down?"

He stopped and took her in his arms. She felt his heart pounding beneath her cheek, felt the tension within him as he held her, but when he spoke his words were light.

"Of course we can. This is your morning. We can do anything you want."

She moved her hands across his chest, up to his face, where

she smoothed the lines across his forehead and around his mouth with her fingers.

"The orchard," she reminded him softly.

"The orchard."

He led her across the lawn to the stone wall. There were wooden steps built against it on each side, but he stopped her when she started to climb them.

"This is much better," he said as he lifted her and seated her on the wall. He scrambled across the steps and lifted her down.

He seemed reluctant to release her, keeping his arm around her, but she felt the tension gradually leaving him as they strolled through the neatly trimmed and evenly spaced peach trees.

"In less than a month," he told her, "when you look this direction from your window, all you will be able to see will be pink." He stopped to break off the end of a low branch. "See? Already the buds are beginning to swell."

"Like me?" she asked, but her accompanying laugh ended in a gasp as the child once again made his presence known.

"What is it?" David asked urgently.

She leaned against him until the spasm ended.

"It's what I wanted to tell you earlier," she said between controlled breaths. "It seems that after waiting so long to be active, your son has decided to make up for lost time." She managed a shaky laugh. "I think I need to sit down for a moment."

David helped her to the wall and settled her onto the steps. She was breathing heavily now. She leaned against the steps and closed her eyes. When she opened them, she saw David staring across the valley, his brow furrowed, with the dark look she had seen so often lately clouding his eyes.

"Don't you think it's time you told me?" she said.

"What?" he asked, too sharply.

"What those men want. Why you are so angry with them."

He passed his hand over her hair and then dropped it to her shoulder. "They are not important. What they want doesn't matter."

She took a sustaining breath before confronting him. "Apparently it does," she said firmly. "You try to hide it from me, but I know there have been many angry words, that there is a serious problem. It's about your nation, isn't it?"

"Eliza," he said equally firmly, "nothing matters now but you and I and our child."

She reached for his hand as she sought the right words. "We spent too many years not talking, hiding our feelings from each other. We can't do that any longer. Please don't keep this from me. I have a right—" She stopped herself. "No, I'm not talking about rights. I'm talking about needs. I need to know. Are they saying you should send me away?"

His averted eyes gave her the answer she feared.

"I see," she said finally. She gripped his hand. "Talk to me, David. Tell me what is being said. It can't hurt any worse than what I'm imagining. It can't hurt any worse than your silence."

He drew his hand away. He turned and leaned against the wall, staring vacantly across the valley while he massaged the furrow of his forehead. When he spoke, his words came slowly and reluctantly.

"I was late coming to you this fall because the legislature was selecting a candidate for principal chief."

"You told me they would do that sometime during the session," she prompted him.

He nodded, still not facing her. "They were impressed by my negotiations following the war, and later in Washington. They liked the stand I took on the railroad and in dealing with the survey. In short, they thought I would probably be able to overcome the fact that my father was white."

She held her breath as she waited for his next words.

"They asked me to stand for election."

"As principal chief?"

"Yes."

She saw his tension in the rigid lines of his body. "That was last fall," she said slowly. Oh, God, did she really want to hear this? "What are they saying now?"

He stood outlined between her and the distant mountains, each feature of his profile in sharp relief. Although she could see his tension, the muscles clenching in his throat and the firm line of his jaw, he remained silent.

She struggled to her feet and stood beside him. She reached out, touching his face and drawing it around to her until she could look into his shadowed eyes.

"Tell me," she said softly.

He gripped her shoulders and pulled her to him. "Eliza," he said, his voice rasping, "they don't know what you've been through, and I can't tell them without jeopardizing your safety."

"Would it make any difference?" she wondered aloud.

He held her tightly, as if the sheer force of his grip could protect her from everything outside themselves. "I don't know."

"What do they want you to do?"

She felt him sigh deeply. "They insist that I be more active now, that I be among the people—" a sound that should have been a laugh broke from him, "showing them what an honorable man I really am."

A chill crept through her, invading the warmth of his arms.

"They want you to go? Now?"

He looked down into her eyes. "I will not leave this hill until after our child is born and you are able to travel with me."

"But they don't want me to travel with you, do they?"

Once again, he didn't answer her.

"That man today," she persisted, "the one you told to leave—what else did you say to him?"

He was silent so long she thought he was not going to speak. When he did, his words were hesitant. "I told him that . . . I thought it would be wise for them to select another candidate."

"Oh, David, no." She tried to twist away from him, but he held her. "All your dreams. All your plans. You can't stop now."

"I will not leave you again."

"David, your people need you. You can't abandon them. Think of the things you told me this summer. You won't be able to live with yourself if you just let them happen, if you don't fight with every ounce of strength you have."

"You need me." His words cut through her, silencing her but not the guilt that ran rampant through her thoughts. Why? Why must he be forced to choose? It wasn't fair. She could not allow it to happen.

"And our son?" she asked. "What will he think when he realizes that his father could have helped save a nation, that his father could have held the highest office in that nation, and that his mother kept him from it?"

"Our son—" The words seemed torn from him. She could not bear the look of pain in his eyes. He took a long, deep breath. "Our son will have the most wonderful mother any child could hope for."

She pulled away so quickly he had to release her. She felt tears brimming in her eyes. She must not cry. "When he learns what was lost because of her, will that be enough for him?" The tears demanded release. She must not break down in front of him. "Will that be enough for you?" she asked as she turned and stumbled up the steps.

"Eliza?"

She heard David calling her, saw him reaching for her. She had to get away, had to return to the safety of her room, had to have time to learn what she must do.

"Eliza!"

Tears blinded her now. She reached the top step and started over the wall.

"Wait!"

Pain knifed through her, doubling her over. Something was terribly wrong. She saw David reaching for her as she gave in to a wave of weakness. She felt the pull of fabric as he grabbed her skirts, but it was too late. She heard his cry, prolonged and agonized, as the ground beneath the wall rushed up to greet her.

Pain was a constant, blinding red cloud enveloping her. David knelt beside her, gripping her hand.

"I've killed our baby," Eliza moaned.

"No. No, you haven't," he protested, his voice hoarse against her cheek.

"Oh, God, please let my baby live. I'll go away," she cried. "I'll go away."

He clenched his hand on hers. "You mustn't say that. You can't leave me. Before God, I won't let you leave me."

There was a weight on my chest, bearing me down into the mattress. I couldn't breathe. I tried to push it away, but Jane held my hands.

"No, Elizabeth, you need the covers over you."

"David? Where is he?"

My voice grated in the silence of the room. "Where is he? He promised!"

Jane smoothed my forehead with icy fingers. "It's all right, child. Don't fret now."

"My baby?" I asked, struggling up in the bed. "Jane, where is my baby?"

"He's all right, dear." Her voice broke as she tried to push me down. "He's asleep now."

I felt the cough building within me. It tore through me,

leaving me shaken and spent. Jane put her hands on my shoulders. "Lie back now."

"No. I have to find David. I have to be with him." I fought against her restraint. "He has to know."

"You'll have to hold her still," a man said from behind Jane.

I had not been aware of anyone else. "Who are you?" I choked out.

He spoke calmly, almost hypnotically. "I'm a doctor. I'm here to help you." Jane held my shoulders. He took my arm and pushed back the sleeve of my nightgown. A blast of cold air assaulted my skin as he positioned the hypodermic, but I barely felt it as he pushed the needle into my arm.

"Is there a child?" he asked as he pulled my sleeve down.

Jane's voice broke. "No."

"It might help if we could contact the man she's calling for. Do you know how to reach him?"

Jane eased me back against the pillows, shaking her head in mute denial. For an instant it was so very clear to me. For an instant there was no other answer. Now I knew why I had at last seen that shadowy form in the flickering candlelight.

"I'm going to die, aren't I?" I murmured. "It's the only way I can be with him again." Desolation washed through me. "David?" I cried out. "Where are you?"

"I'm here."

The doctor was gone; Jane was gone. He reached for my hand, sitting beside me on the bed.

"I've waited so long," I whimpered as he gathered me to him.

"I know." His voice was as soothing as the hand he passed over my hair. I sighed against him, marveling at his touch until that was not enough. I had to see him. I pulled away and reached for his face, smoothing the lines I found there as

I had done so often. As his anguished eyes met mine, I felt a shudder pass through me.

"I'm so sorry," I whispered. "I'm so sorry I spoiled it for you."

He pressed my head against his chest, rocking me, soothing me, murmuring over and over, "It's all right. It doesn't matter now."

I gave in then to the need to cry. Great hacking sobs broke from me, but no tears fell from my burning eyes. It was all so pointless, so futile. I held on to him with all the strength I had. "Must I?" I choked out. Then the words were torn from me. "I don't want to die! I haven't lived yet."

"I won't let you die," he whispered against my cheek. "You can't leave me now."

CHAPTER
13

Elizabeth

My inactivity chafed me. Martha mothered me with juices and aspirin and antibiotics and cough syrup, but now that I could breathe again without feeling as though my lungs were being ripped from me, I longed to be out of bed. A blue jay chattered raucously in the branches of the magnolia outside my window, and the dance of light through the curtain invited me outside, into the warmth of the April day.

I tossed the covers aside impatiently and slipped from the bed, intending to throw open the window and let the fresh breeze play through my room. I found to my dismay that I had barely the strength to make it to the chair. I curled into the wing chair, out of breath, and let my gaze wander idly over the valley below. The view never failed to calm me. Soon I was breathing normally and had regained at least a semblance of composure.

My attention was drawn to the bare spot on the wall. Where was the painting? I still had no idea why or when it had been removed, but I now knew that David must have hung it here after . . . after what?

Frustration welled within me. After all this time, I still did not know.

Tapping lightly on the door to announce herself, Martha came into my room wearing a grim expression on her normally pleasant face.

"Well, young lady, I see you're up again."

I had to smile at her. "Why, Martha, that frown seems unusually severe. Surely it's not caused by my merely walking across the room."

She brought my robe to me and helped me work my arms into it. "You're right," she said. "It isn't. You have a visitor. Do you want to get back into bed, or do you want to sit here while you talk to him?"

Her tone told me I wasn't going to enjoy the visit.

"Who is it?"

"Stanley McCollum."

"Oh, lord, what's he doing here?" I wasn't sure if I was up to dueling with him. "I'll sit here."

She took a blanket from the bed and tucked it around my feet.

"I suppose there's no way I can get out of seeing him, is there?"

"No, there isn't," he said from the doorway.

Martha gave a final tug at the blanket and stepped to one side.

"I'll see Miss Richards alone."

She looked toward me, anger flashing in her eyes, but I gave her a hesitant smile and nodded toward the door. She glared at McCollum but walked stiffly from the room, leaving the door open.

"Well, Mr. McCollum." I spoke as coldly as he had, having trouble repressing my own anger at the way he ordered Martha and me around. "This is certainly . . . unexpected."

"So you do recognize me?"

My hopes for a quick meeting were dashed by his undisguised animosity. Preparing for battle, I smiled sweetly and said in my most saccharine voice, "How could I ever forget your many kindnesses to me?"

"Including keeping you at death's door while denying you medical attention?"

I stared at him dumbly. "What are you talking about?"

"Young lady, I do not appreciate having my professional reputation bandied about this county by an impertinent interloper like you."

I found my voice. "I don't have the slightest idea what you're talking about. I have not been out of this house for days, and I have never discussed you, or my opinion of you, anywhere other than on this hill."

He was paler than usual, his lips white and drawn with the effort of controlling his anger. "I don't know what your game is," he said, "but you're on the wrong track if you think you can play on John Richards's sympathy. I still control the trust."

I was suddenly very tired of this man. I wanted only for him to leave so that I could crawl back into my bed and sleep. I kept my voice as measured as I could. "I haven't seen my illustrious cousin since the day of Marie LeFlore's funeral, and I am sure that by now you know every word that was said between us."

He leaned over me, his face so close his breath puffed against my mouth. "Are you denying that you called him late in the afternoon last week telling him that I wouldn't let you go to the hospital, that you had him bring a doctor to this house to treat you, and that you kept the two of them here until well into the next morning?"

The rage in his voice was like a physical force, pushing me back into the chair. What was he saying? The doctor—yes, I remembered the doctor. But John? Fragments of half-forgotten dreams crowded my vision. I couldn't deal with them and with McCollum at the same time. I forced my words out. "I think you'd better leave now."

He stayed crouched over me, staring into my eyes, his voice low and frighteningly calm. "I have much more experience in this kind of thing than you do. You can't win. Before I'm through with you, you'll regret ever coming to Richards Spur."

I fought down the urge to strike out at him, but with that my control failed. "Martha!" My voice cracked, and I called out again. "Martha!"

I heard her footsteps in the hall as McCollum straightened away from me, a gleam of satisfaction lighting his eyes. He met Martha at the doorway. "I believe Miss Richards is not quite as well as she thought," he said as he left the room.

Martha helped me to the bed. I wanted to sleep, to close myself off from what McCollum had said, from the questions he raised, but the memories of that night tormented me. What was real and what was dream? What was remembered and what was imagined? David. Surely it had been David.

With a moan I beat my fist into the pillow. It couldn't have been John. I couldn't have mistaken them.

Joannie arrived the next morning, helped upstairs by Mack, and settled in with her knitting surrounding her and her crutches nearby. I was selfishly glad to have her with me, but I had to voice my surprise at her being there.

"Oh, I made sure that you're not contagious before I came," she said. "There's no reason for me not to be here."

It wasn't the answer I had expected. Without thinking, I stammered, "When you wouldn't come with Mack before, I thought it was because you'd heard the stories about the house and were afraid to be inside it."

Her eyes misted over, and she stared blankly at the afghan in her lap. When she spoke it was as though it took all of her courage to do so. "Elizabeth, your house is not haunted for me. It has no ghosts except those I bring with me."

Then, as though she had said, and felt, far too much, she shook her head angrily. She looked up at me, and with a

brittle smile said, ''Mack says we're going to have an excep-
tionally good peach crop this year.''

We talked for several minutes about unimportant things
before the edge left her voice and I recognized the Joannie I
had met before. Soon, however, we were gossiping like two
schoolgirls, about her baby, my plans for the house, and
Mack. She always brought the conversation back to Mack,
and I envied her the glow in her eyes when she talked about
him.

While we talked, I shrugged into my robe and climbed out
of bed. I felt too good to be confined beneath quilts.

Joannie looked at me in concern. ''You shouldn't be up,''
she said quite seriously. ''Aunt Martha said I was to keep
you in bed, no matter what you said.''

I grinned at the mental picture of Joannie trying to keep
me down against my will, but, in compromise, I settled on the
foot of the bed with my arm resting on the carved footboard.

''How's this?'' I asked.

Joannie grinned back, then said in a mock whisper, ''I
won't tell on you.''

I don't know who giggled first, but the strain had lasted
too long, and the situation was ludicrous. Soon I was doubled
over, holding my side against the laughter. Whenever I
thought I'd almost controlled myself, I looked at her, trying
so valiantly to bring herself under control, and we were off
again.

The voice from the doorway silenced me. ''Well, cousin,
is it a joke you can share?''

John leaned against the doorjamb with a small package
tucked under one arm and a half smile lingering about his
mouth.

Joannie choked back a giggle. ''Mr. Richards,'' she said
in soft surprise.

''Hello, Joannie.'' He walked to her chair and took her
hand. ''It's good to see you again.''

"It's good to see you, too," she said gently.

I watched the two of them, confused. Neither Martha nor Mack thought well of John, but it was obvious that Joannie didn't share their opinion.

When John turned to me, though, still smiling that half smile, my confusion turned to embarrassment. I felt what little color I had drain from my face. What had happened that night?

He held the package toward me, and it was a moment before I could take it, or speak. When I did, my voice betrayed me.

"Candy for the sickroom, cousin?" I tried to quip. "Somehow it doesn't seem your style."

"Gentle and lovable as always," John said. "I can tell you're well on the way to recovery."

"If you two will excuse me . . ." Joannie had gathered her crutches and was struggling to her feet.

I looked at her in dismay. She couldn't leave me alone with him!

It was John who spoke. "You don't have to leave."

"I think I should," she said to him before turning to me. "I'm a little tired. If you don't mind, I'd like to go to Aunt Martha's room and . . . and lie down for a while."

There was a drawn look about her mouth I hadn't noticed before. "Of course," I told her. "Do you need any help?"

She shook her head. "I'll go down the back stairs. I can find my way."

We watched her leave the room and listened until the sound of her steps died away. Then John said something I thought very strange. "I'm glad the two of you found each other. She needs someone like you."

I started to ask him what he meant, but he took the wing chair, pulled it over to the bed, and plopped himself down in it with a satisfied smile.

"Martha let you come upstairs alone?" I asked.

"Reluctantly, but she had some problem in the kitchen. She's quite a guardian, you know."

"I know—"

"Aren't you going to open your candy?" he asked, interrupting me. "It's the height of bad manners not to offer to share."

Maybe, just maybe, this interview wasn't going to be too bad after all. Perhaps I'd been worrying for no reason. But my fingers trembled as I tore at the paper wrapping.

"I suppose you're going to want the one wrapped in gold paper." The words squeaked out, but with any luck he would blame that on my still sore throat.

"Only expensive assortments rate gold paper, cousin. I'll take anything you give me."

I ripped the paper off. At first I couldn't think of anything to say. He'd brought me a twelve-ounce box of dime store chocolate-covered cherries. Unable to repress a chuckle, I turned to him, one eyebrow lifted slightly. "A token of your esteem?"

"One should give what one enjoys."

I tossed the unopened box to him. "I hope they squirt all over your jacket."

He threw it back at me. "You first."

I was caught up in the game. Without thinking, I joked with him, "You have no way of knowing, so I ought to warn you. When I was little I became addicted to these. I developed the ability to eat a whole box of them at one sitting. Without getting sick."

I pulled the lid off the box. "You may not get *any* of . . ."

The words died in my throat. I felt a band tighten around my chest, squeezing the breath from me. Inside the box, nestled in tissue and gleaming softly, lay a silver hairbrush. On its back a garland of flowers circled an ornate E.

"Martha told me about it," John said, no longer teasing.

I felt tears swimming in my eyes. I couldn't let myself cry

now. Every time I turned around these days, I was crying. I tried to concentrate on something more relevant than an antique brush. When had Martha decided John worthy of her confidence? It did no good.

"Thank you," I choked out before the tears started. They streamed silently down my cheeks. Without knowing how I got there, I found myself in John's arms, my face against his chest. I realized where I was and tried to pull away, but he held me a moment longer, one hand pressed comfortingly across my back and the other moving through my hair.

"You need to be consistent, cousin. I was trying to get used to the fact that you probably hated me. Now, each time I see you, you crumple my shirt."

His words were lightly spoken, but he might just as well have poured ice water on me. I stiffened in his arms. He released me and handed me the box of tissues from the nightstand.

I took a long time drying my eyes before I could look at him.

"Stanley McCollum told me you were here that night."

The change was barely perceptible, but I saw his jaw clench.

"Yes."

"I—I don't remember much of what happened," I said, but what I meant was, *Please, please tell me nothing happened.*

John's eyes were filled with questions I couldn't answer. "You didn't know any of us," he said slowly. "Tom—Dr. Carouthers—attributed it to delirium caused by your high fever."

I couldn't face him any longer. I picked up the brush and turned it over in my hands. "I see," I said lamely.

"I wish I did," he told me. And then, abruptly, his mood changed. "I have to leave now. Someone should check on Joannie. Do you want me to do that on my way out?"

"No," I said, still looking at the brush. "I will."

After he left, it was several minutes before I could even move. Finally, though, I put the brush in its rightful place on the dressing table, gathered up Joannie's forgotten knitting, and went to find her.

She stood near a window in Martha's bedroom staring vacantly into the room. Her face was oddly twisted, and her lower lip was caught between her teeth. A fallen crutch lay forgotten at her feet.

"Joannie?" I spoke softly, not wanting to startle her. "Are you all right?"

She turned toward me, but I don't think she saw me, at least not at first. She seemed almost to cower before me. "It's too much," she whimpered. "Too much."

What could have happened to her in just those few short minutes to cause this? I went to her and put my hand on her shoulder. "Joannie?"

She slid her free arm around me and held on to me tightly. I felt her breath coming in gasps. I had no idea what to do. The only thing I knew was that she needed comfort. I put my arms around her and held her until her breathing returned to normal, and when she released her grip, I eased away from her.

She attempted a smile. "Let's get out of here."

I handed her the fallen crutch and followed her from the room, something telling me to close the bedroom door as we left.

She lowered herself into the corner of Martha's couch and looked up at me, a pleading little smile on her face. "I'm sorry," she said.

"Your ghosts?" I prompted as gently as I could.

She nodded, biting on her lower lip. "I thought they were gone. They're why Aunt Martha didn't want Mack or me to visit—because of the pain they bring—but it's been so long. I try not to think about them, and I can't talk about them—

it hurts everyone too much.'' She doubled her hands into fists and pressed them against her cheeks.

I took one of her hands in mine and sat beside her on the couch. Unclenching her fingers, she gripped mine.

''I stayed here once.''

I started to speak, but she went on, looking past me at the closed door.

''I hid in that bedroom for almost three days.''

''What—''

''Did you ever have the feeling that you ruined the only thing you ever loved? That you were never going to be allowed to be happy?''

''But you have Mack, and soon you're going to have your baby.''

Her face softened. ''I've always had Mack. I've known since I was a little bitty girl that when I grew up I was going to marry him and have his babies, and that we would love each other until we died of old age, and somehow, some way, Mack realized that, too.'' She was rigid again, staring at the ceiling. ''But I may not be allowed to have his babies. I've lost three already. Mack doesn't even want to try anymore. He says that if I lose this one, there won't be another.

''Each time we'd think that finally we could have my leg fixed, there would be a pregnancy, and the delay because of it, and a miscarriage, and then the hospital bills, and always the pain, the loss. Mack says that he is going to see me walking again if it means that we never have children, but, Elizabeth, if I could just carry a baby full term, have a healthy, normal child, I'd wear these crutches forever. But I guess I can't make that kind of bargain, can I? If God lets it happen, it will happen.

''My stepfather—you know my stepfather.''

I shook my head.

''Yes, you do. Aunt Martha warned me that he's back. She

said you chased him off your property for trying to cut your pines.''

That bloated face with its red-rimmed eyes glared at me from my memory. ''Oh, Joannie, no.'' I couldn't stop the shudder that ran through me.

''You do know him. Things were never very good at home after mother married him. He drank a lot. I guess he still does. He and Jim, Aunt Martha's husband, were the closest thing to friends either one of them had. They cut a little pulpwood together, traded a few cows, but mostly they spent their time in the beer joints in Fairview, sometimes alone, sometimes with women. The school isn't that big—the town isn't that big—I couldn't help hearing about it. I don't think mother ever knew. I know Aunt Martha didn't.''

She gave a choking little laugh. ''But it was going to be better. It was in the fall. I was a senior in high school. Mack was in college, at Stillwater, and working there, too. He'd already been notified that he'd been accepted to the College of Veterinary Medicine the following fall. We were going to be married that June, after I graduated.

''It was after school. I'd been out to feed the chickens. My stepfather was home. It was really strange for him to be home that time of day, but he was working on something in the corral. He called me over, and I climbed up on the corral fence and sat on the top rail talking to him.''

Her eyes had that vacant look again, and I knew she was reliving what had happened.

''He had a steel fence post in his hands.'' Her fingers clenched in mine. ''I don't even know what I said, but he whirled around toward me. I've never seen a look like that on anyone's face. It was blind, unreasoning, animal. I saw him swing the post. I knew it was going to hit me, but I couldn't move. I could only watch it as it came closer—

''I guess I fainted. I know I fell off the fence. The next

thing I knew, I was in the house. He and my mother were arguing about whether to take me to the doctor or not. I know now that he was afraid he'd go to jail if anyone found out what he'd done, but he convinced her that it was just a broken leg and he knew enough about broken bones. He put a splint on it, and they put me in bed, but I guess I was too much trouble as an invalid because a few days later he came in from Fort Smith with a pair of crutches and told me it was time for me to get up.

"I wrote to Mack that I had broken my leg. He wanted to come home, but I told him that I was doing fine, for him to stay in school because it really wasn't that long until Christmas."

She beat against the arm of the couch with her free hand. "The closer it got to Christmas, the more I realized that I wasn't going to be healed by then, so when Mack called and told me that he'd been given an opportunity to earn some graduate credit by working over the holidays, I lied to him. It's the only time I've ever lied to Mack. I thought that surely by spring break I'd be back to normal. I told him I was doing fine. I told him that Uncle Frank was thinking about visiting his family in California—that was the truth—and that I'd really like to go with him.

"I know now that a fall from the height I fell won't break the tibia. I know now that a steel bar won't break the tibia unless it hits just right." She took a deep breath. "I know now that it takes six months for it to heal, and that if I had told Mack what had happened, when it happened, I probably would be walking today, but I was seventeen years old, and I was ashamed, and I was scared. I wanted to be perfect for him, and I didn't want to cause any trouble between him and my stepfather.

"Mack came home for spring break. He must have come in during the night, because he was at the house early that morning. My stepfather and Jim were sitting at the kitchen table. They'd been out all night, playing cards and drinking beer. Jim had had a lot of money the last few weeks, and they'd done their best to spend it. I was propped up against the sink, doing dishes, when Mack got there. The back door was open, and the screen wasn't latched. They hollered for him to come on in and at the same time yelled for me to get them some more beer.

"I twisted around on my crutches to look at Mack. He'd had to come inside before he could see me. He was just standing there, staring at me. They yelled again, and I started across the kitchen, dragging this—this leg, and I could feel Mack's eyes on me the whole distance. I wanted to sink through the floor.

"I didn't move fast enough. When I passed the table, my stepfather swore at me. He called me lazy and stupid and slow, and then he shoved me, and I lost my balance and fell.

"I heard Mack yell as I fell. He grabbed my stepfather and yanked him out of the chair and hit him, and hit him, and hit him. Mother heard the noise and came running into the kitchen, screaming at Mack to stop. Jim ran out the door. I heard his tires throwing gravel all the way out of the drive. Mack just kept hitting my stepfather. And then he had him down on the floor, choking him, and hitting his head on the floor.

"I screamed at him to stop, not to kill him. He finally heard me, and he did stop. Mother was still screaming at him, beating on his back. He pushed her away and picked me up. He never said a word, just carried me out the door. My stepfather was still laying on the floor.

"Mack put me in his truck and drove off. He made me tell him what had happened. He swore at my stepfather for doing it, and at my mother for letting it happen, and at himself for not being there, and then he told me he was going to take me someplace where they couldn't find me and then go to the sheriff and make sure the man never hurt me again.

"He couldn't take me to Aunt Martha's because of Jim. He was afraid they'd search his place. Grannie was too old, and besides, Uncle Frank would have told Mother, so he brought me up here."

Joannie looked around the room, again aware of where she was.

"I thought of this place. It hadn't been closed up very long, only a few weeks. Mack didn't even know that no one lived here.

"The back door wasn't locked. Mack brought me up here, and then, because he said it might take a few hours to get things straightened out, he brought up a little firewood and a bucket of water and told me not to worry, because if he had to be gone very long he'd get in touch with Aunt Martha and make her swear not to tell Jim.

"Mack didn't find out until it was too late."

"Find out what?" I couldn't not ask.

"Do you know the big curve in the highway east of Fairview?"

I nodded.

"And the narrow bridge just east of there, the one with the high concrete abutments on each side of it?"

"Yes."

"I don't know where Jim was going when he left our house. It wasn't home; he was going the wrong direction for that. They said he was probably doing eighty when he hit the bridge."

"Oh, my God."

"He didn't die right away," she said in a small voice. "Mack came upon the accident on his way into town. The ambulance had already left for Fort Smith, but the deputy was still there, and the wrecker, and Jim's car.

"Mack stopped to see if he could help." Joannie rubbed her hand across her eyes. "And the deputy arrested him."

"For what?" I gasped.

"For assault with intent to kill and kidnapping." I heard anger in her voice for the first time. "They put him in jail! Mack, who never hurt anything or anybody before in his life, was locked in jail!

"I should have known. There should have been something that told me when it happened."

Her voice lost its intensity. "He couldn't get in touch with Aunt Martha. She was in Fort Smith with Jim. He couldn't tell where I was, because I was still a minor, and my mother and her husband were there demanding that I be returned to them.

"They wouldn't let him post bond, because they knew he knew where I was.

"And I sat here in ignorance while he went through that.

"I'd been here a couple of hours when I heard a car drive up. I knew it was Mack, so I went to the window to call down to him. But it was only Stanley McCollum. I guess he came up here to check on things. And I remember thinking how angry he'd be if he found me in the house, so I looked for a place to hide. He was in the house for a long time, but he never came into this part. I heard him slam the back door when he left.

"It got a little cool, but I was afraid to light a fire in case he came back. I didn't want him to be able to smell the smoke.

"I didn't really worry until it started to get dark. We hadn't even thought about candles or lamps. I sat in the dark and knew that something horrible had happened to Mack."

She looked so lost. I squeezed her hand.

"And then I started remembering the stories I had heard about this house. They were fun to tell, when I was in school. We used to sneak up the road and peer over the wall, looking for shadows in the windows, and we'd make up stories about the colonel and why he haunted the house.

"They weren't fun when I was sitting here alone, and cold,

and afraid. I started listening for noises, but the only thing I heard was my own heartbeat.

"If Mr. McCollum had come back the next day I would have screamed to him that I was here, but he didn't come back. When I realized it was getting dark again, I had to get out of here. If I had to walk all the way to Richards Spur, I had to get out of here. I got as far as the top of the stairs. I was shaking so hard, I dropped a crutch. I watched it slide down to the landing, and there wasn't anything I could do to get it back.

"By the next morning I was half crazy. I hadn't slept. I was out of water. I had pictured Mack dead or maimed so often I had even seen *him* as a ghost in this house. I knew that I was going to die, in that bedroom.

"When I did hear the noises, they were a part of my imaginings, at first, and then I realized that I was hearing footsteps. But by then I knew, I *knew* it was something bad coming. I backed as far away from the door as I could, into the corner, and when the door opened and I couldn't get away, I saw the colonel.

"I started screaming. I couldn't stop. I didn't stop until he shook me and said, 'Joannie, half the county is looking for you. What are you doing here? and I knew he was John Richards and not the colonel, and then I started to cry.

"He held me and let me cry, and then he told me what happened.

"He built me a fire in here, and he got me some more water, and he told me he would help us, but he made me promise not to tell Mack or Aunt Martha that he had anything to do with it, because they wouldn't understand.

"Aunt Martha had told Grannie he had foreclosed on her and Jim, and I knew he was right about what they would think of him, so I never told them he was here.

"But I know he convinced the lawyer to represent Mack.

He probably even paid him, even though the lawyer said he was doing it because he thought anyone who whipped my stepfather deserved a medal.

"And I know he was the reason my stepfather dropped charges and left the county, but I don't know whether he frightened him off or paid him to leave.

"And he probably talked Mr. McCollum into letting Aunt Martha live here.

"And he lent Mother the money to buy out Uncle Frank when he moved to California, but I think that was for Grannie more than Mother. She was so old, it would have killed her to move or to think about anyone other than family owning the store."

I had been staring at the floor, but when she said that I jerked my head up and turned to her. "Joannie, who is your grandmother?"

"My great-grandmother," she said. "Marie LeFlore."

I was speechless for a moment and then I choked on the question. "Louise Rustin is your mother?"

She looked at me in genuine surprise. "I thought you knew."

I found I was still holding her hand. I gave it a little squeeze as I shook my head.

"Maybe I shouldn't have told you, but I've never been able to tell it all the way through before, and you . . . you seem so sure of yourself, and you're not as close to it as we are. . . ." Her eyes pleaded with me. "I didn't impose on you, did I?"

"No, Joannie." How could I possibly say anything else? "You didn't impose."

She gave her head a little shake. "Mack had to quit school. He'll never be a vet, and that's what he wanted most in life."

"It sounds to me as though you are what he wants most in life," I told her.

"I hope so, because there's no way I can make up to him what he gave up." She smiled then, a wistful tremor. "I can only love him. As long as God lets me."

I lay awake long into the night. My thoughts flitted from Joannie, to Mack, to Louise and that horrible man she had married, to John. John, who had helped me with Marie, who had brought me the brush, who had held me . . . who even now I wanted to hold me. . . . John, who hated this house and all David had stood for. John, who had foreclosed on Martha and Jim. Martha had told me that, without actually saying the words. I wondered why I'd never heard her. But he had helped Joannie. Or had he only told her he would? What had she said? *I know he did, even though . . . He probably . . .*

I climbed out of bed and walked to the dressing table. The silver hairbrush gleamed in the moonlit room. I carried it to the bed and lay there, tracing the design on its back with my fingers.

In any event, he had effectively silenced Joannie. Why had he come to the house? It had been closed for weeks. What business did he have here? I remembered the jumble of boxes I found when I arrived. Some of them looked as though they had been searched, rapidly and not too carefully. Surely John wouldn't have had to prowl through the house's possessions. He had the key to the storeroom. He could have used it anytime he wanted.

Unless . . . unless that was the time he chose to use it, and he didn't have another opportunity. When had Martha come to live here? How long after Jim had died? Finally, exhausted by questions I didn't really want answered, I slept.

I was in an old overgrown orchard with Joannie. I was trying to help her escape, and we ran, hiding among the twisted, dying trees. I held on to her hand as we ran, but I tripped on a root and fell. When I reached for her, she was floating away from me. "I have to go," she said as she dissolved into the night. "I have to do this." Then I was alone except for the unknown menace which now stalked me. I ran blindly, not knowing which direction to take, losing my footing, stumbling forward, until I saw the wall. David stood by the wall with his arms outstretched, waiting for me. I ran toward him gladly, but when I reached him, I found that he was John, not David. The unknown force pursuing me grew closer. John's arms beckoned me, and I ran to him, seeking safety, but as he reached for me the voice overtook us, surrounded us—Owen's voice, his words echoing through the night, "There's no place for you to hide, Eliza. I'll find you wherever you are. He'll never have you."

CHAPTER
14

I didn't argue with Martha's admonitions the next morning not to get up, not to get dressed, not to overtire myself. It seemed much easier just to lie in bed, staring at nothing, thinking of nothing. When Martha came back for the breakfast tray, she rewarded my good behavior with a smile. "That's much better," she said before reaching for the tray.

Her smile faded. "You didn't eat your breakfast."

"I don't want anything."

"But you didn't even drink your coffee."

"I don't want anything."

She clucked her disapproval but left me alone.

When the covers became oppressive and I slipped out of bed, the hairbrush fell to the floor at my feet. I picked it up and carried it with me to the wing chair. There, my feet tucked under me, I looked at the long, pine-bordered drive. The young trees that had sprung up sprawled in a disordered jumble on each side of the drive. They were visible now, dark green against the lighter green of the hardwoods which were just starting to leaf out, but in a few weeks, perhaps in a few days, I would not be able to distinguish one tree from the next at this distance. Strange that they were the only pines on the hillside, except the one which stood alone in isolated splendor on the south slope, its color the only thing marking its location for me.

I let my glance wander back up the hillside, to the bare elm guarding the gate to the drive. No color showed on it—even the clumps of mistletoe hanging from its branches were brown. At some level I knew the tree was dead, that it had probably been dead for a long time.

I swiveled in the chair, leaned back, and stared at the bright spot on the wall.

"Did you do this, Eliza?" I spoke in a tone that was half musing, half conversational, not really seeing the wall, not really seeing anything. "Did you sit and watch the seasons change and wonder about the trees? Did you plan? Did you dream?"

A sadness welled within and threatened to choke me. I felt an overpowering need to cry for her and yet no tears would come.

"You had so few moments of happiness. Was it worth it? Why did you go on?" I asked her—asked myself.

Martha brought me fresh coffee and saw that I took what medicine I still required, but soon she left me in silence.

I sat there, hearing nothing but the gently rhythmic *whish* of a branch against my window, seeing nothing but my fingers tracing and retracing the E on the back of the hairbrush.

"You might find this more interesting." John stood beside my chair, holding an oversized book toward me. I hadn't even heard him come in.

A retort was too much effort, even if I had wanted to make one. I took the book. "You came back."

"Martha told me you had a bad case of the dismals," he said as he lifted the lid to the coffeepot beside me, "but I didn't realize how serious it is. You've got a full pot of cold coffee and you didn't greet me with an insult or a verbal attack."

Martha must have decided he was the lesser of two evils, I thought, and John must have thought so, too, but he didn't say anything, as he had never said anything derogatory about Martha in my presence.

He brought the dressing table stool over and sat in front of me, looking steadily at me. "What's caused this?"

I turned the pages of the book idly, not looking at them, but not able to look at him, either. "Nothing is wrong."

He leaned over me, closed the book, and grasped my hands. "Elizabeth . . ."

I couldn't face any questions now. I stared down at the cover of the book, seeing it for the first time. "Stephen Ward," I whispered.

John released my hands and I once again opened the book, this time seeing the lavishly illustrated art book containing color plates of the work of Stephen Ward.

My hands trembled as I turned the pages, only scanning Ward's beautiful landscapes, to the section of portraits. I stopped at the picture I knew so well, a portrait of the young David, painted before the war. He had posed informally, leaning back slightly, at easy attention. A suggestion of a smile softened his mouth, as though he were enjoying a secret joke. His eyes were fixed on something to his right, off the canvas, and they glowed with an eagerness, an anticipation seldom seen in real life, much less in oil on canvas.

Reluctantly I turned the page. David's face stared back at me from the next page, too, but what a changed face. I must have made some sound, for I felt John lean forward. I searched the page for the date of the portrait. 1885. I couldn't believe the face I saw. The hair was liberally laced with silver, the face aged, but it was the eyes, sunken, shadowed, and unseeing, which tore at my heart. They bore no trace whatsoever of his zest for life. An expression of my grandmother's floated through my memory and as I touched the face I spoke without thinking. "Burnt to the socket."

"Explain," John prompted softly.

I let myself glance at him, but the contrast in the too similar faces was too great—too painful. I tried to soothe the face in the portrait with my fingers, but, of course, the picture couldn't change. "It's an expression used to describe a candle that has so completely consumed itself that there's nothing left in the holder," I whispered.

"It's strange you should say that. At the time that portrait was painted, he was already the wealthiest man in the Choctaw Nation and well on his way to becoming disgustingly rich."

"But at what cost?" I asked.

"At the cost of his honor, for one thing," John said bitterly. "He sacrificed his nation, everything for which he had once fought, for his own greed."

"No," I told him. "His problem was much more complex than that. There was a time when the nation forced him to make a choice. I think that was what killed him."

"Elizabeth, he didn't die until 1925."

"Oh, yes, he did." I looked directly into John's eyes, willing him to understand what I said. "He was dead when this portrait was painted, only no one but he knew it."

Sometime during the early morning I gave up any hope of sleeping and curled into the chair, watching the cloud-shadowed moonlit hillside.

"What happened, Eliza?" I asked the night. "What finally brought about that change in him? Did you die giving birth? Did you leave again, thinking that would help him?" I shuddered at the next thought. "Or did Owen find you?" My words were mere whispers. "And why don't I know?"

Martha found me in the chair when she brought my breakfast. She set the tray on the table beside me and stood over me, her arms folded.

"Eat," she said.

"In a while, Martha. I'm not very hungry."

"Eat now," she said firmly, "or I will feed you."

After I had forced down a few bites of egg, a piece of toast, and the orange juice, she relaxed. ''Would you like to get dressed and maybe come downstairs for a little while today?'' she asked with a hesitant smile.

I just shook my head. No, what I wanted most was to sit where I was and do nothing.

''I know you're not through in the library. You could tell me what to do and I'd finish for you.''

''No,'' I said. ''There'll be plenty of time to do that later.''

She ran her fingers across my forehead. ''Well . . .'' she said before she reluctantly left me alone, ''you let me know if you need anything.''

I didn't need anything but some answers, and they didn't come that morning. Who had cried out against dying? Had it been done in the past, or in the present? Had I been given my one chance to be with David again and refused it?

The art book lay on the floor at my feet. I picked it up and took it with me to the fireplace, where a few coals still glowed from the night's fire. Absently I added another log and settled myself on the rug, prodding the fire to life. I sat with my arms around my knees, idly turning the pages of the book on the floor in front of me. Inevitably I returned to the portraits, but I couldn't bear to look at the two faces of David Richards. I flipped past them, deeper into the book, not seeing what was in front of me until a familiar pose captured my attention. It was a painting of a woman standing in front of a fireplace, her arm along the mantel, light and shadow playing across her. The woman was exquisitely beautiful, and blond, and seemed vaguely familiar. I read the caption. ''Amanda Carmichael—1871.''

''Am painting second most beautiful woman in world,'' Stephen's telegram had read. Now I knew. Or did I? Although the fire now blazed beside me, I was suddenly very cold. The pose was identical to the one I thought imbedded deep in Eliza's memory. I tried to push the doubt away, but it refused to go. Had I at some time seen this portrait and forgotten it? Had I used it, built on it, created something that never existed?

I looked at the bright spot on the wall. If I looked hard enough, maybe I would see what I knew ought to be there. Nothing. The paper gleamed in the morning light, once again mocking me. I looked back at the book, turning the pages mechanically, seeing the faces—laughing, tragic, hopeful, despondent, and I realized that they were all faces of persons long dead.

I rested my head on my knees and turned my face so that I faced the glowing coals, hoping their brightness might chase away the shadows inside me.

"Enough of this!" John's voice boomed through the room, startling me. He grasped my wrist and pulled me to my feet, tugging at me and leading me to the wardrobe. He opened the door and began pulling out clothes—jeans, a turtle-necked sweater—tossing them at me, and I caught them as best I could with my one free hand.

"Put these on," he said, releasing my wrist, "and warm socks and boots and a scarf, and be downstairs in ten minutes or I'll come back up and get you.

"Where are your car keys?" he added, almost as an afterthought.

In my confusion, I answered automatically. "On the mantel, beside the others."

He crossed to the mantel and I heard the jingle of keys. "I don't see any others, but these must be the ones," he said as he walked back across the room. He stopped at the door. "Ten minutes. And comb your hair. You look awful."

I don't know why I did it, unless it was because I knew he meant what he said about coming back for me. The forbidden excitement of seeing him again had nothing to do with my actions, did it? I dressed, I brushed my hair, and I even hurried downstairs.

Discordant sounds from the piano in the drawing room

told me where he waited. I stopped in the doorway, a little breathless but also more alert—more alive—than I had been in days.

John stood by the piano picking out a melody with his left hand, a vaguely familiar melody that sounded flat even to my untrained ear.

I didn't mean to start anything—I wasn't sure I'd be able to finish what I started—but he was so confident, so at home in my home, but most of all so vibrantly . . . alive . . . that the words just erupted from me.

"Well, cousin, if you'd kept up your music lessons you'd now be able to dazzle me with a private performance."

His hand crashed against the keys, but when he faced me he wore a rueful grin. "Beethoven himself couldn't dazzle you on this piano. Do you play at all?"

"No." Grandmother's income hadn't stretched to include what she considered frivolities, but I saw no reason to tell John that.

"Then you can't know how badly out of tune this piano is. It ought to be a criminal offense to neglect a fine instrument like this."

The house was deteriorating around us, and he was concerned about a piano? I felt a flash of anger shoot through me. "It ought to be a criminal offense to neglect a house like this."

His eyebrow lifted slightly as he studied me. "Perhaps it is."

Then he grabbed my wrist again, leading me down the hall into the kitchen, where he snatched my jacket from the hook. Martha stood up from the table when we entered the room, but she didn't say anything, just watched us with an expression that warred between concern and confusion, with outrage never far behind.

"Martha," I asked, "are you just going to let him drag me out of here?"

"Dr. Carouthers called," she said. "He says it will be good for you."

"What?"

A jingle of keys meant to hurry me reminded me of the others. "Have you seen my keys?"

"I have the car keys," John said.

"No, the others, Martha. They're not in my room."

"Why, I have them," Martha told me. "You must have left them in my room the day of the—" Remembering John's presence, she bit off her words. "The day we went to Mack's. Do you need them now?"

As I shook my head, trying to remember taking the keys to Martha's room, John lifted my hair, draped my long scarf around my neck, and took me by the arm.

"Come on, cousin. Fresh air and sunshine await you. And if you're really good, I might even let you pick a fight with me."

"Go along," Martha said slowly but firmly.

I was outnumbered. John led me past his pickup truck—pausing long enough to retrieve a paper bag from it—to my car, where he opened the passenger door.

"Get in."

I balked at that. "How far are we going?"

"Not far."

"Good, because the gas tank is almost empty. Besides," I said, feeling my back stiffen, "if we must take my car, I prefer to drive."

"Oh, no," he said, laughing. "I've wanted to drive this toy far too long to miss an opportunity like this. Will you get in?"

With a sigh I slid into the car. John closed the door firmly, walked around to the other side, and placed the bag behind the seat. It was almost funny watching him trying to bend his tall body into my car. In any other circumstance I might have laughed, but I hid the smile I felt building as he maneuvered himself into a space that was barely adequate for my own much smaller frame.

He drove well, without the jerks and stalling I expected because of his cramped posture. We went east from Richards Spur, past the survey stakes, past the turnoff to Mack's. In silence. And it wasn't an easy silence. Soon the lack of words played on my nerves. I spoke more to make noise than for any other reason.

"I understand this is all your land."

"Yes. Are you impressed?"

It was a cynical answer, and it deserved a cynical response.

"That depends on how you got it."

I felt his eyes on me. "Except for what I inherited, I bought it."

I couldn't stop. I remembered Martha's bitterness and Joannie's attempts to excuse him. "All of it? Even the land south of the hill?"

His reply came clipped and cold. "Every acre."

I made a checkmark on my mental scoreboard and leaned back in the seat, my lips compressed and my mind closed. One lie for John Richards. How many more would I catch him in this day? Why was it so important that I do so, and why was I so disappointed when I did?

"I've been approached to sell some of it," he said with a hint of a question in his voice.

"At an enormous profit, I assume."

He laughed softly. "Hardly. A developer wants to subdivide it into ten-acre tracts and build moderately priced homes for people who want to raise their kids in the country but can't get very far from their jobs in Fort Smith or Fairview."

"You refused, of course." I turned around in the seat to face him. "It's probably the last chance Richards Spur will have to be a real town again. How does it feel, John, to watch a town die, to own all those empty buildings and know that you can strangle the last bit of life from a community that has been here since territorial days?''

Unbidden, David's words floated through my memory. *I promise you, when I have finished what was started today, there will be no community to need your church.* He hadn't meant it! Only the stress of the moment had caused him to lash out in anger—as the stress I now felt and didn't completely understand caused me to lash out at John.

I remembered his new building in Fort Smith. That was much safer territory. ''But then I suppose it is better for you financially, and much easier, to destroy tradition and build something to suit your needs and your pocketbook than it is to rebuild.''

His jaw clenched, and I saw a muscle jump in his throat, but when he spoke he did so evenly and quietly. ''I said *if* you were good, I *might* let you pick a fight with me, cousin. I didn't issue an invitation for a full-scale attack.''

His underlying message was, of course, that I hadn't been good. I didn't need him to tell me that. Gran would have been dismayed at my lack of manners. *I* was dismayed.

John ground the gears as he turned south onto a gravel road and pressed his foot against the accelerator. He drove with a grim determination, and I could tell that he had no intention of slowing or turning around.

''I told you the gas tank is almost empty,'' I said, a far cry from the apology I had meant to offer. ''Don't force us to walk home.''

''Maybe I should have left you sunk in the slough of depression. At least then you were halfway civil to me.'' His voice was edged with self-derision which, surprisingly, hurt me— hurt me far more than a scathing attack would have.

''I wasn't depressed—''

He braked the car so hard I had to hold on to the dash as he pulled into a drive. I thought he was going to turn around, but he circled a small, white frame house and drove to a large metal barn surrounded by an array of farm equipment and stopped in front of three elevated tanks.

I opened my mouth to speak a belated apology, but he silenced me. "Just hush for a minute, will you?" he said as he took the keys from the ignition and began extricating himself from the car.

A thin, elderly man in mechanic's blues shuffled toward us from the barn, the frown on his face fading as he saw John unfolding from the car.

"Hello, Mr. Richards. Didn't recognize the car. Can I help you with something?"

"Thanks, Andrew, but I just stopped for some gas."

Andrew noticed me then, and bobbed his head in my direction. Then with a speed he didn't seem capable of, he lifted the hose to one of the tanks as John was reaching for it. "How much do you want?"

John shrugged. "Oh, go ahead and fill it. It can't take much."

The old man nodded as he worked with the hose. "The missus took an apple pie out of the oven about an hour ago. She'd be right pleased if the two of you would stop by the house for a while."

John smiled and shook his head. "Not today. Tell her I'm sorry, but my cousin and I only have a short time. I need to go down to the river. How's the trail?"

"Not too bad," Andrew told him as he replaced the gas cap.

"Your own private gas station?" I asked as we bumped along the pasture trail. If the road wasn't "too bad" today, I'd hate to see it when it was.

John grinned. "One of them."

This time my words weren't malicious. I was genuinely interested. "He seems awfully old to be still working."

"Andrew? I suppose. But he's the best mechanic in the county, and I think it would kill him to quit altogether."

He swerved to avoid a deep rut. I couldn't think of anything else to say, so I sat quietly, and as I did I found myself enjoying the smell of pasture grasses drifting through the open window, watching the tree line marking the river growing closer.

John stopped the car at the edge of the trees, grabbed the bag, crawled out, and pocketed the keys. "Come on."

"What now?" I asked resignedly.

"Don't fight me every step of the way, Elizabeth." Was there a wistful sound to his voice, or was I imagining it because I, too, was tired of the fighting? "I'm going to share something with you."

I groaned inwardly. I didn't want John sharing anything with me; I didn't want to like him any more than I already did. But I stepped from the car. There seemed nothing to do but play this out.

I joined him at the front of the car, and he put his arm around my shoulder, leading me toward the trees. I could have broken the physical contact. A step to the right, a step back would have done that easily. I did neither, because, God help me, I *liked* his arm around me.

"Watch your step," John told me as he guided me through the briars at the tree line, looking up sharply as I choked on a guilty giggle.

Once through the briars and down a short, steep embankment, we were in another world. Large trees filtered the sunlight. Our feet sank into a mattress of leaves, dry and crumbling but soft by the very number of them. The sounds were different, too: a rustle of water, but except for the distant call of a bird, nothing else but the crunch of our feet on the leaves. Gnarled old vines hung from the branches of the taller trees, and young trees grew straight and slender, stretching toward the sun with no ragged outcroppings of lower branches. Discolorations on the trunks of trees and an occasional bit of flotsam lodged in the crotch of a tree showed old high-water marks. The river was low today, and peaceful, and it seemed to sing to me as we walked through a fairy-tale world in which no one else existed.

The tree was ancient. I knew it was our destination the moment I saw it. Sometime, years before, the current had undermined it, and it fell toward the river. But it had held and twisted as it grew so that its upper branches now reached for the sky, while its trunk appeared to grow out from the side of the bank, over the water.

I glanced at John and found him watching me with a wary look in his eyes. "It's wonderful," I whispered, for in the silence surrounding us, whispering seemed right.

His eyes softened. "Yes, it is. Come on."

He jumped up on the trunk and helped me up. Then I held on to his hand for balance as I walked out over the river. Where the tree curved upward I settled myself on the trunk with a contented sigh. John eased down on the trunk in front of me, his long legs dangling, his toes just inches above the water.

"If we're very quiet," he said softly, "the river creatures will forget we're here. Listen."

I leaned back into the curve of the tree and closed my eyes, feeling the play of filtered sunlight on my face, hearing nothing but the hypnotic rhythm of the water beneath me. It was as though the water were drawing all my tension and frustration from me and whisking it downstream. I felt my muscles loosening and my body growing limp.

A loud slap in the water nearby startled me. I started to speak, but John shook his head quickly. He mouthed the word soundlessly, *beaver*, and pointed upriver. I looked but couldn't see anything. A few seconds later I heard another slap from the same direction. Before long the river was alive with sounds—the noises of birds alighting in the trees nearby or searching the soft bank, the rustle of leaves as small creatures ventured forth, the splash of fish breaking water. I watched breathlessly as a raccoon emerged from the woods and scurried to the edge of the water, and then I spoiled it all by coughing.

Once again there was only the sound of the water to break the silence.

"I'm sorry."

"That's all right," John told me. "Sometimes it is so perfect down here that it takes an interruption to remind you there is another world waiting." He reached into the bag he had set in front of him. "I hope you're not very hungry."

I was suddenly aware that I was hungry. I leaned forward and asked suspiciously, "You didn't bring a picnic lunch?"

"No," he said innocently. "I just knew that if you were in your usual good form, you'd need coffee. And since I had to bring that, I thought I might as well bring a couple of sandwiches."

I felt the chuckle growing within me and tried to stop it. It was impossible. "All right," I said. "Coffee. And food. In that order."

John juggled the thermos and plastic cups, and we balanced them before us as we unwrapped sandwiches and picknicked over the river like a couple of kids who had escaped from school. I had never in my life felt so young. As he gathered the wrappings and refilled the cups, I studied his face. He seemed to be genuinely enjoying himself, but there was a watchfulness about him that I hadn't noticed before.

I didn't want to have to say it, but I knew he deserved some word. "Thank you."

For an instant, he seemed almost surprised. "But we're not through yet," he said, reaching back into the bag. "We still have dessert. Were you serious about liking these?"

He handed me the familiar box of candies, and as I held it I could see myself as a child, hiding in the downstairs hall to finish the last piece before tossing the box into the incinerator, licking the sticky sweet filling from my lips, knowing there wouldn't be any more for at least a month.

"Does that dreamy expression on your face mean yes?" John drawled.

"Yes." I laughed. I tore the cellophane from the box and opened it, exposing the candies in neat rows in their molded plastic tray. Remembering my manners, I held them out to him. "Bonbon, Mr. Richards?"

"After you."

I closed my eyes as I bit into the first one. The chocolate tasted strongly of paraffin, the syrup was cloyingly, toothachingly sweet, and the cherry a little tough. It was just as I remembered, and it was wonderful. I held the taste in my mouth, savoring it, and then unconsciously licked my lips to remove all traces of this forbidden treat. I know that I gave a little moan of pleasure as I opened my eyes.

John was watching me with a satisfied smile on his face. "It's been a long time, hasn't it?"

"Umm. My grandmother didn't approve. Proper young ladies did not indulge in such improper foods."

I took another candy before handing the box to John and leaning back into the curve of the tree. I nibbled at the candy, licking the syrup from inside before popping the whole thing into my mouth, all the while wondering about this new side of John.

He looked skeptical. "Well, perhaps not a box at a time."

I had to laugh. "If she had ever found out about that," I told him, "I would have been in serious trouble."

His skepticism faded; his smile faded. "You didn't have a happy childhood, did you?" he asked, but it wasn't a question.

Happy? I thought of the years of being lonely, and confused, and wanting so desperately for my grandmother to show me the kind of love my schoolmates talked about.

I shrugged my shoulders in an attempt to convey indifference. "Not particularly. But then happiness is relative. My childhood was something I had to go through. I got through it as quickly as I could, and now it's behind me."

"That bad, was it?" John's comment was too perceptive for comfort.

I took another candy, not because I wanted it but because toying with it gave me time to avoid answering. And yet I answered.

"Not *that bad*, John. I was raised by a woman who was almost sixty when I was born. I was all that she had left to remind her of her only child. She blamed my father for causing their deaths and was afraid that I would be more like him than her daughter. She wanted—demanded—that I be perfect. I wasn't."

He studied a leaf floating down the river. "At least she didn't blame you for their deaths."

"No. She didn't do that."

He faced me abruptly. "Elizabeth," he asked with an intensity that surprised me, "why was it so important that you have that hairbrush?"

Now I studied a dead leaf floating in the water. What should I tell him? What could I tell him? He waited for an answer.

I spoke to the river. "David gave it to Eliza."

"Do you know that?" he asked, no less intensely.

The leaf swirled beneath me now, torn and half submerged in the water. I shook my head. "No. I know she used it while she was here. I know that she didn't bring anything with her when she came. I know that she thought of it as his gift."

"How do you know?"

The leaf spun madly, caught in a crosscurrent. An inner voice warned me not to trust John, but I had hidden this so long, kept it such a tightly guarded secret, and the events of the last few days had shaken me so much, left me so confused, I felt I had to tell someone or lose all grip on reality.

I looked straight into his eyes as I spoke, half defying him to laugh. "I remember."

His eyes widened slightly, but other than that he showed no reaction. He didn't laugh. Instead, he said softly, "Will you tell me about them?"

I realized that I was holding my breath. I let it out in a long sigh, thankful that at last I could share this story with someone.

"They met during the Civil War. She was only fifteen when she hid him from a troop of Yankee cavalry. He had been wounded, and she nursed him back to health."

The words did not come easily. Even though I wanted to share their story, telling parts of it seemed an invasion of their privacy. I struggled through it, though, groping for a way to convey to John how much they had meant to each other, until the moment after Eliza had fallen in the orchard. I buried my face in my hands.

"And then what happened?" he prompted gently.

I shook my head. "I don't know."

I looked at him and attempted to smile, but I couldn't. "I know the child was born; you've told me his condition. You've told me that she left because—because—" My voice broke. "John, that is not true. If she left, she did so because she thought she could help him by leaving."

He didn't say anything for a while. He poured the last of the coffee into our cups and sat staring into his.

"Can you make yourself remember?" he asked finally.

"I've tried! These last few days I have tried so hard." My coffee splashed on my hand. I concentrated on the slight burn until I felt I could speak calmly. "I can remember things I've already been through, but I've learned nothing new. I can't force it. It has to be triggered by something. A person I recognize, an incident, something tangible like the hairbrush will unlock whatever it is that lets me see these things, and then I can't stop it. I may delay it for a short period of time, but I can't stop it."

"Earlier, when you were eating the first piece of candy, you remembered something. Is that the kind of episode you're talking about?"

"No. No. I knew I was here, with you. I was remembering how it felt to be nine years old, not reliving it, not feeling the incinerator door in my hands or the texture of my dress or the twist of apprehension I always felt when I was late. I know those things existed, I can recall them, but I can't go through them as though they are happening now, the way I can—the way I could in the story I just told you."

I wanted so much to be able to explain clearly, but I didn't know how. "There's no way you can understand." I didn't understand it myself.

"I'm trying," he said. "This may not be a fair question. You said that recognizing a person could trigger . . . remembrance. Does this mean that you see in the people around you now persons Eliza knew?"

I had gone this far. There was no point in denying it. I nodded.

Now he was the one having trouble finding words. "And when you called Martha by the name Jane, it was because you were seeing her as you think she . . . once was?"

The expression in my eyes must have answered him. He paused, but he wasn't waiting for an answer, he was groping for words.

"Do you recognize everyone as someone in . . . Eliza's life?"

"No." I could answer that question. "Sometimes I am very drawn to a person, and I feel that I must have known that person before, but I don't know when. It's that way with Joannie. If she was there, I don't know who she was. My grandmother had no part in Eliza's life. Strangely enough, Louise Rustin was . . . she was the housekeeper. She hasn't changed much."

"Stan McCollum?"

"My—He must have been Eliza's father."

He looked at me sharply. "Doesn't this get confusing?"

"Not usually." I could say that truthfully. "Usually there is a clear definition between what I do and think and feel and what I learn about Eliza. Only once . . ." The confusion of that night haunted me. "John, I don't know who I was that night. I don't know who called out. I don't know who cried. I don't know who you held. I—I don't even know if it was you. Was it you?"

"Yes."

"Why? Feeling about David the way you do, why did you let me—" There were no other words to describe what I had done. "Why did you let me use you?"

John studied his coffee cup for a long while without answering. When he did answer, his voice was as troubled as my thoughts. "I don't know. My first reaction was to try to make you understand who was really with you, but I knew from what you said to Martha that I probably couldn't. You wanted David at that point, not anyone else. Certainly not me."

He tossed the last of his coffee into the river. "In spite of the resemblance, you don't see David when you look at me, do you?"

I shook my head.

"But you do recognize someone," he said intently. "That's the only thing that can explain your actions toward me. Who do you see?"

It had been such a perfect afternoon that I had almost forgotten. Now Owen's possessiveness and cruelty invaded our innocent interlude, forcing me to remember what I knew about the man facing me, and yet it all seemed so far removed from the tranquility of the river and from his attitude of the last few days that I couldn't tell him.

As I looked at him, unable to speak, seeing each familiar beloved feature, wanting at that moment what I knew was not so, he read the answer in my silence.

His mouth twisted. "You see Owen, don't you?"

I could no longer bear to look at him. I stared into the trees, not seeing them, either.

"Of course you do," he said.

How different the silence between us now from that of only a few short minutes before. I felt the too familiar ache at the back of my throat and the heaviness behind my eyes warning me that I was close to tears.

"I don't understand," John said finally. "I am trying. But . . . there has to be some explanation for what you go through. Have you ever talked with anyone else about this?"

Still staring into the trees, I shook my head. "Except . . . once. But I had hidden that so far away, I didn't even remember it. Until after I came here."

"Your grandmother?"

"Yes."

Out of the corner of my eye, I saw him run his hand through his hair. "You said that these incidents have to be triggered by something. Is it possible that what triggers them is actually what causes them? I mean . . . you saw the hairbrush and then you remembered the hairbrush. You knew of Joannie's miscarriages and then you remembered a disastrous pregnancy. You saw a picture of David Richards in a book and then he was a part of your life. Isn't it possible that your mind has taken these instances and woven them into a complicated romantic fantasy?"

His question was so close to the one I had asked myself only that morning that I felt I had to deny it, but all I could manage was a slow shake of my head and a murmured "No."

"Elizabeth, listen to me. Sometimes a lonely child has to create a world in which there is love, romance, and adventure. How old were you when you first saw David Richard's picture?"

"Twelve," I told him, suspecting and hating the direction his words were taking me. "I was twelve."

"Don't you see? When you saw his picture, you had none of those things in your life. It would be natural to build a fantasy on a picture like that. I know. I've done it myself."

I looked at him then, trying to understand what he was saying.

"When I was a boy, I found a picture of a lovely young woman. I invented stories about her, and I endowed her with all sorts of virtues and charms." He laughed reluctantly. "I suppose I even fell in love with her. For a long time she was my world. I talked to her, and in my fantasies she talked to me. I dreamed about her. I made plans including her."

"What happened?" I whispered.

He clenched the cup in his hand. "I grew older. Other things filled my life." He shrugged his shoulders. "And I realized that she was just a picture and that had she been a real person, she wouldn't—couldn't—have lived up to my idealization of her. No one could have. Just as no one can live up to the idealization you have created from a picture and a few pieces of fact about David Richards."

He reached for my hand. "I want you to talk to someone—someone who can help you with this—because I don't think I can. I have a friend in Fort Smith who is a psychologist—"

I jerked my hand away. I wanted to back away from him, but the tree trunk was pressing into my spine. I stared at him in dismay, feeling suddenly very vulnerable. "You think I'm crazy," I whispered.

"No! I didn't tell you to see a psychiatrist. I said I wanted you to talk to a friend who has studied psychology, who understands fantasies and dreams, who may even be familiar with the type of thing you're going through. Wouldn't it be nice to know that you're not the only one who has ever gone through this?"

I struggled to my feet, still staring at him, afraid to take my eyes from him. I held on to the tree for support, but I felt myself swaying.

John swore under his breath. "Why can't I ever say the right thing to you?" he asked.

"Just say you'll take me home, John," I said stiffly. "Our picnic is over."

"Yes, it is, isn't it?" He gathered the remnants of our meal and stuffed them into the bag, then scrambled to his feet and held out his hand to me. If I'd thought I could walk off the tree without his help, I'd have refused to take it, but, inwardly, I was shaking so badly I knew I had to have support. Reluctantly I reached out to him, and he guided me toward the bank.

He jumped down from the tree, dropped the bag into the leaves, and reached up for me. I started to jump, but he caught me about the waist and lifted me down. He didn't let me go. Instead, he tightened his arms around me and in spite of my resistance pressed me ever closer to him. I felt his heartbeat and his words reverberating in his chest as he spoke.

"Please don't think I believe you need medical help."

Again I tried to pull away, but still he refused to release me.

"I guess I said what I did for selfish reasons."

The rhythm of his heart against my cheek, the rush of the river current, the soft forest noises all conspired against me. I felt myself yielding to him, enjoying—relishing—the feel of his hands on my back and the warmth of his body against mine.

He spoke softly. "It's just that when you look at me, I don't want you to see someone else, either good or bad, who failed in his life a hundred years ago. He had his chance. It's my turn now, and I have to live the best way I know—the only way I know. I can't be shadowed by someone already dead. I have to be who I am."

He held me away from him, and the expression in his eyes kept me still and quiet.

"When you look at me," he said softly, "I want you to be able to see me."

I was still hypnotized by his eyes as he bent toward me, until his eyes closed and he touched his lips to mine, gently at first, almost as though waiting for me to push him away. I couldn't refuse him. I sensed a longing in him, a need that I could only wonder at, as I could only wonder at the answering need welling within me.

I swayed against him, a sound catching in my throat. My arms moved to hold him to me. I felt my heart beating violently as his mouth moved against mine, testing, searching, claiming, and without knowing how, or why, I found myself answering the longing I felt in him with my mouth, my hands, my body, not wanting the moment to end.

For that moment there were only the two of us, reaching out for each other, not bound by the past. For me there was only the feel of his hair under my hands, the taste of his skin, the exquisite agony sparked by his touch. I was lost in those sensations, surrendering to them, wanting more, demanding more. My hands moved from the back of his head to his face, my fingers outlining the planes of his cheeks, his jaw. It seemed so right, so natural. I opened my eyes to look once more . . . but when I did, I remembered who I was and where I was and knew that I had to stop.

Reluctantly I tried to push away from him, moaning in protest. He released my mouth slowly but continued to hold me in his arms, and when he pressed my face against his chest, I felt his heart beating as wildly as my own. We stood that way until I was able to breathe almost normally, until my heart resumed a rhythm only slightly faster than usual.

I pulled away and looked up at him. At John. Who was he? I could find no trace of Owen in the eyes that returned my own intense search. Could I have been wrong?

CHAPTER
15

Martha opened the kitchen door for us when we returned to the house. She stepped back to let us enter, twisting the ring of keys in her hands. "I'm so glad you're home." She told me, her voice breaking. "I didn't know what to do."

"Martha, what is it?" I asked in alarm.

She glanced at John, frowning, but I was still caught in the magic of the afternoon. "Say what you have to say," I urged her.

For seconds, the rattle of the keys in her hands was the only sound in the room. I took them from her gently. "Say what you have to."

Her lips twitched as she searched for words. "I was thinking about the keys, how you'd never left them in my room before, and I went to get them. And I remembered your letters, so I was going to get them, too. I'd picked them up at the post office and had just gotten home with them when Mack called and asked me to put the plants in the ground for him. I put them by the telephone. So much happened afterward that I just forgot about them, but I know where I left them. Now they're not there. I went through the house, and I don't think it's my imagination—things aren't where they were. Elizabeth, I think we've been robbed."

I met John's eyes and knew he was thinking the same thing I was.

"Wait here," I told Martha as John and I hurried from the room.

I ran up the last flight of stairs. My hands were trembling so by the time we reached the vault that I couldn't find the right key. I thrust the key ring into John's hands.

He pulled the door open, and this time I didn't need an invitation to walk into the blackness. While John lit candles, I waited impatiently inside, looking at the spot where the paintings should be.

The light flickered, and I saw that the canvas-draped rack appeared undisturbed. I lifted the fabric. "Are they all there?" I asked.

John knelt by the rack and counted canvases. "They seem to be. Just a minute." He stayed on his knees, searching the back of each canvas. "Do you have any idea what was in the missing letters?" he asked while he searched.

The letters. Now what was I going to do? But I had already said too much to retreat into silence. "They have to be replies to the ones I wrote to the Department of the Interior and to the town near where Eliza grew up, trying to find information about her and Owen Markham."

John rocked back on his heels and swiveled to face me. To his credit, he didn't challenge my reasons for making inquiries. "It's strange that a burglar would take something like that. Do you suppose Martha has just misplaced them?"

"No. She's too careful to have lost them. If she says they aren't where she put them, someone has moved them."

"When?"

"I don't know. There's always someone in the house. Except the night we went to Mack's." With a tiny click, one seemingly inconsequential, almost forgotten fact slipped into place. "Oh. Of course."

"What is it?" John asked as he rose to his feet.

"Mack and I came back to the house. . . ." I remembered then that I shouldn't tell John and stopped in confusion.

He smiled, a little grimly, I thought. "I saw the glare from the valley and wondered where Mack got his smudge pots. Don't worry. I won't say anything."

"We didn't take them off the hill," I told him, knowing I sounded defensive, but it seemed such a minor point now. "We came across the top on an old wagon road. When we got to the barn, I noticed a light in Martha's room. When she and I came home later that night, the house was dark."

"That was the night Louise wouldn't let Martha have the supplies unless you came in and signed the ticket?"

I nodded.

John took the canvas covering from me. "The Wards are all here." He shook out the fabric to redrape the rack and then paused. "Do you still have that stack of paintings in a bedroom downstairs?"

"Yes," I said, puzzled. "And I still haven't decided what to do with them."

John reached into the rack, pulled out a small framed painting, and looked at it for a long while. "No. I can't do that." He started to replace the picture and then turned to me. "Would you trust me with this one painting for a little while?"

It was a landscape, but that was all I could see in the dim light of the vault. "Why, yes."

"I don't want you to tell anyone, not even Martha, that I have it."

I glanced around the room then, but nothing in it seemed to have been disturbed, not even the small packet of correspondence from Stanley McCollum that I had hidden on the back of a shelf. How strange, I thought. I had known about the paintings for weeks. I had been able to leave them in the vault and not think about them, but now that I felt they had been threatened they became very real to me and in need of more protection than I had given them.

John might want to challenge the trust, to destroy the house, but he would do it openly, without stealth. In this much, I could trust him. When he closed and locked the vault door and handed me the ring of keys, I slipped the vault key off the ring and held it out to him.

He hesitated, his hand on mine. "Are you sure you want to do this?"

I nodded. "It's safer with you."

Downstairs, he opened the front door and placed the painting outside. "Do you want to check for anything else missing?" he asked.

"I will," I told him, "but Martha and I can do that. Should I call the sheriff?"

"I wouldn't do that now," he told me, "but you do need to let Stan know."

"John, I—"

"I know, but he is still responsible for the house. I'll tell him; you won't have to. Besides, we don't know what is missing. One more day won't make any difference at this point."

After John left, Martha was adamant about wanting to call the sheriff. I knew how she felt. I calmed her, though, and together we began examining the areas where she felt things had been moved. As we went through the rooms and I imagined some unknown person moving my possessions, pawing through the drawers, taking liberties in my home, I felt as though I'd been violated as well as the house.

For the second time that day I felt vulnerable, but that feeling was quickly replaced with rage. How dare someone do that? I would not tolerate it. Unbidden, a small voice whispered within me, *You have no choice.* Maybe not, I thought. Maybe I had to accept what had happened, but I could see that it didn't happen again.

Still, it was not until late that evening that I managed to put thoughts of the burglary from me.

The book of Stephen Ward's paintings still lay on the floor beside the fireplace where I had left it that morning. I opened it to the picture of Amanda Carmichael. With the violence of a spring storm, John's questions surfaced to push all other thoughts from my mind. Had I created that other life?

With the letters gone it would be weeks before I could possibly know what had been in them. Yet I had more facts now. I knew when and where Eliza had gotten her divorce. What had John said? Most lawsuits are public record. One could see them simply by going to the courthouse and asking to.

I felt myself relaxing for the first time since Martha had stammered her suspicion. It was so simple. All I had to do was go to Fort Smith. I would have my evidence within hours. I slipped into bed feeling drowsy and contented.

"I haven't imagined you, Eliza," I whispered into the dark. "I haven't."

When John arrived the next morning, I had already dressed in jeans and a long-sleeved sweater and was downstairs trying to do justice to the breakfast Martha had insisted on preparing.

Martha left the kitchen immediately, and I glanced at John to see how he reacted to what was definitely a resumption of rudeness on her part. He looked after her with an expression I couldn't interpret, then shrugged and reached into the cabinet for a cup. He poured his own coffee and freshened mine before sitting down.

A week earlier his easy familiarity in my house would have angered me into making a caustic comment. Now, although it still bothered me a little, I felt no anger. I thanked him for the coffee and waited for him to tell me why he had come.

"You look rested," he said. "Did you sleep well?"

"Yes." I couldn't help noticing, though, that John didn't look as though *he* had slept well.

He watched while I finished my toast. Twice it seemed that
he was on the verge of saying something, but he remained
silent until I carried my empty plate to the sink.

"Elizabeth, I . . ." he started hesitantly.

"Yes, John?"

"Nothing. It isn't important now." He brought the empty
cups to me. "I need to go upstairs for a minute. Do you want
to go with me?"

I took the cups from him and stacked them beside my plate,
routine motions, but I was both puzzled and curious. "All
right."

He opened the kitchen door, reached outside, and brought
in a framed painting. I saw a blur of pink on the canvas, but
before I could see more he crossed the kitchen and waited at
the hall door for me.

I expected to go back to the vault, but at the stairs leading
to that floor, John stopped. "Where is that stack of odd
paintings?"

I showed him to the room where the pictures were stored.
It was a mixed collection of framed prints, oils, and watercol-
ors I had found as I unpacked various boxes throughout the
house. Some had broken glass or chipped frames, and some
I just couldn't decide where to hang.

John pulled out the first few and placed the Ward behind
them. I bent forward to look at it, but he pushed the others
back in place.

"You don't know anything about this painting," he said.
"You don't really know what is in this stack."

"What are you talking about?"

"Stan McCollum will be out today to take another inventory because of the suspected burglary. I want you to let him
take the inventory in privacy, and if he asks you any questions, although I don't think he will, I want you to tell him
that you have no idea what is in this stack of paintings."

"There are enough games being played with my life without adding another one, John. Tell me what is going on."

"I can't do that now, because I'm not sure myself. I can tell you that this is no game. Forget the canvas is here."

"John?"

"I wish you could trust me in this, Elizabeth. It is important."

Trust him? I could think of all sorts of reasons why I shouldn't, but something in me wanted to trust him.

"Will you be here?" I asked.

"No. I have some business I have to take care of today."

Logic told me to demand an explanation. But it wasn't logic that made me agree. "All right. I'll forget the Ward is here until you put it back in the vault."

After John left I paced restlessly around the kitchen. With nothing to do but drink coffee and wait, my frustration at having my plans for the day interrupted grew by the minute. The knowledge that I was less than an hour away from having proof of Eliza's existence and that I had to put off obtaining that proof because of Stanley McCollum's schedule chafed my nerves. I had no doubt that he would be anything other than his usual condescending, irritating self, and I was in no mood to put up with that kind of treatment.

When I emptied the second pot of coffee, Martha took my cup from me. "What is the matter with you this morning?"

"It's just that I hate being at that man's beck and call," I muttered. "You'd think he'd have the decency at least to let us know what time he's coming."

"Why, child, if you've got something to do, you go do it. I'll be here when Mr. McCollum comes."

"Martha, I can't ask you to do that for me."

"You didn't ask me," she said. "I offered. Besides, he bothers me, but not near as bad as he bothers you."

Grateful for the reprieve, I gave her a quick hug and started out the door. I remembered John's admonition in time to tell her. "When he gets here, you don't have to help him with anything unless he asks. He'll probably want to prowl through the house by himself. I guess," I added reluctantly, "he has the right to do that."

I felt a pang of guilt as I left her there, but that was quickly replaced by excitement. Too many questions had been raised, but now I had enough pieces of the puzzle to look for answers and, thanks to John's whim of the day before, enough gas in my car to begin the search.

It took a while, once I reached Fort Smith, to find the courthouse—the elaborately detailed art deco building was far from what I expected, from what Eliza had seen. It took me several more minutes to find a parking place. By the time I reached the inside of the building my enthusiasm had begun to falter. I stood much too long studying the directory on the main floor. Finally, though, I selected the office I thought would be the right one and pushed the button for the elevator.

My hands felt clammy, and every nerve in my body was tingling as I opened the door to the clerk's office. I was suddenly aware of my fear. What if . . . No. I couldn't even think about that possibility. But as I stood at the counter, part of me wanted to run from the building without asking, without ever knowing.

"Can I help you?" a dark-haired young woman asked from behind a desk across the room.

Now or never, Elizabeth, I told myself. I made my fists unclench. I swallowed. "Is this where I would check on an old divorce?"

"How old?"

"1871."

She grinned at me. "This is the place. Come on around."

She indicated a space at the end of the counter, and I walked around.

"They're in the vault," she said, leading the way into an adjoining room. "Are you looking up family?"

"Kind of," I admitted.

"We get a lot of people through here doing that. Usually in the summer, though. Do you know how to use these books?"

"No. This is the first time I've been in a courthouse."

"It's not as hard as it looks," she said, gesturing toward the stacks of large red volumes lining the walls. "You want the old chancery records, and they're over here."

She scanned the books in one corner, and I felt a little of my excitement returning. She pulled a volume from its rack and opened it.

"That's strange," she murmured. "This is the first one up there and it starts in '82. Let me look."

She pulled several books out and opened them, but her easy smile soon turned into a frown of concentration. "I haven't been here very long," she admitted. "I think I'd better go ask somebody where those records are, because I can't find them."

She left me standing there feeling helpless, knowing that what I needed was probably on the wall in front of me and not having the slightest idea how to begin to find it. The young woman wasn't gone for long. When she returned she was once again smiling.

"I'd forgotten about the affidavit," she said. She pulled a book down and scanned the front page. "The courthouse burned," she told me as she flipped open the pages, "but I can never remember the date. Here it is."

I looked at the words. I read them twice. All records from 1851 to March 17, 1882, destroyed by fire.

"But where can I find it?" I asked.

"I'm sorry," she said, and she really did seem to be, "but there is no place else to look. Those records are gone."

Gone. Destroyed. Nonexistent?

She looked at me curiously. "Can I help you with anything else?"

"No. No, thank you. That was—that was all I needed."

Outside, I walked across the lawn and stood in the shade of a dying elm, looking up at the statue of a Confederate soldier.

"Where do I go now?" I asked the statue, as if he could answer me any more than the dying tree could. "What do I do? I can't just give up." The traffic noises from Rogers Avenue faded away. I heard instead the sound of horses' hooves on packed earth and David's voice asking Wilson, "Have you been saving the newspapers for me?"

"It's worth a try," I said to the soldier. The chance was slim, but there might be something in the old newspapers, if they still existed. I lingered in the quiet near the statue for a few minutes, reluctant to join the rush of the present world.

The newspapers had survived, at least part of them, on rolls of microfilm at the library. The librarian showed me how to operate the viewer and left me with two rolls of film containing issues of the two newspapers in business during the time period I had requested. Not knowing what to look for, I began by reading whole pages of tiny, dim print beginning with the July 9, 1870, issue. By the time I finally gave up I had learned to scan the pages, but when I cranked the last roll back in place and turned off the viewer, I sat with my head in my hands. I really had nothing to show for the afternoon but burning eyes and a throbbing ache in my neck.

There had been an earthquake, in Little Rock, but it had happened sometime in May, not July. There was an article about the Okmulgee Council of Tribes and an editorial questioning whether the nations could be sealed off for the benefit of a few. Even I realized I could have read something about either of those things.

The river had been low in early August, and then swollen, and the first steamer upriver after that had arrived on a Sunday. Coincidence?

There were columns of professional ads on each front page of both papers. Albert Pike advertised boldly and regularly. I didn't see Jeremiah Grimes's name.

The only fact that I had no way of knowing, or imagining, was contained in an article on July 14 telling of construction on Garrison Avenue between Wayne and Green. Kanady's shop and mill were being torn down to make way for an "elegant, massive" block of three-story brick buildings. Was it where I thought it was? Was it still there? I had to find out.

What appalled me was the number of things that had no part in my memory. So much had happened in the time that Eliza had been in Fort Smith. For six months the papers had carried lengthy stories about the war in Europe. Shouldn't that have found its way into her conversations with David? Wouldn't she have been aware of a major fire at the barracks no more than a mile from her house? Was she so locked in her own pain that not even the death of Robert E. Lee penetrated her shell?

Once back in my car, it took several minutes for me to get my bearings on the unfamiliar streets and find the road that led to the river from the end of Garrison Avenue. I crossed the railroad tracks and stopped in dismay. Nothing remained of the wharves or the warehouses Eliza had seen, nothing to indicate they had ever existed, except one small plaque. The Arkansas River stretched before me, much, much wider than it should have been, and devoid of traffic except for a coal-laden barge being pushed downstream by a tugboat.

I turned the car around and began backtracking, out from the river, to the right, then left onto Garrison. The wide street was the same, but I had seen that when John brought Martha and me shopping. Nothing else was familiar. I read street signs, but there was no street named Wayne, no street named

Green. I found a location that could have been the one in the article, that could have been where David asked Wilson to stop the carriage, but it was not a block of buildings, it was one building, and there were no landmarks I recognized.

I could go on to the house. Surely I would recognize something. I didn't even recognize the street to turn onto. Not until I found myself at John's new office building did I realize that I had gone too far.

Determined now that I would find the house, I drove up and down the streets, across side streets, through neighborhoods I had never seen before until, accidentally, I found myself beside the house I sought.

I parked at the curb near the carriage step for a long time, trying to find courage to go inside once more. The house was so beautifully restored—clean and shining as it had been in my memory—but did that new brick sidewalk replace an older one? Had there been porch rails there in 1871? There were freshly spaded flower beds bordering the porch, and young rosebushes on each side of the front steps. Had they been there when I visited the house with John?

Suddenly I wanted to be anywhere but where I was. I started the car and drove off blindly, totally lost, in traffic which was becoming increasingly heavy. I shouldn't have come, I told myself over and over as I made my way back toward the business district and the road home.

I was the second car in a line of traffic waiting for a light when I saw John. He came out of a small brick building in the next block. I was surprised by how relieved I was to see him, how much I wanted to walk up beside him and have him drape his arm over my shoulder and tease me into believing things were all right.

I waved at him, but he didn't see me. Something else attracted his attention and he turned away from me. All happiness at seeing him disappeared when I saw a tall, slender blonde crossing the street in midblock, picking her way through the barely moving traffic, toward John. She joined him on the sidewalk and after a few words linked her arm though his as they crossed the alley and entered the next building.

A car horn honking behind me made me realize that the light had changed and I was holding up traffic. I caught just a glimpse of tables and wineglasses and laughing people through the windows of the building John had entered before turning at the next corner.

It shouldn't bother me, I told myself. She was attractive. And he was—how had he put it?—the most eligible man in three counties. There had been nothing between us but harsh words until yesterday. What was I thinking? There was nothing between us. Nothing. There couldn't be.

I drove home without seeing the beauty of the country surrounding me, without seeing the shabbiness of Richards Spur, praying silently that once I returned to the shelter of David's house I'd be able to push away the doubts of the last two days and see John as I knew I should and not as I wanted him to be.

Martha raised an inquisitive eyebrow when I entered the house, but all she said was, "Supper's almost ready."

"I'm a little tired. I think I'll lie down for a while before we eat," I told her, and escaped to the privacy of my room.

"What has happened?" I asked the now shadowed valley. "I was so sure before. Why can't I be now?"

It was not Eliza I thought of then, or David. It was John. Smiling at a lovely blonde over drinks. Laughing with her. Sharing himself with her. Thoughts of them together haunted me through the evening. My last thought before falling asleep that night was of them. I punched the pillow down numerous times, pulled the sheets loose with my tossing, tried concentrating on a shadow on the wall, but no matter what I did, I kept seeing the two of them. Together.

And I knew that I didn't want John teasing me. I didn't want him calling me cousin. I wanted more from him. Much more than I should. More than I ever could have.

CHAPTER
16

Once the seeds of doubt had been planted, they grew, weedlike, choking out what little faith I had left in myself and in my memories. I turned often to Stephen Ward's book and the painting of David that I had loved since my childhood. A famous artist, a famous subject, and a lonely little girl with the same last name. Could I have created the whole thing just to escape from a life that had no meaning for me? And had my life been any less empty when I found my father's letter?

But it was so real. How could I have imagined something so complicated, so lifelike, when I had no experiences to draw from?

David's books gave me no answers; their verbosity only confused me more.

John's suggestion that I see the psychologist kept creeping into my thoughts. Perhaps I should. Perhaps someone trained could say, "Oh, yes. That's . . ." and give me a latin name for some sort of phobia or delusion that would explain away what had become a major part of my life, and weaken the hold it had on me.

No. I would not do that. Eliza was real. As long as I believed in her, she was real. Soon now, something would give me proof of her existence. Soon now, something would give me proof of my reason for being here.

Joannie's visits were welcome intrusions. When she was with me, I couldn't stay lost in my confusion. I worried about her, though. I didn't want her doing anything to jeopardize her baby.

"It's only a couple of miles across the top of the hill," she told me. "Mack filled in the bad spots so the road is all right. It's an easy ride in the truck, and I don't do anything here that I wouldn't do at home. Besides," she added, smiling wistfully, "I've never had a friend, except Mack. He's my best friend, and I love him dearly, but sometimes I need to talk to another woman, someone my own age who I can share things with—things that he doesn't understand, or isn't interested in." She glanced at me and asked hesitantly, "Will you be my friend?"

"Oh, Joannie." She looked so defenseless, so open to hurt, I had to hug her. "I am your friend."

I had never had the luxury of a close friend, either, and even though there were things I couldn't share with her, I treasured her understanding of the things I did share. It was as though once we started talking, we couldn't stop. By the end of a week, we knew as much about each other's childhood as we did our own. We found a common bond in our early loneliness and isolation, in the way we had had to be careful at home in what we said and how we acted—for completely different reasons, yes, but the underlying fears and uncertainties were the same. But even though I knew that Mack and probably Martha had told her of my delirium the night I was so ill, Joannie never mentioned it. Something warned me not to tell her of my memories, not to tell her about the confusion which tormented me to the point that I no longer slept more than two or three hours at a time or ate more than a few bites of food at each meal.

John's visits were intrusions, too. Disturbing ones. He visited every day. He was always gentle with Joannie when she was there. Surprisingly, he was equally gentle with Martha, when she let him be.

At some point during his visit John would excuse himself and go upstairs. I knew he went to check on the painting, but I didn't understand why. Nor did I understand his attitude toward me. It was as though the day on the river had never happened. Or perhaps, I told myself, it was because he wished that were the case.

He was always polite, always considerate, but there was a wariness about him that I had not seen before. At times I found him watching me, studying me, and I could tell that he had questions to ask, but he didn't ask them.

Gone were the days when he teased me until I snapped at him with an angry retort. Gone were the days when he laughed at my anger until I had to laugh at it, too. Gone were the times when he draped his arm over my shoulder, giving me a quick hug as he did so. And I missed them. I missed them almost as much as I missed the closeness I had felt with him that day on the river.

I haven't changed, I wanted to say to him. *I'm still the same person I was before you made me tell you. You made me tell you!* But he hadn't. He had only given me the opportunity.

Would I never again hear him call me cousin in that slow, mocking drawl? Would I never again feel his arms around me? Would I never again . . .

"You ought to do something about that," Joannie said as I stood on the terrace one morning and watched John drive away.

"Do something about what?" I asked, recalled abruptly from my musings.

"John Richards," she said. "Or more particularly the way you feel about him. Have you tried telling him?"

What was she saying? "Joannie, he's my cousin. That's all. What should I tell him?"

"Oh, flip," she said. "You have to go back at least five generations to find a common ancestor. That doesn't exactly classify you as close kin. Besides, if the way you act around him is any indication of the way you feel about him, you'd better be real glad he's not your cousin."

She was mistaken. She had to be. By now I had almost convinced myself that I just wanted things to be the way they had been. Nothing more. And surely, even that couldn't be seen in what I did.

I tried to hide behind a laugh. "What happened to the shy, soft-spoken girl I didn't even get to meet for three months?"

Joannie's smile faded. "I learned that I don't have to be afraid of you. That you aren't going to hurt me, or laugh at me, or tell me that I must have really done something bad for God to punish me so."

"Oh, Joannie, no! No one would do that." Her twisted little smile silenced me. "Would they?"

"Not many."

What could I say? I wanted to lash out against anyone who would do that to her, but I had no words for her. Instead, I knelt by her chair, reached for her hand, and held it as tightly as I could until her eyes lost their hurt look.

She smiled down at me. "We're avoiding the issue," she said. "What are you going to do about John?"

"Nothing." I dropped her hand. "There isn't anything to do."

"You might try being a little friendlier toward him. Smiling at him occasionally wouldn't hurt, either. You'd do that for a stranger; why not for someone you care about?"

"You're reading more into this than you should, Joannie," I told her slowly. "John and I . . ." There was no way I could explain. "John and I . . ."

"Got off to a wrong start," she finished for me. "I don't know who said the first harsh word—I'm not sure it's important. I do know that you are two nice people, and there is no reason why you can't back up and start over. No. Let me finish," she said as I tried to interrupt. "Have you ever asked him to spend time with you, or have you just let him think that you put up with his visits because you have no choice?"

"I—"

"He's an awfully busy man. Haven't you ever wondered why he spends so much time with you? I have. Maybe . . . maybe he can't see what I can. Maybe you need to do something to let him know he is welcome here."

"I wish it were that simple."

"It might be. I'll bet you've never even asked him to stay for lunch, have you?"

"Now you remind me of Martha," I said, laughing. "She would solve all the world's problems with a good home-cooked meal." I felt my laughter die. "But would she want to solve John's problems?"

"I don't know," Joannie said simply. "But speaking of lunch, Mack will be here for me any minute." She struggled to her feet and together we walked to the terrace gate.

"It's almost perfect up here," she said softly as she looked across the lawn.

"Umm," I agreed wordlessly. As always the beauty of the hilltop filled me with a curious combination of emotions: awe, the rightness of my being here, and a vague, bittersweet longing.

"It's a shame about the elm, though," Joannie said, looking toward the gates. "It was a magnificent tree."

I looked at the tree silhouetted brown and bare against the green of the forest behind it. "I keep hoping I'll look out one morning and see leaves on it," I said.

"I don't think you will, Elizabeth. Would you like Mack to take it out for you?"

"No. That's too much to ask of friendship," I told her. "And," I added, giving her a hug, "I'm not ready to deal with that yet."

* * *

I slept fitfully that night, turning restlessly in my bed until that became unbearable, sitting for hours in the dark in my chair. What did I want from John? The answer had to be that I could want nothing from him. But if Eliza wasn't real, then neither was Owen. And that brought me back to . . . what did I want from John?

"Oh, God," I cried into the dark, "why don't I know?"

There was no obvious sunrise. The sky changed from black to gray, matching the gloom within me. When Martha brought my coffee, a light drizzle had started falling. Martha glanced at the bed and at me, still in the chair, but she no longer lectured me.

"I'm making biscuits this morning," she said. "Do you want me to bring your breakfast up here?"

I succumbed to her gentle pressure. It took so little to please her. "No. I'll be down in a few minutes."

After she left, I stared into the rain. Perhaps Joannie was right. If I could do it for Martha, why not for John? A voice within me whispered *Because you can only deal with emotions you feel are Eliza's,* but I pushed that thought away as I began searching my wardrobe. Blue. *You ought to wear that shade of blue more often,* John had said. No. Not the dress. That would be too obvious.

I found a soft cotton blouse of dusky blue with long, full sleeves and ties at the throat and wrists with narrow cording of the same fabric. Jeans and boots were inevitable; they were now my daytime costume. But I took the sash from the skirt which matched the blouse and tied back my hair. I wasn't pleased with my appearance. Dark circles shadowed my eyes, and my face was too thin, too pale. But I had never worn makeup around the house and I wouldn't start now. The blue blouse was enough, I told myself as I started downstairs, fumbling with the ties at my wrists.

I tied the bow on the left but was still trying to fasten the one on the right, now convinced that wearing the blue blouse was a mistake, as I entered the kitchen.

"Good morning," John said.

He leaned against the counter, dressed in a dark blue suit and tie, and he looked . . . devastatingly handsome, infinitely appealing.

"Good . . . good morning."

"Here. Let me help you with that."

Automatically I held out my arm and he tied the bow at my wrist.

"You look very nice this morning," he said.

I hadn't seen him in a suit since Marie's funeral. "So do you."

Perhaps it was only because he was out of his familiar uniform, but he seemed more distant than usual. "You're not counting cows this morning, are you?"

"No. Not this morning."

How could my voice sound so calm? "I didn't expect you this early," I said as I took a cup from the cabinet. My hand shook—there was no reason for it, but it did—as I reached for the coffeepot. I had made up my mind that this was the thing to do, and I would do it. "I was going to ask you to stay for lunch."

John took the cup from me and filled it.

"But perhaps breakfast would be more in order," I added lamely.

He was so close, too close, almost touching me as he stood in front of me. "I can't stay," he said. "I have appointments in Fort Smith until the middle of the afternoon."

Our eyes met then, and I didn't care what he saw in mine, I only wanted to be able to understand what was in his, and I couldn't.

"Maybe tomorrow?" he asked as he handed me the cup.

I tried to smile. "Maybe."

*   *   *

Joannie didn't arrive until after lunch, and when she came she literally brought the sunshine with her. We sat on the terrace, enjoying the just-washed freshness of the plants around us.

"It turned out to be a pretty day after all," she said idly.

I nodded in silent agreement.

"We were worried for a while this morning, though. The sky had that funny green cast to it."

"How could you see it through the gray and the rain?" I asked.

"It's easy," she told me, "once you've lived through a few tornado seasons."

"I keep hearing about those storms," I said, "but I can't imagine anything that destructive. Do you suppose that was what caused the damage here? The broken windows and the log in the upstairs room?"

"I don't think so. That had to have happened after the house was locked up, and we'd have known about it if another tornado had come through. Besides, the damage wasn't bad enough."

We lapsed into silence, neither saying what was uppermost in her thoughts.

"All right," Joannie said finally. "I stayed away as long as I could, and I've kept my mouth shut as long as I can. Did it work?"

I knew what she was asking but not how to answer her. I looked around the terrace for some diversion until I found one, a perfect yellow rosebud on a long stem. I stepped over to it and broke it from the bush and as I did so the bow at my wrist snagged on a thorn and came untied.

"I was going to give you this," I said, "but now you'll have to earn it. I'm tired of tying these bows."

"All right." She laughed as she retied the bow and held out her hand for the rose. "Did it work?"

"I don't think so."

"Did you ask him to stay for lunch?"

"Or breakfast. I gave him a choice."

"And?"

"And he said he had appointments until this afternoon."

I heard the car engine at the same time Joannie did. She looked at me inquisitively. "Probably not," I told her, answering her unspoken question. "I suspect that one of his appointments is a very attractive blonde."

We both turned to look for the car. My curiosity only deepened as I saw the sheriff's cruiser come through the gates and along the drive. I walked to the edge of the terrace and Joannie joined me as the car pulled up to the front door.

A tall, gaunt deputy with sunken eyes and almost skeletal features, obviously not wanting to be where he was, looked anxiously at Joannie as he walked to where we stood. "Miz Wilson," he said with the remnants of a southern drawl, "I didn't expect to find you here. Are you doing all right?"

"I think so, Wade," she said a little breathlessly. "Is anyone hurt?"

"No, ma'am," he said, and then he looked toward me, but he didn't really look at me. "Are you Elizabeth Richards?"

"Yes."

"I'm going to have to ask you to come with me, ma'am."

The air was suddenly cold on my skin. "Where?"

"To the courthouse."

My first thought was that McCollum had somehow found out about the smudge pots, but that was too ridiculous even to consider. "Am I under arrest for something?"

"Not exactly," he said.

I looked to Joannie for an answer, but she was as puzzled as I.

"And if I choose not to go with you?" I asked.

His hand gripped my arm before I finished the question. "I'm real sorry, ma'am, but I have an order that says I have to bring you before the judge whether you want to come with me or not. The doctors are waiting for the hearing now.''

Joannie's voice cut through my panic. "Let me see that order," she demanded.

The deputy didn't release me. He reached into his shirt pocket with his free hand and pulled out a folded document. Joannie took it from him impatiently, shook it open, and scanned it. Her mouth opened, but she made no sound. She turned to me with stricken eyes.

"What is it?" I asked, afraid to, afraid not to.

"Elizabeth, it's a . . . it's a sanity hearing."

I was beyond thought or feeling, completely numb as the deputy led me to the car. Some instinct made me pause and turn back to Joannie as he opened the door to the caged backseat. "Find John," I begged her.

It wasn't happening. I kept telling myself that throughout the drive. It was a nightmare. In a minute I'd wake up and realize that it was just a dream. It was a mistake. They had the wrong person. Just as soon as we got to the courthouse, they'd apologize for the silly error they'd made.

This was McCollum's work, I thought. He was trying to frighten me away. He didn't mean to go through with this. He just wanted to scare me so that I wouldn't stay to inherit.

John won't let this happen, I told myself over and over. *John will not let it happen.*

The panic had lessened by the time we reached the courthouse in Fairview, but I was still very much afraid. My heart threatened to beat through my chest as we rode the tiny elevator to the second floor and as the deputy guided me down the hallway and into an office.

"Are they ready for us?" the deputy asked a woman seated behind a typewriter.

"Not yet."

We stood and waited, the deputy still gripping my arm. I held my shoulders back and my head high, desperately trying to give the appearance of being calm. The door to an inner room opened and Stanley McCollum came out. As I noticed the gleam of triumph in his eyes, I felt a little of my fear turning to anger. How dare he do this? How dare he put me through this?

The inner office was crowded with men. The deputy guided me to the desk and then stepped back. The man behind the desk spoke.

"Miss Richards, I'm Judge Tomlin. Do you know why you're here?"

After seeing McCollum I was pretty sure that I did know, but that was not the answer the judge wanted. "I have been told that this is a sanity hearing," I said as calmly as I could, "but no, I don't know why I'm here."

"Would you like to sit down?" He indicated a steel straight chair in front of his desk, and I took it hesitantly.

"The man on your right is Mr. Beams," the judge continued in an even tone. "He's the lawyer who has been appointed to represent you. To his right is the district attorney. These men over here," he said, indicating two men seated near the wall, "are Dr. Whitaker and Dr. Carouthers."

"I know Dr. Carouthers," I said.

"Good. They're here to examine you." He cleared his throat and picked up the file in front of him. He didn't read, but he spoke in the same monotone one uses when reading aloud. "It has been brought to the court's attention through the office of the district attorney that you exercise poor judgment and that you are dangerous, or may be dangerous, to yourself or others."

He put down the file. I found that I was holding my breath. I couldn't release it as he went on.

"The purpose of this hearing is to determine whether you should be committed, immediately, to an institution for treatment and protection."

The breath squeezed out of me in a moan.

"Dr. Carouthers, will you go first?" the judge asked.

Dr. Carouthers nodded and walked over to me. He spoke softly. "Do you know your name?"

I looked up at him in amazement, but something in his face warned me to be careful of what I said. "This is serious, isn't it?" I asked.

"Yes, dear," he said as he leaned against the desk near me.

I answered his questions, terrifying in their simplicity. My name, my age, the day of the week, the name of the president, my mother's name, my birthday, my address.

"Elizabeth," the doctor said, sighing. "I treated you at your home one night when you were quite ill. Do you remember that night?"

No. He couldn't ask me about that.

I swallowed, and nodded. "Vaguely."

"You said something that night, I can't remember the exact words, but you said something about having to die to be with David again. Do you remember that?"

My hands seemed to have a life of their own. I clasped them together to keep them still. "I was told you attributed that to delirium."

"I did at the time," he said. "That was before I was made aware of some other facts."

"I thought anything I said to you as a patient was confidential," I said, my voice fading as I spoke.

He looked at the ceiling for a long while before he looked back at me. "I'm in an unusual position," he said finally. "I have to be fair with the court, I have to be fair with you, and I have personal knowledge of importance to this examination." He spoke carefully. "Do you think that you were guided to Richards Spur by some supernatural force to die, to free your spirit to join that of David Richards?"

I shook my head. That wasn't why I was here. That couldn't be why I was here.

"Do you believe you are or were a woman David Richards loved and that the house you now occupy was built by him for you?"

John. The realization stabbed through me like physical pain. I had been calling out to him for help, and he was the one who had done this. Maybe tomorrow, he had said, when all the time he knew that by tomorrow I would be locked in an institution. Well, I wouldn't be. I wouldn't give him that satisfaction. I was fighting for my life now, and I couldn't be concerned with being fair or truthful. Later I could sort through being disloyal.

I held my head up and said distinctly, "I believe the house was built by David for a woman he loved. Whoever she was, she has been dead for a long time. I came to Richards Spur to claim a sizable inheritance. I didn't make the rules, but in order to claim that inheritance I have to meet certain requirements. Dying is not one of them."

He smiled at me. "You've lost a lot of weight. How is your appetite?"

"It's better. Every day it gets a little better."

"Are you sleeping well?"

I knew he could tell from my appearance that I wasn't. "Not very."

"Why is that?"

One more disloyalty. "Dr. Carouthers, you've been in my house at night. Do you really have to ask that question?"

He shook his head and stood up. "That's all I have, Your Honor."

I wanted to sigh and sink back onto the chair, but I couldn't. Not yet.

"Dr. Whitaker, do you have any questions?" the judge asked.

"No, Your Honor, I believe most of the points have been covered."

"Have you reached any conclusion?"

Dr. Whitaker didn't even look up from his notebook. "Yes, Your Honor. I believe, based on what we've heard today, that a commitment, at least for evaluation, is in order."

With a sharp burst of insight, I realized Whitaker's recommendation had little to do with what I'd just said—he'd been determined to commit me all along. I looked to Dr. Carouthers for help. Surely he wasn't in on this . . . this conspiracy as well?

"Dr. Carouthers?" the judge asked.

He looked at me as he spoke. "I might go along with a psychiatric evaluation, Your Honor. Miss Richards may have a mild form of depression, and she probably does have an active imagination, but I see nothing in either of those factors to justify institutionalizing her."

"Mr. District Attorney?"

The man spoke for the first time. "We considered this matter carefully before bringing it to the court's attention. The petition was not prepared frivolously but was based on reliable information brought to us by a concerned, reputable citizen. I have heard nothing here today that would warrant withdrawal or amendment of that petition."

"Mr. Beams?"

"I have nothing to add, Your Honor."

It was like a roll call, and it was over so fast I couldn't assimilate what one had said before the other was through speaking. But one thing was clear; with the exception of Dr. Carouthers, the men in this room were acting together. For McCollum? For John?

"Very well," the judge said. "Miss Richards, it is the ruling of this court, based on evidence presented and the examination held in my chambers today, that you be committed for evaluation—"

"Wait!" I cried. "Please, wait!"

The judge stopped speaking and leaned forward.

I looked to Dr. Carouthers, the only one who had even seemed to care, for help. He shook his head ever so slightly and glanced over my shoulder. I turned to see what he indicated.

My lawyer stood there. My lawyer—if I hadn't been so near tears, I would have laughed.

"Mr. Beams," I asked through clenched jaws, "are you here because there must be a lawyer present, or are you here to actually represent me?"

He studied me for a moment. "I'm here to see that your rights are not violated."

"My rights? Do I have any rights? I was torn from my home. I was brought here with no notice, no time to prepare for this . . . examination, no time to get help, and now it looks very much as though I am going to be sent to a mental hospital because I *might* hurt myself. My God, even someone accused of murder gets a trial. Have I been completely disenfranchised?"

He smiled at me with a picture-perfect copy of McCollum's smile. "You don't really want to go through the embarrassment of dragging this in front of a jury."

"Oh, you bet I do," I said. "You bet I do. If that's an option open to me, I insist on it."

"I think that's an excellent idea," Dr. Carouthers said. "I'm glad you remembered it, Beams."

The look that ran between the two men spoke of long and bitter disagreements. Beams broke the glare and turned to the judge. "Your Honor, in view of my client's insistence, and the mixed findings of the examining physicians, I move that the court refrain from ruling at this time and that the matter be submitted to a jury for determination."

The judge looked at him and sighed. "Motion sustained. Miss Richards, I remind you that you are still under the jurisdiction of this court. Do not leave the county without the court's permission. Thank you very much, Doctors, for your assistance today. This matter is continued until the next jury docket.''

They all stood up, but I was too stunned to move.

Dr. Carouthers came to my side when the others left the room. ''Is it over?'' I asked.

''For now. I'm sorry, Elizabeth. I didn't want to have any part of this.''

''At this moment,'' I told him, ''I'm glad you were here. What do I do next?''

''You'll need a good lawyer, a good psychiatrist, and some money, but not for a while. Right now what you need is dinner and a full night's sleep. Do you want something to help you rest?''

The room grew smaller by the minute. ''No. I just want to get out of here before they change their minds about letting me go.''

Joannie, Mack, and Martha waited in the outer office. Each of them embraced me, but even their love and concern couldn't push back the feeling of confinement creeping around me.

Mack had the sheriff's folded order in his hand. ''I can't believe something like this can happen.''

I took the order from him. ''Not now, Mack. Please.''

If it hadn't been for Joannie, I wouldn't have waited for the elevator. I would have run down the stairs and into the fresh air outside. Instead, I endured the confinement of the small cage as it jolted us to the first floor, and I paced my steps to Joannie's slower movement. When we at last pushed open the door to the parking lot and I felt sunshine on my skin, I filled my lungs with untainted air and raised my face to the sky. ''Thank you.''

''I couldn't find John,'' Joannie said, ''but I got in touch with Mack at the feed store and he came on over. John's supposed to be home by now, but he doesn't answer the telephone."

"He wouldn't have helped anyway," I told her.

"But he could have done something. You shouldn't have had to go through that, especially alone."

I still clutched the order. "Where does he live?"

She pointed to a house on the hill above us. I could barely see the roofline through the trees.

"I need a car. Martha, can I use your car? Would you mind riding home with Mack?"

"Why, child, if you need something done, I'll do it for you."

"No. I have to see John. If it means waiting in his driveway half the night, I have to see him before I go home."

"Of course you do," Joannie said, and I knew she had no idea of the real reason why I did. *Oh, Joannie,* I thought, *how can you still be so innocent?*

CHAPTER
17

As I labored up the hill in Martha's car, missing turns, losing my way, searching for the right street, the emptiness within me grew. "How could he do it?" I asked. I could understand, almost accept, that Stanley McCollum was capable of this kind of treachery. But John? How could he have betrayed me? *Remember who he is*, I warned myself. *Owen could do it. Owen would do it.* But at some point, I had stopped seeing Owen in John.

I found John's driveway and turned in. Martha's car protested at the sharp grade and died. Somewhere, in one of the widely spaced houses, someone was practicing the piano. I heard the sounds of heavy chords being tried time after time, matching the blackness in my heart, muting for me the sounds of birds in the nearby trees.

I patted the dashboard and spoke to the car as I tried the key. "Just a little bit farther." Thankfully, I heard the engine catch. I eased the car into gear and coaxed it up the drive.

Could I really wait for him half the night? It appeared that I wouldn't have to. I saw both his car and his truck parked near the garage.

Even the birds were quiet as I stood at his door. I heard the pounding of my heart in the silence. What would I say to him? I squared my shoulders and jammed my finger against the doorbell. I held it there, listening to the persistent buzz, raucous and irritating though muffled by the heavy door.

The door was jerked open, and John stood there, scowling. My glance swept over him, taking in every detail: the rolled-up shirtsleeves, the tie twisted loose, the hair which looked as though he had been running his hands through it, and the drink he held in one hand.

His scowl changed to a look of confusion. "Elizabeth? What—"

"It's a little early for celebration, cousin," I snapped. "They haven't managed to lock me away yet."

I could no longer bear to look at him. The pain was too great. The words broke from me as I twisted away and stumbled toward the car. "I trusted you."

John grabbed my arm, and it was as though the deputy once again clutched me. It was too soon. My nerves were too raw.

"Let go of me!" I screamed at him. "I've had all of that I can stand today."

I heard the sound of breaking glass and then felt both his hands on my arms. "What happened?" he demanded.

"What happened? What happened?" I began laughing insanely. No. Not that word. I mustn't use that word. I forced myself to stop laughing, but I couldn't keep my voice from rising. "What happened was that your conspiracy didn't work. I'm still free. Tainted, but free. Take care, you said . . ." Oh, God, he had warned me, months before when I first met him. "Take care, you said," I continued in little more than a whisper, "that they don't say there goes that crazy Elizabeth Richards."

I tried to twist away, but he tightened his hands on my arms. "Elizabeth, you aren't making any sense."

I felt something in my hand and realized I still clutched the order. I raised my hand between us. "Have you ever seen one of these?" I asked. "Do you have any idea what this can do to a person?"

He released his grip with one hand and took the paper from me. I still couldn't look at him; I stared at the ground.

"Damn him!" John said under his breath. He grabbed me to him, pressing my face against his chest. "I won't let him do this to you."

"Won't let him? It's done, John." My voice broke. "And you're the only one who could have done it." I forced my hands between us and pushed at him.

"Come inside," he said, "We have to talk. We can't stand out here like this."

"No." I struggled vainly to break his hold on me. "I've talked to you too much already. I'm going home, while I still can, and I'm staying there until someone else comes and drags me away."

I broke loose from him then and ran toward the car, but I wasn't fast enough. He caught me and picked me up. "Put me down!" I cried, kicking and hitting him. "I'm leaving."

"Not like this, you aren't," he said as he struggled to get me into the house. He slammed the door shut and carried me down a short flight of steps to the living room. He dumped me unceremoniously onto the couch, in the middle of a pile of plans and blueprints which he shoved to one side and onto the floor.

He held me against the back of the sofa and stood over me. "Look at me," he said, shaking me. "Look at me!"

I looked at him. His eyes held mine. "I am not your enemy."

I wanted to believe him. Oh, how I wanted to believe him. But how could I?

"Aren't you? Who else could have told them about David and Eliza?" He didn't answer me. "Do you know your name?"

"What?"

"Do you know your name? That's one of the questions they asked. Another was, do you think you are the woman David Richards loved? How did they know to ask that, John?"

"I don't know," he said. "Your burglar, maybe. Could he still have been in the house that night? Or Louise. How much did you and Marie say that she could have overheard? But the hearing is over? They did let you go?"

"For now. I won a small victory. I'm going to have a trial. I'm going to have to convince a jury that I'm not crazy, which is something I'm not too sure of myself, right now. Oh, why am I telling you this?" I cried.

"Because you have to trust me."

"No. I trusted you once before, and if it hadn't been for Tom Carouthers, I'd be on my way to a state hospital right now because I did."

John released my shoulders, but he took my hand. He sat on the arm of the sofa, holding my hand in both of his. "Not a state hospital," he said softly. "Stan couldn't take a chance on the state releasing you. It would have been a private hospital. An expensive one. One that believes in a lot of medication." My hand was numb in his. "I wonder how long he thought it would take me to get you out?"

"Why would he think you'd want to?" I asked woodenly. "With me out of the way, you could go ahead with your plans to break the trust."

"Elizabeth, I—" He bit back his words, drew a deep breath, and exhaled slowly. "Not now." He straightened my fingers along his, massaging the back of my hand. "Let me tell you what has happened, and what I think has happened. You have a right to know what you're facing.

"Stan McCollum has been in charge of your trust for almost twenty years. It had been sitting there, growing, since 1925.

After the first few attempts, no one expected it ever to be distributed; the requirements were too . . . bizarre. At some point, Stan began using your money.''

''You knew?''

''I suspected.'' John shook his head. ''I should have done something, but I didn't care about the money. I filed that suspicion away as something to check on later, to use if I had to, when the time came that I could break the trust.

''Seven years ago, the unexpected happened. A woman came to claim the inheritance. Stan didn't say anything to me, but he was shaken. I suspect that he in some way used the legend of the haunted house to frighten her away, but I can't be sure, because she wouldn't talk about it. The caretakers left at the same time. The house was abandoned.

''Stan had taken so much money from the trust that he couldn't have returned it if he'd had to make an accounting, not without using the bank's funds, and that would have meant almost certain discovery. There was only one way he could get his hands on that kind of money, and I suppose I was the one who gave him the idea.

''Several years ago, I had one of the Wards copied, from a photograph. The artist in Texas who did the work is extremely talented. If he'd had the original painting, his copy would have been good enough to deceive most people. I didn't want that kind of copy, I just wanted the picture, and I was pleased with his work. I told several people about him.

''When we inventoried the house before closing it, Stan was insistent that we photograph, authenticate, and appraise the Wards. The insurance company was reluctant to cover them for full value if they were going to be left in a vacant house, but under the terms of the will they couldn't be removed. Stan was still fighting with the agent about coverage when I got a telephone call from Texas. Someone, the caller told me, was making inquiries about a collection of Stephen Ward paintings.

"I love those paintings. One of the few good things David Richards ever did was sponsor that young man until he could establish himself. I went to the house, helped with the packing, hid the paintings, and when Stan showed up asking where they were, I pointed to the stacks of boxes that filled the upper floors and told him I had packed them as they were brought to me, in whatever space was available at the time.

"He searched for weeks, until Martha needed a place to live and someone was in the house again. By then the pressure was off. He'd forgotten his panic.

"He still controlled the trust. He convinced himself, again, that it would never be distributed. He helped himself to more of the funds."

John closed his hand over mine. "Then you showed up, and one of the first things you did was threaten an audit."

I leaned my head back against the couch and closed my eyes. "Oh, John." It made sense. It made sense! "The burglary?"

"I don't know. I saw his inventory afterwards. Nothing new was missing from it, but what is more important is that nothing new had been added to it."

I remembered my confusion when John left the painting outside the vault—now it made sense. "You tempted him with a Ward? You left one where he could get his hands on it? How could you do that?"

"Let me show you something," John said, standing, pulling me to my feet.

For the first time I became aware of the room and its contrasts. There was little furniture, only the large curved sofa and tables for it and an ornately carved, antique grand piano. One wall was of glass, overlooking the valley; another was dominated by a stone fireplace and filled bookshelves; a third was covered with paintings.

John led me to the wall of paintings behind the piano and stopped in front of a small landscape. Although this was the first time I had clearly seen the picture, I recognized the shades of pink.

"It's your orchard," John told me. "As it was. Or perhaps as Ward wanted it to be. Here is the boundary wall, and here"——he pointed to the edge of the canvas—"is just a glimpse of the mountains."

I touched the canvas. It was like no work of Ward's I had seen before. There was a misty quality to it, an otherworldliness that he had not allowed in his other paintings.

"We have to put it in the vault," I said. "I can't leave it where it is, waiting for him. I don't want him to be able to touch it."

John dropped his arm over my shoulder. "I couldn't risk that, either. I changed the frames on the paintings. This is the original. My copy is what is waiting for him."

He hugged my shoulders. "I'm sorry. Because I'm not a beneficiary, I don't have the right to demand an audit. I have no proof of most of what I've told you, yet. I know Stan is desperate. I thought the temptation of the paintings would be enough. If I could catch him substituting just one of them, I'd have enough evidence to force an investigation. I didn't dream that he'd think of another way out, or that he had the influence, almost, to make it work."

John pulled me to him, holding me close, one hand in my hair, the other moving across my back. "I'm sorry."

For a moment, everything was all right. For a moment I felt safe and comforted, and I gave in to the luxury of not having to think about what had happened or worrying about what was to come.

"You shouldn't have been used that way," he whispered into my hair.

Used. That was the word for how I felt. I wasn't a person to Stanley McCollum, I was an annoyance, a disturbance, a *thing* to be disposed of. No one at the hearing, except Tom Carouthers, had even pretended to care about me. I was a case, a patient, or an interruption that had to be dealt with so that they could go on with their plans. I hadn't been real to anyone, just a pawn to be moved about as Stan McCollum wanted.

I pushed away from John's embrace. "But I *was* used," I said. "You should have told me."

"So you could do what?" he asked. "Confront him? Defend your precious property the way you defended your pine trees? You couldn't speak civilly to Stan as it was. No. I thought it was better that you not know, that I take care of the situation. That I take care of you."

I was so tired, so confused and defenseless. "Well, cousin," I said, "you've done an admirable job."

I might as well have struck him. He dropped his hands from me. His eyes shadowed. I saw a muscle tense in his throat. I wanted to call back the words the moment I said them.

"I didn't mean that," I cried. "I don't know what I'm doing anymore. I don't know what I'm saying. I'm not even sure what I'm thinking. I just don't know how to act around you." I stopped myself. I'd said far too much. "I'm going home."

"Not like this," John said. "You're too upset to drive, and I don't want you leaving feeling the way you do about me right now."

"I don't know how I feel about you right now."

"I know," he said, smiling that strange half smile of his. "Believe me, I know."

I felt there was more he wanted to say, but he laughed. "Tell you what," he said, draping his arm over my shoulder and leading me to the couch. "If you'll give me a few minutes to shower and change clothes, I'll drive you home and take you up on your offer of one of Martha's home-cooked meals."

I forced a tentative smile. "And all will be right with the world?"

"At least better."

I let him settle me on the end of the sofa. He gathered up the rolls of plans and stacked them on the far side of the oversized coffee table, snapped his briefcase shut, and placed it on the floor near them.

"A little music while you wait," he said as he switched on a stereo unit in the bookshelf. The soft, calming sound of a piano refrain pervaded the room.

John left the room, and I thought he had gone to change, but he returned in just a moment with a long-stemmed glass. "And a little refreshment." He held the glass out to me until I took it. "I won't be long," he said.

I sipped the wine while I waited, feeling the tension leaving me as the music eased through me, looking through the glass wall, over the clutter of the town, to the valley beyond. The same valley. The same river. . . .

The melody was so familiar, the same few notes repeated tentatively, gently, that I wasn't shocked into awareness so much as eased into it. Enjoying the feel of the blanket over me, the pillow beneath my head, I opened my eyes reluctantly, puzzled but not alarmed by my strange surroundings. The room was dim, the only light coming from one corner. I turned my head toward the light.

John sat on the piano bench, his elbow propped on the music stand. Massaging his forehead with his left hand, he picked out the familiar melody with his right. I was content to lie there, half awake, watching him. But something about his actions tugged at my memory, and I must have made some sound, for he looked toward me.

"I didn't mean to awaken you."

"It was the music," I said dreamily. "Have I been asleep for long?"

"Not long enough."

I sighed and stretched. "Where did you learn her song?"

"Whose song?"

Still caught in the web of sleep, I answered, forgetting Beethoven, forgetting that anyone ever exposed to classical music had at least heard the melody. "Eliza's. Her mother taught it to her. She told her that the man who wrote it had misspelled her name, but it would always be her song. How do you know it?"

John looked at me for a long time without speaking. Then he smiled. "The man who wrote it was Beethoven," he said, reminding me, but not unkindly, and bringing me fully awake. "He spelled Eliza, *Elise*."

"I knew that," I muttered.

"I know," he said, still smiling. "I played it in one of my earliest recitals. I believe it must have sounded something like this."

He began playing, stiff measured notes, and I could almost see him counting as he played. The notes were the same, but there was no emotion in them, only mechanics, and I felt a twinge of sadness for John.

"I believe I was ten," he said. "I knew the music in my heart, but I had to work a while before I could play it as I felt it."

He began playing then, in earnest, and he played the song as Eliza never had. The music wept, it laughed, it danced, and then it started over, weeping and laughing, repeating, ending with a promise of more to come.

It shouldn't have ended. I was filled with a sadness I couldn't describe when John lifted his hands from the keys, yet the melody played on in my head, in my heart.

He covered the keyboard, crossed the room, and sat beside me.

"You're very good," I said when I could speak.

"No." There was a note of finality in his voice. "I'm competent. Adequate. I could have been very good."

"Why did you give it up?"

"I didn't give it up," he told me. "I had it taken away from me."

I remembered the times I had teased him about abandoning his lessons, and regretted them. How many other things had I listened to and not heard? Martha had told me. "When the horse threw you?"

He held his left hand with fingers extended in front of him and studied it as he talked. "I was told I was lucky. The damage was slight. After all, it was my left hand. I shouldn't be bothered too much by a reduction in dexterity, in strength, in reach. It shouldn't affect me at all in daily life. I'd still be able to work cattle. I'd still be able to ride."

I reached for his hand, running my fingers along his, clasping it in mine, seeing the ten-year-old who had learned to make the music he felt, the sixteen-year-old who had had his dream stolen away. "I'm so sorry."

I don't know what I had meant to say after that, or what I had meant to do. I only know that I had to raise his hand to my lips.

With a groan, John took me in his arms and buried his face against my throat. I felt him tremble as I slid my arms around him. I twined the fingers of one hand through his hair and held him close. It was right, so right, for me to be there, holding him. I kept that thought as I felt his lips trailing across my neck, teasing at my cheek, finding my lips, until I lost all conscious thought. My hands moved on their own, needing to touch him, to bring him closer to me. My mouth answered his exploring mouth with a searching need of its own. My heart hammered within me, *love this man, love him, love him,* while my body moved against his, each point of pressure a brand and a bond between us. John loosened the tie at my throat, and each place he kissed became a wellspring for a molten river running through me. His mouth found the hollow of my throat, and now it was I who trembled.

His words were a husky whisper, muffled by my flesh. "Oh, God, how I want you."

It was as though Owen stood beside me, I heard his voice so clearly: "And by God, I will have you."

For an instant all feeling, my breathing, even my heartbeat stopped, and I could see myself as a person standing above us might have seen me, locked in an embrace, letting my body betray me, ready to give myself to this man who had given me nothing but pain, a lifetime of pain.

"No," I murmured, trying to push away from him, and my own voice stopped my clamoring thoughts. He wasn't Owen. But neither was he David.

"Don't fight me now," he whispered against me. "I've waited so long."

I had waited, too. But for what? Or for whom? Maybe I was crazy after all, because I wanted John. But this wasn't right—not the time, not the place—and it might never be right.

My blouse had worked loose from my belt. John's hands roamed over my skin. His mouth explored more deeply the flesh exposed by the open collar.

"No," I said again, louder this time, the protest as much for me as for him. Freeing my hand, I pushed against him.

John raised his head and looked down at me, his eyes shadowed in the dim light.

"Let me go," I begged, but he made no move to release me. My right arm was still trapped between us, but my left was free. I pushed at his shoulder. "Let me go."

He caught my wrist in his hand. He looked at me as though memorizing each feature before a shudder ran through him. "Why does it have to be you?" he murmured. "You aren't," he said, and I heard anger in his voice and saw it in his eyes as he repeated, "You are not."

He glanced toward my hand, still pressed against his shoulder, and his eyes widened. "No," he moaned as he stared at my arm.

The tie at my wrist had come undone, the sleeve had fallen, and my arm was exposed to the elbow.

John's grip tightened. "Where did you get that scar?"

I saw. I felt him holding me. I heard his voice. But at the same time I was no longer in John's arms. I saw Owen. I felt Owen twisting my arm as he raised the whip. I heard Owen's voice demanding, "His name, Eliza. Tell me his name."

I couldn't cry out, not then, not now. All of the pain of that other time was there, all the fear, all the anguish, mingled with the longing and confusion of the present.

John's voice was insistent. His grip tightened still more. "Where did you get that scar?"

My words were choked from me. "Which time?"

John dropped my arm and pulled away from me. I freed myself from the blanket, which had wrapped itself around my ankles, and struggled to my feet. I stood looking down at him, telling myself I was safe, I was with John, that John wouldn't hurt me, until I could force my legs to move. Then I turned toward the door, knowing only that I had to leave.

"Elizabeth?" John's voice, hoarse and broken, stopped me at the top of the stairs. "Wait?"

I turned to look back at him. He slumped on the edge of the sofa, elbows on his knees, staring toward the wall of paintings.

His words came one at a time, as though he were trying to hold them back but couldn't. "I have something that belongs to you."

He rose slowly from the sofa and started toward me. I took a step backward.

"I won't touch you," he said. "I won't—" He made a sound that should have been a laugh. "For God's sake, you have to know I won't hurt you." He stopped on the edge of the landing and made no move to reach out to me.

"Will you come upstairs with me?" he asked in a ragged voice I barely recognized. "I have something to show you."

I wanted to tell him I knew he couldn't hurt me, but I could do no more than look helplessly into his eyes. Taking a deep breath, I nodded, and John stepped aside to let me go up the stairs before him.

He indicated an open doorway and I entered the darkened room. I heard him behind me, but he stopped at the door. I heard the click of a switch as the light came on at the side of the oversized bed across the room from me.

I turned questioningly toward him.

"Elizabeth," he said, sounding drained as he spoke. "Look over the mantel."

There was a corner fireplace facing a drapery-lined wall, but it was shrouded in shadow. I walked to the chair in front of the fireplace, a deep, welcoming leather chair, which I leaned against as I looked through the dark to see why John had brought me upstairs. There was a painting over the mantel, but its details blended with the night.

Once again I turned toward John, and I saw his hand move over the light switch. "I couldn't leave her in the dark."

Light flooded the room and I looked back at the painting to see my face staring back at me with haunted eyes, my arm resting on a carved white mantel, my scar barely visible but showing past the edge of a rose-colored shawl.

I couldn't breathe. I clutched the back of the chair for support as I stared back at my image. It had happened. It really had happened. And now that I knew, I almost wished it had not.

I don't know how I got there, I don't remember moving, but I was at the fireplace, touching the canvas. It was real. I wasn't imagining it.

"It's me," I whispered.

"That's what I thought the first time I saw you," John said as he walked toward me. He stopped beside me and reached out, but he dropped his hands without touching me. "But it isn't." His voice was low, vibrating with emotion. "I won't let it be."

"I don't think there is anything you can do about it, John," I said, still looking at the portrait. "Look at us. We are identical."

"No. You resemble her. My God, the resemblance is uncanny. Even the scar. Why didn't you tell me about the scar?"

He clenched his hands into fists, but held them stiffly at his sides. "We know nothing about the woman in this painting."

"I've told you about her."

"You've told me what you remember of a girl named Eliza. Can you prove that this is Eliza? Can you prove that Eliza ever existed outside of your imagination?"

Could he really be asking? Could he look at this painting and not know?

"I can't," John said. "I've tried. I've had experts looking for any shred of proof since the day after you told me the story. There is no divorce in Fort Smith, no marriage in Richmond, no record of her father or a plantation, no reference to her in the Washington papers. There was a time when I thought she must have—must have been David's woman, but the obvious answer is that this is the portrait of one of our unknown ancestors, someone whose appearance you inherited, the way I inherited David's."

Again John moved as though to touch me. Instead he turned to the chair and gripped its back. "I did find Owen Markham," he said. "He was a captain in the Union Army. He was with the Department of the Interior after the war. He assisted with the negotiations for the terms of surrender for the rebel Indian nations after the war. He did his best to destroy the nations at that time, an attempt which he pursued actively throughout his career.''

''What happened to him?'' I asked, not really sure I wanted to hear the answer.

John's mouth twisted. ''No one seems to know. He disappeared into glorious anonymity. The last reference to him anyone can find concerns a Senate vote in which he campaigned against the return of the Choctaw Nation's funds.''

''When?'' I asked, knowing what the answer must be.

''July of 1870.''

''Doesn't that prove anything to you?''

He spoke evenly, carefully. ''I have a list of books in which he is mentioned, never prominently, but he is mentioned. My investigators found no reference to a wife, and no record of his ever having owned a home in Washington.''

''What kind of proof do you need, John?'' I cried. ''Look at this picture and then tell me how I imagined this. Why are you fighting it so hard?''

He reached for me again, and this time he did touch me. He grabbed me by the shoulders and swung me around to face the painting. ''Because I can't have you bound by what I once thought of her. Look at her. Look at her, remember what you think you know about her, and then tell me that you honestly believe you are the same.''

I tried to see what he meant. She was softer than I, more gentle, and, while there were times when I felt vulnerable, she looked as though she were totally defenseless.

''What would have happened to her if she'd had to go through what you survived today? Would she be here confronting me, or would they have done what Stan wanted and locked her away?''

I didn't know. I looked to her for an answer. Could she have sustained herself through anger? Could she have lied?

''And you?'' John turned me toward him. ''Could I force

you to marry me? If I told you that was the only way you could save yourself from being committed, if I told you that was the only way you could save David's house, would you do it?''

Was he threatening me? I tried to read the answer in his eyes, but all I saw was a question, a question I didn't understand. I backed away from him, shaking my head, but he still gripped my shoulders, his fingers biting into me.

''Of course not,'' he said. ''The only reason you would marry me would be that you loved me.'' He slid his hands down my arms as he released me. ''And we both know that can never happen, don't we?''

Then I understood his unspoken question, and my heart twisted painfully against the flare of joy I knew I shouldn't feel. With trembling fingers I touched his cheek. ''How long?'' I asked.

''I don't know.'' He looked toward the painting and then back at me. ''Forever, I think.''

Once again I was in his arms, but this was different from the other times. He held me as though he had to hold me but was afraid to.

''My first thought when I saw you was that crazy old man had brought you here just for me. . . .'' I felt his heart pounding beneath my cheek as he continued talking, softly, reluctantly. ''You're not the only one having trouble with this. I don't know how many nights I've sat in this room, talking to myself, talking to that portrait, talking to you, coming to grips with the fact that you are not the same. I fought so hard for my own identity, separate from that of my name, separate from that which people insisted on imposing upon me because of my face, that I had to acknowledge your right to an identity of your own, and I can't let anyone, not even you, take that right from you.''

''I'm sorry, John. I'm so very sorry.''

''Why?'' he asked. ''You aren't responsible for a boy

falling in love with a picture any more than I'm responsible for your falling in love with David Richards. It's strange," he said. "For the first time in my life I almost wish I were more like him."

He squeezed me in a hug, then let me go. "Come on," he said. "It's time for me to take you home."

Only then did I think of the questions waiting for me at home. "Martha will be wondering what's happened to me."

"No. I knew she'd worry. I called her when you fell asleep. I caught her at Mack's. She said something about having dinner with them if you weren't going to need her. She may not even be home yet."

A sob caught in my throat. This man was in turmoil, yet he had worried about Martha, was comforting me. I took the one step necessary to lean against him and slid my arms around his waist. This much he needed. This much I could give him—had to give him. And this much I needed for myself.

I felt his start of surprise before he tried to push me away. He wanted me; his body couldn't lie. But he wasn't going to do anything about it after what had happened downstairs. And did I want him to do anything about it?

Yes! That was exactly what I wanted. What I had wanted far longer than I had been willing to admit. Since when? The day on the river? The day he brought me the hairbrush? Our first kiss the day he showed me the vault? I didn't know; I didn't care.

Now I fought his resistance. I looked up at him and lifted my fingers to his face. "You weren't Owen; never in a million lifetimes could you have been Owen."

"What is this, Elizabeth? A consolation prize?"

I moved my fingers to his lips, silencing him. "You just read me my character. Would I do that?"

He closed his eyes, throwing his head back, and I saw him swallow convulsively. "I—No."

"Then would you—would you quit fighting what is happening between us and kiss me?"

He lifted his hands to my face and searched my eyes. "A kiss won't be enough for me, Elizabeth. Not now."

"I know."

And still he resisted me.

I felt the tension in his body, the need that so clearly gripped him, and I felt an answering need in me. We were so close and yet separated by so much. And for now, for me, that separation was intolerable.

I traced the planes of his face, a face that had grown dear to me in spite of all that had happened, then slid my hands behind his head, drawing him closer to me as I leaned more closely against him. "Make love with me," I whispered.

John's resistance evaporated. Groaning, he pulled me still closer as he rained kisses across my face before capturing my mouth with his.

I wanted him. John. And for the moment I forced away any thought that I shouldn't want him. He wasn't Owen, he wasn't David. He was John, and he was bringing my body to life with each touch of his hands.

I felt the brush of air as my blouse parted, followed immediately by a caress that was gentle yet possessive. "Yes. Oh, yes," I said as I began an exploration of my own, an exploration that led to an ecstasy I had only dreamed of, a togetherness that I feared would never be possible with anyone but John Richards, and a knowledge that most of my former assumptions were wrong. . . . For now, at least, with John's arms around me, my questions seemed unimportant. All that mattered was this love.

CHAPTER
18

We drove home in oppressive silence. By the light of passing cars I saw that John held himself tense, his jaw firmly set, his hands clenched on the wheel. I saw no trace of the gentle, loving man who had so recently held me as John returned me to David Richards's house.

Now I had to admit, if only to myself, that making love had probably been a mistake, but it was a mistake I couldn't regret. Because love was what John had shown me: love, and gentleness, and passion.

In spite of his earlier words, John really didn't believe in what I was going through, but he believed in me. And while he was relieved I no longer saw him as Owen Markham, he knew I still had many unresolved questions about David. "I've been fighting him all my life," John had told me. "Why should I expect the most important part of my life to be free from him?"

Now in the car on the way home, I wanted to do something to comfort John, but there was nothing I could do. I had not asked him to love me; I had only, selfishly, asked him to express that love.

On the road up the hill, John stopped once and peered sharply into the pines.

"What is it?" I asked, glad to have anything to distract my thoughts, to help ease the screaming silence between us.

"Nothing," he said tersely. "I thought I saw something."

Soon we would be at the top. Soon he would be leaving me, going off, alone, into the night. I searched for something to say to him, but everything I thought of carried the reminder of John's last words to me before we left his house. "You're going to have to resolve this, Elizabeth. I don't care how, but you're going to have to do it soon. You're going to have to choose: Life. Or a dead man. Put him to rest. Set us all free." So I sat in silence until we passed through the gates and rounded the still bare elm.

I gasped in amazement. Every light in the house was on. The front doors stood open, and, outlined in the light flooding from those doors, I saw two sheriff's cars.

"No," I whimpered, clutching at John's arm. "Turn around. Take me away from here. I can't go with them."

John stopped beneath the elm, and for a moment the only sound I heard was the groaning of the branches above us.

"I don't think they're here for you," John said softly. "Will you let me find out? I won't tell them you're with me."

I nodded. In this, as in so many other things, I now trusted him.

He drove to the side of the house and parked in shadow. "I won't be long," he said, squeezing my hand.

Even though I expected him to return, when I heard the sound of the car door opening, my heart lurched sickeningly.

"It's all right," John said. "It's safe for you to go in."

He held his hand out to me, but I couldn't move. "Why are they here?"

"You've had another burglary. This time Mack and Martha caught the burglar."

What else could happen before this day was finally over? I took John's hand and let him help me from the car. I needed the strength of his arm as we entered the house. Two brown-uniformed deputies stood at the end of the hall, near the library door. Between them, turned away from me, stood a man. A tall man in a black frock coat, with long black hair tied at the nape of his neck. I recoiled, reaching for John.

Martha came out of the library. She saw me and ran down the hall. "Elizabeth," she said breathlessly, "Mack caught him!" But I couldn't listen to her. I was staring at the figure at the end of the hall, the figure I had seen and said nothing about, the specter in the night that had disappeared when I called out to him.

They turned and started toward us, and I saw his face, the reddened eyes, the bloated features. John's arm tightened on my waist.

"Well, Rustin," John said as they stopped in front of us, "this seems a little sophisticated for you. Who thought up the costume? It is convenient, though. If anyone sees you where you aren't supposed to be, it's a guarantee that nothing will be said. And it's almost as convenient as having a telephone up here and someone at the foot of the hill to warn you if anyone comes up."

The deputy who had come after me was on one side of Rustin. "So far he hasn't said anything." The deputy nodded to me. "But he was carrying a pillowcase full of your things out the back door when Mack tackled him."

"Can I talk with you before you leave, Wade?" John asked him.

"Sure. Henry?" Wade said to the other deputy. "Do you want to take him on in? I'll be right behind you."

The other two left, and Wade looked from John to me. "If it's about this afternoon—" he began hesitantly.

"No. It isn't," John said, interrupting him. "Martha, Elizabeth needs some coffee." He gave me a little push toward her. "And I still haven't fed her supper."

I resented his pushing me away. I resented his not letting me hear what he told the deputy. But Martha advanced on me, taking my arm, chiding John for not feeding me, scolding me for not taking care of myself, and led me to the kitchen, bubbling over with stories of coming back over the top of the hill after supper and surprising the "ghost." It seemed hours before John joined us in the kitchen, alone.

Martha poured a cup of coffee, handed it to him, blushed a deep, mottled red, and then hurried from the kitchen.

John stared after her. "Did you say anything to her?"

"No," I told him, as puzzled by her actions as he was. But there was something more important on my mind. I studied my cup before I spoke. "He took more than that pillowcase full, didn't he?"

"Yes."

"What will happen to him?"

"I suspect that he will be out of jail on bond by morning and out of the state soon after."

"Just like that?" The unfairness of it brought unwanted tears to my eyes. My voice trembled as I spoke. "He can just run away? He can leave people thinking that he was a small-time burglar who got caught, never dreaming he was the tool of an evil man?"

"Stan isn't really evil, Elizabeth. He's greedy and he's weak."

"Don't argue semantics with me, John. The effect is the same. I'm having to fight for my life because of him, and you're telling me there's nothing I can do about him."

John took my hand. "Stan will have to file the complaint on the burglary and give them a list of what was taken from the trust property. He will never mention the Ward. Because of what happened earlier today, you can't mention it. If you were to report the theft of a Stephen Ward painting, he'd deny it, probably replace the painting, and use it as further evidence of your instability."

I tried to pull my hand free from his, but he refused to let me break the contact.

"Wade is a good deputy," John said. "He ought to be sheriff. He wants to be. I told him pretty much what I told you this afternoon and then I walked down the hill with him to the place where we had stopped earlier. What I had seen was Rustin's truck. The painting wasn't in it, but a number of other things were. I don't think they'll show up on the report, either. I think Rustin did the job he was hired to do and came back later for himself. I think he's probably done that several times in the past, which would explain more than anyone other than us cares to question right now. I hope he still has the painting hidden, but it doesn't matter. The truck will be watched, Rustin will be watched, and Stan will be watched. It's just a matter of time before one of them makes another mistake."

Time. It was something I had in abundance. With orders from the court not to leave the county without permission, I couldn't go back to Fort Smith. I didn't need to go back. I was sure I wouldn't find any more proof on a return visit than I had the first time. And with an empty gas tank and no money unless I asked McCollum's secretary for it, I was under virtual house arrest. John recommended an attorney, and I talked with him about my defense, but I couldn't yet submit myself for psychiatric examination, although I knew it would be necessary before I faced a jury.

I could leave. I confronted that thought one night in the dark. I had a little money in a bank in Columbus. Not much. But enough to take me far enough away that Stanley McCollum could never carry out his threat. Far enough away to make a fresh start. But running wouldn't help. I admitted that as the morning sky lightened. I'd be running away from too much more than Stanley McCollum ever to find peace.

As John had predicted, the only items McCollum listed as stolen on the burglary report were those found on Rustin when Mack caught him. No one was surprised when Rustin disappeared after being released from jail the next day, but, according to Martha, there was a lot of talk when Louise closed the store and left, too.

Joannie visited less often than before. As her time grew near, she became more awkward and uncomfortable. I understood her not wanting to be away from home. I didn't understand the tension that existed between her and Martha. Martha denied there was any tension, and Joannie did, too, at first.

"Please, Joannie," I said to her one morning when Martha had left us alone. "Enough people are trying to tell me that I imagine things. Don't you be one of them."

"I can't not tell you, can I?"

"No." I grinned at her. "You *can't not.*"

She smiled ruefully. "I lost my temper. I said some things I shouldn't have."

"I can't imagine you saying anything to hurt anyone," I told her.

"But I did!" Joannie shook her head as though she couldn't believe it, either. "After your hearing, after John called to tell Aunt Martha that you had fallen asleep, she and Mack started talking about going to his house to get you. I told them to leave you alone, that you were where you ought to be. Mack was real upset. He told me that I didn't know what I was talking about, that John was a ruthless man and had probably even had something to do with causing the hearing, and Aunt Martha, bless her heart, Aunt Martha had to remind me that he had foreclosed the mortgage on their farm and put her and Jim out of their home."

"You defended John?"

Joannie nodded.

"But what did you say? What could you have said that was so bad?"

She nibbled on her lip before answering. "I broke my promise to John. I told Mack what he had done for me and what I thought he had done for him, and then . . ."

"Then what, Joannie?" I prompted softly.

"And then I asked Aunt Martha where Jim had gotten all the money he had in the last few months before he died, and . . . and she didn't know about it."

"Oh, Joannie."

"There were a lot of things she didn't know about Jim, but I didn't realize he hadn't told her he had that money. She had signed the deed to John, but Jim had told her it was just to keep them out of court. That hurt her, Elizabeth, and I wouldn't have had that happen for the world. I love her."

"And she loves you," I said. "She knows you wouldn't hurt her intentionally."

"I don't think it matters if I meant to hurt her or not. I did, and I don't know what to do about it."

I had no answers for her. I hadn't meant to hurt John, either, but I had, and I didn't know how to change that. No. I knew what to do. I just couldn't do it.

"Martha wants your love," I told Joannie. "She wants you to need her."

"I do," Joannie said.

"Then why don't you tell her?"

John no longer came to the house. I understood why. I realized he was doing the right thing by staying away. I should have been grateful, but I wasn't.

I found his music books in an upstairs bedroom where they'd been stored all along; I just had never looked. Beginner's books, exercise books, books with the notes so closely spaced than only an accomplished musician could read them, all bearing his name, from the neat block print of the beginner to the bold scrawl of the young man. On each of them, even the earliest, I read in his signature the struggle he'd gone through to assert his identity. In each of them it was John that stood out boldly. Not Richards.

I felt myself drawn more often to the piano, the sound of

John's music still echoing in my heart. I carried the books downstairs, found an early one with the melody I needed so desperately to hear, and began trying to find the notes on the piano that would bring it once more to life.

Why had John practiced here? Why not at his own home? Bits of our conversations kept flashing through my memory at the most inappropriate times. I kept returning to thoughts of the night at his house, thoughts of our picnic on the tree over the river. What had John said? We were talking about my grandmother, and he had said, "At least she didn't blame you for your parents' deaths." Was that what had happened to him? Had his father blamed him for his mother's death?

John wanted me to choose. Why was that so difficult for me to do? John loved me. And I had made love with him. Not David. Not, thank God, Owen. David had become for me the haunted picture in the Stephen Ward book. Even the memory of Owen's cruelty had faded; all I could remember was the anguish in his eyes when he said, "I want you to want me."

It was hopeless. I was in a quagmire of conflicting thoughts, conflicting desires, conflicting needs. Perhaps I was mad. Eliza had prayed for madness. Perhaps I was just fulfilling that prayer. But if that were so, then I couldn't be mad; for if Eliza was real, I was sane.

I crashed my hands on the keyboard. Enough! I would not wallow in these thoughts any longer.

I stormed out to the kitchen just as Martha entered from the outside with a bag of groceries.

"Are there more?" I asked.

She nodded as she put the bag on the table, and I went outside and got the remaining two bags from her car.

"You shouldn't be doing that," she chided when I carried them into the kitchen and began tossing their contents into the cabinet.

"I have to do something," I told her. "I can't just sit around and wait."

Martha sighed and sank into a kitchen chair. "It's about time you realized that. I'm going over to Mack and Joannie's this morning. Do you want to go with me?"

"Oh, yes," I said.

Martha refused to use the road across the top of the hill. She said it was fine for a truck or a tractor but not her car. As we drove through Richards Spur, I glanced at the boarded-over general store. Now the town really was dead. A ghost in stone. Only the church with its leaning bell tower and the squat, ugly little post office had any purpose for being. When we turned off the highway and onto the gravel road around the base of the hill, we passed at least a dozen pieces of earth-moving equipment parked along the side of the road near the bright orange survey flags.

"It looks as though you were right," I told Martha. "They are going to fix the road. But I wonder why they'd even bother, now."

Martha opened the door to the bungalow and called out as we entered.

"In here, Aunt Martha," Joannie answered from the kitchen, where she stood in front of the stove tending the bubbling contents of three large pots.

"I thought I told you I'd take care of that," Martha chastized gently.

"You did. I just thought I'd get it started for you." Joannie turned, and a smile brightened her face as she saw me. "Elizabeth! I'm so glad you came."

"Out," Martha said. "Both of you. Out of the kitchen, out of my way."

I walked with Joannie into the living room and took her crutches from her as she eased herself into a chair.

"How are you?" she asked.

"Just between the two of us?"

She nodded.

Oh, how nice it was to be able to say it and not be afraid of how it sounded. "Sometimes, Joannie, I wonder if I'm not really going crazy. Sometimes I wonder if I need to see a psychiatrist."

"I'm not surprised," she said softly. "With all you've been through in the last few months, what does surprise me is that you've managed to hold yourself together so well. Can I help?"

I sighed and leaned back in my chair. "You do, already."

"Sometimes you just have to talk things out, Elizabeth, to understand them, to put them in perspective. If there's no one you can do that with, maybe seeing a psychiatrist wouldn't be so bad."

"Maybe not," I admitted, to myself as well as to her. "I just can't bring myself to do it yet."

"How's John?" she asked.

I glanced up in time to surprise an impish grin playing across her face. "You never give up, do you?"

"Never," she admitted. "How is he?"

"I don't know," I told her. "I haven't seen him. And," I added, "I'm not going to talk about him. How are you?"

"I'm fine," she said with a contented smile. "But I'm going to be better. I asked Mack to take me over to your house at noon so I could tell you."

"Tell me what?"

"My doctor wants to go ahead and take the baby and not run the risk of my going into labor. I'm checking into the hospital today. Tomorrow morning, I will be a mother.

"I made it," she said, then laughed with joy. "I carried this baby."

The rain started as Martha and I drove home, huge drops that cascaded from low-hanging clouds, overpowering the windshield wipers and making sight of anything past the hood ornament of the car impossible.

The rain continued through most of the night, accompanied by jagged flashes of lightning that lit up my bedroom with their brilliance, and thunder that seemed to rumble from the center of the earth to rattle the windows in the house.

By morning the rain had stopped, but the sky was a dull grayish green. Martha cast a wary glance outside. "I hate to go off and leave you in weather like this," she said.

"You have to be with Joannie and Mack at the hospital, Martha. You can't stay home on a day as important as this one is, and you know it."

"I suppose not," she admitted. "You promise me something, though."

"What?"

"You promise me that if the weather gets worse you'll go to the cellar and stay there."

"Martha." I was both pleased and a little irritated by her concern. "This house has been here over a hundred years without being blown away. It will be here when you come home."

She pointed outside. "That's a tornado sky, young lady. You haven't seen the destruction one of those storms can wreak, so you don't know to be afraid of it. I'm telling you, if it gets worse—"

"If it will make you feel better, Martha, I promise. Now go, and call me just as soon as you know anything."

I wandered into the drawing room. The beginner's book still sat on the piano. I hurried past it to the window. The mountains were dark blue in the distance, but darker still was the sky behind them, a dull blue-black, rent by flashes of lightning. I dropped the curtain in place and faced the piano. It was a simple melody. If a ten-year-old could play it in recital, surely I could pick out the first few notes. I finally found the first nine notes, and I repeated them, time after time, hearing not the noises coming from this piano but Eliza's voice humming them and the music John made when he played them. I found myself being drawn deeper and deeper into the morass of confusion. There was no answer. There was no escape.

"No," I moaned, burying my head in my hands. "I can't go through this again."

Sometimes it helps to talk about it. Joannie's voice sounded in my mind. *How's John? Sometimes it helps to talk about it. How's John? Sometimes it helps to talk about it. How's John?*

I ran from the room. I ran from her voice. I ran from the music still playing in my mind. I ran from me. To Martha's room, where I found myself with the telephone in my hand.

"I have to do this," I told myself, told the room, told the storm outside as I searched through the telephone book. It was too late for John to be at home. The listing for the ranch headquarters stood out in boldface type. I dialed it before I lost my nerve. When a man's voice answered, I forced myself to speak calmly.

"John Richards, please."

"He's not going to be in this morning."

But I had to talk to him. "Can you find him for me? Please? This is . . . I'm Elizabeth Richards. Would you ask him to call me at home? It's important."

A bolt of lightning struck somewhere nearby as I hung up the telephone, and the accompanying clap of thunder shook the lamp on the table in front of me. The room grew dark while I waited with the telephone in my hand. It seemed hours before it rang.

"Are you all right?" John demanded without preamble.

"I don't know. Yes. Yes, I'm all right." I had to say this while I still could. "John, I have to talk to your friend in Fort Smith."

Another bolt of lightning struck nearby. The line cracked and hissed. Only after the static cleared did John speak. "I'll set up a time. I'm coming to see you," he said. "I'm on my way now, but it will take about an hour to get there. I have something to tell you." The line hissed again and then went dead.

John was coming. Wasn't that what I had really wanted? To throw myself in his arms and have him make everything all right? But he couldn't do that for me. I knew, deep down, that somehow I had to make things right for myself.

The air in the house closed in on me and the rooms seemed to grow smaller. I ran down the hall, threw open the front doors, and breathed deeply of the heavy, humid outside air. The mountains loomed in the distance, and to the east I saw the storm raging, but here no rain fell.

I strode across the lawn, splashing through little puddles of collected water, to the low rock wall to the south. I scrambled onto the wall and sat looking over the valley, needing the harsh caress of the rough wind that washed over my face and through my hair.

The problem, I decided as I watched the storm cloud roiling over the mountains, once trimmed of all but the basic issues, was simple to state. Either I had created a fantasy world to fill a need I once had and had let that fantasy consume me, or, by some quirk of fate, I was remembering a life that had really happened. If I had created Eliza's world, I could put it aside. If I had created her pain and her love, then I could be free of them. I watched a distant bolt of lightning spear through the sky. If I were free of them, I could let myself love John, and, oh, how I wanted to do that.

I let my gaze wander over the familiar surroundings, feeling as though I had to see them one last time with Eliza's eyes— the dead elm by the gate, the bright green of the scattered pines along the roadway. I searched the south slope. Only because I had watched so often could I even pick out the solitary pine, hidden now by the clutter of foliage surrounding it. How different from the winter when it had stood as a dull green banner in a jungle of browns.

Dull green? I looked back at the pines. They were bright, with moisture glinting from them. Wasn't it a pine tree? And yet, it had stayed green all winter. The only other tree on this hill—I swiveled around on the wall and looked back at the house. The magnolia gleamed a dull, deep green beneath its garland of ivory blossoms.

No, I told myself as I turned back to the valley. It's a stray, one of the pines that came up from the first ones. They were all over the hillside by the roadway. But that one stood alone.

Marie LeFlore's words played through my memory. "My doll is in the ground. Under the magnolia." What else?

"I'd go to the top of the hill. To the graves."

"No," I moaned, but I was sliding down the hill on the rain-slicked grass, scrambling through briars that tore at my clothes, pushing through the branches of young trees that slapped at my face, denying—denying all the time that it could be.

I saw the blossoms first, creamy cups of ivory against the dull green foliage. I stopped, afraid to go any farther, knowing that I must.

Wild roses and fruit-laden blackberry vines covered a mound beneath the tree, hiding something that glowed a soft white between their leaves. I stumbled toward them, seeing nothing but the dull white gleaming in front of me, calling to me.

"No." I tore at the briars, ripping my hands and my clothes, pushing the vines away until I saw the three marble boxes, placed above ground, one alone, two side by side. All were old and weathered, but the engraving on one was almost worn away. I traced the outline of the word with my fingers. One word. Only one word. ELIZA. The engraving on the adjacent vault I could read. It said simply, DAVID. There were no dates. A stone at the head of the two graves united them. I scraped away the accumulation of dead leaves and dirt, and, knowing that this had to be a dream, traced the familiar words, words that tied them together for all time. NOR DEATH WILL US PART.

"Oh, God." A shudder ran through me as I collapsed against the marble slab, clutching the edge.

Eliza

Eliza felt other people in the room, working over her, tending to her. She was tired, so tired. The pain no longer tore through her, but she was spent. She had no strength left, not even the small amount needed to open her eyes.

"You saved her," she heard Jane say.

"I don't know why," a man answered dully. "There's no chance he'll send her away now, is there?"

"None," Jane said.

"Then he's ruined. And for what?" The bitterness in the man's voice sliced through the fog surrounding Eliza. "Another man's woman and a bastard child. Someone whose every need is going to have to be tended to, someone who will never be whole or normal."

"Could you be wrong?" Jane asked.

The man laughed derisively. "He's going to ask the same question. I was wrong four months ago when I told him she couldn't live through the beating she had taken. I was wrong when I told him the child couldn't survive. God, I wish I hadn't been wrong about that. But no. This time I am not wrong. The damage has been done. There can be no improvement. And I have to be the one to tell him. Will you finish up in here?"

Eliza lay stunned as she listened to footsteps leaving the room. What damage? She forced her eyes open.

"Jane?"

The woman was gathering soiled linens. She stopped and walked to the bedside. "Yes, dear?"

"My baby? Is he all right?"

Jane smoothed the hair back from Eliza's face. "He's fine," she said. "I found a nurse for him. He's with her now."

"I can't even do that?"

Jane's eyes misted. "You used up too much of yourself in giving him life. Rest now, and get your strength back. Someone else can care for him for you."

"I want to see David."

"Let me finish cleaning up in here," Jane said. "Then I'll get him for you."

"Leave that." Eliza's voice broke. "I want to see him now."

Jane looked down at her, a frown creasing her forehead. "Yes, I suppose you do," she said gently. She deposited the pile of linens near the chair and left the room.

At least God had let her baby live. Eliza thanked Him for that and remembered her promise to leave if He would.

He's ruined, she heard again in her mind. *No chance he'll send her away now. He's ruined.*

"No," she moaned. She couldn't let that happen to him.

David leaned over Eliza and brushed a light kiss across her forehead. He smiled at her, but she saw the anguish in his eyes.

"Have you seen him?" she asked.

He nodded without speaking.

"How is he?"

David raised her arm and kissed her wrist. His face was turned from her and his voice muffled by her arm when he spoke. "He's beautiful, Eliza. A perfect little boy."

She closed her eyes and breathed a silent thank-you. "God heard my prayer," she whispered.

She reached for David's hand. "Sit beside me."

He eased himself onto the side of the bed, facing her. She traced the planes of his face with her fingers, memorizing the feel of his skin beneath her touch. No, he wouldn't send her away. He wouldn't let her leave. He'd keep her with him until he was broken and bitter, until the nation he loved was dead, until the love he now felt for her was choked out of him by what it had cost. Had she always known they could not be happy together in this lifetime? It seemed that she must have.

"Remember," she whispered, "years ago, when we went hunting for squirrels?"

"How could I forget? That was the day I learned that you loved me."

She touched his lips with her fingers. "We talked that day about living a life we had already known, in another time, another place. I wonder how many lifetimes we do have that we can spend with each other."

"We have this one," he said. "Years more of this one."

"I want nothing more than to spend the rest of this life with you," she said softly, "but I have to believe that there will be another time for us, another life for us. And you'll love me then, too. You promised." A wave of longing washed through her as she let her fingers slip from his face. "Wouldn't it be wonderful if we could spend that other life here, in the home you've made for us, where I've known happiness that I only dreamed existed?"

"We'll spend all of them here, if that's what you want," he said gently.

"Just one," she whispered. She resented the weakness that dragged her down, drawing her away from him.

"I'm tired," she told him. "So very tired. I don't want to, but I have to rest now."

He touched his fingers to her lips and rose from the bed.

"Kiss me good-bye," she asked.

He bent over her, touching his lips to hers, and she grasped him, holding him to her, needing his strength. "I love you," she told him. "More than life itself, I love you."

He left, reluctantly, and she was alone. She lay quietly, gathering her strength. "God will understand," she said. "He must understand. It's the only way I can leave."

She slipped from the bed and made her way slowly across the room, holding on to the furniture for support, until she reached the dressing table. David's razor still lay beside her hairbrush. She touched it tentatively, and then clutched it in her hand as she stumbled to the chair by the window. A breeze played through the open window, rifling the curtains. In the distance the mountains loomed, hazy, mist-covered, violet shadows.

"Please, God," she whispered, "let me see them again. Please let there be another time for us."

She thought of her baby. She longed to call for him, to hold him just once. "No," she moaned, knowing that if she once held him she might never be able to leave him, and leave she must, for his sake as well as David's.

She glanced around the room, perfect except for the un-made bed and the pile of linens at her side. She drew a sheet from the linens across her lap.

It can't hurt much, she told herself. After what she had been through, the pain couldn't be much. She did it quickly and lay back in the chair, her wrists resting on the crumpled sheet. She looked at the valley below as her strength and her life drained from her. "There will be another time," she murmured. "We will be together again."

Elizabeth

A violent clap of thunder shook the earth. "Oh, God," I moaned, still clutching the edges of the marble slab. "No. No! She couldn't have done that. She couldn't have!"

I staggered away from the graves and stumbled blindly up the hillside. It hadn't ended that way. I wouldn't let it end that way!

I was still trembling by the time I reached the house, unable to unlock my mind from the horror of what I had just learned.

"Why?" I cried. What had happened to the girl who had defied the Yankee captain? What had happened to the woman who finally stood up to Owen Markham? What had happened to let her get to that point of desperation? There was no need for her to have quit. "Eliza?" I screamed at the ceiling. "Why did you give up? You didn't have to!"

Her song kept running through my head, mixed with memories of her, laughing, happy. My breath came in ragged moans. I couldn't think. I couldn't feel. I could only question. "Why did you do it?" I wanted to hit something. I wanted to scream. I wanted to cry, but no tears would come. Her song kept playing through my heart, louder and harsher and more insistent each time it repeated.

"Why?" I cried, flailing out at nothing, at everything. My fist crashed against the piano. I stumbled to the bench and collapsed on it, my head buried in my hands, rocking back and forth, unable to do anything else, and still her music tormented me.

The music book on the piano mocked me with the silly nine notes I had learned. I had to do something. Eliza was dead—not over a hundred years ago, but now, just now—and I had to do something. Raggedly I began picking out the notes. Her death was so senseless. I felt a blind anger at the injustice of it, but my fingers pounded the keys mechanically, repeating those notes, until the discord deafened me, until it drowned out the other music in my head.

A tanned hand covered mine, stilling it.

"Never with anger," John said softly. "With sadness, compassion, love, sometimes with laughter. But never with anger."

I swiveled on the bench and buried my face against him, sliding my arms around him, holding on to him, needing him.

"She killed herself," I told him. "And she didn't have to. They lied to her about the baby. She heard them talking, and she thought—she thought she was the invalid, that she was the one who would be the burden on him."

"So that's what changed him," John whispered. His hands clenched on my shoulders, then moved over my hair, comforting me until I stopped trembling, until I once again breathed evenly. I pulled away from him, shaken, but for the first time in weeks in control of myself.

I looked up at him. "I'm not crazy, John. I didn't make her up. She was real."

"I know," he said, and I heard a sadness, a finality in his voice. "That's what I came to tell you." He picked up his briefcase from the floor and set it on top of the piano. He opened the briefcase and took out a document. There was no life in his voice when he spoke.

"I only got this this morning. I've had my attorneys and both abstract companies searching for any reference to Eliza in Fort Smith. They finally found one."

"What is it?"

John crumpled the document in his hand. "It's an old lawsuit. An 1885 quiet title suit involving ownership of the house we visited in Fort Smith. There are a lot of names, and a lot of dates, but only a few that matter to us."

He handed the papers to me. "The house was deeded to Eliza Griffith in August of 1870. She divorced an Owen Markham in October of 1871. She died March 30, 1872, in Indian Territory, survived by an infant son who was also dead by the time of this lawsuit, and her husband, David Richards."

I stared blankly at the papers. A month ago all I had wanted was a scrap of proof. Now I held documentation of her last year and a half of life in my hand, and it was a burden pulling me down into a place from which I couldn't escape.

"How did I know?" I whispered. "Why do I know?"

His voice droned on. "Gail is coming over Saturday."

"Gail?"

"The psychologist I told you about. She's eager to meet you. She sent you some things to read." He pulled books from the briefcase. "It seems that there has been a lot written about past life recall, through hypnosis, but she has never heard of anyone who has involuntary recall. And there has been a lot written about hypnogogic reverie—that's the term for your intense remembrances—but not in connection with a past life."

His voice broke. "Elizabeth, damn it, even if everything did happen the way you remember, you still have the right to a life of your own."

"Do I, John? I've lived before, here in this house—"

"Not *you*, Eliza. Another woman, another time, another life—"

I heard what he was saying, and I wanted to believe him. God, how I wanted to believe him, but how could I? "I loved here. I died here. I promised to come back, and David knew I would. He made it possible for me to be here, with him, again."

John groaned, and then he had me in his arms, lifting me from the bench, holding me to him. "Look at me," he said, "and tell me you don't care for me."

I tried to do that, but when I opened my mouth to speak, the words stuck in my throat and refused to be said. I couldn't look at him any longer. I buried my face against his shoulder, and tears I had no right to shed slid from my eyes. I felt his fingers on my cheek as he raised my face to his and held it imprisoned. He bent toward me and kissed my tears away with gentle, teasing touches. When his lips met mine they were questioning, pleading, and I couldn't lie, I couldn't refuse. Tears streamed down my face as I surrendered to my need for him, my love for him, knowing that this kiss was the last there could ever be.

He pulled away and looked down at me. He knew. I saw in his eyes that he knew. "Tell me you don't love me."

I wanted nothing more than to reach up and touch his face and tell him how much I did love him, but now I could never do that.

"I—I can't!" I cried. "Don't you see? I promised to come back to him, and he's brought me here. I don't know where he is now, but I'm not free to love you. I deserted him once before. I can't do it again!"

He caught my face in his hands and bent toward me as though to kiss me again. "Please go," I whispered. "Please. Go."

"He's won, hasn't he?" John asked bleakly. "All my life I've fought against him, hating him for the failure I knew him to be, and I suppose I always knew it was a futile war. But he hasn't failed in this. Elizabeth, I can't go on fighting a dead man, not without hope, not without help."

I closed my eyes against the defeat I saw in his face. "Please," I repeated. "Go."

He dropped his hands from my face and without another word he turned and left the room. I heard his steps down the hallway and the sound of the kitchen door slamming shut. I sagged against the piano as a sob tore from me.

I saw him in my mind as he left the house, as he got in his car, as he started around the barns. I had to have one more glimpse of him, even from a distance. I ran to the front door. The wind tore it out of my hands as I opened it. John's car was just rounding the barn, leaves and twigs and dead grass thrown by the wind swirling around it. Soon he would be gone. Gone.

And I couldn't let him leave. I couldn't. No more than I could let myself die when I thought that was the only way to be with David. No more than I could have taken a razor and ended my life. I had to live! And what kind of life would I have if I sent John away? An empty one. As empty as most of Eliza's had been.

"I'm sorry, Eliza," I sobbed. "I can't do this. Not even for you." I felt the weight of my rejection pressing into me. "I'm sorry, David. I love him. Please understand. Please."

And then I was running, feet sliding on the wet lawn, being buffeted by the wind and debris, calling for John, screaming his name. He couldn't hear me. There was no way he could hear me. He was almost to the elm tree. Once past that he would never see me. "Please look back!" I prayed. "Please, don't leave."

There was a deafening clap of thunder as a bolt of jagged light speared from the sky in front of me. I slid to a stop and watched, disbelieving, as the car skidded across the wet grass, as the elm, in slow motion, drifted downward, ever closer to the oncoming car.

The crash of metal and blare of the car's horn released me from my paralysis. I stumbled across the lawn, fought through the branches overhanging the car, and yanked the door open.

John slumped over the steering wheel, his chest pressing the horn. A trickle of blood flowed from a gash on his forehead. I had to get him out of there. "Help me, John," I repeated as I tried to pull him from the car. "You have to help me."

The noise around us was deafening. The roar came from hell itself. I couldn't hear myself; how could he? "Oh, please!" I whispered against his ear.

I breathed a silent prayer of thanks as I saw his eyes open. I helped him struggle from the car, the wind-whipped branches beating against both of us. He stumbled when he put weight on his right leg, and I took his arm and put it over my shoulder. "We have to get to the house!" I screamed against the wind.

John shook his head, clearing it. "It's too late for that," he yelled back. "Look."

I looked in the direction he pointed. Between us and the mountains a whirling cloud advanced on us across the valley, black roaring death sucking up trees and fences and even cattle from the valley floor, spitting out some of them, keeping others.

He shook me back to awareness. "Through the gates," he yelled. "To the left. There's a ditch. We have to get to it."

We ran as fast as his injured leg allowed, through the gates, into the trees, to a small ravine. We threw ourselves into it and stretched out, flat along the bottom, while the debris whistled over our heads. John's body shielded mine, but I still felt the pricks of twigs and stones being thrown against me.

I knew we were going to die. We couldn't die yet! I had just chosen to live. And I hadn't told John. I touched his face with my fingers and yelled at him over the wind, "I love you, John Richards. I love *you*!" We held each other while the forest screamed in protest above us, as the tornado roared through the sky with the noise of a thousand freight trains.

Silence. Wonderful silence. Until nearby a bird began to chatter. Another joined it. Soon the forest was alive with sound. I felt John's body relax against mine and sighed in relief. We were still alive. We were together, and we were still alive. John brushed the twigs from my hair and plucked a leaf off my face. His hand lingered on my cheek. "Thank you," he said softly.

"Thank God," I whispered. I was spent. I had no strength left to do anything but lie there in the ditch holding John, feeling him holding me, until from the highway below rose the sound of sirens.

John stirred. "Let's go see what you have left," he said.

We helped each other to our feet, and, with him leaning on my shoulder, we made our way to the gates.

There was no sign of the elm tree, but John's car lay in a mangled heap blocking the road. I shuddered at the thought of what would have happened to him had he remained unconscious, and felt his hand tensing on my arm as he urged me away from the car.

The house still stood, although draperies hung outside some of the windows, and one of the front doors leaned against the fountain.

One of the barns was gone, but the roomful of smudge pots sat intact in the place they had occupied inside the missing barn.

The cloud had dipped down at the north side of the hill, taking out a portion of the stone wall and cutting a swath through the trees. With the trees gone, we could see what was left of Richards Spur.

As capricious below as it had been on the hilltop, the cloud had taken some buildings completely, left others intact, and damaged still others. The bell tower had finally separated from the church and lay in splinters across the cemetery. The post office was gone. The store didn't appear to have been touched.

"What will you do?" I asked as we looked down at the ravished town.

"Save what I can," John told me. "Rebuild what I can't save."

"Why, John? The town was dying. Why would you want to rebuild?"

He spoke slowly, groping for words. "God only knows. For years I wanted nothing more than to squeeze what life there was left from that town. It was a challenge, like destroying the house. But I couldn't do it.''

John settled onto the edge of the wall. ''We broke ground in the new addition east of town yesterday,'' he said. ''I've already closed the sale on several of the acreages. There will be new families moving in, new life for the town. They'll need a place to shop.'' He looked toward the church. ''A place to worship.''

So it had not been highway department equipment after all. I squeezed his shoulder. ''Do you need to go down there?''

John rested his elbows on his knees, his head in his hands. Then, in a gesture to me as old as time, as familiar as my heartbeat, with strong, tanned fingers he massaged the furrow of his forehead. My breath caught in my throat, trapping my voice and keeping me silent.

''Not now,'' he said finally. ''Help me to the house, Elizabeth. It's time we went home.''

EPILOGUE

David Richards's letter to Stephen Ward was found by workmen renovating the Ward home, and a copy was mailed to John five years after the tornado that marked the rebirth of Richards Spur and the beginning of our life together.

There is no way of knowing how Stephen Ward, staunch Presbyterian and elder of his church, reacted at first to David's request. His reply, if written, has long been lost. But the court records reflect that he acted as trustee of David Richards's estate until his own death in 1932.

And there is no way of knowing how different the life John and I now share would be had we known of the letter earlier. Would I have chosen John and life, or would knowledge of that letter have kept me immobile in the doorway and cost John his life? Distanced by years and the happiness I fought for, I can say I would have chosen as I did. But occasionally, late at night, I wonder.

Was David successful? John says no. Obviously not. Because *he* has me. But he no longer hates David. And he no longer denies his heritage.

Joannie's baby was born healthy and normal. He's seven now. His little sister is three, a month younger than the daughter that fills our hearts and the hallways of our home with joy.

And Joannie is walking—with the aid of a loan we practically had to force on her and Mack. We've widened and smoothed the road across the hilltop, and often on a spring evening she and her entire family will walk to our home for a laughter-and-love-filled visit.

John and I kept only two of the Wards: the pink landscape and the portrait of Eliza. The others are where they belong, in museums where they can be seen. Recently we received an offer for Eliza's portrait. We don't know yet if we will accept the offer, but if we do, her portrait will hang beside the one of David that I first saw when I was twelve.

Stanley McCollum made the mistake John was waiting for and has been convicted of embezzlement, from my trust and from others.

I began working with Gail on the Saturday after the storm and continued even after the sanity hearing was dismissed. She's perceptive, nonjudgmental, and understanding—another friend in a life that for too long had no friends.

Gail asked permission to share my story with some of her colleagues, and I agreed.

More than one theory has been advanced about what I experienced. The most frequent one is reincarnation—that somehow David and Eliza did return to a specific location, and that David planned the return. In that scenario the terms of the trust make sense: Eliza had been a child when he first met her, only twenty-one when she came under his protection—she must be an adult this time. And before, it had taken a year for her to admit her love; he would give her that much time.

Another theory is that the spirits of the two lovers were so strong that anyone sensitive would have felt them.

And there are others.

Working with Gail I explored most of these possibilities. Was this reincarnation? Through hypnosis, I was able to go back, but never with the clarity of the recall I no longer experience. And if we were reincarnations, who were the major players?

David was easy. He'd been here all along, and I didn't need hypnosis to recognize him. I did that on my own, after I almost lost him, although I'm not sure he will ever want to know.

And Owen? Owen was here all along, too, though not where I thought. And no one but Gail and I will ever know of that identification. Revealing it would only bring pain, because at last Owen has found the ability to give love, and in so doing to receive love.

Reincarnation? Genetic memory? Spiritual energy and thought transference? Possession? Or a window in time? All have been suggested. But does it really matter which of those, or none of those, it was?

David and Eliza are at peace.

John and I, with our daughter, are storing up our own memories.